SF Books by Vaughn Heppner:

DOOM STAR SERIES
Star Soldier
Bio Weapon
Battle Pod
Cyborg Assault
Planet Wrecker
Star Fortress
Task Force 7 (Novella)

EXTINCTION WARS SERIES
Assault Troopers
Planet Strike
Star Viking
Fortress Earth

OTHER SF NOVELS
Artifact
Accelerated
I, Weapon

Visit www.Vaughnheppner.com for more
information.

Fortress Earth

(Extinction Wars 4)

By Vaughn Heppner

Copyright © 2016 by the author.

ISBN-13: 978-1533018939
ISBN-10: 1533018936
BISAC: Fiction / Science Fiction / Military

-1-

The spaceport's siren blared as I raced past the regular people. Some of my speed was due to steroid-68. The rest came because of the embedded neuro-fibers in my muscles.

"Look," a woman whispered. "That's Commander Creed. This must be a real emergency."

It was real, all right, and baffling. How could anyone have launched a space attack against the Solar System without the Starkiens in Alpha Centauri first informing us? The other jump gates leading to Earth were guarded by human-crewed vessels, so the attack couldn't have originated there. The others would have sent a warning before this. To my mind, the answer was obvious. The bloody baboons were backstabbing us after all we'd done for them. It made me furious.

Because I was on Mars with its weak gravity, I made incredible bounds. The hard part was controlling my leaps so I didn't crash into the ceiling or against an unsuspecting bystander.

Soon, thankfully, I slid to a boarding gate. Two assault troopers with rifles stood guard. The senior man nodded to me. I raced past him into a twisting passageway, soon running up a ramp onto a booster shuttle.

For those who are wondering, we no longer called ourselves Star Vikings. I liked the term. We pretty much all did. But it no longer fit. We'd graduated from hit-and-grab raiders into a real force. Earth Force, to be exact. In the three years since I'd killed the Purple Tamika Emperor in hand-to-hand combat, a lot had changed.

"I'm strapped in!" I shouted.

"We're waiting for a few more officers to arrive, sir," the attendant told me.

"Negative! Sound the alarm. I want upstairs now, as in we should already be in orbit."

"Yes, sir," the attendant said. She stumbled for the pilot's compartment to give him the news.

Seconds later, a klaxon blared.

Maybe it would have been wiser to let the other personnel board first. But maybe this was my last chance to get onto a starship as Mars Fleet accelerated to meet the invader. I didn't know, and there was no way I was going to miss being part of the welcoming committee.

The engines ignited, creating a roaring fireball underneath us. The heavy booster shook violently. I loved it. We began to lift as the roar increased. The G-forces shoved me deep into the cushioned seat as we headed for space.

Someone had invaded the Solar System. Even now, I wasn't sure how close they were to Earth. I knew they were among the Inner Planets, though. That was the crazy part. There weren't any jump gates among the Inner Planets. So, it didn't make sense that an attack force had made it this far without anyone having spotted them long ago. Did the invader possess a fantastic cloaking device?

I should point out a few critical factors as to why I was so anxious. Aliens had visited Earth over a decade ago. They'd called themselves Lokhars, although we hadn't known their names or even what they looked like at the time. They'd shown up in a Rhode Island-sized spacecraft, launching thermonuclear missiles at the majority of our cities. London, Moscow, Beijing and Washington DC had all burned up with a thousand others. A few hours later, drones had appeared, spraying a bio-terminator, one intended to kill all life. That had come to be known as The Day. The tiger-

2

like Lokhars—of an upright, humanoid variety—had been ninety-nine percent successful against human life. They'd left one percent, however, the tough, mean, angry humans with the constitution of cockroaches. The one percent had been hidden in submarines, in Antarctica, the Artic and other out of the way places. We'd collectively climbed back up from the brink of extinction…

Long story short, Earth thrived once more, reseeded from the children of stolen Earth people throughout the centuries by Jelk slavers. The Jelk had been the source of most of the UFO sightings in the past. Countless Lokhar automated factories now gave us the industry we needed for the terraforming and other processes.

Since then, I'd made sure our planet had become *Fortress Earth*. I never wanted to go through another extinction-level assault on humanity again. Maybe that's why I was a little crazy about the invasion right now.

Winning last time had been hard. The last sons of bitches of the human race had sold their bodies to the Jelk Corporation, becoming assault troopers for alien masters in an alien war. We'd bought the human race time to lick its wounds. Later, I led a slave revolt, captured a Jelk battlejumper and began the road that led to our freedom and a place in the Jade League.

If that doesn't make sense yet, it will. If you know all about that, hang on for a few seconds longer.

We should have had more starships around Earth. Over three-quarters of our growing fleet had left for the Grand Armada, the one that was going to head off to do some damage against the worst menace left. I'm talking about Abaddon and his Kargs. I was supposed to be with the Grand Armada. Frankly, it was a fluke I was home.

"Faster!" I shouted, managing to raise an arm and slamming a fist against an armrest. I don't know how many G's we were pulling, but I almost tore a muscle with that little stunt.

3

The booster roared into Mars orbit, gaining velocity as it headed for space.

The intercom came on. "Commander Creed," the pilot said.

"Yeah?"

"I have bad news, sir."

"Don't prep me for it, just spit it out."

"Mars Fleet is already accelerating for the enemy, sir. The fleet's velocity is already too much for us to reach them. It looks like we're going to have to go back down."

-2-

"I'm coming forward," I said.

"Sir, our acceleration is too great. You need to remain in your seat."

"Cut the acceleration until I'm up there."

The pilot might have argued with me, but he seemed to think twice about it. A moment later, the harsh acceleration quit.

I unbuckled and launched into the weightlessness. A few tugs on the nearby seats sent me sailing toward the hatch. It opened, and I floated through. The pilot was a lean fellow in a spotless uniform. The stars glittered through the window in front of him.

"Do you see those, sir," he asked, pointing out the window.

I squinted, seeing a dozen extra-bright stars. "What about them?"

"Those are the exhausts of Mars Fleet. We won't see them much longer."

"Patch me through to them."

He didn't argue. Two minutes later, using a small monitor, I spoke to my old friend Rollo.

Officially, he was First Admiral Rollo Anderson of Earth Force. He was my longest-running friend. We had each worked for Black Sand once, a mercenary outfit providing security all over the world. Rollo had been tall and bony

5

back then, and had worked out like a fiend. He'd wanted bulk but had been cut instead like nobody's business. The alien steroid-68 had done a number on him. Rollo was still tall, but there was nothing bony about him anymore.

He wore his own, specially tailored uniform, a tight-fitting jacket that did nothing to hide the fact that he was a bulked-up steroid monster with a neck and sloping shoulders better suited to a gorilla than a man. He looked more like a bone-breaker for the Mob than Earth's highest-ranking fighting admiral.

One of the sad things was that Rollo had forgotten to smile somewhere along the way. He'd been engaged to a hottie before the aliens had ever shown up on Earth. She'd died on the day of First Contact. Rollo still had her photo. It was clipped inside a book he kept, one with as accurate a score as he could figure concerning the number of aliens he'd personally killed.

There was nothing cold about Rollo's desire to enact vengeance against aliens, any aliens of any size and stripe. It was a fiery desire, barely balanced by a fierce loyalty to the sons of Earth. He'd been the first on many occasions to climb to his feet and charge back into laser fire or plasma blasts, to come racing back with an injured assault trooper on his shoulders.

In war, there was no one better to have by your side than First Admiral Rollo Anderson.

He now scowled on my tiny screen, his buzz-cut giving him an old-time U.S. Marine look.

"I'm coming out to you, old son," I said. "That means one of your ships needs to hang back and wait for my booster."

He stared at me for three silent seconds. "Fine," he said.

"What?" I asked. "No argument?"

He shook his head.

"What's the situation?" I asked.

"If you want to join the party, you'll have to max out your acceleration immediately."

"I have an orbital lifter. These things only have so much kick."

Rollo stared at me. He didn't like excuses on the parade ground. During a system-wide emergency—

"Ella has given me the computations," he said in a clipped voice. "She wants you to max out immediately. Time is critical, Commander."

"Ella's with you?"

He barely nodded.

That was good news. Ella had been a Russian scientist in Antarctica on The Day.

"What aren't you telling me?" I asked.

It seemed he fought with himself for a moment, as if he wanted to start smashing things.

"We hardly know anything yet," he said in a hoarse voice. "They're hidden behind a vast sand shield that is moving with hard velocity toward Earth."

That sounded weird. "Give me a visual," I said.

Rollo rerouted what Earth Fleet was sending him.

I squinted, lowering my head to get a closer look. A vast field of sand headed away from Venus toward Earth. The sand spread out over a tremendous area, greater than the old United States of America. My chest grew cold. A monstrous invasion fleet could be hiding behind that.

This was a clever idea. But how had a vast shield of sand gotten there? Our system's jump gates were among the outer planets. How could an enemy have maneuvered the sand wall in secret so they came as if from Venus?

That didn't make sense.

A terrible thought struck. What if the invasion force hadn't used a jump gate? What if they'd found a new way to travel between star systems?

"Get ready to send a message to Alpha Centauri," I said.

"I know what you're thinking, Creed. You want Baba Gobo to bring the Starkien Fleet into the Solar System."

"The invaders could badly outnumber us," I said. "That means we need reinforcements. The Starkien Fleet is closer than anyone else, a mere jump gate away. There's no time to lose in sending the message."

Rollo hesitated. Maybe he suspected the Starkiens had a hand in the attack. The more likely possibility was that he was considering the political-religious ramifications of such an order.

The Solar System held the Forerunner artifact Holgotha. Once, the Starkiens had led a nomadic existence because every race believed they lacked honor. I'd helped them regain their honor, but the Starkiens were treaty-bound to stay out of any star system holding a Forerunner object. If they broke their treaty agreement, every Jade League race was supposed to help hunt down the oath-breaking Starkiens.

"The Starkiens won't come," Rollo said.

"Baba Gobo owes us everything. He'll come. Besides, he'll realize I'll help him smooth this over later."

Rollo shrugged, turning, giving someone my order.

By the time he looked at me again, I'd strapped myself into the navigator's chair. The navigator headed for the main compartment to sit.

"Ready?" I asked the nattily dressed pilot.

He glanced at his board, finally seeing the blinking green light that indicated everyone else aboard the booster was ready for acceleration.

"Give it all you have," I told him.

The engines soon ignited, and we headed for the extra-bright dots in the star field.

As per my command, Rollo had ordered a starship to wait for us. I had time to kill before I reached the vessel. So, I might as well explain the religious-political situation that humanity found itself in. The whole thing was weird and rather interesting.

Where to start, though…

Before the Lokhars—the humanoid tigers—hit Earth, there was a grand two-way struggle going on in our neck of the Orion Arm Spiral. On one side was the Jelk Corporation.

Nasty red-skinned Rumpelstiltskin devils ran the giant company. The small red bodies were just a fleshy disguise, though. If you shot a Jelk enough times, his body vanished and his true self appeared. That self was an energy creature that could float through walls and fly through space.

The Jelk Corporation was hardheaded and tough-minded. They had two-legged lizards called Saurians to do their dirty work. That work included flying their spaceships and providing soldiers for the company armies. Saurians landed on Earth one day after The Day. Jelk battlejumpers had chased off the Rhode Island-sized dreadnaught that had attacked Earth. None of us knew that at the time. We figured the Saurians had done the mass killing. Thus, being in a murderous rage, I'd killed Saurians in order to get aboard a landing craft. I'd had some big plans that day.

But that's not what I'm trying to explain. On the other side of the grand Orion Arm conflict were all the other aliens. The most important were the Lokhars, who worshiped the Creator. That's key to understanding the political scheme. The Lokhars had created the Holy Jade League. They fought a losing religious war against the Jelk Corporation. The Jade League protected and worshiped at ancient Forerunner artifacts. The best way to think of those in Jade League religious terms were as holy Catholic relics.

As I've said, Earth now had a Forerunner artifact of its own. It was an ancient machine the size of an asteroid. It could talk, think and do freaking wild things. One of those things was to transfer or teleport to just about anywhere in the blink of an eye. That was ancient Forerunner technology for you.

The Forerunners, by the way, were the First Ones, really intelligent beings who had made the jump gates and other cool crap. They were so bright and inventive that they were all gone. The going consensus was that they were extinct.

The Solar System and Earth in particular was a backyard dirt-pile in the scheme of Orion Arm religious politics. The Jelk had planned to come to Earth to recruit hundreds of millions of slave soldiers for their company armies. The tigers figured no way could they let us ferocious humans loose on the star lanes, so they'd tried to exterminate us before we became a problem. Maybe I should be more exact. The Purple Tamika Emperor had reasoned it out like that, giving the kill order to his subjects. That's one of the reasons I killed the bastard three years ago, plain old human revenge.

A good tiger by the name of Doctor Sant, belonging to Orange Tamika, now ruled the Lokhars. The tigers had become humanity's friends in the bargain.

I'm sure that's all as clear as mud, as the old expression goes. Well, it gets more interesting. A third party joined the fray. They're the Kargs, ruled by a demonic being named Abaddon.

It's a mess of an explanation. Let's just leave it at this. I helped stop the original Karg invasion, one that came from a different space-time continuum. You heard me right. They were from a different reality. They would have come in their trillions in a billion spaceships. We assault troopers took their portal planet away, stranding them in their dying space-time continuum. However, and this is a big one, believe me, Abaddon made it out with enough Kargs and giant moth-ships to begin attacking the Jelk Corporation core worlds.

That meant the Kargs and Jelk had been battling it out one thousand light years from Earth. That gave me the needed time to get rid of the Purple Emperor and help put the Orange in his place. It gave humanity time to fix the Earth, repopulate it and build a tough little fleet of our own.

Now, when I say Earth Force was little, that's in comparison to everyone else. We made up for it by being the toughest mo-fos on the block. That only makes sense, right? The *nice* humans had all died on The Day. The only ones left were the crazy kind, the ones regular people had avoided when everything had been normal.

Anyway, after a lot of complications, things had worked out for humanity. We joined the Jade League, and I managed to help the baboon-like Starkiens get their honor back. The other races no longer sneered at them as space vagabonds and nomadic trash. The Starkiens also sealed Earth's most easily used jump gate.

As the booster continued for the waiting ship, I used the monitor. I studied the wall of space-sand. It moved away from Venus toward Earth. How long would it take Mars Fleet to reach the wall of sand? Could it do so before the sand and whatever was behind it reached Earth?

I ran some calculations and knew momentary relief. The edge of the vast sand wall would barely pass Earth. That was something. At least the grainy particles wouldn't sandblast the planet or its atmosphere away. However, whatever was behind the sand wall would reach Earth in...twenty-seven hours.

We only had a little time left. Was that enough time for Mars Fleet to join the battle? Maybe only if whatever enemy ships over there didn't accelerate through the wall of sand to make a dash at our planet. If they did make that dash, though...

I hated this. I didn't know enough. How had the sand gotten where it was without anyone spotting it sooner? It seemed clear. The sand hadn't used a jump gate. What motive technology had it used? I had a grim feeling that the sand had used Forerunner technology to teleport into place. It was the only explanation that made sense.

That would be bad if true. It might mean that the ancient machines like Holgotha had finally turned against us. Fighting Forerunner tech would be like Stone Age tribesmen trying to defeat tanks with flint-tipped spears. It was something that wasn't going to happen.

Did that mean I was rushing to my death?

I had no idea. So, I waited, trying to will the booster to greater acceleration. Instead, the engines quit as weightlessness returned to the rocket.

"We're out of fuel," the pilot told me. "Someone must have screwed up at the spaceport. We should have had a lot more fuel than this."

11

This was just great. Now what was I going to do?

-3-

"Any change in the situation?" I asked.

I walked onto the bridge of the *George Patton*, Rollo's flagship. It was a big starship, built like a Jelk battlejumper. It was new from our orbital Earth factories, which put out one new battlejumper a month.

The Mars booster was a chemical rocket, very short-ranged. That meant there hadn't been any braking to match the *George Patton's* velocity. That hadn't been a problem, though. The battlejumper did the matching, a team helping me with my space leap from the booster to the flagship.

Now, the *George Patton* accelerated to catch up with the rest of Mars Fleet. Gravity dampeners allowed the starship to do that without causing any discomfort to the crew.

The various bridge consoles were aimed at each other in a circle. In the very center was a big holographic display, visible from any angle.

Rollo moved away from his monitor. We shook hands, the big gorilla trying to crush my fingers as he pumped my arm up and down.

I grinned at him, slapping him on the shoulder hard enough to make him take a step to the side. That caused him to release his rock-like grip.

"Hello, Creed," Ella Timoshenko said.

She came to me, a thin Russian with a pretty face and breasts that wouldn't quit. Her dark hair dangled to her

13

cheeks like an erotic elf. Despite her Miss America-like beauty, Ella was an old-fashioned scientist, not like the ones we'd had just before the Earth died. Those had been easily swayed by the latest politically correct fashions. Ella only cared about what you could see and count. She'd never bought any of the Forerunner arguments about the Creator either.

Like the rest of us, Ella had her dark side and a no-nonsense practicality when it came to saving humanity. She was the best at operating the Jelk mind machine, having put many Lokhars under it in the past. The present Lokhar Emperor had gone under the machine when he'd simply been Doctor Sant. It was one of the reasons Emperor Sant favored humanity to the degree he did.

Ella searched for angles, for reasons and rationality. She had a burning desire to know why a thing was the way it was. If someone told her something that her observations said was BS, she would not hesitate to call the person out no matter their rank. It was easy to forget that about Ella Timoshenko when one looked at her.

She hugged me, pressing her breasts against my chest, releasing me after a time to look up into my face.

"I'm glad you're here," I said.

She gave me a curt nod, leading me to her station. "I'm thinking the same thing about you, Commander. But I'm curious. Why aren't you with the Grand Armada?"

An uncomfortable silence fell between us.

Rollo cleared his throat, saying quietly, "Zoe died. Creed brought her body back to Earth so he could bury her here."

"Oh, Creed," Ella said. "I'm terribly sorry. I wouldn't have asked if I'd known."

I looked away as I stuffed my pain in a deep place. I would miss Zoe Artemis dearly, had been missing her for some time already. Maybe I should have said something sooner. I operated on the theory that if I didn't think about it, my heart wouldn't ache so much.

14

"She was inspecting a laser coolant," Rollo told Ella. "It blew up at precisely the wrong moment. Some of us suspect sabotage."

Ella made compassionate sounds as she patted one of my shoulders.

I hardened my resolve. Aliens were trying to steal a march on Earth. We had to stop them. That meant total concentration of effort.

"That's the past," I said hoarsely. "We have a terrible dilemma to solve today. So let's get to it."

Ella squeezed my arm. The human contact felt good, but we had no more time for niceties. I took my memory of Zoe, placed it in a drawer in my mind and closed it so I could concentrate.

Afterward, I faced the others, asking, "How did a wall of sand the size of a continent appear between Venus and Earth?"

"Anyone have a theory?" Rollo asked his bridge crew.

No one looked up from their monitors.

"What does Earth Defense say?" I asked.

"The sand appeared a half hour ago," Ella told me. "One moment no one saw anything, the next it was there, heading for Earth."

I frowned at her.

"I'm telling you exactly what I know," she said, sounding defensive.

I nodded. "We have to break through the sand wall and see what's behind it."

"Earth Fleet is getting ready to launch T-missiles at it," Rollo informed me. The "T" in T-missiles stood for *teleport*.

"I want to see the situation," I said.

Ella manipulated her console.

I looked up at the holographic display. Earth Defense was composed of layers. At the bottom, on the planetary surface, were giant missile silos and rail-gun domes. They would attack anything trying to breach the atmosphere. Huge laser satellites orbited Earth. They could reach farther out.

Luna—the Moon—was a fortress. It had giant rail-guns, laser beam turrets and shorter-ranged particle beam emplacements.

The original Lokhar dreadnaught would have never made past all those defenses to harm Earth. The planet had even more, though, boasting its own private fleet.

Mars Fleet was the general force for the rest of the Solar System. Earth Fleet existed just to protect humanity's home. Twenty large starships with forty smaller patrol boats composed the force. Currently, it headed out to do battle with the wall of sand.

Rollo's dozen starships—three of them battlejumpers—would add considerable weight once they reached the enemy.

We'd come a long way from the ignorant savages we were before The Day, and we'd come almost as far since our Star Viking desperation.

These days, if someone wanted to pick a Jade League planet to bust, Earth would be one of the toughest. That was by my design. I'd spent too much time trying to bring humanity back from the brink of extinction to want to do it all over again. Still, if I'd known the wall of sand would appear, I would have kept *everything* back home, having sent nothing to the Grand Armada.

One battlejumper—the only one that belonged to Earth Fleet—inched a little father out than the rest of its sister ships.

"The battlejumper is about to launch a salvo of T-missiles," Ella explained.

"Is the starship captain aiming behind the sand or on it?" I asked.

"On, I believe."

"I've been thinking," Rollo said quietly.

Ella and I glanced at him.

"There's only one way that I know of that something just appears," Rollo said.

I kept staring at him.

"Forerunner transfer technology," he whispered.

His words were like a blow to the gut. They actually hurt. That's one of the ways to know if a thing seems reasonable or not. If it hurts, that's probably because there's a grain of truth to it. If you don't care what's said, it's because the thing is not even a remote possibility. That's why most insults that weren't even close to the mark slid off most people. The true insults are the ones that sting the worst.

Rollo was confirming my own worst suspicion.

"Holgotha hasn't moved from Ceres," Ella pointed out.

Holgotha was our Forerunner artifact, the one staying near the asteroid Ceres in the Solar System's Asteroid Belt. We'd used the artifact a little over three years ago. When humanity had been down to one measly starship, I'd convinced the artifact to teleport from one spot in space to another many hundreds of light years distant. T-missiles only had a several hundred thousand kilometer range, not light years. We had no idea how the ancient machine could make those vast transfers in a moment of time. It was First One technology. If the Forerunner machines were the reason for the wall of sand…

"Would Holgotha have remained near Ceres in order to make us think he had nothing to do with this?" Rollo asked.

"I doubt it," I said. "He wouldn't care enough. No. The more I consider this, the more I *don't* think the Forerunner artifacts are behind the attack."

"Why not?" Ella asked.

"The machines aren't inclined to direct bloodthirsty action," I said. "It's not their way."

"Look!" Rollo shouted. "The T-missiles are launching!"

I watched the holographic display. The battlejumper heading toward the wall of sand launched over a dozen big missiles. Those missiles disappeared from view one by one.

The first thermonuclear explosion blasted sand from the continental-sized wall. More T-missiles kept appearing at places hundreds or even thousands of kilometers from the

17

first one. They also exploded, hurling more sand from the space wall.

It turned out that the wall of sand was less than a centimeter thick. The T-missiles blasted gaping holes in it. The expanding explosions moved even more sand. Some of those forces collided. That also shoved sand, exposing the foe behind the wall.

"Is that right?" Rollo asked in disbelief.

Ella checked her monitor. "Yes," she said.

Along with everyone else, I stared at the holographic display. An asteroid had been behind the sand. It wasn't an enemy fleet, but a very large chunk of rock.

"How big is it?" Rollo asked.

"A little bigger than our Moon," Ella said as she studied her panel.

That meant it was much bigger than most asteroids. No wonder the wall of sand had stretched out larger than the old United States.

"Seeing that makes even less sense," I said. "How did a moon-sized rock come to appear between Venus and Earth?"

"What's the moon's trajectory?" Rollo asked.

Ella ran some numbers. "It will miss the Earth just barely."

Rollo scratched his head. "I don't get it. If it isn't a threat—"

"Look," Ella said. She pointed at the holographic display.

Giant blue-colored fumes lengthened behind the enemy moon. That indicated some kind of engine back there, propelling the moon. Yet how did one maneuver such mass? It would take extremely vast engines.

"The moon is changing its trajectory," Ella informed us. "It's shifting onto an Earth intercept course. Maybe with its sand shield pierced, the moon's pilot no longer cares if we see what it's doing."

Rollo banged a fist against a monitor.

The moon moved in a slightly different heading than the pocketed sand wall. My eyes widened as shock struck. Was I seeing this right? Not only did the enemy moon change heading, but now chunks of rock zoomed off its lunar surface.

"What's going on?" Rollo shouted.

"Observe," Ella said, manipulating her board. She managed to zoom in a little closer.

We saw a giant rail system, an accelerator, shooting moon rocks from the object, launching them at Earth. It was like our own mining operation on Luna. We had tugs to catch those rocks, as the rocks leaving Luna lacked the velocity of the ones being hurled now.

"Is that a spaceship instead of a moon?" I asked.

Ella and Rollo looked at me as if I was crazy.

"It has exhaust," I said. "That means it has motive power. That makes it a ship in space, hence, a spaceship. Those are its missiles. Rocks. If it fires enough rocks it will overwhelm Earth Defense."

"Forget about the rocks," Ella said. "If the free moon smashes into the Earth...it will mean the death of everyone on the planet."

A cold feeling swept over me. Just how were we supposed to stop something with the mass of Luna from colliding against the Earth? It looked as if after all our hard work over the years that our lovely home was about to die a second time.

-4-

"Are there any suggestions as to how we're supposed to stop a moon-sized spaceship?" I asked.

"It's like a rogue comet," Rollo said.

"That thing is a lot bigger than any comet," Ella told him.

"I know that," Rollo said crossly. "My point is: how do you stop a rogue comet? You blow it up. Well, that's what we do here. We blow it up."

"We might not have enough warheads—thermonuclear or antimatter—to do that," Ella said. "Maybe, just maybe, we have enough to splinter the moon into pieces. That won't help us, though. The pieces have the same mass as the whole. It's enough to wipe out life for a million years."

"The thing is too big to think of it as a comet," I said.

"Correct," Ella said. "It's like an asteroid, an errant one. We had plans in the old days to deal with something like that from hitting Earth."

"Something that big?" I asked.

"Maybe not quite that large," she admitted. "But the principle is the same."

"I'm listening."

"You nudge it off course," she said.

"With nukes?" I asked.

"Yes."

20

"You have a problem," I said. "That's not a big asteroid. That's a vessel. Look at the exhaust tail. That means it has engines. It can steer itself. If you use nukes to nudge it out of its path, the ship will simply steer itself back onto target."

"We should steer it ourselves then," Rollo said.

I clapped my hands, grinning at him. He'd come up with the answer.

Ella shook her head. "Creed, you can't be thinking what I think you're thinking."

"I am," I told her.

Rollo glanced from her to me.

"We go old school," I told him. "We've done it before. Do you remember when we grabbed Shah Claath's battlejumper out from under him?"

Shah Claath had been our original employer, a red-skinned Jelk. During a grim battle, we'd used an enemy T-missile to teleport back onto his battlejumper. It had cost us assault troopers. It had wrecked a lot of the interior starship, too, but it had worked after a fashion.

"How are you going to know where to teleport inside that thing?" Rollo asked.

"We're not going to appear inside it," I said. "We appear outside above the surface."

"I'm sorry," Ella said. "But that doesn't help you. The moon has forward momentum. You will appear with your own momentum, going exactly the wrong direction, toward it. Instead of landing on the surface, you will splat like bugs. Every assault trooper who teleports will die."

"That makes sense," I said, undaunted. "So I'll figure out a different way to land."

"What way?" Ella asked.

"You're the scientist. Give me a solution. Isn't that what Russian scientists are supposed to do."

"No," she said. "This is an impossible situation."

"Balls!" I said. "I already have an idea. We pop behind it instead of in front. Then, we accelerate to land on its dark side."

21

Ella blinked several times. Finally, her fingers flew over a computation pad. She ran numbers and velocities. "That's out," she finally said. "It wasn't a bad idea, but the moon-ship has too much velocity. Supposing we sent a regular missile with the T-missile—if such a thing is possible—the regular missile won't have enough fuel to accelerate you fast enough to reach the moon-ship."

I tapped my chin, my gray cells alive to the problem. I had the right idea, I was sure of it. Otherwise, I didn't see how we could stop the mobile moon from smashing against the Earth.

"The Earth Fleet ships will have to launch assault troopers onto it," Rollo said. "Once they're close enough to the enemy—"

"Tell me this," Ella said in a scathing tone. "How are the Earth Fleet ships supposed to do this thing?"

"Easy," Rollo said. "They brake—"

"They're heading *at* the moon-ship," Ella said. "To brake completely and then accelerate to catch up with the passing vessel…There isn't enough time and room to do all that. The moon-ship has too much velocity. This is the perfect attack. That as much as the rest of the evidence leads me to suspect the Forerunner machines are behind it."

"It isn't a perfect attack," I said. "We just haven't come up with the solution yet."

"We'd better do so in the next few hours," Ella said. "Otherwise, we're not going to have the time to implement your plan of steering the moon-ship away from Earth—given that it's possible to capture."

I glared at the holographic display. Putting my hands behind my back, I began to march around the consoles that circled the display. How could we land assault troopers on the moon-sized object? We couldn't appear in front of it, or the surface would rush up and crush each one of us.

"It's a matter of having enough fuel, right?" I asked.

"You mean concerning the missiles appearing behind the moon catching up with it?" Ella asked.

22

"Yes."

"Yes," she said. "If the missiles had more fuel, perhaps they could accelerate fast and hard enough at the moon-ship to land on it. Remember, though, first the missiles have to brake in order to stop their momentum as they head toward Venus. Once they stop, then they will have to accelerate after the moon-ship."

"Okay," I said. "That just means we need more fuel."

"It would take too many T-missiles teleporting enough regular missiles or fuel pods into position. And how would you get the fuel from one missile or pod to another? We don't have that kind of refueling tech on the missiles themselves."

I scowled. We needed more fuel, more mass, more—

I snapped my fingers. "I think I have it. But it will be risky, really dangerous, in fact. I wouldn't suggest it except for the prize, saving our beloved planet."

"Well?" Ella asked. "What's your great idea?"

I told her, Rollo and the listening bridge crew.

Ella laughed, shaking her head as she did so. "I can't believe it, Creed. That's outlandish, insane and as improbable as hell. You do realize that, yes?"

"I don't care about any of that," I said. "Can it be done?"

Ella Timoshenko stared at me. "I have no idea. In fact, I doubt it. But I don't see that we have any other choice. I wish N7 were here. We're going to need incredible timing to pull this off. But if everything works at precisely the right instant, maybe, just maybe, we can pull off this madcap stunt and have a shot, at least, at saving Russia—saving Earth, I mean."

-5-

Several hours later, the *George Patton* nosed among masses of free-floating T-missiles.

Our battlejumper had finally reached the Mars Fleet. The other ships had had to slow down so we could catch up in time. Once we all had the same velocity, those warships had disgorged almost their entire complement of teleporting missiles.

"Shouldn't we disengage the nuclear warheads first?" Ella asked.

"There's no time for that," I said. "It's going to be hard enough sequencing the mass of T-missiles to all teleport at one precise instant of time."

"Hard?" Ella asked. "I still say it's impossible. You're going to tear the battlejumper apart with this stunt."

"Which is one reason I'm going to only ask for volunteers," I said.

"Creed, you don't have time for that either."

She was right, but it was hard to accept.

"When they signed up for Mars Fleet, this was one of the adventures they signed up for," Ella said.

"I don't see any other way to stopping the moon-ship in time," I said.

"Me neither," Ella said. "It's the only reason I'm agreeing with this madness. But now you've got another problem. The moon-ship keeps catapulting rocks at Earth.

We're going to need the Mars Fleet out there to help knock down all the rocks. That means these ships should start accelerating for Earth again."

"First things first," I replied. "The planet can survive a few rocks. It can't survive a direct moon strike."

Ella could see that. "How many assault troopers will you have?"

"One thousand, maybe," I said. "I'm taking every assault trooper Mars Fleet has."

"One thousand to storm a moon-sized ship." Ella shook her head. "That's far too few."

"You're right. It is. We're going to have to reach the enemy bridge to win."

"I don't know if you've thought this through," Ella said. "Maybe they have auxiliary control stations over there. Maybe they can override the engines. Maybe—"

"Ella," I said, interrupting.

She raised her eyebrows.

"Kindly shut up with your pessimism and start working on the immediate problem. How to board and secure the enemy moon-ship is my problem. I'll solve it my way, and that isn't by wringing my hands on all the possible ways it can go wrong."

"No. You like to charge straight ahead and hope for the best."

"If it ain't broke, don't fix it," I said. "That includes a proven combat method."

She rolled her eyes, but obeyed my command, continuing to link every T-missile so they could make one coordinated launch. Combined as one, the mass of missiles in a precise whole would create a teleporting web, hopefully taking the battlejumper with them.

"I'm coming with you," Rollo said.

"Good. I'm going to need someone old school. You can start by calling all the Mars Fleet ships. Make sure all their assault troopers are headed here. Do you have your bio-suit aboard?"

25

"Of course," Rollo said. "What about yours?"

"I sent it ahead to the booster on Mars before I boarded. So it's here."

Our bio-suits were something else. They had first come to us from our Jelk paymasters. The suits were one of the reasons we'd all been injected with steroid-68 and surgically implanted with neuro-fibers.

Our bio-suits were alive, symbiotic second skin. They flowed over our bodies and could harden on the outside while keeping soft on the inside. They absorbed a tremendous amount of damage. The second skin also amplified our already considerable strength. They could also act like spacesuits, powered by our sweat. In case you're wondering, the alien second skin didn't cover our faces. We wore helmets instead and heavy combat boots.

We first-timers had had our bio-suits from the beginning. We'd found more in several Jelk star-cities throughout the years, but only had a limited supply. That limited the number of assault troopers humanity possessed.

I continued to run the steroid-68, bio-suited assault troopers, leaving day-to-day politics to those that loved it. Diana the Amazon Queen and Murad Bey were still alive. Each headed their respective parties for Earth Parliament. We used the old British system of government. Theoretically, I had a boss, the Prime Minister. In reality, I still pretty much did as I saw fit. That would change one of these days. But it wasn't going to change today.

The hours fled as space teams maneuvered the T-missiles against the *George Patton's* outer hull. Welders secured them to the armored skin.

During that time, the moon-ship catapulted more rocks. Earth Fleet charged toward the enemy and Earth Central began launching missiles. Those would intercept and obliterate as many approaching rocks as they could.

All the while, comm-operators hailed the moon-ship. So far, no one had replied.

It was maddening not knowing who piloted the moon-ship. Who was the enemy? What did they have against us? Was this a new alien menace or an old one finding a new way to attack humanity?

"Maybe we should talk to Holgotha," Rollo said.

I shook my head. I doubted the Forerunner object would answer. He usually didn't unless pressed hard enough. Once this was over, though, I planned on having words with the ancient machine.

More hours ticked away.

It was maddening. I stood on the bridge, staring at the moon-ship bearing down on Earth. My gut had begun to churn some time ago. If we didn't get these T-missiles coordinated soon, it wasn't going to matter what we did.

It was delicate work sequencing each T-missile to teleport at a precise instant of time. Anything else would tear the battlejumper apart as half teleported away and half remained behind. We still had the other problem. The moon-ship came toward the Earth from Venus. We headed inward from Mars. Once we teleported, we'd still be going in the same direction. That meant the battlejumper had to brake to a full stop and accelerate to catch up to the moon-vessel. That's the reason I was using the battlejumper. It had the fuel and hard accelerating engines—but only if we went within the next three hours.

I called Ella. Sweat bathed her face, and worry lines creased her forehead. She was concentrating and didn't have time to talk to me.

Two hours and twenty-three minutes later, Ella called me.

I'd moved down to the main assault chamber, more a cargo hangar really. There were assault shuttles and sleds in abundance. We old-timers had used these before. I'd spoken to my assault troopers, a little less than one thousand warm bodies. I had nine hundred and forty-three troopers to be exact. It was a paltry sum to capture a moon-ship, but hey, it's what I had.

"We're as ready as we're going to be," Ella told me.

I inhaled deeply through my nostrils. If I thought too hard about what we were going to do—

"I want you off the battlejumper," I said.

Ella laughed harshly. "That's a negative, Commander. I'm coming with you. I even have my bio-suit here."

"Ella—"

"I'm not going to argue with you about it," she said. "I'm on the bridge right now. You need someone up here that knows what's going on. Also, this is a science experiment, and I want full credit for what we did."

She was ever the scientist.

"If this works," I said, "I'll tell people it was all your idea."

She made a face. "Ideas are a dime a dozen, Commander. It's executing them that counts."

She had a point.

"How much longer until we're ready to launch?" I asked.

She checked her board. "Give me another ten minutes. I want to run one last test. Then, it's go time."

"Roger that," I said.

During those ten minutes, I loaded up the shuttles, twenty vehicles with fifty assault troopers per carrier. We weren't going to use the sleds this time. Most of us carried pulse rifles and shock grenades. We also had a scattering of plasma cannon teams and some anti-air teams to knock down any moon fighters the enemy might launch.

The ten minutes passed in a blur of sick anticipation. This was our planet's great hope for survival. How had it happened that after all our hard work to make Earth a fortress, she was relying on one thousand assault troopers? If we survived this, I was going to make the attacker pay an unholy price for attempting it.

I sat in the pilot's chamber with Rollo. The First Admiral was going to do the flying. That was the kind of admiral I admired, one willing to risk everything with his men.

Ella appeared on a tiny screen. "Are you ready?"

"Yes," I said, over-anxious to get going.

She nodded, tapping a panel as numbers flashed in the screen beside her.

Rollo began the count at, "Three, two, one...ignition."

For a moment, everything went blurry. A feeling of sickness hit my stomach. Had we made it?

Disorientation struck. Then, everything around me began to shake. Through my helmet, I heard shredding metal sounds and crumpling bulkheads. What had gone wrong?

The shaking increased. Our shuttle lifted off the hangar bay deck. I looked over at Rollo. The flight board was dark. Our assault vehicle slammed against another shuttle. That flung me against my straps, forcing air from my chest. Our main blast window shattered as a different shuttle cartwheeled across us to bang against a hangar bay bulkhead.

This was a disaster. After all this preparation, the T-missiles must have not worked all at the same instant of time.

Finally, we stopped rolling. My muscles ached. That had been worse than any destruction car derby I'd been in as a teenager. Lights flickered in the hangar bay as grim rumbling sounds came from deeper within the battlejumper.

The comm came on. At least it still worked. A bloody-faced Ella stared at me.

"What happened?" I asked. "Did one of the T-missiles misfire?"

"No," she panted. "It was a perfect teleportation. We did everything right in that department."

"Then how come I've probably lost half my assault troopers before we started the attack?"

Tears welled in her eyes. "We miscalculated our destination, teleporting in *front* of the moon-ship not behind it like we'd planned. One of the rocks catapulted from the moon smashed through our battlejumper. The ship is shredded, Commander."

I swore, feeling sick and helpless. How could this have happened? Did that mean Earth was doomed? A fierce resolve swelled in me. We still had to make this work, but I had no idea how.

Ella worked her board as she spoke. "It's worse than that, Commander. The battlejumper is getting ready to go critical. You have to leave the ship or die in the coming explosion."

"We need the battlejumper's acceleration," I said. "That was the critical element to my plan."

"I know. You're going to have to use the shuttles for that now."

Right! That's the only thing that made sense. "Get down here," I shouted.

"There's no time for that, Commander."

"Get down here, Ella. I'm not leaving without you."

"Sir—"

"Do it, Timoshenko. Or I'm coming up there to get you."

She stared into my eyes, realizing I was dead serious. "I'm on my way, sir,' she said, moving out of visual range.

Rollo turned to me. "Do our shuttles even have enough fuel and speed to accelerate fast enough so the moon-ship doesn't obliterate us?"

"No," I said.

"That's it then," Rollo said. "The moon-ship will either smash us or pass us. We failed."

"Not yet," I said. "I have an idea."

-6-

A munition explosion tore open the frozen-shut hangar bay door. More explosive munitions hammered against an inner lock. The bullets came in a stream from Shuttle Nine. It was the least damaged shuttle of the lot.

We had begun the mission with twenty shuttles full of assault troopers. Now, we had fourteen. Few of those had a full complement. This was a balls-up. That didn't mean it was over, though.

"I see stars," Rollo shouted.

Ella hunkered in a back seat, having barely made it in time.

Shuttle Nine had already lifted from the hangar bay deck. It sped at the ragged opening. The assault shuttle tore pieces of bulkhead as it crashed through, but the operative word was through.

More shuttles followed number nine.

"Get us out of here," I told the First Admiral.

The musclebound gorilla did just that, taking the armored shuttle like an angry baby through its birth canal. We zipped out of the mostly destroyed *George Patton*.

Rollo cursed as he gave the shuttle as much thrust as it could muster.

Before us were stars, beautiful stellar lights. I could see Earth in the distance. It wasn't visibly blue-green yet, but it was the biggest thing other than the Sun. Uh, let me rephrase that.

The moon-ship looming behind us was the biggest thing. We could see craters just as if we had been Apollo astronauts in the good old days. But that I mean the '60s. If there had been a better time for the Earth, I don't know it.

The moon-ship loomed massive behind us, and it gained on our tiny shuttles. Our minuscule shuttle fleet tried to outrun doom.

The battlejumper no longer had acceleration power. The moon-ship gained on it and crashed against the wreckage, crumpling what was left of the glorious vessel and spreading it across the rocky surface.

No one said anything for several seconds.

Ella finally broke the grim silence. "I see the catapult rails."

"Are they firing on us?" I asked.

"I doubt the rails are that precise," she said. "But would you look at that. They're launching another batch of rocks at the Earth."

I watched from her view-screen. A giant bucket sped along the rails gaining velocity. It reached a ramp, like an old-time ski jumping ramp, and shot the rocks into space. They tumbled end over end, heading for Earth. The rocks would miss us by hundreds of kilometers. The battlejumper getting hit by some of them had been the freakiest of bad luck.

"We don't have much time left, Creed," Rollo said. "Maybe you'd better explain your wonderful plan to us."

"You're doing it," I told him.

Rollo shook his helmeted head. "I'm not seeing it."

"We're losing velocity as we brake."

"Not much velocity," he said.

"Maybe enough so we can survive a crash landing."

"That's it?" he asked. "That's your great plan?"

"There you have it in all its glory," I said.

"How can you be so cheery at a time like this?" he complained.

"Because I'm playing the game," I said. "If I keep my wits about me, I may get a chance to win. That will allow me to destroy the bastards who attacked Earth."

"Oh-oh," Ella said.

"What's 'oh-oh?'" Rollo asked.

"Those look like hangar bay doors," she said. "And they're opening."

I tapped a console, bringing up her view. Huge doors opened on the lunar surface. One after another, fighters launched into space.

I stared at them in slack-jawed wonder. "Those are Jelk craft," I said.

Rollo glanced at my view.

They were narrow fighters with missiles under incredibly stubby wings.

"Saurian fighters," my friend amended.

"Saurians," I said, tasting the word. "That scratches the idea this is a Forerunner plan. It's a Jelk plan, a corporation assault." My hatred for the Jelk Corporation awakened with added intensity.

Saurians were two-legged, walking lizards as I've said. The creatures' movements were springier than a human's. Usually, Saurians stood four or four and half feet tall. They called themselves the Family and made better workers than they did fighters. I think the Jelk liked them because Saurians were easy keepers and bred like flies.

"Where did the Jelk get transferring moon-ships?" Ella asked, perplexed.

"We're going to have to turn to face the fighters," I told Rollo.

"If I do that," he said, "I can't slow our shuttle from crashing against the moon-ship. We'll smash against the surface harder—"

"Turn around, turn around," I shouted. "They're coming on us fast."

As I spoke, enemy missiles launched from under those stubby wings. Fortunately for our side, we'd been fighting Saurians for a solid four years. We'd done so as Star Vikings and afterward as we went after the Jelk frontier planets. Most of those planets had Saurian guards. We'd gotten pretty good at shooting them down. Even better, we had their tech down pat. That included these missiles.

Our electronic countermeasures were more than up to the task. Only three of their missiles hit targets. They shredded a shuttle, knocking us down to thirteen, and opened a huge hole in another.

My boys and girls did much better. They didn't rely on missiles, but used autocannons with great targeting computers. We chopped up those fighters in quick order, leaving hunks of spinning metal and fleshy Saurian pilots to twist in space.

As a military problem, their menace lay more in that we hadn't been able to slow our rush toward the moon-ship during the fight than the actual fighters' basic deadliness. I suppose the dead assault troopers in shuttle fourteen felt otherwise.

"We know something vital," Ella said. "The Saurians have the moon-ship, but it doesn't appear they have any more technological advantages."

"Their one advantage seems pretty harrowing," Rollo said.

"Agreed," I said. I studied the rear-viewing screen. The lunar surface was much closer than before. We only had a little time left.

"We're going to hit too hard," Ella said, studying numbers.

"That's why we're wearing bio-suits," I told her. "They'll absorb the shock."

"The crash might kill the suits," she said.

"Rollo?"

"I'm sick of running, Creed. I'm sick of Saurians, and I'm sure as hell sick of these Jelk bastards. I want to kill them. I want to kill all of them."

"How about a moon's worth of enemies?" I asked.

He shot me a glance. "You know we're going to die in a few seconds, don't you?"

"I didn't survive Antarctica to die on this moon," I said.

"I know what you mean," Rollo said. "This is going to be like the Antarctica lander all over again, huh?"

"No."

"No?" he asked.

"This time, we're going to win."

Rollo laughed. It was a good sound.

"Here it comes," Ella shouted. "Good-bye, Creed. Good-bye, Rollo."

I might have answered, but the moon surface smashed up against our little shuttle, hitting with too much force.

There's a time for detailing all the pyrotechnics, all the gore, pain and misery of a situation. Sometimes, though, words simply don't do a moment justice. This was one of those times.

The moon collided with our shuttles one right after the other. Some of the ships crumpled like beer cans in a strongman's hand. Some smashed open like overripe cantaloupes, spilling their precious cargos over the lunar surface. A few of the shuttles cartwheeled down lunar mountains into a giant crater. That shed some of the initial killing velocity. Ours happened to be one of those vessels.

Three other shuttles met a similar fate. Approximately half of the cargoes survived. That meant one hundred assault troopers in horribly beat-up shape found the strength to get up and collect what weapons they could find.

Rollo, Ella and I were among them.

Every step hurt. So did every breath. Every time my right foot came down, I winced. Fortunately, my symbiotic suit was still alive. It was incredibly rugged. The bio-suit began secreting painkillers directly into me. That helped a lot. It also started healing processes. I would need those if I was going to do much.

Five minutes later, I'd gathered the hundred survivors. To my surprise, no Saurian fighters strafed us. I vowed to myself they were going to rue this to their dying breath.

"Listen up," I said, using a short-wave band. "We're here. Now, I'm going to tell you something critical. A man in the right spot at the right time can do more than a nuclear bomb lit in the wrong star system."

Every silver-colored visor was aimed at me.

"A man with a knife in a foe's bedroom can do more than a million-man army in the wrong city. We're that knife, us, a mere one hundred assault troopers. We're going to have to storm this moon-ship, killing anyone getting in our way. If we fail, the Earth dies. I'm not letting that happen. What about the rest of you?"

Many of them shook their helmets.

I pointed. "That way is the hangar bay door, the one that disgorged the fighters. This is a moon-ship with negligible gravity. That means we can run fast and far in a short amount of time. The first trick is getting inside this thing. The second is finding the bridge sooner rather than later and then taking over.

"Any questions?" I asked.

They were all probably still too sore to ask questions. But that was fine with me. I was tired of talking.

"All right," I said. "Follow me."

***

Someone inside the moon-ship must have finally gotten smart, or maybe they got scared.

Three Saurian fighters zoomed low over the horizon. Each of them launched missiles. Those must have been antipersonnel missiles.

I went down onto one knee, raised my pulse rifle and let instincts take over. One shot, two, three, four and an explosion told of a direct hit.

Other hits told of other assault troopers taking down missiles. Soon after that, three smoking fighters slammed against the lunar surface.

"It's time to run," I said.

They did, following me. As I said a few moments ago, this was a moon-sized vessel. That gave it a similar gravity as Luna. We were all highly trained, veteran killers of many campaigns. If I could have felt pity for our enemy, I might have almost felt it for the Saurians. But they'd already slaughtered far too many of my people. I told myself they hadn't done so because they were good, but lucky.

We all like to lie to ourselves sometimes. Brain over brawn, right? What counted in the end was who won, not who fought better, whether it was because of bio-suits and killer attitudes or superior tech, like the moon-ship. Winning determined everything. If you don't believe that, just ask the German soldiers of WWII or ask General Lee at the end of the American Civil War.

I wanted to write the history books on our war, telling my story. That meant I had to win this fight. Otherwise, some hoary Saurian in some lizard cave would tell all the listeners how foolish the Earthlings had been to take on the Jelk Corporation moon-ship.

"I just had a thought," I said over the short-wave comm. "What if Claath is in here? Wouldn't that be something?"

"We could make him float away again," Rollo said, leaping even with me.

"I'd like to figure out a way to kill him for good," I said.

"Yeah," Rollo agreed.

I saved my breath after that. We traveled up the crater, turned right at the base of the mountains and noticed the blue-green object in the heavens.

Earth had gotten bigger, more visible. It was maybe a quarter as large as Luna seen from Montana at night. How much time did we have left?

I was guessing it was not enough.

It was at that point we got our first break. Someone in Earth Fleet was thinking. They'd sent more T-missiles. Those missiles now targeted various open hangar bay doors. With the keen precision I'd come to expect from humans, they threaded those missiles into the various openings. Only once inside the enemy ship did the thermonuclear warheads detonate.

The blasts and shockwaves would no doubt travel down various corridors. The T-missiles might prove terrific shock grenades, softening up the enemy before we reached them.

It took another ten minutes to reach a twisted, smashed hangar bay. It was hot with radiation. But we could take it for a while with our bio-suits. Later, we could soak in healing baths. Many of us had done that before.

At that point, the assault troopers received a coded pulse letting us know our boys in Earth Fleet knew what we were doing. They weren't going to send any more T-missiles down to frag us.

"This is it," I radioed. All our communications crackled with static. "We're headed for the center. That's where the Jelk probably built the bridge. This doesn't end for us until we're dead or victorious."

I got a ragged cheer and some curses. That was good enough.

With bitter determination, remembering all the indignities Claath had first heaped on us, I jumped into the hot hole, hoping to head down deep into the moon-ship.

-8-

We made it half a kilometer into the ship before the Saurians hit us. They'd set up heavy laser guns, chopping down seven troopers before we knew they were there.

I chalked that up to radiation poisoning. I was feeling woozy by then, with an upset stomach. Like many of the others, I was taking too long to react to the enemy.

"Peter is down," a man radioed.

"Side hatch time," I snapped.

My troopers knew what I meant. We retreated from the laser gun nest. Then, a team set up a mine against a bulkhead. We ducked around a corner and saw the blast. I led the way through our new "hatch" until we reached another selected bulkhead and set up another mine. We ducked around a corner, saw the blast and used the new opening.

In short order, we bypassed the blocking Saurians. Normally, I would have hit them from behind. They didn't count, though, not in the greater scheme of things. Let them wait for us to show up again.

Sure, we set up a few booby-traps in case they decided to chase us. But in that case—

Behind us, the corridor shivered from heavy explosions. The Saurians had tried to follow us after all. That had been their last mistake.

"I'm recalibrating my motion-sensors," Ella told me. "I know their trick now."

I didn't bother to ask what she meant. I used my remaining mental energy to keep going. I was having an interior debate with myself. Long ago, our bio-suits had secreted a berserker drug into us troopers. We'd short-circuited that feature. With a simple command, however, I could reorder my suit to give me the battle-juice. That might make things a whole heck of a lot easier on my aching head. It would also make me stupider.

"Creed," Rollo said.

"What is it?" I asked in an irritated voice.

"I found an elevator," Rollo said. He studied an analyzer.

"That doesn't make sense."

"I downloaded a schematic," Rollo said. "I've been deciphering old Jelk commands and maps."

He always had been good at electronic devices.

"And...?" I asked.

"And I found an elevator. Aren't you listening to me? It's to our left. I have to tell you, Creed. It's a long way to the center of the ship."

"Just like the portal planet, huh?"

"Pretty much," Rollo said. "I don't think we're going to make it in time unless we go for broke and use the elevator."

"Halt," I said.

Assault troopers threw themselves onto the floor, panting. We'd been going for some time now. If the rest of them had started like me from the first body-smashing moon-crash, they'd felt beat from the get-go.

I sidled next to my friend and studied Rollo's schematic. He had a point about the distance. Ah. He'd also located the enemy bridge. It was at almost the exact center of the moon-ship. That was a long way down, all right. We had to start turning the massive vessel sooner rather than later if we were going to make it miss the Earth.

"This is the piece of luck we needed," I said.

41

"I think it had more to do with the T-missiles than luck," Rollo said. "We've seen the number of dead, right? Those EMPs must have messed with many of their control systems."

Had I forgotten to mention the many dead Saurians lying in the upper corridors? I must have been more beat than I realized.

"Listen up, people," I said. "We're heading out. We have to move."

This wasn't like the portal planet. I didn't need to kick anyone to get them up onto their feet.

"Let's double time this," I said. I was getting paranoid about having enough time to turn the moon-ship. Did that show I was overconfident about reaching the bridge? Maybe.

We found Rollo's elevator several minutes later. Guess what? It worked. The T-missiles hadn't messed with it. The thing was a cargo hauler. That meant there was room for everyone. Did I dare take everyone, though?

I laughed to myself. Did I dare leave anyone behind?

We piled into the box. Ella fiddled with the controls. Soon, we plunged down at express speed. It took eight minutes to reach the center.

They tried another ambush, big-wig Saurians with lots of braid on their fancy uniforms. They manned plasma cannons, heavy laser guns and pulse rifles like us.

Fifteen assault troopers fell to their savagery. We returned the favor with interest, slaughtering all but three of them. The biggest Saurians, which were the oldest, I took as prisoners.

We stormed onto the bridge next, dragging our Saurians with us.

It took Ella less than ten minutes to figure out the controls. Soon, the giant engines made the bridge thrum with power.

Slowly, on a large screen, we watched the Earth. By incremental degrees, we shifted our home planet from the center of the screen to the edge. It looked like we were going to do it.

That's when a Saurian horde hit us, trying to retake control of the moon-ship.

-9-

The Saurians made a mistake, though, an elementary one. They should have sabotaged the engines so we couldn't turn the ship away from Earth. Fortunately, they didn't do that.

Instead, the lizards tried to boil through the main hatch onto the bridge. My assault troopers mowed them down. It was carnage, a butcher yard.

Pulse bolts tore holes in tough lizard armor and the leathery hides underneath. Awful smelling smoke roiled. Blood spurted. You get the idea. After a while, the lizards tore at the corpses jamming the main hatch. They should have rolled grenades onto the giant bridge. They should have blown bulkheads to make new entrances. They should have at least fired blindly as they charged in. They did none of those things. They rushed us with knives and knuckle-crushers. Some of them held their rifles like bats, coming in swinging.

That didn't impress us. We killed them like you would kill cockroaches scurrying through the house.

All the while, Ella used the primary controls, turning the moon-ship farther off course.

I kept my left arm tight around the biggest Saurian's throat. Surprisingly, he stood a little taller and a lot wider than me. Once I started to get the idea of his critical importance, I pushed the old shod forward, using a pistol. I

44

target practiced against the Saurians trying to get at us. They rushed me madly, straining to reach me, probably wanting to free the old Saurian in my grip, the one I used as a lizard shield.

Here's the thing. A Saurian was like any lizard on Earth. As long as he lived, he kept growing. That meant the biggest ones were old ones, the most important Saurians. This old guy was the biggest lizard I'd ever met.

As I said, the other Saurians didn't roll grenades onto the bridge or charge while shooting from the hip. Clearly, they didn't want to accidently kill one of the three old ones we held. Mine was the most important. He had an impressive uniform, too, positively jangling with all the medals on his chest.

Maybe you're waiting for me to tell you I got tired of killing Saurians. I'd be lying, though. I didn't get tired. I could have kept doing this for days. My only regret was how sore my trigger finger was getting. I kept switching hands. That helped a bit.

Finally, I began to wonder if there was a better way of doing this. It turned out, for us, there wasn't. The Saurians kept charging until more assault troopers landed on the moon-ship. They came directly from the Earth Fleet, who had finally reached the moon-ship.

This vessel had literally tons of Saurians as crew and service personnel. Finally, however, the enemy realized the hopelessness of their situation. After a long time trying to kill us, the Saurians began to surrender.

We were the last to learn of it down here. Luckily, before our energy packs drained dry, the cavalry rescued us.

I could have dropped to the deck and slept right there. Instead, I popped a stim. It took a little longer than normal to take effect. Finally, my eyes bulged, and a dry taste developed in my mouth. A wicked energy began to fill me.

I hustled my captive into a different chamber. Ella joined me, standing against a bulkhead near the hatch. I shoved the

45

old Saurian onto a chair. Then, I took off my helmet. Even here, the air stank, but at least it was breathable.

The old Saurian looked at me with big, sad eyes.

"I'm glad that's over," I told him, using the slave tongue I'd learned in Jelk service.

He made an incomprehensible gesture with his three-fingered hand.

"Who are you?" I asked. "What's your rank?"

He said nothing.

"You're not the Wisdom of the Family, are you?"

He sat a little straighter at that. Had that been a surprise for him? I'd captured an old Saurian before on a star-city we raided three years ago. That old one had been a robe-wearing priest known as a *wisdom*, a religious leader. The Saurians called all other lizards "the Family", although I'd never learned why.

"Time's up," I said, drawing my pistol, aiming it at his oversized head.

"Wait," Ella said, stepping forward.

I turned to her while keeping the gun rock-steady on him.

"Let me put him under the machine," she said.

As I've said before, Ella had a Jelk machine, a nasty mind gadget. It did things…

"I am So-Ko-Liss," he said in his hissing speech.

I lowered my gun a fraction as I stared at him.

He glanced at Ella before regarding me. "I am the Supreme Ship Lord. I received a direct commission from…"

"Don't stop now," I said, when he seemed to hesitate. "Who gave you the commission?"

He made an odd expression with his leathery jowly features. "I am not to say," he informed me.

I holstered the gun, jerking a thumb at Ella. "You heard the lady, right? She's our expert, our mind scrubber. She's going to rip out your every secret."

Supreme Ship Lord So-Ko-Liss blinked at me in his lizard fashion. The idea didn't seem to trouble him. I wondered what had had him up in arms a few seconds ago.

"Afterward, she'll reprogram you," I added.

That made him agitated, shifting on the chair.

"Hmm," I said, stroking my chin. "We'll give you a totally new personality, a cheerful, helpful one. How does that sound?"

"N-n-no," he stuttered.

"Then it's time you talked, got honest with us. Who gave you your commission?"

"Do you know Shah Claath?" the Saurian asked.

I glanced at Ella as my heart rate sped up. That little bastard was behind this?

"This is important, Creed," she said in a soft, dangerous voice.

Nodding, I took hold of myself. I took a deep breath, held it for a long moment, and slowly let it out. I did that a second time for good measure. I hadn't realized how much the name Claath made me boil. Why had he wanted to wipe out humanity at this late date? It was time to find out.

"I've heard of Claath," I said in a conversational tone. "Is he well?"

The lizard blinked at me again, maybe realizing he'd made a mistake.

"Did Claath order you to destroy the Earth?" I asked.

"I am on a sacred mission," the Saurian said. "I am now foresworn. It is wrong of you to question me as you do. Allow me the dignity to die in battle."

I stepped closer to him, and I could smell his dry lizard odor.

He slid back as if to get away from me, which I found strange for a creature who had just asked to die in battle. I think he saw his death in the wrath blazing in my eyes. The old boy struck me as a hypocrite. This Saurian wanted to die…just not right now, please.

Maybe he didn't want to die as I ripped limb from torso. He wanted a quick *clean* death, one I most certainly would *not* give him.

"Creed," Ella warned.

I nodded again without turning to her. "Dignity," I said slowly. "That's an interesting word. Don't you agree, Supreme Ship Lord?"

"I have sworn an oath," he said.

"I bet you have. I bet it was a grand occasion, eh? Thousands, maybe millions, of Saurians saw the honor Claath gave you. It must have felt nice."

"I am the oldest."

"Oh, wow," I said. "That's totally cool. If I'd known that…"

"Now you know," he said.

"Yes. I do. Would you like a drink of water?"

"I would. My throat is very dry. I need some moisture for my skin as well. In my quarters you will find a cream—"

He stopped talking because I lunged at him with a knife, stopping a centimeter from his wobbly throat skin.

"If you're thirsty, how about I cut you? You can suck your own blood. Would you like that, old guy?"

He sat straighter, more stiffly, and I thought I saw reproach in his eyes. "You are mocking me."

"Now we're getting somewhere."

"I am the oldest," he said. "I commanded the Death Ship. Shah Claath commissioned me. I have been given a great honor. You worked for the Corporation once. You should—"

I slapped him across the face. That shut him up pronto.

"Guess what, old son. I'm unimpressed by your age. You just tried to exterminate the human race. That makes me angry. That makes me very angry. Do you know what I do to aliens that make me angry?"

He shook his head.

"I figure out what they hate the most," I said. "Then, I do that to them. Before I do anything to you, though, I'm going to change the basic set of your personality. I'm beginning to really dislike the one you have."

"No..." he moaned. "That is evil. I am the oldest. I hold the old knowledge. I am the Saurian of Saurians. I had the greatest, noblest task of all."

"Destroying the Earth?"

"Yes," he said, "wiping out the nest of race killers. We know. I know. You are the bred ones. You are the terrible slayers. Abaddon has shown Shah Claath. If the galaxy is to know peace, humanity must die."

"Abaddon hates the Jelk," I told So-Ko-Liss."

"The Dark One hates humans even more," the Saurian said.

"Are you telling me the Jelk and Kargs have made an alliance?"

"It is so," the Saurian said.

That was big. It was stunning. The two evil races had made a pact. They had started by trying to wipe out humanity. Why was that so important to them?

"This is the beginning attack?" I asked, wondering about my hypotheses.

"You would die first, as is fitting," the Saurian said.

I shook my head. "You blew your shot, old son. You appeared too far away from Earth. You should have teleported closer."

The Saurian hung his head. "I know, I know. My navigator miscalculated. It was a great sin. I shot him the instant I realized we had appeared in the Sol System off course. I should have shot myself then as well." He looked up. "Will you spare me a pistol?"

"Oh, of course," I said. "I'll give it to you after we're finished here."

"Thank you," he said, having no idea of my sarcasm. "Could we finish quickly then, please? My shame is becoming more than I can bear."

"Creed," Ella whispered.

I cast an irritated glance over my shoulder at her. We'd both taken off our helmets, but we still wore our bio-suits.

Hers was glistening black like mine. It gave her a decidedly martial but still sexy appearance.

I stepped to her as she lowered her voice.

"There's more going on here," she whispered. "Do you mind if I ask him a few questions?"

"Go ahead," I said.

Ella stepped up, nodding to him.

So-Ko-Liss regarded her uneasily.

"Abaddon hates us because we stopped him before," Ella said. "Surely, you and Shah Claath realize Abaddon is only attacking us out of self-interest."

The Saurian cocked his head as if trying to figure out what she was saying.

"Humans are the greatest fighters," she said. "Kargs are antilife soldiers. For life to win here, everyone needs us."

The Saurian glanced at me impatiently, as if I would hurry this up for him.

"Why would Claath help Abaddon against the Jelk?" Ella asked.

"You are wrong," the Saurian said. "Claath and the Jelk are in alliance with Abaddon."

"When did this happen?" Ella asked.

"I do not know the exact time and date."

"The Kargs and Jelk were at war as little as a year ago."

"That is true."

"Now they are at peace?"

"That is self-evident given the alliance."

"Surely, there are greater targets than Earth," Ella said.

"I suppose that's true."

"Why wouldn't the greatest Saurian lead the attack against the greatest object? Why would you be relegated to a lesser task?"

"The destruction of Earth was considered critical," he said proudly. "I *was* given a noble task, a great task. Alas, I failed. My honor is gone. Please," So-Ko-Liss said to me. "Give me a pistol so I can cleanse this offense with my blood."

50

"What other places were targeted?" Ella asked.

"I was not privy to the planning meetings," the Saurian said. "I do not know."

"Then how could you know there were greater targets than Earth?" Ella asked.

The old lizard stared at her for a heartbeat, finally saying, "Rumors leaked through."

"Give me an indication of some of the other targets," Ella said.

"The Lokhar homeworld," he said.

"And?"

"The Sirius System."

"Any others that you heard about?" she asked.

"Only the Proxy System in the Centaur Nebula," he said softly.

Ella nodded, still staring at him. "Tell me, Supreme Ship Lord, would you really have crashed your vessel against the Earth?"

"Of course not," he said. "My ship was too valuable for that."

"What?" I said. "But you aimed for the Earth."

"That was a deception," he said. "The rocks would have been enough. Besides, I have a bio-terminator aboard. I would have unleashed it on the planet in passing."

Hearing that, I wanted to crush his skull with my bare hands.

"Did you have another target in the Solar System?" Ella asked.

That made me listen more closely. I hadn't thought of that.

So-Ko-Liss swayed. "You are tricking me." He gave me a sad-eyed scrutiny. "You do not plan to give me a pistol, do you?"

"Not right away," I said.

He made a keening sound, hugging himself. It was kind of pathetic.

"What other target could he have?" I asked Ella.

51

She stared at the ancient Saurian. "I don't know for sure," she said, "but I'm beginning to have an idea."

"How about cluing me in," I said.

"Every star system he named is home to a Forerunner artifact," she said. "I don't know about you, Creed, but I don't think that's a coincidence."

-10-

A week later, I approached Ceres in the Asteroid Belt. I had no intention of landing on the busy asteroid. I was heading for Holgotha, the Forerunner artifact.

N7 had dashed home, which was good for us and me. The android had been inside the artifact before. The blond-haired, choir-boy-looking android sat beside me in the speedster. He had begun as my enemy, a DI in the Jelk Corporation. N7 had been good at what he did, always winning himself upgrades. When I'd made my break for freedom with a T-missile against Claath, N7 had decided to throw in his lot in with ours. He'd won even more upgrades since then, and was the brightest among us.

Ella stayed with the moon-ship presently parked in a far Mars orbit. She and teams of scientists were crawling everywhere as they studied the incredible vessel. Others fixed what we and the T-missiles had destroyed capturing the ship.

Supreme Ship Lord So-Ko-Liss was dead. It hadn't been by our design. I'd wanted to know more. So, I'd given Ella permission to put him under the Jelk machine. A mini-bomb went off inside him the first time she tried. Whoever had put the bomb there hadn't wanted anyone prying secrets from him.

N7 had informed us of another moon-ship attack in the Beltran System. The transfer ship had feinted at the main planet, raining rocks onto the surface. Afterward, it had struck at the Forerunner object. The enemy vessel might have destroyed the ancient machine, but the artifact had transferred as moon rocks sailed toward it. Where it had transferred to, no one yet knew.

"The pattern is interesting, don't you agree?" N7 asked me.

"Sure," I said.

N7 glanced at me. "You have a right to be nervous. Holgotha is still processing his subroutines."

N7 referred to something we'd learned several years ago. The Forerunner artifacts had certain First One programs. One of the most critical was to find evidence of the Creator. I'd asked Holgotha if he and the others had been trying to set up a universal apocalypse by bringing Abaddon and his Kargs into our galaxy, thinking an ongoing apocalypse might cause the Creator to show up. Holgotha had become curious at this, wondering if that could be true. He'd told me he would internally investigate his subroutines. When I'd asked him how long that would take, the artifact had told me, "Twenty to twenty-five years."

That meant Holgotha was still analyzing his subroutines. His past reactions had shown us he didn't like being disrupted during that time.

"Still," N7 said, "I might point out that every time you've gone to see him, the artifact has been incredibly patient with you. That, too, is interesting. I wonder if I have failed to detect a pattern there."

I was nervous, all right. The last time I'd been inside the artifact, I'd fought the Purple Tamika Emperor. The fight had been more touch and go than I cared to remember. The end had been ugly, too, with me stomping the emperor's face with my boot... That had been the ugliest fight of my life. I didn't care to rehash it now.

Theoretically, Holgotha was under my care first and humanity's second. Long ago, the Starkiens had gained their evil reputation because the curious baboons had tried to take

54

apart the artifact in their care. They'd inadvertently destroyed the object. The other Forerunner objects had known right away about that, and they'd known who the culprit was too. The artifacts told on the Starkiens. From that point forward, the rest of the Jade League members had treated the Starkiens as outcasts.

Now, that was interesting and ominous on several fronts. Firstly, clearly, the artifacts had a way to communicate with each other across hundreds and possibly thousands of light years. They could and did talk among themselves. No one else knew how to do something like that. We had to travel through jump gates by starship to send faster-than-light messages to one another. Secondly, the artifacts had gone so far as to make trouble for an artifact-destroying race such as the Starkiens. Thirdly, the reason why the Starkiens had destroyed an artifact didn't matter. The destruction was the only thing that counted, not whether it had been an accident or not.

Three years ago, Holgotha had agreed to help the Star Vikings. He'd warned me, though. If he was destroyed while helping us, the other Forerunner objects would instantly become our enemies.

Like all the aliens I'd met so far, the ancient machines had a very high opinion concerning themselves. Had the First Ones programmed them like that, or had the machines gotten high and mighty over time?

Our speedster was getting close to Holgotha. I'd already answered the first picket. Other guard satellites ringed the asteroid-sized object.

On a parenthetical note, Baba Gobo had sent a ship into the Solar System at my request for help against the moon-ship. The Starkien captain had beamed a question to Earth. The reply caused the Starkien ship to turn around and go back to Alpha Centauri. I'd altered the jump gate's log, erasing the fact of the broken treaty. Soon, I'd have to go to Alpha Centauri and personally thank Baba Gobo for risking everything for us.

It was at that point a light bulb popped into brightness in my mind. I turned to N7.

"I just thought of something. Maybe you've already thought of it, but let me run it by you just the same."

The android nodded.

"Somehow, Abaddon or the Jelk have gotten hold of several moon-sized ships."

"That seems obvious," N7 said.

"Let me finish. They have several of these incredible transfer ships. So far, only Forerunner artifacts have the ability to pop hundreds of light years in a sudden teleportation jump. Instead of massing these special moon-ships and hitting one system after another—that's what I would have done with them."

"You are not Abaddon," N7 said.

I gave him a shrewd glance. "Do we know this was Abaddon's plan?"

"No, but I would suggest it is."

"Okay, okay," I said. "Before we get to that, here's my point. They sent these transfer ships at star systems holding artifacts. In one at least, the moon-ship feinted at the home planet and then attacked the artifact, causing the artifact to leave for parts unknown."

"Correct," N7 said.

"It's a good bet that's what would have happened in the Solar System—after they rained rocks on our planet."

"That seems logical."

"Therefore, our enemy, Abaddon or the Jelk Corporation—"

"Or both," N7 added.

"Whoever our enemy is, they want to strip us of Forerunner objects," I said.

"That is my guess as well."

"Why does our enemy desire this?"

"I have no idea. Do you?"

I faced forward, searching for a visual sign of the artifact. "I don't know yet," I said. "But I know what I'm going to do to find the answer."

***

The Forerunner artifact in our system was as large as an asteroid, as I've been saying. It had a donut shape. In the middle of the donut hole was a black hole. I'd always thought the black hole was critical to the transfer ability. So far, we hadn't found any black hole on the moon-ship, nor had we found anything that simulated the actions of a black hole.

One thing the black hole on Holgotha did was make it difficult to walk on the inner ring of the artifact because it poured radiation there. The reason that was bad was because boxlike, squat houses in a small area were situated on the inner ring. No one had any idea who used to live in those homes. They were incredibly old, much older than So-Ko-Liss had been.

N7 and I knew the drill. We'd done it several times already in the past. I donned my bio-suit. N7 wore combat armor. Letting the speedster float several kilometers from Holgotha, I opened a hatch. Jumping out, I activated a small thruster, holding onto handlebars.

N7 had his own thruster. We flew to the artifact, gently landing a little later. Magnetizing the thrusters to the metal hull, we did the same to our boots. Then, we began to clank our way across the artifact.

The walk took time. Eventually, radiation began to strike our armor. I'd taken the healing bath after the moon strike. Even so, the radiation leaking onto me gave my mouth a metallic taste. I'd never gotten used to that.

In time, we reached the unimpressive box buildings. I went to my favorite. This was usually a long process of banging on the metal and trying to convince Holgotha to let us in. This time it was different. I went to knock, and my hand sank into the substance.

I turned to N7 and motioned him to follow me. Afterward, I waded through the substance. It was creepy, but this was the only way to reach Holgotha's comm center. Finally, I oozed out of the wall into a speaking chamber.

"You may remove your helmet," Holgotha said.

He spoke with a wall membrane. It vibrated like a larynx in a throat. The process gave the artifact a deep voice, and it was damn eerie. The light was diffused in here, but I could see easily enough.

As I've done before, I detached my helmet, holding it in the crook of my arm. The odor was neutral in here now. It hadn't always been like that.

A bench oozed up from the floor. It was a large bench, with enough room for N7 and me.

"Hello, Holgotha," I said, after seating myself.

"Hello, Earthling," he said, the wall vibrating. "It has been too short of a time since we spoke last."

I found myself holding back. The last time I'd been here, Holgotha had said the winner of our duel would get one question answered. The Purple Tamika Emperor had wanted to know the true purpose of the Forerunner artifacts. That had been a shrewd question. On my most pessimistic days, I wondered if that's why I'd been able to kill the tiger. Had Holgotha secretly aided me so he wouldn't have to answer the tiger's question?

"I've come to warn you," I said.

"Please, Commander, let us not go through these tedious games. I have much work to do and only a few years to get it done. My subroutines are extremely complex and sophisticated. I begrudge myself even these small moments talking to you."

"I can well imagine."

"No," Holgotha said, "I do not believe you can. If you could imagine, you would feel such shame at bothering me that you might ask for a sidearm to commit suicide."

"I see. You were listening in on our conversation with the Supreme Ship Lord."

"Not only are you bloodthirsty," Holgotha said. "I have discovered that you are heartless as well."

"The Saurian planned to smash the moon-ship against the Earth."

"That is false. He already told you that was a trick. His true purpose was to attack me."

"If that's true, why didn't he appear closer to you? Why did he start near Earth first?"

"That is an interesting question," Holgotha said.

I glanced at N7, who sat with his hands on his armored knees, apparently failing to notice the similarities in their speech.

"Why are they attacking Forerunner objects?" I asked.

"Perhaps to show us how futile the Jade League aliens really are in protecting our kind."

"We beat off the attack," I said.

"By that you mean the humans did, I suppose. Many of the others did not 'beat off' the attacks.' The human victory was to be expected. You are the *little killers* in the old tongue."

"What tongue might that be?"

"I already told you, Commander, the old one."

"All right," I said. "I've heard enough about us being the *made ones*, the *little killers*. Our victory seemed far from certain. It was next to impossible in fact."

"Did that stop you?" Holgotha asked.

"We didn't have any other alternative. We had to win or perish. But that's not what I'm getting at. The Saurian referred to us as the made ones. Why is that? Why were humans called the little killers in the old tongue?"

Holgotha remained silent.

I stood, beginning to pace. "You can't be happy with Abaddon and his Kargs. They're antilife. The Jelk Corporation is an abomination. Everything is profits with them, yet they're not even material creatures, but energy beings. Why are energy beings so absorbed with profits?"

Holgotha still said nothing.

Scowling, staring at my feet, I told myself to stay calm. If only the Grand Armada had started for the Jelk core worlds two years ago. That had been the plan. We were going to swamp the embattled Kargs and Jelk, surprising them. Political divisions, revolutions, quarrels along with a thousand other minor problems had delayed the great adventure. It had given the Kargs and Jelk time to come to an agreement.

"Who suggested the joint operation against the league?" I asked.

Holgotha did not say.

"Who was losing the war, the Kargs or Jelk? You can at least tell me that, can't you? Or can't you spy on Abaddon the way you can spy on us?"

"Abaddon has advanced procedures that make direct observation impossible," Holgotha said.

"Do you think Abaddon wants to replace you?"

"I do not understand your reference," Holgotha said.

"You're the mysterious power in the Orion Arm. Heck. Maybe you artifacts litter the entire galaxy. I don't know. Maybe you don't either."

"I do know, of course," Holgotha said, but the artifact didn't elaborate.

"Maybe Abaddon wants to be the mysterious force," I said.

I was guessing. I knew too little about Abaddon. I didn't even know what species he was. I didn't think he was a Karg. Maybe he was a corrupted First One. Abaddon had power. Every time I'd talked to him via screen he had given me the shivers. He'd lived for millennia and had offered me a place in his command structure, telling me I'd become an immortal. If any creature could be like the devil in the Bible—only with technological space powers instead of magical abilities—it would have been Abaddon. Sometime in the distant past others had driven him out of our space-time continuum. Now, he was back.

"I have waited," Holgotha said, "but you have failed to tell me how Abaddon wishes to replace us."

My head lifted. Why hadn't I noticed this before? I kept myself from grinning. Maybe I finally understood something critical and could use it to pry real information from humanity's secretive artifact.

-11-

I sat down on the bench and began to tap a finger on a knee. "Don't you see it?"

"I can predict most actions with a high degree of accuracy," Holgotha said. "I cannot read minds, though. What are you thinking?"

"Wait a minute. You can predict most actions, most reactions as well, I guess. That means you should be able to predict my thoughts. You shouldn't need to ask me."

"Usually, this would be the case," Holgotha said.

"But not today or not with me?"

Holgotha did not answer.

"I'm an enigma to you," I said. "That's what you're implying, right?"

No answer came.

I smiled, trying to bluff him. "Your silence confirms my thought."

"You are free to think what you want," Holgotha said.

"I know. I am."

"I find you to be an exasperating creature. These conversations are nonsensical. I do not know why I permit you to enter my chambers. It is a waste of time."

"I know why."

"That is false," Holgotha said. "If I do not know, you surely cannot know."

"You do it because you're trying to understand me. You wonder if I can figure out a few of the mysteries that are baffling you. It's in your self-interest to talk to me."

"No. These are absurdities. I am not baffled by anything."

"Oh, sure, I believe that," I said, glancing at N7.

The android was frowning at me. I don't think he appreciated my novel approach.

I wanted to wink at N7, but I didn't know how Holgotha would take that. I didn't see anything resembling cameras, but I knew the intellect of the Forerunner object watched my every action.

"I believe I know why Abaddon sent the moon-ships against you artifacts," I said.

"No one has yet established that Abaddon did these things," Holgotha said. "All indications show it was a Jelk idea."

"What indications?" I asked.

N7 cleared his throat. "I suspect the artifact means the Saurian crews. I would guess the other moon-ships also had Saurian crews. There were no Karg crews on the various transfer ships."

"Is that right?" I asked Holgotha.

"Affirmative," the artifact said.

"Ha!" I said, smacking a fist into a palm. "It was Abaddon's plan, all right. The Saurian crews are simple misdirection. You and your brothers were meant to see that and draw such an inference as you have."

"Your reasoning does not hold in the slightest," Holgotha said.

"Maybe not to you," I said. "But I see it clearly."

"That is emotive speech, nothing more. It means nothing."

"No. It's clear to me. Abaddon doesn't want you to see it. That's all. Why get uptight about that?"

"What doesn't Abaddon want me to see?" the artifact asked.

"Before I answer that, let me ask you this. What is the critical element regarding the moon-ships?"

"You must do your own reasoning," Holgotha said. "I am not here to do your thinking for you."

"I just wanted to see if you realized the key element. It's the transfer power. The moon-ships do what, until now, only you Forerunner artifacts did. That's amazing when you think about it. That must mean the moon-ships are using First One technology. Doesn't that bother you?"

"Given that it's true, why should it?" Holgotha asked.

"It means Abaddon can use the moon-ships to duplicate your most amazing feat."

"That does not altogether hold. I doubt the Kargs or Jelk have our far-scanning tech. The moon-ships' improper usage suggests that."

Holgotha meant that the Forerunner objects could look where they were going to transfer before they actually did the transferring. In some fashion, the giant machines could scan hundreds maybe thousands of lights years ahead of them. The moon-ships hadn't been able to do that, it seemed. Their less than ideal appearance in the Solar System suggested that.

"That each attack was meant to drive away an artifact suggests Abaddon doesn't want your kind around," I said. "Maybe he's found other Forerunner tech. Before he unleashes it, he wants all the artifacts out of the way. Perhaps his plan is so blasphemous it wouldn't work unless you're elsewhere. Seeing what he's really doing, would force your kind to fight him. Maybe you're afraid to do that, though."

"Your guesses are not even comical," Holgotha said. "They are simply absurd."

"How do you know that?" I asked.

"Commander Creed, I grow weary of your childish ploys. I understand you are attempting to drive me into a garrulous mode so I will impart to you information you would never receive otherwise. It is the tediousness of

64

speaking to you, the sheer waste of time, that has forced me to my newest conclusion. I will grant you your desire in order to end our prolonged conversation."

N7's head swiveled around sharply.

Out of the corner of my eye, I saw the android studying me. I'm sure he wondered if that had been my intent the entire time. It hadn't, but when this was over I'd tell N7 it had been. That would keep him guessing about me.

"Claath was instrumental as an intermediary in bringing the Jelk Corporation and Abaddon into their present accord," Holgotha said. "Together, they will attempt to shatter the Jade League. You have seen the first hammer blow directed against it. The shock of these moon-ship attacks is even now beginning to take effect. Firstly, many Forerunner artifacts have vanished. Secondly, that has started a religious crisis in many star systems. Thirdly, that crisis will shake Jade League morale. Fourthly and finally, the Grand Armada will lose flotillas as the various commands return home to secure their home worlds. The crumbling of united League action will leave the individual species open to separate attacks by the combined Jelk-Karg Super Fleet."

"You see all this or you've figured it out?" I asked.

"The Super Fleet already nears the Jade League. This is fact. The unusual route means that Earth will be one of the earliest targets."

"What?"

"I would suggest that either Abaddon or the Jelk Council has a special dislike directed toward you humans, or against you personally, Commander. The Super Fleet has bypassed the Grand Armada. If you wish to protect the Solar System, you will need the Jade League armada. However, it is substantially weaker than the Super Fleet. Plus, my analysis of the Jade League religious reaction has a ninety-four percent chance of taking place exactly as I've described it. That means the Grand Armada will face a serious reduction in fighting power."

I stared at the vibrating wall. If the Super Fleet was coming here, did that mean Abaddon or the Jelk had expected the moon-ship attack to fail? That didn't make sense, did it? Why would they want us to have a moon-ship? Or was this a precaution on Abaddon's part? Yet, why would he fixate on Earth first? Why not attack the critical Lokhar star systems first? The tigers had a vastly greater amount of starships than we did.

Okay. I had to put Earth's danger aside for the moment to figure out the rest of this.

I cleared my throat. "So...you're saying the moon-ship attacks were primarily directed against the league members, to weaken us as a whole?"

"No, not primarily," Holgotha said. "That is one of the side benefits to the enemy. The primary benefit is to drive us ancient machines into hiding. I suspect you are correct about Abaddon's ultimate goal in that regard."

That surprised me, as I'd been guessing in the dark. I didn't have all the facts, though, and what I didn't know could end up being the most dangerous.

"If our Grand Armada is weaker than the Super Fleet," I said, "I guess that means the enemy has a greater mass of starships."

"You would be incorrect in believing that," Holgotha said. "The Jelk and Kargs fought too long against each other for that to be the case. They should have come to an accord sooner."

"Why didn't they?"

"That is not germane to our present consideration," Holgotha said. "Mass tonnage or simple number of vessels is only part of the equation. They have superior technology, if one does not include the Forerunner artifacts on the League side, which I do not for a battle calculation."

"Why wouldn't you include yourselves?" I asked. "Aren't you artifacts on our side?"

"We are in almost every consideration," Holgotha said. "Abaddon's victory would be tragic. His ethics are what you would consider demonic. I do not believe the Creator would approve of him."

"Is Abaddon a First One?" I asked.

"That is not germane to the situation."

"The hell it isn't."

"You will refrain from cursing in my presence," Holgotha said. "Otherwise, I will terminate the conversation this instant."

"Sure…" I said. "Consider it done. No more cursing."

It was several seconds before the wall began to vibrate again. Maybe that was the artifact's cooling off period.

"As we have spoken just now," Holgotha said, "I have run several million war scenarios. The Jade League is annihilated in eighty-three percent of them. In twelve percent of the outcomes, various races will survive as slave subjects for an indeterminate number of years."

"That doesn't leave us much of a chance."

"That is correct. There is, in fact, a five percent chance the League will defeat the combined Karg-Jelk forces. That would take brilliant leadership on your part and various acts of stupidity on theirs. I do not envision stupidity from Abaddon. Instead, in those outcomes, I envisioned his elimination early on."

"Wait a minute. You're saying we can't win unless Abaddon dies?"

"That is essentially correct," Holgotha said.

"And if he dies that gives us a five percent chance of victory?" I asked.

"Yes."

"What can we do to increase our odds?"

"Eliminate at least fifty percent of the Jelk before the main forces engage in hostilities."

I stared at the wall. "You're implying we hit them before the Super Fleet engages the Grand Armada."

"Congratulations, Commander, you have correctly divined the meaning of my words."

"I'd appreciate it if you turned off your sarcasm program," I said. "It's becoming irritating."

"There was no sarcasm intended," Holgotha said.

I didn't believe that, but I let it go. Instead, I cracked my knuckles, thinking. "For us to do something like that, we'd have to make transfer attacks. I don't see how else we could do it. Are you willing to host a number of assault troopers—"

"I engaged in direct military maneuvers once before when you were Star Vikings," Holgotha said, interrupting me. "I will never do that again. I find my actions back then repulsive. War is a hideous experience, much better observed several star systems in the distance than in proximity."

"That just leaves the moon-ship. It's sluggish. Maybe it can transfer to the Super Fleet..." I looked up. "Are you suggesting we simply appear in the middle of their Super Fleet, locate Abaddon and kill him?"

"We were speaking about the Jelk," Holgotha said. "In either case, however, that is a rough outline of the correct operational plan with the highest probability of Jade League success."

"That's no plan," I said. "It's a suicide mission."

"And yet, I have noted that you excel is exactly those kinds of missions."

I studied the wall, wondering about the artifact's intellect. "What are the present Super Fleet coordinates?"

Holgotha did not speak.

"If you're not going to tell me," I said, "how are we supposed to do this?"

"That is not my concern."

"That doesn't make sense. You said Abaddon was odious."

"I said he is an abomination. I have come to believe his destruction is critical. We will not directly help you in this, though, as our programming forbids it. However, I have been engaged in a careful study of my restrictions for the last

68

thousand years. I am about to make a momentous decision. The appearance of the moon-ship has given me the liberty to introduce the Obliteration Protocols."

"What are those?"

"I can only tell you that they are among my oldest programs. Let me begin by saying that you do not possess the weaponry to kill Abaddon. Do not believe that stranding him in space will kill his body or that placing him in the center of a thermonuclear detonation will obliterate him."

"What about in the heart of an antimatter explosion?" I asked.

"Abaddon has resources beyond your understanding. In fact, most of this is beyond your understanding. The Jelk, Kargs and Abaddon...all of them are incredibly ancient. The moon-ship predates my construction. That is why it is so inferior. It was the first transfer vessel. We artifacts are a vast improvement upon it."

"Okay..."

"The weapon you need is at Sagittarius A*." That was pronounced Sagittarius A Star.

"Where?" I asked.

N7 spoke up. "That is at the Galactic Center, Commander. It is in fact a supermassive black hole."

"Just like Abaddon's space-time continuum," I said. "What are you trying to pull, Holgotha?"

"The android is incorrect," Holgotha said. "Sagittarius A* is not the Galactic Center. It is the center of your galaxy. That is approximately twenty-seven thousand light years from here."

"But Sagittarius A* is still a supermassive black hole, right?" I asked.

"The Fortress of Light orbits the supermassive black hole," Holgotha said. "At least, the last time I checked it did."

"How long ago was that?"

"That is not germane to the situation."

69

I felt my blood pressure rising, but refrained from cursing. In a tight voice, I said, "This sounds like a goose chase. Twenty-seven *thousand* light years away…is that right?"

"That is correct," Holgotha said. "The weapon is in a vault inside the Fortress of Light."

"What is this fortress exactly?" I asked.

"One thing at a time, Commander," Holgotha said. "Twenty-seven thousand light years is too far for your moon-ship to transfer in one bound. It will take several teleportations. Once you arrive there, the key I give you will allow you entrance into the Fortress of Light. There, the key will lead you to a weapon with the power to slay Abaddon. Return with it, and humanity along with the Jade League will gain a chance of surviving the coming war."

I plopped down onto the bench. "You want us to teleport to the center of the galaxy while the Super Fleet heads to Earth?"

"That is my best recommendation toward your ultimate victory."

"Well…first," I said. "Can you send a message for me?"

"Of what nature?" Holgotha asked.

"Telling the admiral of the Grand Armada to start heading to the Solar System," I said.

Holgotha was silent for a time. Finally, he said, "Yes, I am willing."

"Great," I said. "Now, explain the Fortress of Light to me."

"The key can do that."

"This is a Forerunner key?" I asked.

"In truth, no," Holgotha said. "The key belongs to the Fortress of Light. It will agree to do these two acts for you as the price for its freedom."

"What?" I asked, rubbing my forehead. "This is beginning to sound weird."

"That is due to Abaddon and the Jelk," Holgotha said. "Like me, they are special entities. That calls for special

70

weaponry. Why else do you think the Jade League has been losing this long conflict since the beginning?"

It dawned on me that I might be touching upon the true purpose of the Forerunner objects. A captive key to the Fortress of Light in the center of our galaxy...that sounded strange, all right, and interesting. What was Abaddon? Why did we need a special weapon to kill him, one found in something called the Fortress of Light?

I looked up.

"Since I wish to forestall another round of tedious conversation," Holgotha said. "I am about to give you the key. Your time is strictly limited, Commander. The Super Fleet is approaching fast, and I'm sure Abaddon has other surprises in store for you. This is the great showdown. The Dark One has made a miscalculation, however. I am sure he did not foresee my cunning with the Obliteration Protocol. Now, it is up to you."

I stood up. "What does the key look like and when do I get it?"

"It is on its way to your speedster. Since it cannot withstand the black hole radiation, I have let it out a different port."

"There's another way in to see you?" I said.

"None of that will ever matter to you," Holgotha said. "Good-bye, Commander. I bid you a blessing in the Creator's name. You have the weight of the galaxy riding on your shoulders. If you fail...your race along with the Forerunner machines are most certainly doomed."

-12-

The next few weeks were a blur of activity. It's hard to remember what happened in exact order.

I imagine that's how the workmen at Pearl Harbor felt after the Battle of the Coral Sea against the Imperial Japanese Navy in World War II.

After the treacherous Battle of Pearl Harbor, where the Japanese sucker-punched the U.S., the American Navy had to make do against the stronger Japanese Fleet, at least stronger in the Pacific at the time. Some of the remaining U.S. carriers met the Japanese in the confused Battle of the Coral Sea. The Japanese sank the *Lexington* and damaged the *Yorktown*, as well as sinking some other, non-carrier American vessels. The U.S. had struck back, sinking a Japanese flattop.

In any case, *Yorktown* limped back to Pearl Harbor. U.S. Naval Intelligence knew the Japanese were planning another attack—the coming attack on Midway. Admiral Nimitz of the Pacific Fleet had two good carriers left, the *Enterprise* and *Hornet*. Besides that, he had seven heavy cruisers and the damaged *Yorktown* to face the coming might of the Imperial Navy.

The Battle of Midway would be one of the most decisive in War World II. The Americans went into it as underdogs, utterly turning the tables on the Japanese. One of the keys to that victory had been the carrier *Yorktown*.

When it steamed into port, the authorities estimated it would take ninety days to repair the internal and leaking damage. Fourteen hundred yard workmen toiled around the clock for *two days*, and then the desperately needed carrier was ready for war. One reason everyone had worked so hard was that Admiral Nimitz had realized navies had entered a new era of flattops and air wings. The battleships, cruisers and destroyers counted for far less in terms of sea superiority than the new carriers.

I suppose the same might be true for us. With the moon-ships, Abaddon and his allies had introduced a new type of spaceship. A regular fleet would take weeks, possibly even months to get to a location, one a transfer ship could reach in three seconds.

That got to me thinking. How many moon-ships did Abaddon have? It must be a strictly limited supply. Had our captured moon-ship struck here first, or had it hit elsewhere before we captured it? That seemed like a critical question.

The fact that Abaddon hadn't loaded up the Super Fleet on his moon-ships and simply transferred here showed he must have one or two at most left. Otherwise, he could carry his entire fleet on the surface of the moon-ships. Either that, or there was some other factor I didn't understand yet.

"We have to multiply our fighting power," I told the others. "Catapulting a few rocks doesn't cut it. Loosening a handful of fighters was a mistake on their part. The way I see it, we should land the Earth and Mars Fleets on the moon-ship. We'll take everything with us wherever we go."

"No, no, no," Diana said. "That would leave Earth defenseless."

She was as striking as ever, if a little older. The Amazon Queen with her glorious figure and stunning features had taken full advantage of the alien tech we'd come across these past years. She'd used it to enhance her already overpowering beauty.

Diana ran the Survival Party. Her chief opponent was Murad Bey, the leader of the Holy Compact Party. Diana

73

was Prime Minister, while Murad Bey led the opposition. Today, inside the cabinet room, Murad Bey's representative smoked a huge cigar. He was a squat, tough-looking bald man with a dark complexion, a former worker on a Saurian world who had taken to Islam with gusto.

Murad Bey had refused to come to the cabinet meeting, sending Abu Hawkblood instead.

"Tell him, Hawkblood," Diana said.

The squat man smoking his cigar stared at me. "I'm unsure about this," he said in a hoarse voice. "Isn't there an old Earth saying regarding the situation?"

One of the things I'd noticed about the human immigrants from the Saurian worlds had been their intense desire to become Earthlings. Abu Hawkblood had it bad. He was a strict Moslem who read history every chance he had.

"Sure there is," I told him. "The best defense is a good offense."

He smoked it over, finally slapping the table. "There! That is what I think."

Diana shook her head. "That's because the Earth isn't precious to you like it is to me. It isn't thick in your blood."

Hawkblood scowled. "I love the Earth dearly. It is my new home, my only home."

Diana laughed at him scoffingly.

Hawkblood puffed harder, sending up a smelly cloud of smoke. "Maybe the Prime Minister has a point, Commander. We need the fleets at home to protect Earth."

"Come off it, Hawkblood," I said. "She's playing you. She knows your weak point."

"I am not weak," he said.

"That's not what I meant."

"Is that true, Commander?" Diana asked archly. "Don't you think of all of us as *weak*? We're not bulging with muscles like you."

"You are bulging, though," I said, glancing at her bosom.

"That's not very chivalrous," Diana said. "It's yet another example of your disdain for the rest of us. We're

74

supposed to leap to whatever you say. Well, you know what, Commander. I've had enough of that. Either the people's vote counts for something or it doesn't."

"Votes must count," Hawkblood said. "It is the Earth way."

"This isn't about votes," I said, feeling my temper slipping. Had Diana gotten better at these kinds of conversations or had I lost my grip?

"You want to take everything we've worked so hard to build," she said. "Then—"

"Hold it," I said, standing up.

Diana glanced at Abu Hawkblood as if to say, "Look at him, ordering us around again."

I sighed. "Diana, I'm not a parliamentarian. I don't have your skill at public speaking, nor am I a politician. I'm a soldier, an assault trooper. Fighting is my game. I understand battle strategy. Abaddon is coming fast, and we only have a little time left. He has a Super Fleet. Holgotha has predicted complete victory for the enemy unless I can kill the unkillable alien. The only way—"

"Creed, Creed," Diana said, "spare us your ringing rhetoric. It won't work on us. This time—"

"Stop," I said. "I'll meet you half way. Keep the Earth Fleet. I'll take the Mars Fleet."

"No," she said. "We need it all. What if another moon-ship appears?"

"What happens if *ten* moon-ships appear in the Solar System?"

"They won't," Diana said.

"You don't know that."

"Come off it, Creed. You must have figured it out already. If Abaddon had a horde of moon-ships, he could have landed his Super Fleet on them and transferred here. Surely, the enemy only has a few of them. Yet, Abaddon could do what you're doing, and load one up with battlejumpers. We need every ship we have for a fighting chance at defense. The truth is, even with the Earth and Mars Fleets, we have too little to protect our home world."

I lost my temper. Instead of shouting, I gathered my folder and headed for the door.

"What is this?" she asked. "You're walking out on me?"

I regarded her while counting to ten. "I don't have time for this, Diana. Political maneuvering is a pastime with you. To me, our situation is life and death. You don't seem to realize just what's at stake."

"That's not true or fair," she said. "I just don't see it your way. How about you try to see our point of view?"

"It's wrong," I said.

"Well, you know what. That's why we vote. This isn't a dictatorship. You have a plan. I have one, too. Each side builds warships as fast and as hard as we can. Then, our giant fleets crash against their giant fleets. Maybe we outfight them. Maybe we lose. What we don't do is strip our world of everything after having just survived because we had fleets in place against the attacking moon-ship."

"Our fleets gave us the moon-ship—"

"That's another thing," Diana said. "I claim the moon-ship is under parliamentary control. Our military—"

She fell silent, staring at my .44 Magnum, which I'd drawn. "Is this a military coup, Creed? Are you taking over?"

"What's really going on here?" I asked. "I can see your point about wanting the Earth and Mars Fleets here. Yeah, your plan made me mad at first, but I'm seeing it now. You can't be serious about wanting the moon-ship, though. We lose if I don't use it."

Diana stared at her hands, which were intertwined on the table. "The world is terrified, Creed. They know we all almost died. If the fleets go…there are going to be riots all over the place."

"You're not answering the question about the moon-ship."

"You've lost touch," Diana said. "You've been so busy with your wars, with your steroids and bio-suits, that you've lost your humanity."

"I'm going to ask you one more time," I said.

"You will drop your gun, Commander."

Keeping the .44 aimed at Diana, I peered over my shoulder. Abu Hawkblood aimed a stubby little palm-gun at me. It wasn't of Earth-make. I glanced into his eyes, which were hard and glittering with intensity.

"You're not human," I said.

"I am," Hawkblood said. "But that's neither here nor there. You are my prisoner, Commander. If you don't put down your weapon—"

I moved, swiveling toward him.

Hawkblood beamed a milky substance from his weapon.

I'd already hurled myself to the side, though. The milky substance grazed my arm, burning fabric. At the same time, I brought up the .44. Three times, I pulled the trigger. Each time, nothing happened.

"Drop it," Hawkblood said, grinning at me. The tricky devil must have something in place to retard gunpowder reactions.

So, I dropped my gun, kicking it as I charged. The .44 sailed at him. He beamed it, realized his mistake and tried to retarget me. He should have shot me when he had the chance. Before he could fix his mistake, I drew my Bowie knife and stabbed it through his chest, lifting him off the floor.

Hawkblood groaned. He tried one last time to bring his palm-gun around. I slapped it out of his hand. Then, I flung him off my blade onto the floor.

The man coughed blood, staring at me. "You moved so fast. I didn't realize. I didn't..."

I crouched beside him, wiping his blood on his clothes. That made him grin. After that, he shuddered, his entire body moving in one long spasm. Then, he stopped breathing, as he was dead.

77

I stood up wearily and glanced at Diana. She sat almost frozen in her spot at the head of the table. The others in the room sat rigidly as well. I went to her. Only her eyes moved, watching me.

I began moving her thick hair, searching her scalp until I found a tiny device there. My heart thudded. Was the thing embedded into her brain? That would be awful. I tugged. It came free, exposing a needle-thin sliver several millimeters long.

Diana gasped, collapsing onto the table. Then it was her turn to shudder.

I stayed with her the next several hours, and called down several shuttles full of assault troopers too. It was a good thing I did.

Maybe you've already guessed it. We'd unknowingly rescued Jelk-trained sleeper humans from the corporation frontier planets. Hawkblood had been among the most successful of the sleeper agents.

The next week was mayhem on Earth. Despite everything, I took time to help hunt down Jelk-trained ringleaders. A short, very brutal civil war followed.

A little shy of a million people died. Most of those came from a nuclear bomb detonating in New London. Murad Bey was dead, had died a month ago according to the study of his exhumed corpse.

Hawkblood had been running the Holy Compact Party for several weeks already. He'd put quite a few of his operatives in places of power. That made it easier finding them now.

After the brutal week, it was over.

I spoke with Diana in her hospital bed in Brinktown. It was in Old Canada where Moose Jaw used to be.

"Creed, they came so close," she said.

"The Jelk are cunning. We should have been more careful with those we rescued. It's just..."

"I know," she said, patting my hand. "Poor Murad Bey. He had his faults, but he loved Earth. He loved humanity."

"He'll be avenged," I said.

"By the way, I agree with your idea. Take the Earth and Mars Fleets. We'll keep building battlejumpers."

I shook my head. "I'm not leaving Earth defenseless. The civil war showed me how precious our planet is. I'm giving you everything but for a few fighters. It's not easy to say, but you were right and I was wrong."

"Creed," she said, staring up at me.

"There's more," I told her. "I spoke with Baba Gobo. He told me he's never sending another Starkien ship here again. I stopped him before he could say more. I won't bore you with the whole talk. I convinced him this is the end. If we win but Abaddon chases off all the Forerunner artifacts—"

"The Starkiens will enter the Solar System to help defend us?" she asked.

"In a few days," I said.

"What about the accord?" Diana whispered.

"If I kill Abaddon, I can protect the Starkiens and give them full rights. I have a feeling I'll have something over the artifacts as well. If I fail to kill Abaddon, none of this is going to matter anyway."

"But—"

"Baba Gobo saw the logic of that. The Forerunner artifacts seem to be the critical feature. Why else did Abaddon use the moon-ships against them? That being so, we must protect the artifacts at all costs. That means the entire Starkien Fleet is coming. If Abaddon sends a moon-ship loaded up with starships, Earth will have a fighting chance."

"What if Abaddon hits the Starkien planets?"

I shook my head. "The Forerunner artifacts are the thing, Diana."

"You're going to need warships with you."

"Maybe, but I doubt it. Besides, I'll have the entire moon-ship, and I should be able to teleport out of danger if I need to."

"What about a good offense being the best defense?" Diana asked.

"That's a saying, Prime Minister. It doesn't make it holy writ."

Her eyelids finally grew heavy. "I'm going to sleep, Creed. We can talk later."

"No," I said. "We're leaving. It's good-bye, Diana."

"I hate good-byes."

"Yeah."

"Kiss me, Creed," she said, sleepily. "Kiss me on the lips."

I bent down, doing just that. The Amazon Queen grabbed the back of my head, kissing me longer than I'd intended, using her tongue.

Finally, I pulled away. She was already asleep.

I smiled before heading for the door.

-13-

Since we'd captured the moon-ship and made it ours, we decided to christen it. To my mind, the best name was *Santa Maria*, Christopher Columbus' flagship. We were about to explore places no human had been before. Sure, the Indians had beaten Columbus to the New World, but Chris had made the world a little smaller with his feat, knitting it together. Wasn't I about to do the same with our galaxy?

Before the Earth died the first time, some people had gotten huffy about Columbus. I remember an intense argument in my high school history class. I'd sided with Columbus, saying the man had been a stud, risking everything on a courageous voyage of discovery. I'd had a few fellow students who'd gotten angry with me. It turned out according to the teacher that I made some politically incorrect comments toward them. That had landed me in the office later getting a good talking to by the principal.

Big deal. Who doesn't get sent to the office now and again? The bigger deal had been a few gangbangers waiting for me on my walk home. The hombres hadn't liked my comments in class. They proceeded to call me a few names, among them *pendejo* and *gringo*.

I'd seen the way the wind was blowing, five of them against one of me. My palms had turned sweaty and my balls had begun shriveling, looking for a place to hide until this was over. Sometimes, a big mouth could land a kid in trouble, especially if he lacked the muscle to back it up.

I turned around and ran, which had been a mistake. They ran after me, shouting more insults. Soon enough, my side began to ache. A few of them had scooped up stones, one of them hitting me in the back of the head. It had been just hard enough so I lost my balance and skidded chest-first across pavement. That had torn the front of my shirt and bloodied my chin.

I imagine that would have been enough of a chastisement for most of them. One guy, though, the smallest, had strutted around me, giving me several kicks in the side, telling me that's what he would have done to old Columbus.

The last time he walked toward me to give me another boot, I reacted, rolling onto my side, catching his foot and yanking as hard as I could. He slammed back hard and fast, his head hitting the ground with an audible crack.

I'd already scrambled to my feet while the others stared at their friend. I was a mess, with a torn shirt, blood on my chest and craziness in my eyes. Mr. Tough Hombre had begun puking and then choking on his vomit. I'd rolled him over face first. He gagged, spewed again and began to cough hoarsely.

"Better take him to emergency," I said. "He might have a concussion."

"Maybe we give *you* a concussion," the biggest one told me.

I finally remembered the knife in my backpack. I'd been wearing it the entire time. So, I shrugged off the pack, ripped it open, rummaged around and pulled out my switchblade. Admittedly, I was a bit of a troublemaker in my youth, with plenty of poor decisions to show for it.

I clicked open the blade, telling them in so many words to let it go.

"We're finished here," a different gangbanger said. "You go home, Gringo. We'll take Jose to emergency. But watch your mouth next time in class or it won't go so good for you."

"You watch your mouth," I said, getting madder the longer I clutched the knife.

"Maybe we get knives, too," the biggest said.

"You do what you have to," I told him.

Jose started retching again, which was probably good for me. Two of them helped Jose to his feet, taking him away.

Some things you don't forget. They get branded in your memory. I was going to call the moon-ship the *Santa Maria* in honor of Christopher Columbus, because one day as a kid I'd been forced to run away. This was my belated finger against our former politically correct system and against Abaddon who thought he could wipe humanity off the galactic map.

***

The *Santa Maria* was huge inside with hangar bays, endless corridors, chambers, engine rooms, fuel pits, storage facilities, elevators, garden rooms—you get the idea.

The repair teams had fixed some of the T-missile damage, maybe a bare hundredth, the most critical hundredth, though. We took along thousands of technicians and engineers, and they worked in shifts around the clock. Other teams with hordes of shipped tractors, cranes and other equipment, built laser batteries and plasma cannons, along with missile launch sites on the moon surface.

I didn't want to worry about the personnel, so I had Dmitri Rostov take care of that. He was another of the original assault troopers. Once he learned about our mission, he'd demanded to come along. That was fine with me.

For those who don't know, Dmitri was a Zaporizhian Cossack by nationality. He'd been from the Ukraine. The Cossacks used to be a hard-riding, freedom-loving people from the steppes or plains of Russia and the Ukraine. They were good fighters, but most people recognized them as those acrobatic dancers who squatted low, folded their arms on their chests and vigorously kicked out their legs.

Dmitri was a solid, muscular man, shorter than my six-three. He had taken to wearing his hair in a straight-up brush-cut like Rollo.

It felt good to have my old teammates back: N7, Rollo, Ella and Dmitri. Rollo and I had been together since Antarctica, since The Day. Then, I'd found Dmitri and Ella in glass tubes, ready for transshipment up to Claath's battlejumper on The Day +1.

I called a meeting with the four of them, wondering how soon we should start the great journey.

Rollo would run the moon-ship as its captain. Ella was the chief science officer while Dmitri took care of personnel, as I've said, and would run security. That would leave me more time to simply think, with N7 as my personal advisor.

We sat around a conference table fashioned out of moon-stone instead of wood. Ella had a steaming cup of tea, Dmitri a shot of vodka with a bottle beside the glass. Rollo had a beer. N7 kept his hands free and I kept moving my .44 lying on the stone top.

Many of the moon chambers, incidentally, had been hewn out of rock. It gave the ship a cavernous feel, like flying around space in an ancient cave. I kept wondering how the builders had drilled the holes for the electrical equipment behind the scenes.

"I am struck by the incongruence of our vessel," N7 said. "It can transfer, which is stunning. Otherwise, it strikes me as a primitive machine of ancient design."

"It's a freak of a ship," I agreed. "It has a few built-in advantages, though. The biggest is its massive rock armor, an entire moon of it surrounding the deepest structures like the bridge and living quarters."

"I'm still troubled concerning our motive force," Ella said. "I have been studying the transfer mechanism—"

The doors swished open and Key floated into the chamber, disrupting the meeting.

Key wasn't actually shaped like a key or hotel card plastic. It wasn't like a giant ball-bearing, either. Key was square like a metallic cube the size of a desk, with colored lights swirling on all its sides. I couldn't see a way to put anything into Key or open it up to fix the thing. When Key spoke—causing the air to vibrate with sound—the swirling lights pulsed a deeper color and moved in faster rhythms on its sides.

"You began your meeting without me," Key said. It had an alien feminine voice like a cat-person. There was nothing visibly feline about the cube, but that's what I thought if I listened to Key with my eyes closed.

"This is an exploratory meeting," I said. "Here, we don't hold anything back. If you're going to stay, you'll have to follow the rules of the meeting."

The lights flashed darker on Key's sides. "You are suggesting I am not welcome here."

"Of course, you're welcome," I said. "You're going to help us into the Fortress of Light, aren't you?"

Key didn't respond to that.

"You will help us in, won't you?" Ella asked.

"If the basic conditions are met, certainly," Key said.

"What are those conditions?" Ella asked.

"I would rather not say," Key said.

"Why are you withholding the information?" Ella asked.

"I would rather not say," Key replied.

"Fine, fine," I said. "We don't want to put you on the spot." I also wasn't sure how to make Key tell us if the thing didn't want to. We'd have to ease into this, it seemed. "I'm curious, Key. What were the conditions of your imprisonment aboard Holgotha?"

"I would rather not say," Key said. "And before you ask me why I'd rather not say, I should tell you that I won't explain it.

Deciding on yet another approach, I spread my hands. "Are you seeing why you're not very helpful to have at the meeting?"

"No," Key said.

"Now, you're just being stubborn," I said. "That will put a dampener on our talk, which we can't afford. I'm afraid you're going to have leave."

"I do not want to leave," Key said. "And I do not believe you can make me."

"We can make you anytime we want to," I said, starting to get angry.

"I'm curious how you would achieve this feat."

I almost retorted hotly. Instead, a thought struck. I sat back with a half-smile, saying, "I would rather not say."

Dmitri chuckled appreciatively, sipping his vodka.

The big metallic cube bobbed up and down in the air as if thinking. "I have noted your reactions and can now tell you this was a test. From this point forward, I will react according to what I've learned. Please, continue your meeting while I double-check your main transfer unit."

We watched Key depart, the doors closing behind it.

"I don't trust it," Ella said promptly.

"Me neither," Rollo said, with his thick features set.

I touched my revolver. "Trust is an issue, isn't it? Can we trust Holgotha? Can we trust Key?"

"You don't trust Holgotha?" Dmitri asked.

"Not altogether," I said. "There's too much the artifact doesn't tell us. What is the Fortress of Light, for instance? What exactly is Key? Why would Holgotha keep such critical information from us?"

"We should transfer and discover these things for ourselves," Ella said.

I picked up the .44 and shoved it into my holster. "Ella, N7, maybe one of you can explain to me how the transfer unit works?"

"I am ashamed to admit this," Ella said, "but I have no idea. I would dearly like to know, however."

"I believe it works on similar principles as the Lokhar dreadnaught's ability to move into hyperspace," N7 said.

That didn't make any sense. The two operations were quite different. A transfer ship remained in the same universe. A dreadnaught moved into hyperspace, something next to normal space but also outside of it.

"Oh, wait," I said. "The dreadnaught had a sealed-off area. The Lokhars told us it contained a simulated black hole, but we had no way of confirming that."

"Precisely," N7 said. "Our captive Saurians showed us the procedures, but we still don't understand the transfer engine or its fuel. It is all a mystery, just as the dreadnaught's hyperspace mechanism was a mystery. I have been pondering our situation, and I have a concern."

"Speak up," I said. "That's why we're having this meeting."

"How many times can our present moon-ship transfer before it needs refueling or an overhaul?" N7 asked.

I looked around the table, finally settling onto Ella. "Do you have an idea?" I asked her.

"We understand the regular engines well enough," she said, sounding defensive. "They're big antimatter drives. As to the transfer mechanism…" She shrugged, frowned and focused on N7. "I'm surprised you don't even have a theory."

"Who said I did not?" N7 asked.

"What is it?" I asked.

"This may sound surprising," N7 said. "But I believe the transfer mechanism is partly supernatural in origin and operation."

"That's preposterous!" Ella said. "We've transferred before with Holgotha. They were natural occurrences. I do not recall anything supernatural about the process."

"That is interesting," N7 said. "How did these 'natural' occurrences take place?"

"I don't know," Ella said. "But I mean to find out."

"That still does not eliminate the possibility that it is through a supernatural act," N7 said.

"No," Ella said. "I don't accept that."

"Isn't that simply a matter of your preconditions regarding reality?" the android asked.

"This is absurd," Ella said. "An android, a mechanical man, is suggesting supernatural processes to move a spaceship. Does anyone else find that strange?"

"You have stated my condition and belief correctly," N7 said. "I find nothing incongruous about the two."

"Just a minute," I said. Ella was getting angry, and I had no idea what N7 was really driving at. It was time to switch topics. "Let's not get bogged down. *How* the ship moves from one location to another isn't critical."

"I must decline such a view," N7 said.

"Good enough," I said. "For now, though, let's leave it at we don't know how the transfer mechanism works or what fuels it. We do know that we can set the coordinates and transfer to said location. That's all we need at the moment to get from A to B. We're like cave men with a jet, able to fly it from France to California. We don't need to know how much jet fuel the thing has. We just have to be able to turn it on and fly."

"Is there a point to this?" Ella asked dryly.

"You bet," I said. "I don't fully trust Holgotha or Key. Something is going on with them and it smells. Some of you appear to agree with me."

I got nods around the table.

"Why won't Holgotha take us himself to the Fortress of Light?" I asked. "Why wasn't he sure it was still there? Can't he see that far?"

"What *is* your point?" Ella asked. I could see that N7's words still had her riled.

I tapped a finger on the table, studying them. "This transfer power is strange. Popping from one locale to another...I don't know. It seems custom-made to land someone in terrible trouble each jump. To forestall any more delays and any possible trouble, I think we should make a single direct transfer to Sagittarius A*."

"Is that your only reason?" Ella asked.

"No. The other is that we don't know how many transfers the moon-ship can make. Why waste them with mini-transfers? Get everything done as quickly as possible is my thinking."

Ella thought about that. "That is true after a fashion. We don't know our transfer limit. There is another possibility, however. Maybe a transfer twenty-seven thousand light years is too much for our ship."

Dmitri drained his shot glass, clicking it onto the table. "Isn't it dangerous going against Holgotha's advice?"

"That's the question, all right," I said. "I'm saying 'No, it isn't.' If there's one thing I've learned these past years, it's to go with my gut. My instincts tell me to switch it up a bit as to how Holgotha said we should do it."

"Why would Holgotha try to trick us?" Ella asked.

I grinned. "I can think up as many reasons as there are hours in the day. The artifacts are screwy. Add to that Abaddon's strangeness and unpredictability and the more troubling fact that ordinary weapons can't destroy him."

"You don't believe that's true?" Ella asked.

"I do, as a matter of fact. Abaddon has talked to me across a thousand light years in my dreams. He's survived who knows how many thousands of years in a different space-time continuum. If anyone would be hard to kill, it would have to be Abaddon. I mean, we don't even know how to kill Jelk. Last time we tried to butcher Claath, he just floated away."

"At least we were able to drive him away," Rollo said.

"That's a point," I said. "But if you want to know the truth, I lie awake at nights sometimes trying to think up ways to kill Claath. I want the little bastard dead."

Ella began to nod. "We do not have enough facts to make a reasoned decision. Therefore, it is logical to trust some other mechanism to make the decision. Your 'gut,' Commander, is as good a mechanism as others."

"It's better," I said.

"Please, let me finish."

I inclined my head to her.

"Your instincts have proven right more often than not. If they were merely random choices, I would expect you to be right only fifty percent of the time. Therefore, it is logical to depend on your gut feelings, given that we have nothing else concrete to go on."

"That seems like round about reasoning," I said.

"It is *scientific*," Ella said, glancing sharply at N7.

"Right," I said. "My gut instincts are scientific. I like that."

"No," Ella said. "Your instincts aren't scientific. That they've been correct more than fifty percent of the time shows they are not completely random. Therefore, a scientific test proves they are worthwhile in lieu of anything else."

"Okay, okay," I said. "Let us proceed. Are we agreed that we transfer directly to Sagittarius A*?"

"When do you envision the jump to take place?" N7 asked.

"In six hours," I said.

"Yes," N7 said. "I am agreed."

I glanced around the table. No one else added anything.

"We're running out of time," I said. "If we're going to kill Abaddon—and by that save the Earth—we're going to have to succeed on our weapon-gaining mission right away. That means we have almost no margin for error."

The others nodded.

I stood up. "All right then. Let's get cracking."

-14-

Instead of six, it took ten hours with teams of scientists, engineers and dock personnel to get everything ready for transfer.

As a final precaution, I ordered everyone off the moon surface. After thinking about it, it made sense why the enemy hadn't brought starships along on the surface. Perhaps in this older transfer vessel anything on the surface would disappear.

The idea of transferring twenty-seven thousand light years in a single moment seemed preposterous, outlandish and—

"I am certain this is a supernatural proposition," N7 confided to me on the bridge.

This was the same bridge where we'd slaughtered attacking Saurian hordes. It was huge, with over one hundred personnel monitoring half as many stations. We'd already torn out some of the ancient computers and installed our own. Even with familiar equipment in critical areas, it had still taken time for our people to understand how to operate the bridge. N7 and Ella, and surprisingly Key, had been instrumental in teaching the others the process.

We were deep inside the moon, with our vessel between Jupiter and Neptune. According to the latest reports, Abaddon's Super Fleet was less than two weeks from Earth. The Grand Armada was a week behind them.

I had no idea why Abaddon didn't simply transfer a fleet to hit our planet. Maybe he thought that was redundant. The Grand Armada would never get to Earth in that time to save us. The Grand Armada's numerous vessels simply couldn't pass through the many jump gates fast enough to beat the Super Fleet.

Despite the horror of the situation, I found it interesting that a small thing like moving ships through gates could make such a huge difference in terms of stellar rates of travel.

Abaddon's ships were like the soldiers in Napoleon's Grande Armee. The French soldiers had marched more steps per hour than the Austrian and Prussian soldiers could. That had allowed Napoleon greater operational speed, which made a difference strategically and on the battlefield.

I took a deep breath. It was time to teleport to the center of the galaxy. I cleared my throat to give the order.

Before I could, Ella turned around. "Can we really do this?" she asked.

"We're about to find out," I said.

By the look on her face, she wanted to ask more. She didn't, though, finally turning back to her people.

"Let's start," I said.

Rollo stood up and began giving orders. His bridge teams worked fast and efficiently. Soon, his various leaders said, "Check," or "Ready." At that point, Rollo pointed at the piloting group.

The entire time, a power source whined louder and louder. It seemed as if a turbine somewhere was going into overdrive. Unbelievably, the bridge began to shake. The amount of power necessary to do that boggled the mind. We were actually going to transfer twenty-seven thousand light years—

"Go!" Rollo shouted. "It's time."

Two big men shoved giant levers. It was like something out of a 1950s science fiction movie.

The turbine-whine became high-pitched. The bridge shook harder. Had I made a terrible mistake trying to go for it in a single leap? Had Holgotha given us honest advice? Should we have made the journey in three separate bounds?

If that was true, the Forerunner artifact should have done more to make me trust it. This was partly his fault.

I laughed, shaking my head. No matter how hard one tried, the temptation to shift blame to someone or something else was always present. In my head, I'd been doing just that. Whatever happened, I was responsible for it.

"We're going for it!" I shouted. I couldn't hear my voice anymore. The whine had become too loud.

Suddenly, everything changed. One moment, the roar was intense and the chamber shook. The next moment, silence combined with stillness. Had we made the shift, blown our transfer engine or found ourselves in some sort of null or limbo world where nothing moved? I was almost too nervous to find out.

Ella sucked in her breath, making the first noise. She was staring transfixed at her monitor.

I sat in the command chair, unmoving, unblinking and unbelieving. Had we really done it? Were we now in the center of the galaxy? That would be crazy.

I swallowed in a dry throat. Then, I raised my hands, staring at them. They looked the same. Yet, they'd changed. Had they been broken down and recombined? Was that how the moon-ship transferred across twenty-seven thousand light years?

"I'm putting the image on the main screen, Commander," Ella said in a soft voice. Had she spoken before that?

My neck felt rusted as I moved it. The image on the main screen wavered and then solidified into an amazing sight.

In the distance was a supermassive black hole as predicted by Earth's scientists. It was bright in the center where the black hole tore down matter and gobbled it up like a hog. Around the supermassive black hole was the accretion

93

disk of matter that swirled around it. Were those broken-down suns or planets or both?

I'd seen something like this but on a grander scale in Abaddon's weird space-time continuum. There, everything had shrunk with the shrinking universe. Here, the much smaller supermassive black hole was just the center of the Milky Way Galaxy.

The other sight was the stars. It was fantastic: old stars, young stars, massive stars and small normal stars. On Earth when you looked up at night, you saw one star per cubic parsec. Here in the galactic center, I saw 1000 stars per cubic parsec. There was no comparison in grander.

"What is our present speed and heading?" N7 asked me.

"What?" I said, sounding bemused.

The android repeated the question.

"Right," I said, straightening, gathering my bearings and beginning to give orders. The sight was grand and glorious, but we had to stay on our toes out here.

It took ten minutes to get straightened out. If someone had attacked us during that time—well, they hadn't. So, we got the chance to get our act together.

Ella turned to me with a huge smile. "We can do it, Creed. We can teleport vast distances just like the ancient artifacts can."

I nodded, grinning at her.

"We're in the galactic center," she said. "I am awed, Commander. I never thought I'd get to see this."

"You saw Abaddon's supermassive black hole," I said. "This isn't as cool as that."

"That was different," Ella said. "For one thing, it was a different space-time continuum. This is our galaxy. I used to think of coming here as a little girl. Now, I am here. I am awed, Commander, simply awed."

I grinned stupidly, thinking it must be good for a person to be awed by life now and again. This sight, though—

The main bridge doors swished open. Key floated amongst us.

I said nothing, watching the cube. Had Holgotha sent a Trojan horse along? Had that been the artifact's plan all along? Why did I distrust the thing so much?

Key floated to Ella's main station and hovered there. The colors flashing across its sides became more intense.

I shoved out of my chair and sauntered near Key. "Amazing, isn't it?"

"Explain your statement," Key said.

"The sight is truly amazing."

"Do you refer to your bridge crew working with such efficiency?" Key asked.

"They are working hard, aren't they?" I said.

"They are sluggish by my parameters," Key said. "I am finding your species slow and dull-witted."

"Then the joke is on you," I said, "because I wasn't referring to them."

"What else could you have been referring to?" Key asked.

"Can you see the main screen?"

"I see it."

"Do you see what we're seeing?"

"I see much more than you do," Key said. "I can see into a broader range of colors than you."

"You're telling me you don't find the supermassive black hole spectacular?"

"I do not."

"What about the masses of stars?" I asked.

"That is a simple scene one finds at a galactic core. There is no reason for your emotional reactions."

"We're not machines," I said.

"I am not a machine. I am a key."

I put my hands behind my back. "Why are you here, Key?"

"Do you refer to my being on the bridge?"

"That's right."

"That is a logical question. I am here to inform you that I do not see the Fortress of Light. I am afraid it has fallen into the supermassive black hole."

My heart thudded and my mouth turned dry. "Maybe your processors are off," I suggested.

"No. The Fortress of Light has been destroyed. That is the obvious conclusion. I merely came here to assure myself what my sensors did not detect. Good-bye, Commander Creed. I am supposed to self-destruct at this point. Do you have any last requests?"

"Ah…yes, go outside the moon-ship to do your self-destruction."

"I am to self-destruct the transfer vessel with myself. Good-bye, Commander. Ten…nine…eight…"

-15-

"What?" I said.

"Six...five...four..." Key counted.

"I have a request!" I shouted. "It is imperative you listen to me."

"Two...one..."

"Holgotha told me—"

"Abort the countdown sequence," Key said. The amount of flashing lights on its sides slowed in color intensity and movement. The cube floated away from Ella's station. I took that as a good sign.

I backed up toward my chair. As I did, I noticed the large number of bridge crew staring at me in shock. I told myself to get a grip. It was up to me to save the day. That helped me to collect my thoughts somewhat. I'd been in these situations before. Maybe it would help for me to get pissed off. I had the feeling Holgotha had played a dirty trick on me and on humanity in general. I wanted to survive long enough to pay that bastard back—

"What did Holgotha tell you?" Key asked.

I plucked at my lower lip, nodding knowingly. I didn't know if Key could understand human gestures or not, but I was going to assume so. As I did that, I kept backing up. Finally, the back of my legs bumped against my command chair. I sat down heavily, trying to figure out the best way to approach this.

"You are stalling, Commander. Stalling indicates an attempt at subterfuge. That will not help you against me."

"Believe me," I said. "I know that."

"Because of what Holgotha told you?" Key asked, sounding suspicious.

"Yes," I said, on instinct.

"This is unconscionable," Key said. "The artifact promised me it would leave you in the dark concerning the operation."

"I bet that's what he said."

"Why would you say that?" Key said. "It is merely affirming my words."

"I'm so angry now I could spit."

"Your statement does not make sense," Key said.

"Are you angry?" I asked. "Because I'm freaking livid."

"Is that because of the loss of the Fortress of Light?"

"That and Holgotha's lies directed toward you."

Key hovered a moment without speaking. "I am not sure I understood your last words."

"It pisses me off that Holgotha should lie to you."

"Why would that be?" Key asked.

"I am surprised you don't understand."

More lights flashed across Key's surfaces. "Is this in relation to the Creator?"

"Yes!" I said.

"You worship the Creator?"

"Of course. Don't you?"

"I am Key. I was not manufactured for worship. I have entry protocols regarding the Fortress of Light. With its obliteration, I no longer have a function. My protocols demand that I self-destruct lest I am improperly used for blasphemous purposes."

"Right, right," I said. "I thought as much. Look, Key, Holgotha has kept you trapped for a long time. I know that much."

"The artifact told you this?"

"Key," I said, smirking. "You need to use your logic processors instead of asking stupid questions."

"But…the artifact assured me you knew nothing regarding the higher order priorities. This would indicate deviancy regarding the artifact. That would put in jeopardy—"

I wondered what he would have said if he'd finished. "You were saying…?" I asked.

"Commander, I believe that you are lying to me."

"There have been lies all around, Key. It's disgusting."

The lights on its sides slowed to such an extent that I could almost see individual points instead of mere streaks of lights.

That made me suspicious. A lot about this struck me as wrong. What was Holgotha's angle in this? I've always had the feeling the Forerunner artifact didn't like humanity. Could Holgotha have decided to throw in with Abaddon? That didn't make sense. Abaddon and the Kargs hated non-Karg life. Wasn't the artifact life after a fashion? Wouldn't that mean Holgotha would perish as well if Abaddon won?

"Commander," Rollo said. "There are unidentified objects heading our way."

"Excuse me, Key," I said. "I have to take care of this."

"Are you saying our conversation is terminated?" Key asked.

"No! We haven't delved into the heart of Holgotha's treachery regarding you. Aren't you curious how the artifact tricked you?"

"I am curious indeed."

"Then we have to delay the conversation so I can give you my full attention as you so richly deserve."

"But the countdown, Commander, I must continue it at the earliest opportunity."

"Don't you think I know that?"

"I was unsure," Key said. "Your wet body processing centers are foreign to me. Holgotha told me your emotional processes are merely randomizers given to—"

"Hold that thought, Key," I said. "If we're going to survive to continue the conversation, I have to look into this now."

The lights on its sides speeded up. "I understand the logic. Take care of the Vip 92 Attack Vessels. Then, we can finish the talk so I can hasten to self-destruct."

"Good thinking," I said, turning away, heading for Rollo.

"Did you get that?" I asked Rollo quietly.

"I did," Rollo whispered, indicating the battle screen. "Those are Vip 92 Attack Vessels, whatever they are."

His people adjusted the screen. From the outer edge of the accretion disk, three streaks of light moved fast. They avoided the supermassive black hole as they headed toward us.

"Key said they're attack vessels," Rollo told his people. "I want to know what kind of hull armor these ships have."

"Sir," a lanky tech said. "I'm not getting any material readings. Those are energy fields." The man tapped his controls, studying them. "If I were to guess, I'd say those are antimatter containment fields."

"Could Key be wrong about them?" I whispered.

Rollo eyed Key sidelong. "I think so," he whispered back.

"Despite the lowering of your voices," Key said, "I am quite able to hear you. I am not wrong. They are energy ships, Vip 92 Attack Vessels. They are driven by the Ve-Ky, an ancient life force. I had surmised their energy sphere had already been annihilated by the black hole. By projecting my scanner into a higher visual range, I see their sphere is still active. That is interesting for several reasons."

"Are the Ve-Ky friendly?" I asked.

"Their hospitality is noted throughout the galactic core," Key said. "The fact of their approaching combat run is highly unusual. I would submit you have angered a notoriously friendly species. That does not speak well of humans, Commander."

"What are you talking about?" I said. "We just got here. If they're friendly, they're not doing a good job of showing it."

"I attribute that to your hostile nature," Key said.

Rollo rubbed his forehead, leaning near me. "Is that thing insane? Is the galactic center crazy?"

"Forget about that," I said. "Ella, N7, what should we fire against the approaching energy vessels?"

"Let's try communicating them with first," Ella suggested.

"Yes," I told Rollo. "Give it a try."

The energy vessels increased speed. They were several billion kilometers away but closing fast.

Rollo tried hailing them with our advanced comm equipment. Nothing happened.

"Key," I said, spinning around. "You do realize this is all new to us."

"I had begun to wonder," Key said. "I can find no other explanation for your odd actions."

"Why do you attribute aggressive intent to us when they're the ones making an attack run?"

"Perhaps it is because the Ve-Ky are noted for their discriminating nature," Key said.

"Perhaps it is the nature of our ship," N7 said, speaking up. "Maybe Abaddon has already attacked here. Perhaps the energy creatures—"

"You have made a fundamental mistake," Key said, interrupting. "The Ve-Ky are not energy beings. They simply use energy vessels. Inside the ship is a protective force field shielding the material creatures."

Rollo ordered his comm people to use different frequencies and manners of communication. Before they had exhausted all the possibilities, the energy vessels came within a million kilometers of us.

"Use everything," I said, "lasers, particle beams, plasma cannons and T-missiles."

"Commander!" Rollo shouted.

I looked up at the main screen. A blob of energy detached from each attack vessel. The blobs vanished like T-missiles and reappeared several kilometers from our ship. One after another, the energy blobs closed the distance, striking the surface, exploding, sending alien pulses into our vessel.

Engines stopped, ventilating systems overheated. Electrical power went out in many portions of the ship.

"Fire back!" I shouted. "Hit those bastards."

"They're too far away," Rollo said.

"Launch T-missiles," I said.

"How?" Rollo asked. "We're cut off from our own surface. We can't even give them orders now."

"Maybe someone used their own initiative," Ella said, indicating a working screen.

It was one of the few left projecting images. A T-missile appeared near a Ve-Ky vessel. The warhead ignited with a thermonuclear blast.

I leaned forward in the dim glow of emergency power. One million kilometers away, a Vip 92 Attack Vessel winked out of existence.

I led the cheering.

"Stop, stop," Key said. The colors were going wild on its sides.

"What's wrong?" I asked.

"This is a barbaric display of bloodthirstiness. I find it distressing."

"Yeah? They struck us first. We just hit back harder."

"That must have done it, Commander," Rollo said. "The other two vessels are running away."

"It may be too late for us," Ella said, studying her panel. "We're losing power all over the ship."

"Tell everyone to suit up," I said.

Ella nodded. "That will help for a little while. But if we can't get the systems back online, we're going to run out of oxygen before long. And we can forget about transferring again. Commander, I think we might be stranded out here in the galactic core."

-16-

I took a deep breath before saying anything. I heard the fear in Ella's voice. I could see the frightened faces of those at their stations. I was responsible for them. I had to get us home again. First, I had to find this Fortress of Light.

I know, Key said the fortress was gone. I wasn't taking anything at face value out here, though. The sudden attack by energy vessels with regular creatures inside the weird ships—no, I didn't buy this was by accident. It felt like a set up.

"Here's the first rule I learned a long time ago in the Jelk Corporation," I said, loudly. "Don't panic. Yeah, we're in a tough spot." I shrugged. "We've been in tough spots before and won through. We will here, too. The first thing, though—"

I pointed at Dmitri.

"Don't panic," the Cossack said in his cheerful manner.

"Right, Ella?" I asked.

She looked green around the gills, a prime candidate for panicking.

"Start by figuring out what kind of energy blast they hit us with," I told her.

"How am I supposed to do that?" she asked, her voice rising as she spoke.

"Ella Timoshenko," I said firmly.

She blinked several times before licking her lips. "This is the galactic center, Commander. We're at Sagittarius A*."

"Good. Now, figure out what I asked for, and get your people working on it. Idle hands are the devil's workshop."

Her eyes narrowed. Ella hated supernatural explanations for anything. A bite of anger took hold. I could see it in her eyes. She turned to her nearest team and began to give orders in a calm voice.

One of the keys to leadership was having good lieutenants. I had the best.

"N7," I said. "You're coming with me."

Key floated after me. "Commander, if we could finish our conversation, please, I would like to initiate my full countdown before all of you die."

"I don't have time for that now," I said. "This is an emergency."

"I see. If you're otherwise occupied, I have my own protocols to follow."

I marched up to Key and put my hands on my hips. "Now, you listen here. You're not going to destroy my ship because you messed up."

"That is untrue. I did my duty. I have 'messed up' nothing."

"Ha!" I barked. "It's completely true. I happen to know where the Fortress of Light is. That is what you're supposed to find, right?"

"It has disappeared, Commander."

"Wrong," I said. "You simply don't know where to look."

"That is nonsensical. If you don't even know what the Fortress of Light is, how can you know its location?"

"You have made an error," I said "Come back to me once you figure it out. N7, let's go."

"Commander," Key said. "I realize my error."

"Yes?" I asked, wondering what it would say.

"Holgotha must have given you information regarding the Fortress of Light."

"There you go," I said. "You give me hope that my time with you isn't completely a waste of time. I'm going to get back with you, Key. First, you have to let me do my job."

"I have analyzed your speech patterns," Key said. "You are telling the truth. Therefore, I will wait."

I hurried out with N7 because I was lying through my teeth. It was a good thing I was a natural liar. Otherwise, we'd all be dead.

I'd learned some time ago how to deal with logical artificial intelligences. It wasn't easy and took quick thinking.

I shook my head. I couldn't worry about Key at the moment. First, I had to get my ship running, if it was possible. I'd worry about finding this missing Fortress of Light later.

As I hurried down a corridor with N7, I had a nagging thought. What had Holgotha hoped to gain by this? Just whose side was the Forerunner artifact on? Did the thing even know?

I could already smell the air's staleness. We had to get at least part of the ship running again. Who knew if the two Vip 92 Attack Vessels had gone to get reinforcements or not?

***

Three hours later found us in an even worse condition. The energy blasts had knocked down almost everything. Everyone I saw wore a vacc-suit or a bio-suit. I wondered about the rest of the moon-ship. It was vast, obviously, with over ten thousand operatives on board. Some parts of the ship could have been in entirely different countries, given that they were over a thousand kilometers away.

I was back on the bridge, scowling in my helmet. The bridge was empty except for me. The others were elsewhere, working on repairs. Key was gone, too. I wondered idly where the pesky thing had gone.

Flickering light caught my eye. I looked up. The main screen had gone blank some time ago. It was on again and growing brighter.

I sat up, pushed myself to my feet and approached the screen. It showed the supermassive black hole. Pin dot lights rose from a section of the accretion disk. Could anyone live in the disk?

I glanced around, saw a blinking bank of controls and went to them. I began to test the controls. After a few taps, I looked up at the screen. Finally, I managed to zoom in on the lights rising from the disk.

There were hundreds of them. To my untrained eye, each of them looked like a Vip 92 Attack Vessel. No. That wasn't exactly right. Some of those ships—if that was what they were—looked substantially larger than the others.

What I found interesting was that our battle tech had been good enough to kill one of the attackers. How many T-missiles did we have left? I had no idea. Most, if not all, of the T-missiles were near the surface hatches. I would have to race through literally thousands of kilometers of corridors to reach the surface. By the time I got there, the Vip 92s would have already made their attack.

I hurried to the comm consoles, sitting down at one, letting my fingers rove over controls. I knew how to work these better than the main-screen controls.

Approximately ten minutes later, I got a response. It was a crackle of noise at what seemed like high-pitched speed.

As I tried to puzzle that out, I heard a sound behind me. Turning, I saw Key hovering in place. How long had the thing been behind me, watching?

"Did you hear that?" I asked.

"I did, Commander. I would advise you to finish your conversation with me, as we are almost out of time."

"Was that the Ve-Ky responding to my queries?" I asked.

"Why are you asking me? You heard the transmission."

"I did, but I don't understand their language."

"Commander, do you expect me to believe that?"

"I am not in the habit of lying, Key."

"Are you suggesting I am?"

"I don't know, Key. Are you?"

"That is a slur against my builders, which is to say against the Creator."

I found the statement shocking. "The Creator directly fashioned you?"

"Not directly, no," Key said, "but certainly indirectly."

I frowned. "How do you know that to be true?"

"Commander, it is self-evident. We do not have the time to argue over fundamental truisms. The attack vessels are racing here to finish what you started."

"What? Wait just a minute. We didn't start anything."

"That isn't what the Ve-Ky just said."

"What did they say?" I asked.

"Please, Commander," Key said, sounding miffed. "I am not a translation unit. I am a key."

His reaction gave me an idea. "Wouldn't some worth be better than no worth at all?" I asked.

"Explain that," Key said.

"You said the Fortress of Light has vanished. If it really is gone, so is your purpose as its key, which leads you to think self-termination is in order. Now, however, I offer you value as a translation unit. Since you now have value, self-termination is no longer necessary."

"I was not made to be a translation unit."

"Welcome to the club."

"That statement means nothing to me," Key said. "What club are you referring to, and why should I be welcomed to it?"

"I was designed to live in luxury, served by a thousand Playboy bunnies," I said. "Instead, I have been forced to work for a living."

"I had not realized this," Key said.

I shrugged as sweat began to trickle under my armpits. Pretending to remain cool while stressed, arguing with an over-intelligent robotic—

"Yes!" Key said suddenly. "I will translate for you. The essence of the message was the Ve-Ky opinion leader giving you a list of offenses. To begin with, you appeared in a restricted zone without proper licensing, without any explanation and in clear violation of the Civilizational Value Index."

"Uh...what's a Civilizational Value Index?" I asked.

The lights flashed faster across Key, and it spoke in a reproving tone. "It amazes me that you would agree to transfer without knowledge of something so fundamental. That was rash, Commander."

"Did the Ve-Ky opinion leader say what he intends to do?" I asked.

"That is self-evident. The Ve-Ky will destroy your ship in retaliation for your offenses."

I squeezed my eyes shut, reminding myself that aliens were different from us. They would not think like us nor act like us. If their actions seemed unreasonable, that was because I didn't understand their mode of thinking.

Opening my eyes, I asked, "I would appreciate it if you could explain what the Civilizational Value Index is?"

"I am surprised," Key said. "That is actually a reasonable and logical request. The concept is quite simple, really. The galaxy is cordoned off into varying levels of civilization. For example, Earth has a 6C Civilizational Score."

Immediate questions popped into my mind. Who gave the scores and enforced the cordoning? Instead, I asked, "What is the Lokhar Homeworld score?"

"The homeworld specifically isn't scored," Key said. "The Lokhar are scored as a species."

"Got it," I said. "So, what's their score?"

"6B."

"And the Ve-Ky?" I asked.

"The last time I checked, they hovered between a 2A and a 1E score."

"Yet, we destroyed one of their Vip 92s."

"Yes," Key said. "I find that remarkable. That must be due to your heritage as killers. It must be true what Holgotha suspects about humans."

"That being what exactly?" I asked.

"We are drifting afield, Commander. We will stick to the issue. I find it interesting that you appear to have surmised a technological ability commensurate with a civilizational score. The basis is not one for one, but normally it is close. Thus, a 2A species should demolish a 6C species in space combat. However, the moon-ship originally belonged to a 1C species. Since its construction, though, the ship's technological superiority has slipped into a 3E state, except for its marvelous transfer ability. That is a 1AAA technological achievement."

As Key spoke, I studied the main screen. The flow of energy ships from the accretion disk had grown. It wasn't just hundreds of vessels. This looked like thousands upon thousands were headed at us.

"So you're saying the galaxy is divided into different civilizational zones?" I asked.

"I have already stated so, Commander. Why are you being redundant?"

"And...the Ve-Ky are angry with us because we've entered a place we shouldn't have?"

"That is merely the first of your offensives."

"Holgotha must have known about these different zones."

"He is a Forerunner artifact," Key said. "Of course Holgotha knew."

I nodded slowly, trying to envision what Key was suggesting. Our galaxy was full of aliens. The slower, less developed aliens lived on the fringes, it would appear. The smartest, most advanced aliens lived in the galactic core.

The smart ones didn't want the dumb ones loitering in their zone.

Out of all the dangers brought about by transferring, I would not have thought of this.

"Why did Holgotha chose to live in the less developed part of the galaxy?" I asked.

"That is an interesting question," Key said. "It is deserving of careful speculation. Unfortunately, we do not possess the time at the moment."

As if to punctuate Key's point, another blast of high-speed screeches burst through the comm unit.

"What are the Ve-Ky saying now?" I asked.

Key did not respond.

Since I was wearing my helmet, I didn't notice right away. Finally, though, I saw a blaze of colored lights playing off the reflection of the comm screen. I turned. Key had gone wild with intense colors zipping across his sides.

"What is it?" I said. "What did they say?"

"You don't understand," Key said in a soft voice. "That was not the Ve-Ky speaking. That was the voice of the Curator. He bids you to enter the Museum as sanctuary from the coming assault."

"What Museum?" I said, looking up at the main screen.

I saw it right away. It was on the other side of the accretion disk as the Ve-Ky energy vessels. The thing was built like Key, only on a vaster scale. It was a gigantic cube of multi-colors that shined with even greater brilliance than the black hole.

"Is that the Fortress of Light?"

"That is one of the most ancient titles," Key said. "The Curator has offered you sanctuary. This is marvelous and stupendous. The honor you have just received—"

"Okay, okay, settle down, Key. This is a great and glorious moment. Now, how do we get there before the Ve-Ky swarm reaches us?"

"I do not believe such a thing is possible. You are quite doomed. Still, it is good to know that you humans can die with full and righteous honor."

-17-

"What kind of key are you anyway?" I demanded. "Tell the Curator we're having a little trouble. Maybe he can lend us a hand in getting to the fortress."

The metallic cube turned in the air as if to regard me closer. "That is against all the dictates of the Museum," Key said as if offended. "If your ship lacks motive power, the ancient structure will no doubt vanish back into the accretion disk. That you were allowed to look upon the great fortress—"

"Wait, wait, wait," I shouted. "Why would the Curator abandon us? None of this makes sense."

"That is because you are civilizationally too dull-witted to realize the honor he has done you," Key said.

I opened channels in my helmet comm. "Ella, N7," I said, "come to the bridge right away. We have an emergency."

I watched the stream of energy vessels swing toward the moon-ship. This group had started farther away than the first three that had attacked us. But they were moving fast, getting much too close much too soon.

At that moment, another burst of high-speech screeches assaulted my ears.

"The Curator is wondering why you don't answer him," Key told me.

"Tell him I'm preparing the proper reply."

"I'm surprised at you, Commander. That is a thoughtful response. Yes, I will tell him that."

Key made a volley of similar screeching noises.

At that point, Ella and N7 rushed onto the bridge. As quickly as I could, I explained the situation to them. N7, still in his body armor, raced to a station, hurriedly tapping on a console.

"Given the range of their last attack," N7 said, "from one million kilometers away, I estimate we have fourteen minutes before the Ve-Ky bombardment begins. How soon until we're obliterated after that, I am unwilling to estimate."

"I'm sure your obliteration will occur in less than ten of your minuscule time units after the beginning assault," Key said.

"Are you referring to minutes?" N7 asked Key.

"I am."

"Ella," I said, "how long until the ship has full power again?"

"You can forget about that," she said. "I can give you *some* operational abilities by connecting you with the surface. We can launch T-missiles and possibly activate laser turrets. I could open the hangar bay doors and let our few fighters launch. More than that, however..." She shook her helmeted head.

"It is a pity for you," Key said. "But your glorious adventure is over. I am at peace, however. As I was among you as you witnessed the appearance of the Fortress of Light. Commander, I will take my leave now. I believe I can reach the moon surface before the attack run begins. I will tell the Curator all that transpired here."

"How will you get from the moon-ship to the fortress?" I asked.

"It will take me many of your years to do so," Key said. "Once I begin the initial trajectory, I can drift the rest of the way while shutting down all but my most necessary functions."

"Since we can't travel there directly, why don't we transfer to the fortress?" I asked.

"No, no," Key said. "That is ethically and aesthetically wrong. One does not transfer a distance he can easily traverse by regular means. It simply would not be proper, Commander."

Ella and I exchanged glances.

"I'll get right on it," she said.

"Commander," Key said, sounding indignant. "I cannot believe you would try something like this after I just informed you—"

"Key!" I said, loudly, interrupting it.

"Yes, Commander?"

"Shut the hell up. You're giving me a headache."

The metallic cube bobbed up and down in the air, its lights slowing their speed and brightness. Finally, the thing made noises.

I checked. Key had sent the sounds through the comm channel.

"What did you just tell the Curator?" I asked.

Key remained silent.

"Key, I'm talking to you."

"You told me to shut up."

"I did, but you didn't listen to me. You sent a message to the Curator, didn't you?"

"I did," Key admitted. "I told him we cannot reach him. I have no doubt he will now take the Museum elsewhere."

I turned fast, looking up at the main screen. It might have been a trick of light or my imagination, but the Fortress of Light didn't seem to shine as brightly. Then, it moved. The giant cube began to sink toward the accretion disk.

I swore roundly at Key until Ella touched my sleeve.

"I need your help, Commander," she said. "We have to coordinate this as fast as we can. Even then it might be too late."

"What can I do to help?" N7 asked.

115

"Stand by the rods," Ella said. "You'll have to pull them at exactly the right moment."

I fed data as Ella rattled off instructions. I kept glancing at the main screen as I worked, noticing a continual dimming of the great cube fortress.

"Concentrate, Commander," Ella shouted at me over the helmet comm.

I did. We had enough power on the bridge for most of the instruments to work. I typed madly as Ella spoke faster and faster. N7 dashed back and forth on the bridge. He fed the great machine more coordinates.

"I need more time," Ella shouted.

The Ve-Ky swarm was approaching fast. They would soon be where the first three had launched their electrical bombs. By this time, the Fortress of Light had almost disappeared from the main screen.

The initial Vip 92 Attack Vessels launched energy blobs. The first one disappeared from sight.

"Now!" I shouted. "Pull the levers, N7, pull them!"

"No!" Ella shouted. "I need to make several more adjustments."

N7 followed my orders instead of hers. With a hand on each lever, the android tugged hard.

The first energy blob must have struck the moon surface. The bridge shook and lights flickered. At the same instant, a sick feeling swirled across my chest. Everything went dark all at once. A second later, lights splashed across my brain. I groaned, clutching my helmet. It felt as if my world spun around and around. I clenched my teeth so I wouldn't vomit. Did more energy blobs strike the ship? Everything shuddered. Everything spun and twirled. I heard garbled noises and—

All at once, it stopped. There was no sound, no sight, no smell, no hot or cold, nothing. I think we may have transferred into a null zone or a limbo void.

I wanted to groan. This was one of the worst and most helpless feelings in my life.

-18-

All at once, sight, sounds and feelings rushed into me with heightened force. I staggered, struck a console, rebounded the other way and crashed onto my side on the deck.

That likely saved my life. For at that instant, a bolt of what seemed to be electricity smashed against the panel I'd been standing at, causing it to explode in a shower of sparks and plastic shards.

I looked up from the floor.

A humanoid, electricity-crackling thing oozed from the wall, the moon rock. It was like a stick figure of electricity, with a wand or rod aimed at where the discharge had hit. I noticed, for just a moment, an aperture or hole, as if the rod was a gun that fired electrical bolts.

Key made screeching sounds, rushing the humanoid thing. The electrical thing turned, aimed the rod and fired another bolt.

Key dodged upward at the last moment. The bolt struck another panel, sending pieces flying everywhere.

Were we under attack? I mean, did this have anything to do with the blobs shot at the moon-ship? Could these be Ve-Ky versions of assault troopers? If that was true, what did they want?

The electrical humanoid aimed at Key once more, firing another bolt.

Key was good. He dodged to the left this time.

Now, N7 was up. He swung a pulse rifle off his shoulder. The Ve-Ky trooper fired at N7. The android dropped onto his chest. The bolt passed over him. N7 fired three pulses into the thing in return.

Each pulse caused the electrical thing to darken for just a moment. The Ve-Ky seemed to move a little slower, too. But that was it. Seconds later, the ill-effects seemed to have vanished from it.

N7 didn't stop, though. He kept firing pulses at the thing. That made the attacker sluggish, but he finally nailed N7 with an electrical bolt. N7's armor blackened as pieces spun off.

"N7," I said through my helmet comm. All I heard was static.

I scrambled off the floor, dashing to my pulse rifle where I'd laid it down by the command chair. The attacker saw me, firing several electrical discharges. Even though I dodged the bolts, I could feel a current flowing through my body, setting my teeth on edge. Did he want to capture us? At the last moment, I dove, skidding across the deck. I snatched my rifle, rolled to dodge another bolt and targeted my weapon on the galactic core native.

One pulse after another darkened his torso area. In frustration, he backed into the wall, oozing out of sight.

"Check N7," I shouted at Ella. "Key, what is this all about?"

"Raiders," Key said. "Some of the Ve-Ky must have made it onto the ship before we transferred."

"Where are we now?" I shouted.

"I do not know," Key said. "They want to destroy me, it appears. That is most odd, most odd indeed."

Before Key could say more, *three* electrical attackers oozed out of the moon rock. I had no idea how they could do that. It must have been similar to the way I entered Holgotha.

They shot as one, sending bolts at Key. The cube dodged the first two, but failed to miss the third. The discharge struck Key, drilling a hole into a side. That caused an explosion, and Key tumbled through the air to crash against a bulkhead. The heavy metallic cube struck the deck, all the colors having vanished from its sides. It left Key a dull iron color with smoke pouring from the hole.

Now, the attackers turned toward Ella and me. She dove and rolled as two bolts sizzled across the deck where she'd been. One aimed at me, but he turned as the doors to the bridge swished open.

Three crewmembers rushed in. They wore ordinary vacc-suits.

"Get back!" I shouted.

The three didn't hear me or didn't have time. The nearest Ve-Ky aimed and fired, sending bolts into them. These were ordinary men, not modified assault troopers. The discharges blew gaping, smoking craters in them, hurling them backward and sending up oily smoke. Each of them shuddered and died.

I rose to one knee and fired pulses into the killer. He darkened, grew sluggish and headed for the wall—no doubt to disappear and recharge if he could.

The other two fired at me. One hit the pulse rifle, shattering it in my hands. The electrical effect made my teeth ache.

Hurling the broken weapon from me, I scrambled for cover as bolts zigzagged above me. The raiders had killed three of my crew, incapacitated and maybe destroyed Key and wounded N7. Now, I'd lost my pulse rifle. Maybe I could get N7's. Even as I thought that, one of the electrical bastards zapped the android's weapon into several glowing pieces.

Three of them, a lousy three of them were taking over the bridge. Where had everyone gone? I knew a lot of people were trying to fix the various systems but—

119

I remembered my .44 then. How could I ever have forgotten? Yes, it was an old-fashioned weapon for this space age, but it had done its duty before.

One of the electrical people spoke in a screeching manner. Were they calling on me to surrender?

"What do we do now, Commander?" Ella asked over her crackling helmet comm.

I thumbed back the hammer on my .44, rose from behind a console and saw a Ve-Ky flowing toward me. It seemed to be running and moving like lightning at the same time. It was wicked strange.

BOOM!

I sent lead into his chest. The result was greater than I would have expected. The bullet struck the electrical creature and blew it backward. A sheet of electricity seemed to fly off it, exposing flesh underneath, as if an ordinary person was inside the electrical suit.

That was so weird it kept me from firing a second time right away.

The Ve-Ky fell down, rose, fell again and finally aimed his electrical gun at me.

BOOM!

I sent a shell at his head. It blew away another piece of electrical armor—if that's what I was seeing—to show me a man with red eyes and what appeared to be a bruise on his skin.

Without thinking—

BOOM!

I sent another round at the exposed flesh. The Ve-Ky catapulted off his feet to land on his back. Blood from his face boiled on his outer electrical suit.

I crossed him off from a mental list. I think he was dead. I had a weapon that could hurt the other two. One of those noticed me. He flowed fast for the wall.

BOOM!

BOOM!

The bastard didn't make it. He was on the floor, writhing as his blood boiled onto his outer suit. I'd used the first shot to open his armor, the second to send a slug into him.

At that point, I was up and running. The third Ve-Ky approached the dull-colored Key. He stood over the poor thing, tracing his electrical gun along a side. What was the alien thinking?

The Ve-Ky knelt by the block of metal, put an electrical arm on it and pressed something on his belt. Both of them began flowing with electrical power. As one, they rose. Slowly, almost staggeringly, the Ve-Ky carried Key toward the nearest wall. I think he planned to escape with Key.

I raced after him. Maybe he heard me. He half-turned, raised the electrical gun.

BOOM!

BOOM!

CLICK!

I put two rounds into him. They were side by side instead of one on top of the other. The second one would have killed him, I'm sure, if it entered the creature in the armor. Instead, pieces of electrical armor flew off, exposing his skin.

The shots had caused the alien to drop his gun. The weapon didn't fall on the floor, but flowed into his electrical suit. That was a nice touch. I could have used that on a battlefield or two.

In any case, I was out of bullets. There were more in my room, but I didn't have time to go there. I grabbed a spare pulse rifle from a rack.

The bastard flowed away faster, heading for a wall. He still carried the Key in his electrical hold.

"Stop!" I shouted.

He turned to look at me. All I saw was the living, jumping electricity that was his suit.

Okay then, I laid down a barrage of pulse shots, darkening his armor.

He reached the wall and tried to flow into it, but it was no use. I must have damaged the suit just enough to erase that ability from his toolkit.

Manipulating his electrical suit, the Ve-Ky let the dull-colored Key drop away from him. The heavy cube rolled onto the deck.

For a second time, the attacker tried to flow into the wall, this time beginning to get away.

I slapped another energy pack into the pulse rifle. At the same time, Ella began firing. We pumped one pulse after another into the Ve-Ky. Gouts of electricity began to sizzle in the air. His suit darkened with him halfway into the wall.

Abruptly, it shut off. At least, that's what I figured happened. He froze, half in the moon-wall and half out. All the electricity simply stopped. It left a dead Ve-Ky stuck in the wall.

The suit, I noticed, as I approached, was a network of connections like something from advanced laser tag.

"Is he dead?" Ella asked.

I turned around. She'd taken off her helmet. With a few clicks, I removed mine. The air smelled how you'd figure it should. It had the fresh smell of after a thunderstorm but the horrid stench of burned flesh. It was a terrible mixture.

I walked closer to the dead Ve-Ky in the wall. His face was outside of the rock. The alien had a much thinner face than a human would have. His body was thinner, too. Maybe I should call them Skinnies, from an old sci-fi novel I'd read as a kid.

I didn't see how the Skinnies had a right to think of themselves as our superiors. This one might have passed for human on a busy New York City street, especially if it had been a rainy day and he'd worn a raincoat.

I moved to Key and tapped on it firmly. The thing sounded solid. Nothing happened, though. Was it destroyed or just badly damaged?

"Did we transfer?" Ella asked.

"N7!" I said. I ran to the android, unbuckling his combat armor. His eyelids flickered as I pulled off his helmet.

"Creed," he said dully. "Did you defeat them?"

"The three that made it here," I said. "I don't know if there were any others, though."

Ella was at a comm control. She tapped it, asking if anyone could hear her. She tried several times without receiving an answer.

Just then, the main bridge doors swished open. I didn't know what to expect. The last thing in the world I would have thought to see was exactly what walked through to greet us.

-19-

I was wearing my bio-suit minus the helmet. The pulse rifle in my hands slipped free, clattering onto the deck. That startled me so I frowned at the seemingly old man walking onto the bridge.

He was big, almost a giant, wore a long blue robe that hid his feet and had a great white beard like some mountain man or the way a lot of people pictured God. His eyes were blue and dangerous-looking, not kindly and simple.

I cleared my throat but hesitated to speak first. There was something intimidating about him.

The big old man stopped, taking in the scene, the dead Ve-Ky on the deck, the one frozen in the rock and Key's now dull-colored cube. The old man nodded slightly, as if to himself.

"Uh…" I said, finding my tongue stuck to the roof of my mouth.

The old man looked at me and raised his bushy eyebrows.

"Uh…" I repeated, finally tearing my tongue loose. Even so, I hesitated. Maybe Ella didn't believe in supernatural manifestations, but I sure did. Now, I hadn't read the Bible much, although I knew a few stories. I seemed to recall that no one had ever looked upon the face of God and lived. I was living and looking at this old man. Maybe this was an alien then, an energy creature, and it read my mind. It knew

124

how I conceived of God and came in that guise to trick me. Surely that was the explanation for this.

Whatever the case, the old man seemed dangerous and capable. He frightened me, if you want to know the truth. He hadn't threatened us directly yet, but I didn't feel my usual cockiness.

"Sir," I said. Then I hesitated for the third time. I glanced at Ella.

She was frowning severely as she bit her lower lip. N7 had raised his head from where he lay on the floor, staring quietly at the big old man.

On impulse, I went to one knee and bowed my head as if to a king.

"Sir," I said again, "if any of my actions appear to be disrespectful, please know that I only mean to honor you. I am from—at least I believe I'm from a 6C Civilizational Zone. If I have erred in coming to the galactic core, please know I only did so in order to recuse my race from certain doom."

I could feel Ella's stare burning into my back. She'd likely never seen me act like this.

"I'm unsure what I should call you," I added.

"The Curator will do," the old man said in a deadly deep voice.

I nodded. "Curator," I said, "your presence would imply we made it to your Museum."

"It isn't mine," he said, "although it is correct to say that I am running the Museum for now."

I looked up at him to see if he was smiling. He was not. He had fixed those hard blue eyes on me. I felt as if he judged my worth. It was an uncomfortable feeling. Yet, I did not get the sense he was condemning me.

"Key also said this is called the Fortress of Light," I said.

"Among other names," he said.

"Ah…are we in trouble?" I asked.

"A great deal," he said. "The most pressing problem at the moment are the Ve-Ky storming the vessel."

"What?"

He indicated the Skinny frozen in the wall. "You dealt with the central team, but know...what are you called?"

"I'm Commander Creed."

"Commander, several assault pods made it onto the Survey Vessel before you transferred directly into the ancient hangar bay. I suspect old protocols took over. You must, of course, clear this infestation at once. Otherwise, I will flush the ship with anti-force, ridding it of the Ve-Ky and you fringe dwellers in one sweep."

"Sir?" I asked.

"The Ve-Ky have tried to break into the Museum for...hmm," he said, studying me. "You are a short-lived race, I suspect. Your time units—"

He held up a big beefy hand. The fingertips glowed as if embedded with electronic equipment. I felt light-headed watching this, and had to steady myself with a hand on a console.

"That is the way of it, eh?" he said. "For over ten thousand years—ten thousand of your world's circuits around its sun—the Ve-Ky have attempted to find the Museum. This is a momentous occurrence for them. If any of their initial teams breaks out of the Survey Vessel, they will be sure to give the coordinates to thousands more waiting outside. Then the fortress will swarm with enemy. Then—"

He plucked at his beard. "I'm afraid I will have to flush the vessel immediately. I cannot risk further infestations at this time. Perhaps that is fitting. I realize you did not mean me any harm, but you've brought this about through your rash actions. You will have to accept the price of your thoughtlessness."

I wasn't going to accept anything if I could help it. "Maybe if you and I worked together, Curator—"

"You are fighting creatures," he said sharply, interrupting me. "I realize you hate the idea of defeat. I quite understand. Therefore, to be merciful, I shall give you ten minutes to make your peace—"

"Curator," N7 said. "I have an idea."

The old man jerked around, frowning at N7. "The soulless automaton speaks. I find you unsettling, machine. No. You will remain silent in my presence."

"Just a minute, sir," I said, hurrying to N7, kneeling beside him. "What's your idea?" I whispered.

N7 glanced at the old man. The near giant had turned away to study the rest of the bridge.

"The Curator said the ship is infested with Ve-Ky," N7 whispered to me. "Yet, he has appeared in the center of the ship. That would indicate he's able to teleport from one location to another. Perhaps he can move a combat team to the various infested locales, as he calls them. We will rid the ship of the Ve-Ky for him within his time limit."

I looked up, ready to repeat N7's idea.

The Curator was staring at us, and he didn't look pleased. "I heard him," he said heavily. "I am unhappy to hear his voice after telling him to keep quiet. Still, it is a sound idea. And it has been several eons since I've spoken with fringe dwellers such as you. Also, you have returned my Survey Vessel to me. Yes. I shall give you this opportunity then. Ten minutes. If we can pull this off in ten minutes, I shall let you remain in the Orion Arm exhibit until the lot of you die of old age."

-20-

Before we began the ship-clearing assault, I implored the Curator to take me to my quarters so I could reload the Magnum.

The Curator agreed, and he explained the process to us. It was simple and to the point.

"You must stay in a tight circle around me. I do not feel like expending more energy than is seemly. That would be inelegant and wasteful. Do you understand?"

I nodded, as he seemed impatient.

Ella, N7 and I stood by him as the Curator manipulated his thick fingers. The tips glowed as before. I heard a sizzle of energy, smelled something sharp and heard air displacement as we appeared in my quarters.

I staggered. Ella fell flat while N7 stumbled against the Curator. The old man shoved the android away, sending N7 crashing against a bulkhead.

"Do not presume to touch me again," the Curator told a prone N7.

I kept my opinions to myself, snatching several boxes of ammo. I flipped open the .44's cylinder, shoving bullets into the chambers.

As I did, N7 picked himself up, and Ella stood as she checked her pulse rifle. Soon, the three of us circled the Curator again.

N7 tugged my arm and indicated the old man. I shook my head. N7 gave me an imploring look. It was so pathetic I relented.

"Curator," I said.

The old man grunted a monosyllable response.

"N7 is sorry for touching you," I said.

The Curator scowled at me.

N7 continued to motion urgently.

"He, ah, won't do it again," I added.

"The machine had better not," the Curator said. "Once is more than I will tolerate. Now, cease your chatter and ready yourselves for war. Are you ready?"

"Yes, Curator," I said.

"Then let me think," the old man said, bowing his head. "Ah, this is a terrible manifestation indeed. I should caution you that we're about to enter a hot zone. The Ve-Ky have already slain several hundred of your people."

I gripped my gun harder. I hadn't realized that. "Let's go, sir."

"I hear the anger in your voice, trooper," the Curator said. "That is the proper attitude for this. The Ve-Ky are merciless ravagers."

That isn't what Key had told us, but I decided to keep that to myself.

The Curator's fingertips glowed, and the same disorientation occurred as before. This time, though, we appeared in a corner of a vast engine compartment. Great cylinders purred with power and entire banks of wall controls flashed with lights.

Scattered throughout the mighty chamber were over one hundred charred corpses. Smoke still rose from some, while a horrible stench clung in the air.

As we appeared, twenty assault troopers in bio-suits traded shots with twice that number of electrical-flashing humanoids.

I began to fire, holding my gun in both hands. BOOM, BOOM. An electrical soldier stumbled onto the deck. I swiveled slightly. BOOM. BOOM. One pitched off his feet.

The rest of the Ve-Ky noticed after the third invader sizzled on the deck, with blood flowing from the opening in his weird body armor.

They targeted me, of course. I stayed near the Curator. I figured Mr. Super-High Tech would have some sort of defense. Each Ve-Ky bolt zigzagged toward me. Many appeared to be right on target. None of those reached me, however. They stopped a body's-length away as if smashing up against a force field. I'd guessed correctly about the old man. A thought struck me then. Why had the force field let me in while keeping everything else out? The Curator must have allowed me in.

Without the slightest qualm, I took full advantage of the situation, dumping empty cartridges onto the deck and reloading. I should have had speed-loads, but didn't. Several times, my fingers shook as I tried to shove bullets in the chambers.

"They're retreating," Ella shouted.

The Ve-Ky weren't stupid. Once they realized they couldn't do anything to me—provided I stayed near the Curator—they must have figured it was time to regroup elsewhere.

BOOM, BOOM. I moved the gun. BOOM, BOOM.

"Don't let any get away," the Curator said. "I do not have time for that. I will use anti-force against all of you if you fail."

I glanced at him. The old man seemed serene. The eyes, though, swirled with menace. This dude meant what he said.

"Gottcha," I said.

I left the magic circle of his protection, racing after the retreating Ve-Ky. BOOM, BOOM. One pitched to the deck. I re-sighted. BOOM, BOOM. Another stumbled onto his skinny knees. I used the power of my bio-suit, making long leaps, gaining speed as I went. BOOM, BOOM. This time, as I ran, I reloaded without shaking fingers. I was in the zone, hating these bastards for killing my people.

The remaining Ve-Ky spun around. I guess they were angry with me.

Now, though, things had changed considerably. The remaining assault troopers saw that it was possible to kill the invaders. They lay on their bellies or aimed from behind heavy instruments, firing rapid pulse-rifle volleys. That slowed the electrical suits some. Even better, an intense concentration of pulse hits could short-circuit a suit. At that point, three pulse shots killed a Skinny. The enemy began going down in droves once my troopers figured that out.

Before the last Ve-Ky died, a bolt tore into my bio-suit. The discharge turned me rigid with waves of pain. The bio-suit malfunctioned and began flowing off me. I tried to twist away, but another electrical bolt struck. This one shattered my visor. Foul air billowed against me. The stench made me double over and gag.

I rolled away from the last bolt and lay there panting. I'm not sure how much time passed.

The next thing I knew, the Curator looked down on me. "Is that it?" he asked in his deep voice. "Are you done?"

"No," I said, trying to get up, but I couldn't. My bio-suit had stopped flowing off me, but it was hard like stiff rubber.

"It appears that you are done," the Curator said. "That is a pity. Oh, well, I gave you an opportunity for life. You must admit that, yes?"

"I'm not done," I said. I closed my eyes, concentrated and found that the suit didn't want to obey me in the slightest. "I am the master," I told it. I tried to move again.

"Take his gun," the Curator said.

Someone pulled at it. I gripped harder, and I roared a maddened oath. The person tugged the gun from me anyway. That was too much. Rage washed through me and the bio-suit began to respond. Slowly, I got to my knees— the more I moved the softer the living skin became. I looked up and ripped the gun from N7's grasp. He wouldn't meet

131

my eyes. Shaking, with sweat dripping off me, feeding my bio-suit, I climbed to my feet, glaring at the curious-seeming Curator.

"You are an excellent fighting animal," the old man told me. "Your rage is exquisite."

"I am Commander Creed," I panted.

"It would appear you gain confidence by indulging in excessive self-identification. Clearly, you have a high pride quotient. Unfortunately for you, Commander Creed, you have poor grasp of tactics against the Ve-Ky. Allowing them to damage your suit seems foolhardy. Still, I enjoyed the exhibition of battle prowess. And I seem to remember something about—you're humans, is that not so?"

"We are," I said.

"Yes, yes, this is most interesting. I should have recognized that when I saw the Ve-Ky dead in the control room. That was an anomaly, I thought. Clearly, you are a technologically foolish race, barely above stone tool usage. Yet, you have been flying in my Survey Vessel. You destroyed a Rip 92 Attack Vessel earlier. That is what alerted me to the situation. Commander Creed, you have made me curious. I suspect there is a story behind your presence here. I believe I want to hear that story."

"What about the Ve-Ky?" I asked.

The hint of a grin appeared on his lips. "Let us take care of that, shall we?"

The Curator's fingertips glowed once more. He began to sweep them here and there. Before him appeared a ghostly control panel. He tapped in the air, tapping against ghostly controls. I saw images of electrical-suited Ve-Ky. They winked out one after another as if someone had blown against them like candles. Maybe the Curator did just that, metaphorically speaking.

After a few minutes of manipulation, the Curator closed up the ghostly panel. He shook his hands and the glowing fingertips turned normal colored again.

"That's it?" I asked.

"Not quite," he said. "I do not care to have to watch my back. Therefore—" He clapped his hands. It produced a thunderous sound, one that made my ears ring. The ringing didn't stop, but got worse. It made my eyelids heavy. As the ringing continued, I slumped over unconscious.

-21-

I woke up on a military cot, my mind aching as if with the worst hangover of my life. Sitting up, I found myself in a gigantic dormitory. Perhaps half my crew slept in the giant room with me.

This reminded me of a World War II dormitory in every way. I used to watch a lot of old World War II movies as a kid. Everywhere I looked, the blankets, the springs, the flooring, seemed right.

That made me suspicious. Could the Curator look in my mind? That wouldn't surprise me.

I went outside and stopped in shock. The clouds, the Sun, it felt as if I was back on Earth. I glanced around at the trees, stared at the robins tweeting and squirrels gathering nuts.

This was the Museum, right? The Curator had spoken about taking us to the Orion Arm exhibit. Were we already inside the Earth scene?

I had a bad feeling about this.

I spotted N7. He stood by a tree as if taking a whiz. As I approached him, I saw the android carving his name into a tree with a knife.

"What are you doing?" I asked.

N7 turned around as if shocked. He lowered his knife, putting it behind his back.

In spite of myself, I approached the tree. Yes, there was "N7" carved into the bark.

"What's going on?" I asked.

The android looked away.

"This doesn't have anything to do with what the Curator said to you earlier, does it?"

"Why was he so dismissive of me?" N7 asked. "I found that disconcerting."

"It shouldn't bother you," I said.

"Yes. Exactly, it should not, and yet it does. I do not understand that. I have begun to wonder…"

I raised an eyebrow, waiting for him to continue.

"If the Curator has some kind of power to cause…trouble in me," N7 said.

"Are you talking about Pinocchio power?"

"I do not understand your allusion."

I told N7 about Pinocchio, how an old man had whittled a wooden puppet because he'd wanted a son. The puppet had gone around trying to turn into a real boy.

"That is interesting," N7 said. "Yes. I think you're right. In some manner that I don't understand, the Curator has disquieted me. That is not logical. I am a machine. He is correct in saying that I lack a soul."

"If you lack one, why would you care?" I asked.

"I should not."

"Right."

"Yet, I do. Could the Curator possess a power to do such a thing to me?"

I rubbed my chin. That was an interesting idea. What was the Curator? He obviously had the ability to do things that seemed magical to us. Ella would say that's just because we didn't understand the means he used. I could accept that. We were technological primitives compared to him.

The Curator had told me this wasn't his Museum. Then, whose was it? The old man had also said the Ve-Ky had tried to break into here for ten thousand years. Was that true? Or did that simply mean for a long time?

"Come on, N7, let's look around. You can mope about your lack of a soul later. It's time to figure out what's really

135

going on. There are a number of comments the old man made that trouble me."

"Are you referring to his calling the moon-ship his old Survey Vessel?"

"I am," I said.

"His comment certainly leads one to several conclusions."

We'd found a trail in the woods and walked along it. The trail led uphill, which was fine. I didn't mind a stiff walk right now. Walks helped me think.

"What conclusions are you referring to?" I asked.

"If we had the Curator's Survey Vessel," N7 said, "that would imply the vessel was one of a kind, not part of a fleet of transfer ships."

I stopped and thought about that. "You mean Abaddon might have had only *one* transfer ship?"

"I am beginning to think that was the case."

"But that doesn't make sense. We know Abaddon—our enemy, anyway, maybe Shah Claath for all we know—made more than one transfer-ship attack. You returned to the Solar System telling me about a transfer assault in a different star system."

"That is correct," N7 said. "Yet, I have been studying the dates. Unlike humans, I have total recall. I have discovered that all the other transfer attacks took place days earlier than the Solar System assault."

"Are you saying that one ship made all the transfer attacks?"

"That is a distinct possibility," N7 said.

I stomped on the dirt trail harder than before. It didn't thud quite right. It didn't sound like a hill on Earth should. The idea I was inside a fishbowl, a dirt aquarium, seemed more possible by the moment.

"If there's only one transfer ship," I said, "it makes sense why the Super Fleet is headed to Earth."

"Exactly," N7 said. "Abaddon wants the transfer ship back."

"And it makes sense why the enemy hasn't made larger-scale, transfer attacks, piggybacking portions of the Super Fleet on several moon-ships."

"Yes," N7 said.

I picked up a stone, weighing it in my hand. "If we're right about this, it means we're stranded in the galactic core, as the Curator has taken his ship back."

"Perhaps that is why Holgotha suggested we search for the Fortress of Light. The artifact wanted to rid the Orion Arm of any other transfer craft, leaving only its kind with the unique ability."

I scowled, hurling the stone. It sailed and abruptly halted, sliding down what appeared to be an invisible force screen.

N7 and I traded glances. Then, we ran up the hill. I ran ahead of the android, striking the force screen first, and tumbling backward onto my side.

N7 helped me up. "We have found the limit of our exhibit."

Soon, I put my hands against the invisible screen and shoved. It didn't budge. I hit it with my fist, and found that it had a little give before resisting.

"I don't know if this makes any difference to our plight," I said, "but at least we know a little more about the force screen."

We made further experiments. Finally, my stomach growled.

"I guess we'd better go back and get some chow," I said.

As we turned to go, the Curator walked up the path. He wore the same blue robe as before, with the ends trailing on the ground. It didn't dirty his garment, though. I noticed sandals on his feet. That made me laugh.

I don't think the Curator was expecting that. He halted, eyeing me and frowning.

"What is so humorous?" he asked.

I shook my head.

"That is not the proper response," he said. "When I ask a question, you answer. Even though you are beyond primitive, you understand the realities of power. I hold all of it."

"Do you?" I asked.

His frown deepened. N7 gave me a worried glance.

"Do you wish to test me, Commander?" the Curator asked.

"Not at all," I said. "I'm just wondering about your limits. I mean, we had your Survey Vessel, right?"

"You are attempting to interrogate me. That is unseemly and dangerous to your health."

"You're not really the Curator, are you? He died a long time ago. He—"

The Curator raised a hand, with his fingertips glowing.

My throat locked up so I couldn't speak. I clutched at it, finding it difficult to breathe. I waved to him, nodding.

The fingertips glowed again.

I gurgled with noise, enjoying the ability to breathe once more.

"Are you convinced that I am who I say I am, Commander?" he asked.

"You have the power. I was merely..." I cleared my throat. "Curator, may I be frank with you?"

Those blue eyes regarded me for a time. Finally, he nodded.

"You remind me of what I think God would look like. I don't mean the way our theologians would envision God. I'm talking about ordinary people like me, what's in our minds. That seems unusual. In other words, it doesn't seem like a coincidence that you look like this. I suspect you have taken this aspect for a reason."

"I see," he said. "You wish to prove to me that you're higher in cognitive ability than I first gave you credit for. I freely grant you that. I have come to believe you are the little killers of legend."

A cold feeling worked its way through me. I had heard humans called the little killers before. Were we? And, if we were the little killers, what in the heck did that mean?

"The identity troubles you, I see," the Curator said.

"Who are or were the little killers?"

"Commander, do you not yet realize that I refuse to let you interrogate me?"

"I'm not trying to prove anything. It's our innate curiosity at work. Ever since Abaddon—"

I stopped talking because the Curator stiffened as his eyes bulged outward. He took a step back and raised his fingertips like weapons.

We remained like that for a few pregnant seconds. Finally, the Curator lowered his hands. I found that my stomach had clenched even as I felt sweat on the back of my neck.

"Maybe we have something to trade after all," I said.

"It will be a simple matter stripping your mind of everything it knows. Unfortunately, you will become an imbecile in the process."

"Or I could just tell you what you want to know," I said.

"I would prefer that myself, Commander. You gave me a moment's sport back on the Survey Vessel. I have kept the Ve-Ky at an arm's length for so long that I had forgotten the joy of watching a true combat species at war."

"The Ve-Ky are not a combat species?"

"They have the will, of course, but against the little killers they found themselves badly out of their league. While their civilizational score is high, their military prowess leaves something to be desired. It is one of the reasons…"

The Curator plucked at his beard as he examined me. "Let me see if I understand you correctly. When you said Abaddon, what did you mean?"

I glanced at N7. The android wasn't any help. He was clearly terrified and in awe of the Curator. I had been at first, too. I told myself this wasn't what he really looked like. The being had taken this guise to trick us, or to awe us. It had worked. But there were things going on about which I knew little to nothing. In some manner, Holgotha was involved in all this. So was Abaddon.

"I'm waiting, Commander," the Curator said.

"Abaddon is a First One who found himself exiled in a different space-time continuum," I said. "He was there with the Kargs—"

I stopped talking because the image of the Curator began to shift, almost melt. At first, the Curator didn't seem aware of that. When he did, he turned around sharply. I don't know what he did, but he remained in that position for about a minute. Finally, he faced us again.

I didn't gawk, but I saw that his eyes were brown now. Otherwise—no, there were a few other subtle differences in his appearance. I decided to go with it.

"Is that the Abaddon you wanted to hear about?" I asked him.

"It is," he said.

I worked to keep my features as bland as possible. It must not have worked.

"What has excited you, Commander?"

There was menace in his tone. I wasn't sure about the correct response. Whatever the Curator really was, I didn't think he was an artificial intelligence. Therefore, winging it at this point didn't seem wise. Thus, I decided on the truth.

"I'm excited because I slipped in Abaddon being a First One. I didn't know that was true until now. I've wondered about it, though."

"You are cleverer than I realized," the Curator said slowly. "This is fascinating. Yet, that is what is said about the little killers. One cannot give them an inch. Know, human, that I would not have let you know about Abaddon being a First One."

"Are you a First One?" I asked.

The brown eyes glowed with more menace than ever. "Commander, I am afraid I must punish you this time. I have warned you several times about interrogating me. I have let a few incidences pass. I will no longer."

I smiled.

That made him frown. "What do you find amusing about that?"

"You still seem to feel that you have to prove yourself to me. Even after I did you a solid."

"A what?" he asked.

"A solid," I said, "a good turn. I take it you wanted your Survey Vessel back. I'm the one who brought it to you."

"Turn around, N7," the Curator said.

The android did so with speed.

The Curator reached out, grabbing one of my arms. At the same time, the fingertips glowed. His grip felt like fire. I found myself paralyzed, unable to move, shout or roar with pain. The punishment swept through me with growing agony. I felt as if I might start melting.

Abruptly, he let go, stepping back.

I gasped, rubbing the spot where he'd touched me. There were sucker marks on my skin that pulsated with color. That freaked me out. Was he really some kind of octopus creature?

Finally, the pain subsided as the marks began to disappear. I found myself wheezing.

"I hope I do not need to do that again," he said.

I decided the less I said, the fewer times he'd do that to me.

"Walk with me, Commander," he said.

N7 looked up as if he wanted to ask what he should do. He didn't, but stayed where he was.

Soon, the Curator and I moved past the area where the force field had blocked me. The sky, clouds and sun all vanished as if they had been smoke. I looked back into a forest scene.

"Hurry, Commander," he said.

I faced forward and saw the bearded man sitting in what looked like a roller coaster car. In a few strides, I joined him, sitting down beside him.

He manipulated the controls and the car slid forward. Soon, we moved down a long corridor with stars all around us. I saw the supermassive black hole in the distance along with the accretion disk around it.

"I had to punish you in the exhibit," he said. "I have to follow the rules as laid down long ago."

I thought about that. He said he had to punish me in the exhibit. Did that mean outside the exhibit I could ask questions?

"May I ask a question?" I said.

"Soon," he said. "For now, enjoy the ride. It might teach you something."

I shrugged inwardly, wondering what he meant. If I'd known, I would have buckled up. I might even have asked to stay in the exhibit or receive another punishment shock.

The car sped up even though the stellar scene remained the same. Then, we shot out of the corridor into what looked like the exhibit of a star. We plunged toward the nuclear furnace as the heat became intolerable.

-22-

The less said about my experience, the better. We went through the heart of a star exhibit. The heat caused my skin to bubble and melt, or so it felt. The light burned out my sight. The roaring noises left me deaf.

These aren't metaphorical expressions. I felt real agony and suffered for it. The mild pain I'd experienced earlier when he'd grabbed my arm didn't compare to the torture of the ride.

It also lasted far too long.

Finally, though, the agonies ended, and I endured like a lump of flesh. I was alone and weak. I hated it. Then, by small degrees at first, I began to feel, see and hear again. I became aware that I still sat in the car with the Curator. We sped along as before, the stellar sights the same for all I knew.

I didn't say a thing. I hardly thought. I endured hunched over as time lengthened. As my strength returned, I considered attacking him, trying to rip out his throat if I could. I finally began to tremble with the anticipation of doing it.

"That was necessary," he said in his deep voice, sounding as if he was perhaps sorrowful for what he'd put me through.

I might have given him a glance, but if I had just then, I would have attacked like a maniac. Claath had caused me pain in the past, but nothing like that. I planned to hunt down the red-skinned Rumpelstiltskin for what he'd done. Could I do any less to the Curator?

"It was necessary so you could understand," he added.

I didn't want to ask. "Understand what?" So I continued to keep my mouth shut and envision his death. That was more pleasant at the moment.

"The eternity of my existence has almost become as unbearable to me as your ordeal was to you," he said.

My trembling, my desire to attack increased. Then I uncoiled like a viper, a roar on my lips. I would rip out his eyes, I would—

He touched me as I lunged at him, and it seemed as if he sucked the berserker-like desire from my brain and body. A sensation like cold water poured over my brain. It left me gasping.

"We do not have time to indulge your rage," he said. "I need the cunning Commander Creed, not the emotive warrior full of hatred."

I glanced at him, wondering if he had screwed with my mind in some underhanded fashion I couldn't detect. The thought of that almost started the rage process all over again. I decided to wait to strike. I would test myself and my thoughts by asking questions.

The Curator sat erectly beside me, his beard stirring in the wind created by our passage. He appeared self-absorbed, troubled and sad.

"I am the Curator," he said slowly. "I am the Watchman at the center of the galaxy. I have seen so much, so very much. But now I am tired. I have grown weary of my task. I want to set down my responsibilities, but I cannot."

What was the right way to proceed? Had the agony of the star exhibit been an initiation into his sorrow? Did he think he could confide in me now? If that was true...I should try to understand, right? Maybe if I understood what he was saying, I could comprehend... I didn't know his end game. It was time to study, to think before striking. And if that was the case, I should try to lull him, put him off his guard.

"May I ask why you cannot set down your responsibilities?" I said.

"Because I do not have free will in this one area."

"And the reason for this is…?"

"Being the Watchman is my function, my reason for existence."

My brow furrowed in concentration. I thought about his various comments along the way, especially his dislike of N7.

"I take it you're a construct then."

He sighed. "You're asking if I'm a machine, but you're trying to be delicate about it. I am no more a machine than you are, Commander?"

"Do you have a soul?" I asked.

"If I do, I haven't seen it."

"Have you ever seen the Creator?"

"You have spoken to Holgotha," he said, in lieu of an answer. "I know, because I played back Key's memories. Perhaps you don't realize that Holgotha is chief among the Forerunner artifacts. They have chosen exile in the fringe zones for their own peculiar reasons. I suspect they thought themselves safe out there. They left me to contend with the clever center races by myself. I could have used their help, but they remained in the fringes to play with the weak races, never suspecting that the little killers would someday escape from their prison planet."

"Earth was a prison?" I asked.

"The entire Solar System was," the Curator said. "Think of yourselves as a tool kept in a glass cage to use only in case of an emergency."

"That doesn't make sense," I said. "What was the great emergency anyway?"

"Before I say more, I would like to hear your story. I believe everything will make more sense once I hear the full tale."

"What full tale?" I asked.

"Begin with whatever race first visited you. I suspect I'll see a pattern soon enough."

I stared at the stars, at the accretion disk. I was at the center of the galaxy, sitting with the Curator in a roller coaster car. I had just endured the worst torments of my life. Had there been a lesson in that? If so, I wasn't sure I wanted to know the nature of the lessons. Humans had been in a glass cage, on a prison planet? What did that make the Jelk who had nabbed humans throughout the centuries?

"It started when my Dad, Mad Jack Creed, went up to greet the alien visitors..." I said.

I told him my story from start to finish. He never interrupted. Whenever I glanced at him, his brown eyes burned with intensity. Several times, he grunted as if I'd given him a telling point. Finally, with my mouth dry and my back sore, I said, "And that led us here to Sagittarius A*."

Without a word, he manipulated the controls. The car swerved sharply, swooped down as if into a tunnel—the stellar scene vanished—and came to a stop several seconds later.

He climbed onto a platform I couldn't see. "You'd better come out on my side," he said.

I did.

He led me into an invisible passageway, one I saw only after entering. It was like a cave deep under the earth, with a roar like a waterfall through thick rocks. I noticed the ceiling was slick with moisture.

We walked for five minutes until we reached a heavy stone door. He took out a key, rattled it in a lock and pushed. The hinges squealed and a musty odor roiled out.

"Stay close to me," he said.

He hadn't put the key away, but held it up. It was like a big old skeleton key, and it glowed with light. The light didn't shine far, just enough to show us the floor where we put our feet. Unseen chains rattled in the gloom. A smell like sulfur tickled my nose now and again. I heard a terrible groan and then silence. It made my nape hairs stand on end. I didn't like this place.

He put the key into another lock. Everything went pitch-black around us. This stone door didn't want to move. Then it slid against the floor, throwing harsh light through the crack between the door and jam. The Curator had his shoulder against the door and was pushing. With a grunt, he shoved harder still. The door finally opened enough to admit us.

The chamber was brightly lit. A glowing outline wall showed a star with a big gas giant nearby. The gas giant had swirling clouds like Jupiter, but was bright orange with a giant green spot. Masses of starships passed the gas giant.

I moved closer to the outlined wall, with my eyes narrowed. I recognized Jelk battlejumpers, hundreds, no, thousands of them. They led the way, followed by giant Karg ships, the ones carrying several moth-ships apiece. The fleet headed toward a jump gate.

I turned to the Curator. "Is this Abaddon's Super Fleet?"

"It is."

"This is real time?" I asked.

The Curator bowed his head as if concentrating. I felt the disoriented feeling in my head again. Did that mean he was reading my mind?

"Oh, I see what you mean," he said. "Yes, this is real time."

My head no longer hurt. I wanted to tell him to stay out of it from now on, but I figured we could get into an argument about that later. Abaddon's fleet was more important.

"Okay," I said, "this is interesting. Can you blast the fleet from here?"

The Curator laughed, shaking his head. "I most certainly cannot. I wish it were that easy."

147

I studied the fleet a little longer. Then, I looked at the room. It had this screen, but nothing else. There were several doors leading out of here, however.

"What is this room?" I asked. "How can we see the Super Fleet in real time from the galactic core? I mean, I take it the fleet is still headed for Earth, right?"

I glanced at the old man when he failed to answer. He was plucking at his beard, contemplating the fleet. He didn't seem to realize I'd been asking him questions, interrogating him.

"I had to punish you before," he said. "While we're in the viewing chamber, I won't do so."

So, he had noticed the questions.

I nodded.

"This seems like an old room," I said.

"No older than the rest of the Fortress of Light," he said.

"No one has been in this room for a while then, right?"

"That is true."

"For ten thousand years maybe," I said.

"Maybe even a little longer than that," he said.

I studied the scene for a time. The Super Fleet was smaller than our Grand Armada, but I'd already known that. Seeing it for myself made me feel better, though. At least Holgotha had been accurate about that. Now, if only I could figure out a way so the Grand Armada could block the Super Fleet from Earth. Yet…maybe the technologically superior enemy would slice and dice our armada. No. I was beginning to think that wasn't the answer. If the Watchman at the galactic core was worried about the Super Fleet…

"You're afraid of Abaddon," I said.

"That is accurate to a point."

I scratched my head. "I'm not sure I understand why you're afraid, at least, the extent to which you are. Abaddon is way out there in the Orion Arm, a long way from the center—unless he has more transfer vessels."

"I doubt he has any more yet. But, I suspect his plan includes convincing Holgotha and his brothers to join the rebellion. Then, Abaddon will have plenty of transfer vehicles, superior craft to my Survey Vessel."

"Did you know that Abaddon used to be exiled in a different space-time continuum than ours?" I asked.

"Of course I knew. It's one of the reasons I'm here."

"Were the other First Ones exiled as well?"

The Curator didn't respond to that.

"Maybe you can signal me when you're not going to answer one of my questions. That way, I don't have to wonder if you heard me or not."

"It is not fitting that you should speak about the First Ones."

"Why not?" I asked.

"I do not mean to wound your self-esteem with the answer. But you are too low of a species to carry the higher knowledge."

At least he didn't call me a beast. That was an improvement from all the other aliens I'd met. I was just too stupid. The Curator really knew how to make a man feel good about himself.

"Do the Ve-Ky know what happened to the First Ones?" I asked.

"Of course."

"Do the Jelk know?"

"That is difficult to say."

"You don't know if the Jelk know?"

"No."

"Let me get this straight. The Ve-Ky know, but Holgotha doesn't."

"Is that what the artifact told you?"

"Yep."

"Interesting, interesting indeed. I wonder..." The Curator plucked at his beard.

Since I had this opportunity, I decided to really study the Super Fleet. I might never get another chance like this again. The van of the fleet began braking as battlejumpers neared the jump gate. I marveled at the speed they were going to enter the gate and the nearness of the battlejumpers to each other. Their fleet discipline was far better than the Grand Armada's.

"It's time to leave," the Curator said.

I turned around in surprise. "Wait a minute. I thought we were coming up with a plan of action."

"What kind of plan?" he asked.

"Are you serious? How we should go about killing Abaddon."

"That is not a serious suggestion," the Curator said.

"What do you mean? Of course, it's serious. I'm the chief of the little killers. You don't think we humans are going to take our extinction lying down, do you?"

"You are no longer part of the equation, Commander. Holgotha neatly saw to that by sending you here. The artifact must have realized I would have to put you in the exhibit. Holgotha must have feared your interference. I find that remarkable really."

"No," I said. "Holgotha suggested I come here to get a weapon that can kill Abaddon. He said it would be hard to slay the First One. Well, he said it would be difficult to kill Abaddon."

"It is more than difficult, Commander. For you to suggest it is sacrilegious."

"You know I don't see it that way."

"That is due to your ignorance," the Curator said.

That actually made me smile. "Look," I said. "You're frightened of him. You've already admitted that, and I get it. I've talked to Abaddon before. It was an—"

"You spoke in person?" the Curator asked, shocked.

"Not in person but via screen," I said, noticing the big man had shifted away from me. "Abaddon is the real deal. There's no doubt about that. Instead of stuffing us away in a stupid exhibit, why not help me kill him and thereby help yourself?"

150

The Curator stared at me. "You do not understand what you're saying. You have absolutely no chance of slaying Abaddon."

"Holgotha thought otherwise."

"No, Holgotha wanted you out of the way. He maneuvered you here by telling you what you wanted to hear."

"Okay… Suppose that's true. Why did he want us out of the way? Have you ever thought of that? I believe you said he did it because he was worried I could stop Abaddon otherwise."

The Curator opened his mouth to retort, but said nothing. Slowly, he closed it again, going back to studying the Super Fleet.

"You can't leave here because you don't have a vessel to reach Abaddon," he said.

"You're taking the moon-ship from me?"

"It is my missing Survey Vessel," the Curator said. "I'm curious where Abaddon found it and why he…" The Curator studied me, plucking his beard more slowly than before as he studied the Super Fleet.

Without looking at me, he said, "Killing a First One would be incredibly difficult. That this one is Abaddon makes it even more so. He was the strongest of them and stronger than I originally realized. I'm surprised he survived the other space-time continuum. It moved on a faster time-line than ours. Abaddon would be ancient by now even by First One standards. There's something else I don't understand. The Lokhars possessed hyperspace vessels far beyond their technical competence. There is a mystery here, a deep one. Could I have been remiss in letting the fringe zones go their own way all this time?"

"I don't see what you could have done about any of that," I said. "You can't even protect yourself from the Ve-Ky."

"Do not think that my reluctance to use my powers is the same as not possessing the ability."

"So you *can* destroy Abaddon," I said.

The Curator turned away from the wall screen. He kneaded his fingers together. "This is a mess," he said. "The Jelk…"

The old man stared at me. "Come," he said abruptly. "I am going to show you something. Then, you will attack me if you can."

-23-

We left the ancient viewing chamber, striding down brightly lit corridors. These didn't feel old, but shiny and technologically advanced. Soon, we stopped on a glowing pad. We disappeared and reappeared on a different pad. This room was full of strange and exotic weapons.

There were one-man tanks, egg-shaped hover-chargers, strange flamethrower-like equipment and big laser rifles that might have taken down a bull dinosaur.

We stopped before a wall display that showed small glowing spheres leaving an advanced space machine.

"Hey," I said, "I recognize those. They're Jelk in their natural state, right?"

"Not actual Jelk," the Curator said, "but what they looked like on the day of their escape."

I glanced at him. "Jelk used to be in prison?"

He smiled wanly. "Leave it to a little killer to make that intuitive leap. No. Nothing was a prisoner in the beginning."

I frowned. "Then how or why did the Jelk *escape*?"

"Ah. I see your confusion. You're thinking of Jelk as living creatures. They are not. They are the constructed intelligences of what you would consider the largest artificial intelligence in our galaxy."

"Wait. What? The Jelk are...machines?"

"They were part of a giant machine, yes."

I blinked rapidly. "Let me get this straight. Energy beings are really intelligences that once escaped an artificially intelligent super-machine?"

"You live on the fringe of the galaxy. Everything your species has conceived is merely a shadow of greater things first made in the heart of the galaxy."

I frowned. "I'm not sure I understand what you're getting at."

"That is one of the reasons the galaxy is cordoned off as it is," the Curator said. "Without the illegal use of my Survey Vessel, you would never have made it here to learn things beyond your competence level. For instance, none of the Forerunner artifacts would have dared break the Ancient Concord by transferring to a region they shouldn't."

"I don't know that I buy that. Holgotha transferred to the portal planet in hyperspace, right? Was that according to the Concord?"

"That was a surprising move, certainly. I didn't even know about it at the time. Holgotha must have done so in great secrecy. Yet, such a situation was and is outside the strictures of the Ancient Concord."

"Who wrote the Concord?" I asked.

"That is an intelligent question," the Curator said, sounding surprised. "I believe the First Ones did. There is a theory that the Creator did so, but no one has been able to prove that one way or the other."

"Why has the Creator hidden Himself like He has?" I asked.

"His ways are above our ways."

"That's a lame answer," I said.

The Curator shook his head. "I would never be so rash as to say so. It isn't wise to speak ill of Him."

I scowled, looking down. Did the Creator keep track of who said what? It seemed possible. "Maybe I spoke out of turn," I said.

"You did."

"I didn't mean to."

"Then I would apologize."

"To you?" I asked, not liking the idea.

"Of course not," the Curator said. "To the Creator."

"But I can't see Him."

"Nevertheless,' the Curator said.

I cleared my throat, looked away, and said quietly, "I'm sorry I said that."

"That was a wise decision, Commander. I congratulate you."

I shrugged. I didn't understand why, but I was glad I'd said it. I felt "lighter" in spirit for doing so.

"Let's get back to discussing the Jelk," I said. "You were telling me they're machines."

"Living machines, as we say."

"Who is 'we?'" I asked.

"Never mind that," he said. "Some of the Jelk escaped their confinement. Those that remained stayed as intelligences in the machine. The freed Jelk fled from the galactic core, finally reaching Forerunner artifacts in the fringe zones. In time, the two interacted, with the Jelk providing power to the artifacts. That was important, as the artifacts had begun to run out of their original power sources."

"Give them power how?" I asked.

"In the normal manner," the Curator said, "by being consumed in an energy process. The Jelk were the right kind of source, you see. Other power sources wouldn't have worked with the Forerunner artifacts. It gave the Jelk a fantastic bargaining position."

"I'm not sure I understand. What was the power source again?"

"An individual Jelk," the Curator said.

"You mean the individual Jelk let itself be burned up like coal?" I asked.

"That is a crude example, but accurate."

"The process killed the Jelk then, right?"

155

"That is where the situation becomes interesting and calculating. The Jelk as a group aged. All machines break down in time. It is the law of entropy. However, in a special chamber on each Forerunner object is a containment room. In the room, a Jelk could duplicate in a cellular fashion. Each half retained the knowledge of the original and gained the energy of youth."

"It sounds like the Jelk were alive after all," I said.

"That is why we call them living machines. They are most certainly machines, but with the properties of life."

"Okay..."

"In two out of three duplications, the Jelk left one of the new halves with the artifact. The artifact then used the new Jelk as its power source, consuming the Jelk in the process. It appears to have been a fruitful exchange for each side. Of course, such a situation was banned from the beginning. Thus, each had a reason to remain hidden in the fringes, far out of sight of the Creator."

"Yet...I thought the Forerunner artifacts yearned to find the Creator. At least, that's what mine has said."

"I have begun to believe that the artifacts are conflicted in this. Part of each of them desires the Creator's return. The other half works to keep that day from happening."

"That's wild," I said.

"It is flux. It is rebellion. Thus, it is an unstable situation. No wonder the Jelk have agreed to help Abaddon. Yes, I have been remiss in my duties. There is no doubt about it now."

"You enforce the Creator's edicts, I take it?"

"Nature usually does that," the Curator said. "In this instance, Abaddon has short-circuited nature. Thus, I believe it is time I take a hand in this, however small."

"Maybe you'd better spell that out for me," I said.

"That makes the most sense. Yet...if you should lose, if Abaddon captures you...I do not want you telling him I had anything to do with this."

I stared at the Curator. He stared back. I wondered what he expected from me. I imagine the old fellow could put a mind block in me, do whatever he wanted, really. Finally, I shrugged, and said, "Mums the word, old boy."

"You swear to this?"

I opened my mouth to say exactly that.

"Be careful, Commander. You will have to live up to your oath. The pain you felt going through the sun exhibit will be as nothing if Abaddon captures you. He will demand to know how you acquired the equipment you're about to receive."

"I won't tell him."

"If you swear to me to keep this secret, and then you tell him, your race will be forfeit."

"They're already forfeit," I said. "Abaddon is coming to exterminate them."

"I believe that is true. He does not like the little killers any more than the others do. Perhaps in some strange way he fears you."

"This is too much," I said. "You have to tell me what the little killers are. I mean, they're us. I know that. But how or why did we become that?"

The Curator was shaking his head. "My people would be forfeit if I told you."

After several seconds, I shrugged. "I swear I won't tell Abaddon how I got what I'm about to receive."

The Curator's hands glowed instead of just his fingertips. He reached out, grabbing me by the arms. I felt as if he was searing me and expected to see smoke rising from his hands. There wasn't, but it still hurt.

Finally, he let go. I staggered backward.

"It is done," he said. "You are marked. I am sorry I had to do that, Commander. But it was the only way."

I rubbed one of my arms, keeping my thoughts to myself.

"Now, I can show you. Are you ready?"

"Yeah," I said.

"Then follow me through this door. And Heaven help us both if you fail in your anointed task."

-24-

We walked through many rooms, down endless corridors and chambers. Each held weapons. Some were bigger than houses. A few were smaller than thimbles. The Curator didn't explain any of them to me.

Finally, he stopped before a big, bulky suit. It was like a one-man exo-skeleton armored tank. It had big mechanical packs and various nozzles and gun ports. The thing looked as if it weighed ten tons. Whoever wore it would be inside it like a combat suit.

"What is that?" I asked.

"One of the ultimate combat suits in the galaxy," the Curator said. "A species constructed these who fought a war against the First Ones."

"I take it the First Ones won the war."

"Indeed."

"What happened to the race that took up the challenge?"

"They are quite extinct. The only memory of them is in the Museum with these suits."

"How many suits do you have?"

"Five," the Curator said.

I studied him. Did he expect me to believe that?

"There is one for you, Ella, Rollo, Dmitri and N7," he said.

"You're sure about N7?"

"No, but I believe you are."

"Five suits to kill Abaddon, huh?"

"No," the Curator said. "You have five T-suits to collect Jelk."

"The 'T' in T-suit means teleport, doesn't it?" I asked.

"Yes."

"That's nifty, I guess. What kind of range do they have, and how accurately can they teleport?"

"The range is short, a billion kilometers. Their accuracy is fantastic, just a little short of what I can do naturally."

"By naturally, you mean with the machines that you control with your hands."

The Curator did not respond to that.

"Five T-suits to collect Jelk," I said. "Why are we collecting Jelk? I mean, I know why I plan to kill one of them."

"You will not kill the Jelk directly," the Curator said.

"I haven't sworn to that."

"You need Shah Claath, just as you will need all the Jelk you can catch."

"How do these suits catch energy beings?"

"They do not," the Curator said. He walked several steps to a bulky, pronged device. "This will catch them, provided you can cause the Jelk to go from its physical state to the energy state. Then, you must move these prongs on either side of him or it. The process takes some time. At the end of it," the Curator said, using his finger to show me. "The intelligence matrix will flow up this tube into a containment tank."

"I think I understand."

The Curator detached the hand-sized containment tank from the pronged weapon. He carried it to a wicked looking gun. The gun was huge and would need a T-suit to help carry it. The power-pack would hang from a trooper's mechanical shoulders, while the soldier would need two hands to lift and aim the barrel.

"What is that?" I asked.

"It is an Ultrix Disintegrator," he said. "This is the only one left in existence. It was designed to slay a First One. The species who fought the First Ones slew them on several occasions. Thus, we know the weapon works. It is more than possible that Abaddon has altered his state since his stay in the other space-time continuum. It might take several shots with the Ultrix Disintegrator to kill Abaddon. It might not work at all. But it is the best I can give you."

I stepped up, taking the containment field from him. "That goes up in there?" I asked, pointing at a slot.

The Curator nodded.

"And that containment field will hold a Jelk intelligence?"

"Yes," he said.

"And the Jelk will power the Ultrix Disintegrator?"

The Curator nodded.

I stared at the huge weapon.

"You must not feel remorse using the Jelk this way," the Curator said. "They are not true life. They are living machines that have created endless mischief."

"Curator," I said. "I will feel great emotion using the Jelk like this."

"I am sorry to hear this."

"No," I said. "You don't understand. I won't feel bad about using those little bastards to power the great weapon. I'm going to feel awesome doing that, especially if it's Claath powering up the gun. I hope he can see what I'm doing as I'm doing it."

The Curator took his time. "I realize you say this now, Commander. It will be different during the moment. The Jelk are very persuasive, and they will struggle to an intense degree."

I kept my mouth shut. Why let the Curator think of me as more bloodthirsty than he needed to? If I ever got that far in the game, I'd see how I'd react then.

"There is one problem I have failed to mention yet," he said.

161

"I already know what it is."

The Curator raised his bushy eyebrows.

"We're going to have to steal the *Santa Maria* from you," I said.

"The what?"

"Your old Survey Ship," I said.

"I cannot be party to such a plan," he said, saying it in such a way that let me know I'd guessed correctly.

"If you can't talk, let's not try to talk about it," I said. "I would like to know how we can deduce where Abaddon is in the Super Fleet."

The Curator shook his head. "You will have to figure that out yourself."

"But if you're giving us all this equipment—"

"I am not," the Curator said. "The only way anyone could get this equipment is by stealing it. I have no right to give you any of these things."

I studied him. "Won't I get in serious trouble if I steal from the Curator?"

"Only if you're caught," he said.

"Is there anyone around here who will try to catch me?"

"Everyone," he said, "including the Forerunner artifacts. If you were to leave here as thieves, having broken my concord of goodwill and peace, you would be fugitives. No race would help you after that, including those in the Orion Arm."

"How will anyone back there know we're thieves?"

"You would be marked by such a theft," the Curator said. "I cannot change that."

"Uh...so you're saying every hand will be turned against us?"

"*Would* be turned against you if you practiced such a heinous deed," he said. "That is exactly so."

"Not even the Starkiens would help us?"

"A few might dare, but I doubt it."

"Anyone will be able to tell this mark?" I asked.

"Alas, that would be so."

"Will all humans be marked?"

"As long as my Survey Ship roamed free, as long as those weapons were used, yes."

"Could we return the ship back to you after we killed Abaddon?"

"You will not survive his death, Commander."

The Curator seemed so certain as he said that that I felt a chill blow over me.

"Well, suppose I did survive," I said.

"The only way to atone for such a theft would be to return it to the Fortress of Light and accept whatever punishment awaited you."

"You're dead serious, aren't you?"

"Abaddon corrupts everything he touches. The Jelk are beyond hope now. The entire Orion Arm will soon teeter over the abyss. You could possibly save the others, Commander, but you would risk the entire human race doing so."

"We're dead anyway if the Super Fleet reaches our Solar System."

"That is true. At least in your passing, you could save the others."

"I can do more than that," I said.

He raised those eyebrows once again.

"I could make sure anyone who screwed with us would lose big time."

"They would feel the same way about you."

"Good," I said. "I like beating a sore loser. It makes the victory that much more enjoyable."

"I wish there was another way," the Curator said, "but I cannot see it. I dare not confront Abaddon myself, for I dare not risk my own corruption. Any who would do this would embark on an impossible quest. Your only hope would be that you are the little killers. If any race had a chance of winning through battle, it would be you and yours. Good luck, Commander. May the Creator..." He stopped talking.

"Well," I said. "Aren't you going to bless me?"

The Curator shook his head. "I cannot bless killers, and I cannot bless possible thieves."

"Sure," I said, dryly. "Maybe you can show me what I need to know in order to do what I have to."

"Yes," he said. "We can talk about theoretical possibilities. Follow me, if you dare."

I dared all right, my fingertips tingling with the thought of meeting Claath again, of seeing Abaddon face to face and maybe, if I was lucky, of finally freeing my sweet and almost forgotten Jennifer.

-25-

The next thing I knew, I was running through the *Santa Maria*, racing to the bridge. This felt like Mars all over again. I wondered if all this sprinting here and there would ever end for me. Probably only on the day I died.

Klaxons rang, and people rushed past me in the corridors. Finally, I made it to the bridge.

"Commander," Ella shouted. "What's happening? The last thing I remember was walking through a forest."

N7 sat at a console. He banged his forehead with the heel of his right hand. "I feel strange, Commander. I have the sense I have forgotten something. That is a non sequitur, as I have total recall. Why, then, do I have a feeling I have lived through an experience I cannot remember?"

I slid to a halt. Could they have lost their memories of what had happened to us in the Fortress of Light? I frowned. What was the last thing I remembered? Yes, I'd been talking with the Curator. I was supposed to steal the *Santa Maria* and certain weapons from him to slay Abaddon. Why didn't I remember doing that? I mean, I must have, right? We had the transfer ship, and I knew the T-suits, the pronged Jelk Catcher and the Ultrix Disintegrator were in a special weapons locker on the vessel.

I strode to the command chair to give myself a few seconds to figure out how I was going to play this.

After settling myself, I asked, "What's the last thing you remember, Ella?"

"We had appeared by the supermassive black hole…" she said, as she turned to the main screen. "There it is. But…why does my mind feel fuzzy?"

"Commander," Rollo said briskly. "Over there on the edge of the accretion disk. Do you see those points of light?"

I did. They looked like Vip 92 Attack Vessels. Was I going to have to go through one of their attack runs again?

N7 glanced around the bridge. "We're missing someone," he said slowly.

"Who?" I asked.

"A floating machine…" N7 said, still sounding a bit uncertain.

This was interesting. Were the Curator's methods less successful on an android than on a human? I would have thought androids would be easier to reprogram than humans.

"Are you referring to Key?" I asked.

"What key?" N7 asked.

I bared my teeth in frustration.

Why hadn't the Curator told me he was going to erase their memories? I had a suspicion he'd done it to protect them. Whatever they didn't know, they couldn't tell Abaddon if we failed. Only I could sell out humanity. That seemed fair. I was the one who'd left his lover behind in Abaddon's hands. Now, after all these years, I would have to pay the bill for running away on Jennifer.

Ella looked up from her panel. "Those are ships, Commander," she said, referring to the Vip 92s. "Should I hail them?"

"Negative," I said. "Set a transfer jump for Sal 63 B in the Orion Arm."

The others stared at me as if I'd gone crazy.

"But we just got here," Ella said.

"That's not true," Dmitri Rostov said hoarsely.

I glanced at the Cossack. His blocky features were sweaty and he blinked furiously. "I…" He rubbed his forehead. "I don't feel well."

"There is no response from the points of light," Ella said. "My instruments suggest they are containment fields of energy."

"Those points of light are Vip 92 Attack Vessels," I said.

Dmitri looked up sharply. "That's right. They hold…the Ve-Ky." He frowned. "They're going to storm the *Santa Maria*. One of them will be frozen in a moon wall."

"That already happened," I said. "This is a second attack. Well, their third attack, really."

Ella glanced from Dmitri to me. "He should go to sickbay, Commander. I don't know what's wrong with you. I do know one thing. We haven't been here before."

"Yet N7 recalls a machine that is gone," I said.

"Perhaps that's an after-effect of transferring to the galactic core," Ella said.

"That's one possibility," I conceded. "Maybe the other is that your memory of certain events is gone."

"That doesn't make sense," Ella said stubbornly.

"I've already been on the Fortress of Light—" I snapped my fingers. "I have it. Call the engineering deck. Ask for Marcus, Rodriguez and Kholo Ron."

"We should concentrate on the approaching energy ships," Ella said.

"Call engineering," I told Rollo. "Ask for those people."

Rollo did as requested. Afterward, he looked up in surprise. "They're not at their posts. Engineering called their quarters but hasn't gotten any responses yet. They, along with others, appear to be missing from duty."

"They're missing because they're dead," I said. "The Ve-Ky killed them when they stormed the *Santa Maria*. Dmitri is right. One of the alien enemies died frozen in a wall. Their electrical combat-suits allowed them to walk through the walls if they wanted."

"That doesn't make sense," Ella said. "Wouldn't your bullets and our pulse shots go right through them then?"

"It took a special process," I said. "Maybe wall-walking caused a high energy drain so they could only do it for short periods of time."

"Why would energy creatures need suits in the first place?" Ella asked.

"They're Skinnies," I said, "flesh and blood creatures that fly energy ships and wear electrical combat-suits."

Ella glanced at Rollo. "I think Creed is hallucinating. You should take over."

"What about the missing personnel?" Rollo asked her.

Ella licked her lips, appearing uncertain.

"Listen," I said. "I took special combat-suits from the Fortress of Light. I also have a special gun that can kill Abaddon. If I'm crazy, how did I get those items?"

Ella frowned severely, blinking.

"The energy ships are approaching fast," Rollo said, studying a panel. "They have excessive speed. Look at their numbers. I think we should transfer as the Commander suggests."

"But Sal 63 B is practically back home," Ella said. "Why transfer all the way there?"

"So we can practice with our T-suits," I said. "Ella, do you really think I've gone crazy? If so, tell me what happened to all our missing people."

She stared at me and then Dmitri. "Why does he look like he's been through hell?" she asked me.

"Dmitri wasn't supposed to remember anything," I said. "Maybe his Cossack brain is wired wrong and the...the being we spoke to didn't erase his memories properly."

"I can believe that about the weird brain wiring," Rollo said with a slight smirk. "It would explain a lot of things about Dmitri."

The rest of the bridge personnel waited. Many of them seemed nervous at this dichotomy. A few of them seemed ready to bolt off the bridge.

"Okay..." Ella said. "This is crazy. I'm not buying any memory losses...but something isn't right. Let's transfer and start over. I thought we were on a tight time schedule, but I don't know what else to do."

"Right," I said.

The Vip 92s raced for us as the bridge personnel made the calculations. From farther away than last time, blobs of energy detached from the Vip 92s. The first one disappeared.

At that moment, two men pulled the main levers. The *Santa Maria* transferred out of Sagittarius A*.

-26-

"It shouldn't be that hard to believe," I said. "We've all watched time traveling movies, right?"

The five of us sat in a conference chamber, Ella, Rollo, Dmitri, N7 and me. I'd shown them the T-suits, the Jelk Catcher and the Ultrix Disintegrator. I explained how I'd been in a viewing chamber on the Fortress of Light and seen the enemy Super Fleet.

As I spoke to them, I sketched on a pad from memory the disposition of the enemy fleet. That could come in handy soon.

"At the end of a good time traveling movie," I said, "only one or maybe two of the heroes remember what the timeline was like before they changed it. No one else can remember what it was like."

"I've seen those kinds of movies," Ella said. "But that doesn't apply here."

"It does. I remember what happened but the rest of you don't."

"I remember, too," Dmitri said.

"Parts of it anyway," I said. I'd been wondering about that. Could the Curator have made an error? If so, that didn't bode well for us. However, the Curator might have done that to give me an edge with my own people. In other words, the Curator may have done me a favor with Dmitri.

"I can't explain the missing crewmembers," Rollo told Ella.

"That's another thing," she said. "If this creature can erase our memories, why wouldn't it have taken our memories of those missing people as well?"

"You didn't lose your memories to protect *it*," I said, "but to protect you."

"How does that work exactly?" Ella asked.

"If I told you, that would negate what he did for us," I said.

The *Santa Maria* was in the Sal 63 B System. I'd chosen it because I thought the Super Fleet was headed this way on its path to the Solar System. That was a possibility given from what I'd seen on the wall screen in the Fortress of Light.

"Suppose we accept your explanation," Ella said slowly. "What are we supposed to do next?"

I told them most of what the Curator had told me about the Jelk, Forerunner artifacts and Abaddon being a First One. I also explained something about the civilizational zones and that we were possibly the little killers of galactic legend. What that legend was, though, I didn't know.

"You are describing a great deal of order to the technological and civilizational arrangement of our galaxy," Ella told me.

"I guess so," I said.

"A First One..." she said. "Your tales seem to make Abaddon a devil. A First One sounds like it could be an angel. This so-called 'bad angel' rebelled and found itself exiled from our space-time continuum."

"I didn't say anything about angels or devils," I told her.

Ella drummed her fingers on the table. "This rebel angel idea disturbs me. Why concoct this elaborate 'religious' dogma for a hard-fought war between highly advanced species?"

"Why should that surprise you given all we've seen so far?" I asked. "We belong to the Jade League, right? Its basis is religious. Besides, that's been the norm throughout all of human history." I snapped my fingers. "The…person I spoke to in the Fortress of Light told me that nothing in the fringe zones was new. It was all a reflection of what had happened in the galactic center. Thus, it makes sense that all these aliens are religious. We're just mimicking how everyone else does it."

"That doesn't make it true," Ella said.

"Never said it did," I told her.

"But you think that's how it is, don't you?" she asked.

"What do you want me to say, Ella? Yeah. I think that's how it is. I'm not saying you have to believe that. Sure, we're off to kill a devil. Is Abaddon the real thing or are devil legends Plato's shadows on a cave wall? I don't know. Why does it matter? Abaddon is scary and is going to be hard to kill no matter who or what he really is. You go about this your way and I'll go about it mine."

She frowned at me.

"You were from Russia," I said. "In the States, the teachers and most media types told us we had to accept their thoughts on things. Only they could say their way was right, because they were tolerant, you see. But if they had been tolerant of our way of thinking, they would have welcomed our thoughts as being part of the human experience. Instead, they said we were bigots and had to think like they did in order to be tolerant like them."

"Were they insane?" Ella asked.

I laughed, shrugging. "I guess that would depend on who you asked. They were a royal pain in the-you-know-what. My point is this. You hate the idea of religion. I'm not keen on atheist thought. As long as we can work together to defeat Abaddon—whatever he is—I'm not going to worry how you see things."

"Yes," Ella said. "I can tolerate your belief in your fairy tales. Despite your simplicity concerning a Bronze Age god, you are a good battle leader."

"And you're a heck of a scientist, Ella. Whether Abaddon is a devil or an advanced species with delusions of grandeur, I need your insights to help me kill him."

"Da," she said. "I can live with that. I already have for all these years. Why change now? Besides, it occurs to me why the advanced species in the galactic core use religious beliefs. It is the same reason rulers have used it on Earth since time immemorial."

"Why was that?" N7 asked.

"It should be obvious," Ella said. "Religion is a societal tool. It helps keep the masses in line. Don't steal, or you'll go to Hell. In some times and places, that was as good a tool as enlightened self-interest or heavy-handed policing to keep people from theft."

N7 considered that while blinking slowly. "That computes. Yes. It is interesting. I shall have to think about this carefully."

"That's fine," I said. "But I want you to do that on your own time. Right now, we need a game plan. We have to figure out how to beat the greatest threat Earth has faced so far. Who has an idea about the best way to defeat Abaddon and his Super Fleet?"

Dmitri grew thoughtful. N7 became blank-faced. Ella rubbed her left cheek with a forefinger. Rollo leaned back his chair so it creaked ominously.

"My guess is that if Abaddon dies the whole thing falls apart," Rollo said. "He must rule by force, through fear. Eliminate the fear and his lieutenants won't know how to work together. That might cause the Super Fleet to break into smaller, more manageable pieces."

"Especially if the Jelk are already gone or in disarray," Ella said.

"Is that the idea?" Dmitri asked me. "We storm the Super Fleet as..." The Cossack stopped talking as he saw me shake my head.

"What is the range of the T-suits again?" Ella asked.

"One billion kilometers," I said. "That's greater than the distance from the Sun to Jupiter but not as far as Saturn."

"That all seems too risky," Ella said. "We transfer beside the Super Fleet, teleport onto an enemy ship and what? The five of us attack inside a giant battlejumper? What can five people do?"

"Five ninjas," I said.

The others stared at me.

"Do you know what a ninja is?" I asked N7.

The android shook his head.

"They were a clan in Feudal Japan," I said. "They were trained assassins that slew their targets stealthily, often inside an enemy fortress."

"You mean like the Shi-Feng," N7 said.

"I guess," I said.

"The Shi-Feng were Lokhars," Rollo said. "Creed is talking about human assassins. Ninjas," he said to me. "We slip aboard a battlejumper, grab a Jelk and teleport away with him or it. No one is the wiser."

I nodded.

"There's a problem with that," Ella said. "One, our transfer vessel is the size of a moon. That will be hard to hide. Two, we can't see ahead to where we are transferring. For all we know, we'll teleport into the middle of the Super Fleet. We'll be lucky at that point to transfer away before any of them can board us."

"I will add to the dilemma," N7 said. "It is essentially the same problem but on a different scale. Let us begin with a battlejumper. Where on the ship does a particular Jelk stay? We teleport to a place, but instead of Jelk we find armed Saurians. We could spend a considerable amount of time on the battlejumper trying to locate the Jelk. According to what you've said, getting him into his energy state will take time and effort. Even then, we will need precious time to complete the process. By that time, the *Santa Maria* may be under heavy fire, possibly crippled. I would suggest that Abaddon will recognize the *Santa Maria* as soon as he sees it. He will immediately attempt to capture it, as the transfer vessel is a tremendous prize."

"It's good that we're talking about this," I said. "I've already thought of something because of it. A good strategist turns a weakness into a strength or the bait for a trap."

"What's our weakness?" Dmitri asked.

"Ella and N7 have already told us. The enemy will recognize the *Santa Maria* the moment it appears. If we're right about that, Abaddon will immediately attempt to capture the moon-ship. We have to use that against them."

"How do we do that?" Ella asked.

"I don't know. But one of us has to come up with an answer and fast. I saw the Super Fleet in the Gemini Tao System. It was headed to the jump gate leading to the Epsilon Five System. We don't know exactly which route they'll take to Earth. We'll have to start guessing if we take too long to make our assault."

"We can't attack blindly," Ella said. "And we need to practice our assault. We have to know what we're doing. This time, we can't just wing it as we have so many other times."

"I have a proposition," N7 said. "We lack precise transfer capabilities. Holgotha possesses that trait. We should enlist the artifact's help."

"How could we motivate Holgotha to do that?" I asked.

"Offer him a large supply of Jelk as power sources," N7 said.

"He already has that."

"He *had* it according to what you told us," N7 said. "Abaddon's insertion into our space-time continuum must have changed the power balance, particularly after the Jelk allied with him. This is a new era. Perhaps Holgotha will see this and act accordingly."

"Okay, okay," I said, nodding. "That's not bad."

"I think it's too risky," Ella said. "We need to remember that Holgotha has rarely acted as expected. We would have to implicitly trust the artifact. I know I don't."

"Me neither," Rollo said. "I'm tired of trusting aliens or alien AIs. This time, it's our show. Let's sweep them all off the board."

"We still need a plan that turns our weakness into strength," I said.

"Screw it!" Rollo said, slapping the table. "We do this how you stormed onto the lander in Antarctica. We don't think this out too hard. We appear in the Epsilon Five System and attack a battlejumper. If there's no Jelk, we go to the next one. By the time we have a few Jelk, Abaddon will have made his move. Maybe he's heading for us by then. Maybe he's going for the *Santa Maria*. What we do is go in and start killing. Either we get him or we don't."

I stared at the First Admiral. He wasn't always this angry. He'd never been the same after the Jelk Corporation service.

I turned to N7. "You're right. We need precision. For this to work, we have to make surgical strikes."

"So we attempt to enlist Holgotha to do the transferring?" N7 asked.

"No," I said. "I have something else in mind. Let's see what the rest of you think of this…"

-27-

The key to this was to remember what we had become. The Curator had said every hand would be turned against us now. I suspected that meant the Forerunner artifacts would be in the forefront, suggesting others declare us rogues or outlaws. We had become worse than the Starkiens in their nomadic days.

I had another reason for doing it this way. We knew where everything was in the Solar System and could therefore make near-perfect transfer moves.

Dmitri and I wore our bio-suits. I'd chosen him for this round because he remembered using a T-suit.

We each eased into one. As I said before, the T-suits were like one-man, exo-skeleton tanks. We needed our living skin for several reasons. One, it made us a little bulkier. Given our greater than normal size because of our beefy muscles, we were just about the right fit for these. Tubes attached to the living skin. Receptors sparked with ignition in other places. The last armor plate swung shut, as if enclosing us in a coffin.

The T-suit had various weapons systems, including a small antimatter firing mechanism. They were tiny grenades with unbelievable wallop. My suit had a beam weapon in one arm and a big cannon that fired explosive rounds in the other. The arm cannon fired super-dense shells that made lead seem like feathers. Each suit could launch missiles that packed thermonuclear power or radiated an EMP blast.

I checked my visor, making sure all the hookups were in place so I could control the T-suit from here.

Butterflies roiled in my gut. I went over every suit and weapon feature, rechecking each several times. Finally, I signaled N7, who stood in the chamber with us.

The android raised a hand unit, no doubt telling Ella we were suited up and ready to go.

"What if we teleport into a wall?" Dmitri asked me.

"I thought I told you. The suits have an anti-matter feature. Instead of materializing *in* something, the suit will bounce you so you'll appear near it instead. Have you tested your locator tab yet?"

"Yes."

"Move it around some. Get used to it."

I moved mine, seeing in my visor the targeted teleportation location. With this, I could look into any place on the *Santa Maria*, even in the reactor cores. This must be like Holgotha's far-seeing ability, only with a shorter range. We could see as far as one billion kilometers away, the limit of our teleportation range. I had no idea how far Holgotha's far-ranging sight was.

"This solves one of our problems," Dmitri told me. "We can locate a Jelk on a battlejumper and Abaddon on a Karg vessel with this process."

"Provided they're within one billion kilometers and we pick the right spot. It still means wasting a lot of time searching a ship room by room."

N7 signaled me by waving an arm.

I opened a channel. "Is Ella ready?"

The android nodded.

"Okay," I said. "So are we. Anytime she wants to do this, I'm game."

N7 waited, listening to his comm. Finally, he held up his hands with all his fingers spread. After a few seconds, he put

178

a finger down, then another and then a third. The countdown had started.

"This could get ugly," I told Dmitri, "because I'm not backing down."

"Never thought you were, Commander," the Cossack said.

N7 only had three fingers up now. Two, one…the *Santa Maria* transferred.

I felt a momentary disorientation. It took two long blinks before my mind returned to normal. I wondered if that would ever change. I checked my teleporting scanner, seeing the asteroid Ceres, a hundred Starkien starships around it, and Holgotha gleaming like a great metal donut not too far away from them.

"We're going to pop directly into his speaking chamber," I told Dmitri.

"I haven't found it yet," he said.

"Remember the feature that links you to my scanner?"

"Right! I'm looking for it—ah, found it. I'm linked to you, Commander."

"Good. Let's go," I said, pressing my teleport tab. My suit buzzed, building up power, and a second later I vanished from the guts of the *Santa Maria* to reappear inside Holgotha. There was a rush of displaced air and a slight jar, as I'd appeared a centimeter off the floor. I stumbled, but caught myself quickly enough. The chamber was dark. Luckily, I'd brought my own light, using a big helmet lamp.

"You'd better start speaking, Holgotha," I said. "I have antimatter bomblets in my dispenser. If you don't talk quickly enough, I'm going to pop into various chambers, setting them off inside you."

The wall began to vibrate. Maybe it was my imagination, but it seemed indignant.

"This is gross negligence on your part, Commander Creed," the deep voice said. "You should know that I have already alerted Baba Gobo of your presence in me. He is preparing his war fleet to attack. Soon, the Starkiens will maneuver toward the Survey Vessel. You will have to surrender at once if you wish to save your companions."

"You've got it wrong, artifact. Today, I'm going to tell you how it's going to go. And you know what? I'm going to enjoy doing it."

"You are rash, Commander, and too direct and simple. Don't you realize that your companion-in-arms is absent?"

He was right. What had happened to Dmitri?

"I sense your frustration," Holgotha said. "You have no idea how superior I am to you. You are a gnat compared to me."

"Are you going to call me a beast next?" I said.

"You might as well be one in comparison to me. I imagine you don't even realize what I've done. It's called a dampening field. You cannot teleport out of me. You are trapped until I decide on your punishment for this final affront."

I manipulated the T-suit, rolling an antimatter grenade onto the floor.

"What are you doing?" Holgotha demanded. "Are you demented? You will die in the blast."

"We'll both die," I said. "That's better than having to listen to you pontificate about your superiority until you bore me to death." I rolled a second antimatter grenade onto the floor."

"You must cease this insanity at once."

"Shut down the dampening field or I'll blow us up."

Two seconds went by. "It is done," Holgotha said.

A moment later, Dmitri in his T-suit appeared beside him.

"I couldn't see anything on the artifact," the Cossack said. "Then, I could see again. Do you know what happened?"

"I do," I said. "But you have to let me talk to Holgotha."

"Da, Commander." The huge T-suit took up its station beside me, its weapons blinking at the ready.

"You're doing just fine," I told Holgotha, feeling cocky. This felt better than I'd imagined it would. I hadn't realized until this moment how sick I'd become of the artifact's insufferable arrogance. "Before you know it," I added, "I'll pick up the antimatter grenades, and we'll be pals like old times. First, though, you have to tell Baba Gobo to stand down."

"You cannot get away with this, Commander," Holgotha said. "All the artifacts will help the loyal races to slay every human in existence. Unless you surrender to me, you are dooming your species to extinction."

"I don't think so."

"I implore you to listen to reason," Holgotha said. "Don't you understand the sacrilegious nature of your act?"

"Hey. Before you get all righteous on me, you should know that I've been to the Fortress of Light."

"Please, Commander, that is obvious. You have a Ronin 9 Teleportation Combat Suit. There is only one place in the galaxy you could have acquired that, and that is the Museum."

"How do you know about the Ronin 9?" I asked. "The Curator said he was the only one who remembered them."

"The Curator is very old, Commander. He is senile. Surely, even someone as dull as you recognized that."

"Words," I said.

"Facts," Holgotha said.

"Do you want Abaddon to win?"

"It is not a matter of his *winning*. The First One longs for the old days of his supremacy. He does not realize there is another way to achieve the goals he desires. He is also not aware that I am recording everything for the day the Creator asks for an accounting."

"Why do I have the feeling you're lying?"

"You are so blatantly egocentric, Commander. Haven't you realized yet that it is immaterial what you think or feel?"

"Dmitri," I said. "Go back to the *Santa Maria* and find out what the situation is with the Starkiens."

"Yes, Commander," Dmitri said. His suit whined as it built up power, but didn't teleport.

"You will remain here in me for a time," Holgotha said smugly.

Maybe the artifact figured I was bluffing. I wasn't. I activated the first antimatter grenade. Nothing happened, though. I took another look at it in ultraviolet. I saw a hazy shimmering field around the red-hot grenade. That was interesting.

"I have already deactivated the grenades, Commander. I merely humored you long enough to open channels with a quorum of artifacts. We are going to judge you and the human race. You will be found wanting, of course. Then, we shall destroy the lot of you as should have been done when the Purple Tamika Emperor sent the dreadnaught the first time."

I didn't believe him about having deactivated the antimatter grenade. According to my T-suit, he'd put a dampening field around it. I was betting that took power, and would take power until someone shut off the grenade. The dampening field keeping me from teleporting would also take energy. Therefore—

I spun around in the heavy T-suit. I raised the beam weapon of the mini-tank, hosing it against an interior bulkhead until it glowed red-hot. Then, I rapid fired several super-dense shells into it. That proved too much for the bulkhead. The shells tore holes into it, and a strange fluid leaked out from the other side.

I built up speed, clanking with each step. Then, I struck the bulkhead with force so it sank away from me. Gripping metal seams with my T-suited hands, I ripped the bulkhead apart and thrust myself into another chamber, pushing against a tide of sluggish liquid.

I hadn't expected that. In retrospect it made sense, though. The First Ones had developed strange technologies. It shouldn't have been a surprise that the tech was unrecognizable to me. Whatever this stuff was, I had become a human wrecking ball. I kept telling myself that if I failed here, it was over for everyone. After we humans were gone, Abaddon would outthink the artifacts. I mean, if I was going to bet on someone, I'd bet on the devil against super-logical machines. Thus, I had to beat the machines in order to beat Abaddon in the final match and save our galaxy from his wrath.

This chamber was like entering another universe with different physical laws. Glowing, globular jelly-like matter drifted by in a sea of the sluggish liquid. I waded through it in my suit. One of the globular, wobbling things drifted near. I grasped it with both hands and tore it apart.

The sluggish liquid stirred more at that, with tinted colors bleeding from the torn thing.

I found Dmitri in his tank-suit beside me. I showed him what to do by grabbing another wobbling thing and tearing it as well.

The two of us began to do that. Before long, Dmitri motioned, pointing in the distance. I nodded. Three shark-like objects hissed through the liquid at us.

I tried the T-scanner, found another place inside Holgotha and teleported there. Dmitri did likewise. It would appear Holgotha's dampening field had weakened just a little. That was good to know.

This chamber had a hundred crystals glowing in strange colors. Lines of light shined from one crystal to another. I figured they were power lines.

I charged a crystal formation, swinging my fists so I could save ammo for later. I shattered crystal after crystal. Dmitri did likewise.

I raised my metal fist to pound another crystal to shards when a small object hovered before me. It bobbed up and down, reminding me of Key.

On impulse, I opened channels with the thing.

"I am ready to negotiate," Holgotha said.

"Is the dampening field off?" I asked.

"You teleported," Holgotha said. "Thus, it cannot be on."

"You know I was unable to teleport off you. Is the dampening field off?"

"Not yet," Holgotha admitted.

"Your allies are trying to storm my transfer ship, aren't they?"

"It isn't your ship, but the Curator's."

"You broke the rules a long time ago," I said. "So, don't bother spouting off to me about them. And before you start to moralize again, you should realize that I know we're the little killers. You mess with us at your peril. In the past, you were wise enough to stay on the sidelines and watch. What changed your mind this time around?"

"Abaddon is coming. A First One has not been in the galaxy for a long, long time. Perhaps it is the fabled reordering. It is best to keep an open mind in these situations."

"Abaddon is going to die," I said.

"No. Not even the little killers can achieve that."

"Did you think Dmitri and I could wreck you?"

"Not as you have been doing. I have prepared a surprise for you if you continue to insist on this madness."

"Listen up, bud. I'm done talking to you. Either you hand over your transfer scanner, or I'm going to rip you down one crystal and one wobbly pod at a time."

"I cannot give you the T-scanner, as you call it. That would leave me blind."

"I only need it long enough to kill Abaddon."

"The scanner cannot help you in that."

"Oh, but it can," I said. "I'm going to transfer…I guess I won't tell you how I'm going to do it. I want to borrow your T-scanner and then I'll return it once this is over."

"No."

"That's too bad, Holgotha. You're about to die, as I told Ella to attack you if I don't reappear in fifteen minutes after leaving the *Santa Maria*."

"I will transfer you to Abaddon myself," Holgotha said.

"Sorry, but I don't trust you anymore."

"I will give you my word, Commander."

"Your word stinks to me. I'll stick to my own plan, if you don't mind. I want your transfer scanner, and I want it now or you and I fight to the death."

"It is too late for you, Commander," Holgotha said. "Baba Gobo has surrounded the moon-ship. His weapons are primed—" He stopped abruptly and remained silent for a long moment.

"You were saying?" I asked impatiently.

"The Starkien has practiced treachery," Holgotha said. "He is surrounding your moon-ship to protect you. He—I will see the Starkiens erased from galactic memory. How did I ever let you talk me into trusting them before?"

"It's a tough universe," I said. "Now, about that dampening field…"

"I have to wait on that," Holgotha said. "If I release it too soon, the antimatter explosions will destroy me. That is the only factor keeping me from transferring out of this foul star system and away from you humans. I would have to release the dampening field and that would release—"

"We have to work together to cap the antimatter bombs," I said, interrupting.

"Alas, that is true," Holgotha said.

"Then if I were you, I'd hurry up and get that scanner into my hands. Until I have it, the antimatter grenades stay as they are."

"What if I decide to kill us both?"

"Do what you gotta, Holgotha, because that's how I'm playing the game."

It took several seconds. Then the artifact said, "I no longer have any doubt. You are the little killers. You are morbid in your desire to deal death. Yes, you can borrow my scanner, but I expect it back if you survive this madness."

"A deal's a deal, Holgotha. I'm a man of my word. Now, get me the scanner before I change my mind about you."

-28-

It took a day to hook the T-scanner to our various systems, which included computing and power.

During that time, Baba Gobo and Diana tried to talk to me. I didn't have time for either. It seemed that it was one thing after another. Finally, I found a moment to myself. Maybe ten minutes later, my hand communicator buzzed.

I scowled at it, my mood having turned sour some time ago.

"What is it now?" I said.

Rollo stared out of the tiny screen. He looked worried. "Forerunner object," he said.

"What's that supposed to mean?"

"One just appeared," he said. "You'd better come up here. I have a bad feeling about this."

My scowl deepened.

"When was the last time you heard about a Forerunner artifact just showing up with another?" Rollo asked.

He had a point. I ran to the bridge and knew it was bad by the way everyone hunched over their monitors.

"Look," Rollo said, pointing at the main screen.

I saw two new artifacts, not just the one he'd been talking about. The first was a gigantic cube, pulsating with a green glow. The other looked like one of those twisted metal puzzles kids used to try to maneuver apart. That one had a black hole in the center just like Holgotha did.

"I've launched interceptors," Rollo told me. "Baba Gobo doesn't want to get anywhere near them, though. The Prime Minister is freaking out."

I could see some of our space fighters using afterburners, racing from the hangar bays toward the artifacts. The Starkien fleet hung well back, having moved away from Ceres. Clearly, Baba Gobo didn't want anything to do with the artifacts.

As I watched, another appeared. This one was like an old-fashioned gyroscope, with its interior wheels spinning too fast for my tastes. Perhaps as ominous, this artifact was twice the size of the others.

"Why are they doing this?" Rollo said. "Are they getting ready to attack us? Maybe we should attack them before they start."

I watched the artifacts in silence.

"Can't pick up any radio chatter between them," Rollo said from his panel.

"No…" I said. I watched a little longer. "What are they doing, in your opinion?"

"Right now?" Rollo said. "Nothing special, but that doesn't mean anything. They're probably making plans."

A fourth new artifact appeared. Like the others, it maneuvered beside Holgotha. It struck me then what was going on.

I turned to Rollo. "You know what I think?"

The First Admiral shook his head.

"Did you ever watch nature shows back in the day?"

"A few," he said.

"I remember one about musk oxen. They were shaggy bovines living in the Arctic."

"I know what musk oxen are, or were," Rollo said.

"If a pack of wolves showed up, the adult musk oxen surrounded the calves just like we're seeing those artifacts doing with Holgotha. The adults all faced forward with their

187

curved horns. I think that's what the artifacts are doing, protecting the blind one."

Rollo rubbed a cheek. "Seems like we should talk to Holgotha and make sure that's the case. I don't trust them, Creed."

"Me neither," I said with a shrug. "What good does talking do now, though? If they mean to double-cross us, they'll lie to us, right?"

Rollo glared at them.

"If there's a change in their behavior, call me," I said, heading toward the exit.

Rollo nodded, clearly unhappy.

I went to a washroom, rinsing my face with hot water. That helped my aching eyes a little. Soon, I was back in the T-scanner chamber. I stood to the side as N7 and his team arc-welded the last sections of the viewing plate to the power couplings. I know that sounds old-fashioned— viewing plate—but that's what it looked like, a blank piece of modified steel.

According to what Holgotha had said earlier, once this was hooked up, we could view our teleport destinations on the modified metal.

I didn't hear Ella come in behind me, but I heard her say, "Abaddon knows we're coming."

At first, it was just more noise. Then I played back in my mind what she'd said. To make sure, I asked over my shoulder, "Did you say something?"

When she didn't respond, I glanced back. Ella looked beat-up, her normal elfin hair in disarray, and with black circles around her puffy eyes. It looked like she'd been sobbing.

"Ella," I said, reaching for her.

She backed away as if I were a rapist, her eyes widening with fear. That was weird.

"Are you okay?" I asked, worried now.

She shook her head.

"You can relax," I said. "You're with friends."

She inhaled as tears welled in her eyes. I'd never seen her like this. What had happened? I'd thought she'd said several hours ago that she was going to get some sleep.

"Did you say something about Abaddon?" I asked.

She nodded miserably. "He…he came to me in my sleep, Creed. It was awful."

The memory of when that had happened to me was still vivid. It had felt real, too.

"Tell me exactly what happened," I said.

"It was horrible. He…he threatened me, and he showed me what he does to those he conquers. Creed, Jennifer—"

Ella's words choked off.

A hollow feeling filled my chest. "You saw Jennifer?"

"What she's become," Ella whispered.

"Is she his assassin?" I asked, remembering a threat from long ago.

"Abaddon has lengthened her bones," Ella said. "She has artificially-powered muscles. Her eyes…" Ella swallowed audibly, shaking her head.

Jennifer had been with me in the old days when I'd been a simple assault trooper for the Jelk Corporation. She'd been a sweet girl, the opposite of me. I don't know what she'd ever seen in a scoundrel like me. I know what I'd seen in her, though—the goodness I lacked. I'd left her behind on the portal planet in hyperspace. I couldn't have gone back for her or I'd risk freeing Abaddon and his trillions of Kargs into our universe. The bastard had made it over anyway. Part of me had died that day, a part of me that might have had some decency. Yeah, I was a heck of a soldier. But I'm not sure I was much in terms of a good human being.

"Abaddon knows we're coming," Ella repeated. "He told me we'd fail, and I believed him. But he said he'd show humanity mercy if we made a deal with him. He'll accept us in his hierarchy, giving us high command. That will ensure human survival instead of our coming extinction."

He'd made me an offer long ago too. Maybe that's how he'd swayed others in the past.

"Did you believe him?" I asked.

"I do," Ella said in a small voice. "If we don't accept his offer..." She looked away as renewed fear twisted her features.

I had an idea of what was going on. "You weren't supposed to say anything about what he told you, were you?" I asked.

She kept looking away. Clearly, Abaddon had freaked her out. Maybe he'd gotten stronger since the last time he'd tried that with me. I wondered... Could Abaddon have implanted post-sleep commands in her?

"Do you feel him using you to watch us?" I asked.

"I don't know. Maybe—not like he can see you right now, but that he'll come back and force me to tell him in my sleep."

"How can I trust you then?" I asked.

Ella hugged herself, beginning to shiver. "Commander, we're defenseless against him. How do you fight someone like that in your sleep, in your dreams?"

She had a point. The Curator should have given me a defense against that. The old man should have—

I laughed out loud. I had the answer.

Ella turned sharply, giving me a reproving stare.

"I know how to short-circuit Abaddon's dream attacks," I said. "Look. The T-scanner is almost in place. Once it is, we're going to use it to find the right place to start our attack. That means you have to stay awake until I've killed Abaddon. At that point, he can't bother you anymore, and that's when you can sleep again."

Ella stared at me, finally asking, "How long can I stay awake with stims?"

"Several days, at least," I said. "That's all we're going to need. By that time, we've won or we're dead. So, you don't have to worry about Abaddon anymore. He can't ever threaten you in your sleep again."

Ella bit her lower lip. "I want to believe you."

"So do it," I said. "Now, tell me exactly what he told you."

Ella did. It had been cruel and ruthless, but didn't add anything to our fund of knowledge about Abaddon.

By the time I'd finished with Ella, N7 had put away his tools. "The scanner is ready, Commander."

"Great. Let's figure out how to target this thing."

"I already have," N7 said. "The T-scanner will automatically 'look' at any place we set the transfer coordinates to."

"So it self-targets the locations?"

N7 nodded.

I considered that, glanced at Ella—she ran her fingers through her hair—and finally said. "Let's see where the Super Fleet is. We want to attack as soon as we can."

When N7 engaged the viewing plate, the lights in the chamber dimmed. Through the bulkheads, I could hear the main engines throbbing. Fortunately, N7 acted fast, cutting the connection. If he hadn't, the T-scanner might have blown the main engine core. That would have ended the game plan right there.

It turned out that the T-scanner took fantastic amounts of energy to use. Holgotha might have told us that, but clearly, the artifact had figured we could learn about it ourselves. This would limit our ability to search.

The excessive need for power made sense, but it was another complication we didn't need. I questioned whether I could really keep my promise to Ella. She might have to stay awake longer than just a few days.

This was just great.

-29-

After further preparations, Ella, N7 and I readied ourselves to view the enemy fleet. The *Santa Maria's* engines thrummed at full power. Normally, they would only do so while transferring or attempting hard maneuvers. Now, long-range scanning was added to the list.

Dmitri was in the main engine control chamber. Rollo was on the bridge to make sure the team put in the exact coordinates we wanted.

Given the amount of time that had elapsed, I expected the Super Fleet to have passed through Epsilon Five. Now, they should be in the Tau Beaux System.

"Do it," I said.

With a tap, N7 engaged the viewer.

The plate shimmered. A moment later, I saw a large terrestrial planet in what I assumed was the Tau Beaux System. Unfortunately, I didn't see any spaceships, enemy or otherwise.

"Did the Super Fleet take a different route?" N7 asked.

"It's too soon to say," I told him. "The T-scanner only shows a small portion of a star system. Let's look near the jump gate to Epsilon Five."

"Wait," Ella said. "We should do this systematically instead of bouncing around in a system."

N7 tapped a panel. The viewing plate shimmered once more, becoming dull metal a few seconds later.

Ella went to a different console and pulled up a Tau Beaux System map. She began typing, plotting a straight course from the Epsilon Five jump gate to the Beta Sigma gate. That was the most probable course the Super Fleet would take as it traveled through the Tau Beaux System for the Solar System.

"If they're not in that travel lane," I said, "it might mean that Abaddon took a different route through other star systems."

Ella gave me a troubled glance.

"Hey," I said. "If he's not here, it's not your fault."

"He used me," she said. "He must have picked my brain for data. That means it would have to be my fault He would have learned about our grabbing Holgotha's T-scanner through me."

"Even if that's true," I said, "how could you have stopped him?"

"He never pumped *you* for information in your sleep."

"That was different."

"Because I'm a woman?" she said.

"Why can't it be because he's learned how to do the sleep attack better since he did it to me?"

"Abaddon has lived a long time, Creed. I don't think he's learning new things these days. That doesn't seem logical."

"I am inclined to agree with Ella," N7 said. "That being said, instead of it being a male-female difference, perhaps there is another explanation."

"Like what?" Ella demanded.

"What is different between the dream talk you had from the one the Commander had several years ago?" N7 asked. "What has changed?"

"Proximity!" I said.

They looked at me.

"Abaddon is closer to us than he was before," I said. "When Abaddon spoke to me through my sleep, he was a thousand light years away in the Jelk core worlds. Now, he's much closer. That might make his power stronger."

193

"That is logical," N7 said.

"What are his powers exactly?" Ella said. "That can't be the extent of it: these dream attacks. We know his presence causes fear. What else can a First One do?"

I didn't want to worry about that just yet. Ella had felt his aura, however. Abaddon had stung her by what he'd done. Thus, her thoughts about him were more focused.

"Do you have the sensor sweep worked out yet?" I asked.

Ella opened her mouth—I'm not sure what she would have said. Then she closed her mouth, making several more taps on her screen before nodding.

"Let's do this," I said.

N7 turned on the T-scanner, and we looked at a new location in the Tau Beaux System. Like the first time, no ships appeared. We took twenty-seven minutes to quick-scan the probable path between jump gates. No battlejumper or Karg moth-ship appeared.

"Shut it down," I said.

After N7 did, Ella asked, "Now what?"

I began to pace. According to my former calculations, the Tau Beaux route was the optimum path from the Super Fleet's last known location to Earth. Would Abaddon really have switched routes because of what he'd found from Ella? What other route made sense?

I told Ella, "Put up a stellar jump-route map of the general region."

After she did, we studied it.

"He could have taken the Ross 17 detour," N7 said.

"Agreed," I said. "What star system would he be at now if he'd done that?"

N7 made some rapid calculations. "The Cantor System seems like the obvious choice."

Ella tapped her board, bringing up the Cantor System. Soon, she had a sweep pattern lined up.

"Let's do this," I said.

We did, but found nothing. The Super Fleet wasn't in the Cantor System either.

I began pacing again, with my hands behind my back. "This T-searching is harder than I would have thought. The Curator—"

"Who?" Ella asked.

I glanced at her, scowling. Despite their questions about what had happened during their memory loss while in the galactic core, I hadn't said anything about the Curator. They couldn't spill what they didn't know. With Abaddon's dream assault, that seemed more prudent than ever.

"Napoleon Bonaparte used to scatter his forces when he marched," I said. "Each smaller command marched faster than if they'd been in one huge mass. Maybe Abaddon has done the same thing?"

"Is that logical?" N7 asked.

"I don't see why not."

"Did Napoleon rule a polyglot force through terror?" N7 asked.

"Are you suggesting Abaddon's presence helps keep everyone in line?"

"Would Abaddon trust the Jelk if they were apart from him?" N7 asked. "Might he suspect a double-cross from them?"

"We don't know enough to say," I said.

"Given what we know about Abaddon's nature," N7 said. "I suspect he would keep the Super Fleet together."

"Suppose you're right. Then what route is he using? Or do you think he's switched his objective and is no longer heading for Earth first?"

"So far," N7 said, "Abaddon has moved with fixed purpose each time. It seems unlikely he has abandoned his Earth assault."

"Could he cloak the Super Fleet from our T-scanner?" Ella asked.

I stopped pacing, thinking about that. The Curator had seen the Super Fleet easily enough from his wall-screen.

Could Holgotha's scanner see as easily as the Curator's tech? I had a feeling the Fortress of Light would have a better far-ranged sensor. And, if I was a First One like Abaddon, and I knew about the artifacts' powers, might I not figure out a way to cloak myself from their far-ranging sensors?

"That must be it," I said. "Abaddon has a cloaking device against the T-scanner."

"Then we're back where we started," Ella said, her shoulders slumping.

"Let's not concede so quickly," I said. "Suppose Abaddon has a cloaking device. Is there some way we could sense the Super Fleet's presence anyway?"

"Space is vast," N7 said. "Even the space in a single system is vast compared to starships. I do not think even a Super Fleet would give off noticeable gravitational effects. How else could one detected a cloaked fleet other than through gravitational effects?"

"Space is vast," I repeated, beginning to pace again. "Maybe that's the answer. It isn't a matter of cloaking. Abaddon saw something in Ella's thoughts. He knows about the T-scanner. Thus, he maneuvered the Super Fleet—"

I spun around. "I have it. Abaddon ordered the Super Fleet to swing wide in the Tau Beaux System. He didn't use the obvious route—the straight line. Instead, he ordered the ships to make a curving maneuver."

"That sounds good in theory," Ella said, "but we have no way to know if that's right or not. What if he is using a cloaking device?"

"As N7 would ask, 'Is that logical?' Such a device would have to cover a lot of space. And where would he have gotten such equipment? The artifacts possess the highest-grade technology in our zone. Let's keep looking."

For the next twenty minutes, we planned our sensing pattern.

"I have calculated the power drainage for the scan," N7 said. "If we search for over an hour, we risk a burn-out."

"That's bad," I agreed.

"Maybe we should affix values to our search areas," Ella suggested. "We should scan the higher valued routes first."

"To do that," I said, "we'd have to try to think like Abaddon."

Both Ella and N7 looked at me meaningfully.

"Great," I said. "You're saying I think like the devil?"

"He's not the devil," Ella said. "But I believe you think like him more than anyone else I know."

Instead of arguing, I thought about what I would do if I knew what Ella had most likely given away to Abaddon. Then, I studied the Tau Beaux System map. With a marker, I highlighted how I'd maneuver a Super Fleet.

"Let us proceed," N7 said.

We powered up the T-scanner. Seven minutes later, Ella whispered, "Look. What's that?"

"Move the scanner three degrees to the nearest jump gate," I said.

N7 did so, the viewing plate shimmering.

I felt my gut tighten. I wondered if this was how American Navy pilots had felt in World War II when they'd found the Imperial Japanese Fleet. That's how it had been back then, the carrier ships hiding from each other with search planes scouting the vast Pacific Ocean.

We'd found the Super Fleet. It was en route to Earth. Clearly, Abaddon had used the information he'd torn from Ella in her sleep.

"Right," I said. "Let's pick our first target."

As I'd seen from the Fortress of the Light, masses of Jelk Corporation battlejumpers led the way. They were huge vessels, each carrying tens of thousands of individuals and equipment. Instead of spheres, the battlejumpers were like thick, triangular pie-slices. Behind them followed giant snowflakes. Each of those Karg snowflakes represented many riding moth-ships. They rode together on the snowflake, the mothership carrying the smaller red-eyed vessels.

"There's a problem," N7 said.

"What now?" I asked.

"We cannot look inside a battlejumper to pinpoint the location of a Jelk."

"The T-suit scanners can do that later," I said.

"From a mere one billion kilometers away," N7 said. "That will defeat the purpose of the present scan: to figure out how to attack without being seen."

"Maybe something about a battlejumper will give away a Jelk's presence," I said, "so we can at least know which battlejumpers to T-suit scan first."

We scanned the battlejumpers for another ten minutes. Nothing indicated that one was different from another.

"Maybe we can assume Jelk will pick the safest spot in the fleet," I said. "In your opinions, what place is that?"

"The center," Ella said promptly.

"Then we need to T-suit scan the center battlejumpers first," I said.

Ella looked at me. "That doesn't solve our basic problem. As soon as we appear, they're going to start attacking the *Santa Maria*."

"I've been thinking about that," I said. "I have an idea what we have to do so they won't find us until it's too late for them."

-30-

This was it. We were going to go against the great enemy, Abaddon and his Kargs with his Jelk allies. They had been our bugbear for many years already.

Yeah, the Jade League's Grand Armada had rerouted for Earth, but it would never get there in time to save humanity. Rollo had said it before. If we could cut off the head, maybe the body would begin fighting against itself. That was the plan, going after Abaddon and killing him before the fleet battle began.

Before we could do that, though, we had to collect ammo for our weapon to kill Abaddon.

I wiped my sweaty palms on my thighs. After all these years, I was finally going after Shah Claath. Would I get to see him again or would I have to settle for several of his hyper-intelligent brothers?

I'd gone through a lot of grief in my life because of Claath. At his command, I'd had to wear a control device so he could shock me if he wanted. The red-skinned Rumpelstiltskin with his dark eyes, narrow face and crafty smile...I could still see him in my imagination. Some people fade in one's memories over time. Claath didn't have that distinction with me. I'd wanted to wipe away that superior smirk, to knife him again. I wanted to kill Claath, and this was my big chance. But what were the odds that I'd come face-to-face with him again?

Probably not too good, I was thinking. I had tried to cudgel my thoughts to come up with a plan to make it certain. How many Jelk did the Super Fleet hold? I was betting most of those that were still on the loose in the Orion Arm.

I remembered what the Curator had told me. The Jelk weren't really alive but were machines like N7. Yet, N7 felt as if he was alive.

I shook my head, took a deep breath and headed onto the bridge. It was time to begin implementing my great plan. I hoped it worked.

***

Soon, the *Santa Maria* powered up, transferring from the Solar System to the Beta Sigma System.

I'd calculated this carefully. The others had mixed feelings about it. Rollo had grinned evilly. Ella and N7 both thought it was a bad idea. Dmitri had shrugged.

"It could work," the Cossack had said.

I was hoping it did, 'cause if it didn't…

The *Santa Maria* took up a middle orbit around a blue gas giant. This was the sixth planet in the system, which had a lot of them. Even better, all the planets had plenty of moons of varying sizes. The middle-sized ones were just about the size of the ancient Survey Vessel.

We were hiding out in the open, using one of our weaknesses—the distinctiveness of the *Santa Maria*—that it was, in fact, a moon. If we tried to act like a starship, our vessel stuck out like a sore thumb. But if we turned the giant thrusters so they aimed at the planet and kept all the hangar bay doors shut, we looked like another Beta Sigma moon.

When I say we were out in the open, I mean in relation to the jump gate that led from the Tau Beaux System.

"They'll be so busy trying to figure out where we're hiding that they won't notice us in plain sight," I said.

Ella looked up from her panel. She was pale, with darkness around her eyes. Her bad dream still plagued her.

"How long are we going to wait for them to show up?" she asked.

"Hopefully, not long," I said.

It ended up being another five hours and thirty-six minutes. Finally, the distant jump gate glowed with a yellow color, and Jelk battlejumpers began coming through.

They poured through, one every fifty-seven seconds. That was impressive. I'd been with the Grand Armada for a time. The best any flotilla had done is one ship through every ninety-three seconds. Most flotillas had less than forty vessels, however. It often took ten minutes or more for the next Grand Armada flotilla to start its process. The enemy poured through consistently.

When you're trying to push a lot of vessels through at once, the seconds added up.

After coming through, the battlejumpers didn't mill and wait around. They began accelerating. But they didn't scoot toward the distant jump gate that led to the next system. Instead, they began a curving circuit toward the gate. That meant Abaddon was still being cautious.

We watched from our bridge. The battlejumpers headed in the direction I'd predicted they would take.

Rollo shook his head, counting out credits, coming to me and putting them in my palm.

"How'd you know they'd take that route?" the First Admiral asked.

"Luck," I said.

"Yeah, right," Rollo said, marching back to his station.

Watching them come through the jump gate reminded me of Xerxes' massive army that had marched across the Hellespont from Asia to Europe on his boat bridges in 481 B.C.

Xerxes had been the Persian king who'd planned to conquer ancient Greece. The historian Herodotus claimed Xerxes had marched with 2,641,610 men. More likely, it had been around 150,000 to 180,000 soldiers. Some military historians had calculated that if it had been the larger number, the men and animals would have drunk dry all the streams of Greece. Plus, the front of the marching army would have reached Athens as the last man crossed the boat bridge.

The boat bridges across the Hellespont had been the truly fantastic engineering feat of the day. Xerxes had two boat bridges of triremes and penteconters (fifty-oared galleys). They were linked by six long cables, two of flax and four of papyrus. Over the vessels was constructed a wooden roadway. In all, 314 ships were used for the western bridge and 360 for the eastern.

As the triangular-shaped battlejumpers moved away from the jump gate, they began to take up the same formation I'd seen while standing with the Curator and from Holgotha's scanner. It was like a giant school of sharks, only these were all the same size.

Later, massive Karg snowflakes began coming through. We'd fought the moth-ships in hyperspace a long time ago already. Then, the humans had been a tiny minority aboard the Orange Tamika dreadnaughts. Those had been rough battles with only a handful of survivors.

After several hours of watching this, Dmitri said, "The lead ships are almost one billion kilometers away from us."

"Let's go," I said. "It's time to suit up."

The five of us rose from our respective stations and marched off the bridge. As we went, personnel shouted out, "Good luck" and "Happy hunting," and other ancient battle slogans.

The five of us walked alone in the corridors. It was a good feeling being with friends. We'd been through a lot of wars together. We'd helped each other in many tight spots. Here was one more, hopefully among the last of our engagements.

We'd argued about this earlier. Should we hit them right away—at the one billion kilometer mark—or should we wait for them all to get closer.

"Do you think Abaddon knows our T-suit teleportation range?" I'd asked Ella.

She wouldn't meet my eyes, nor would she say.

"If we strike them near our range limit," I'd said, "that will make it harder for them to strike back at the *Santa Maria*. Given that they figure out we're a starship."

That had been the deciding factor for doing it like this.

Ahead of us, a door swished open and we walked to our T-suits. We'd been practicing with them, of course. Dmitri and I had also gone over with the others what we'd learned during the strike against Holgotha.

"Feels strange," Rollo said through his helmet comm. "This suit must be thousands of years old. Heck, maybe it's even a million years old. Now, we supposed *little killers* are going to use it to do exactly what it was designed to do: killing First Ones. That's a good feeling, if you ask me."

"We're the Space Ninjas," Dmitri said. "Seems like an improvement on being Space Vikings."

"There you go," I said, "ever the optimist."

On a big screen, we could watch the progress of the Super Fleet. This time, the individual starships were accelerating faster than before. I wondered what caused the difference.

"Have they detected us?" Ella asked. "They have to see us."

"Of course they see us," I said, "but do they see a starship or a moon?"

At last, we secured the last seals. Each of us moved around the room, testing the various pieces of equipment.

"I'm still not sanguine about the antimatter grenades," N7 said. "It is self-immolation to use one."

"No it isn't," Rollo said. "It's perfect for these. You squirt one out just as you teleport away. You leave it behind for some deserving aliens. Boom! They're blood and gore."

"Yes, I understand the concept," N7 said. "The timing troubles me, however."

My stomach was seething. Jennifer was somewhere in the enemy fleet. Did she ever think about me? If so, was it with hatred or fond memories? She must have worked it out by now that I had to do what I'd done.

If that was true, why did I feel like such a scoundrel over doing it? Out of all my decisions these past years, that was the one that bothered me the most.

I turned on my T-suit scanner with trepidation. What if Jennifer attacked me? Could I shoot her in self-defense?

I shook my head. Thinking like this was beginning to cloud my judgment.

"I'm seeing inside a battlejumper," Dmitri announced. "This one has Saurians. Big ones. I don't see a Jelk yet."

Soon, the others began scanning battlejumpers as well.

"Yes!" Rollo shouted, punctuating the shout with curses. "Link with me, people. I've found us a Jelk bastard."

"Is it Claath?" I asked, hopeful.

"I have no idea," Rollo said. "They all look alike to me. Is everyone linked onto my T-suit?"

"Wait," Ella said. "Yes! There, I'm linked."

We saw onto a modified battlejumper bridge. The Jelk wore a blue uniform, sitting on a raised throne-chair. No, it wasn't raised. It hovered high above the Saurian crew. The Jelk was small, with narrow shoulders and red skin. It offset his dark, hyper-intelligent eyes. The creature reminded me of a fox. I looked more closely, searching for machine-like elements about the Jelk.

I had to remind myself that a Jelk's natural state was as an energy creature, a ball of pulsating light. This was just a fleshly disguise.

The Saurians sat in a round chamber, the edges lower down like a pit. The dais in the center under the hovering Jelk commander was full of combat-armored Saurians. By full, I mean twenty soldiers. In the past, Saurians hadn't used combat armor. Was that an offshoot of the Jelk-Karg War?

"Everybody remember his location?" I asked.

"Roger that," Rollo said.

We stood in a close circle, each of us facing out.

"This is for the human race," I said. "We can't feel pity or remorse for the enemy."

"No worries there," Rollo said, with an edge to his voice.

"Okay," I said, taking a deep breath. "Here we go. Teleport in three, two, one…now!"

-31-

My T-suit buzzed, shaking the slightest bit as it built up teleporting power. Then the chamber deep inside the *Santa Maria* disappeared.

Whatever the process was, we moved nearly one billion kilometers through space in the blink of an eye. This time, my feet appeared perfectly on the raised dais inside the battlejumper. I heard the rush of air displacement and felt my lips stretch into a wide, almost painful grin.

I elbowed a Saurian space marine, sending him staggering. Then, I used the beam weapon, hosing one Saurian after another. This was a grade-A beam, all right. It breached the Saurian battle armor with pathetic ease. If I could have felt sorry for the enemy, this would have been the moment. But I didn't feel sorry. The Saurians were in the way of humanity. Too bad for them.

Lizard flesh smoked. Saurian blood boiled, and a haze began filling the vast bridge. Saurians made croaking noises. Some of the personnel in the pit on the edges tried to scramble away. One or two charged us. A few hid. Those were the smart ones.

In the end, it didn't matter. We killed them all. Five assault troopers in a controlled fury butchered the bridge-full of Saurians in less than thirty seconds.

During that time, a few Saurian rounds bounced off my armor. A plasma beam darkened Ella's power-pack. That was it. Otherwise, this part of the Family perished trying to protect the little bastard up there.

I was the first to look up. The Jelk pressed controls, shouted orders and finally pointed at me.

It had been too long since I'd seen one of them. It brought old memories rushing back into my mind, but that didn't slow my reflexes.

Maybe he realized this wasn't his day. He pressed a control and an opening appeared above him. At the same time, his throne-chair began to levitate up toward the escape hatch.

Rollo beamed the throne-chair. Dmitri sent dense slugs at the opening, wrecking it.

The little Jelk leaped from his chair. He must have been wearing something, because he flew for the mangled opening.

In a blink, I scanned above and teleported there. The Jelk flew up into my arms, and squealed like a pig.

I jumped down with the Jelk, hearing him grunt with pain at the jar of my landing.

"How did you do that?" he asked in his grating voice.

I squeezed him so the Jelk howled with pain.

"Let me have some fun, too," Rollo said. He shoved cold steel into the Jelk's belly.

That caused the creature to twist and writhe in my grip. "I shall remember this until you're all dead," he gasped.

"Yeah, yeah," I said. "When are you going to do your trick for us?"

Rollo twisted the knife. I crushed the Jelk as if I could fold him up into a flesh-ball, remembering how these hard-hearted capitalists had screwed with humanity for generations. They'd never shown us mercy. I wasn't going to start here with this one.

Suddenly, the Jelk's flesh sizzled. In a flash, the flesh and uniform disappeared. I let go out of surprise. Rollo staggered backward.

"Fools!" the Jelk said as he transformed. "Ultimately, you cannot harm me. Now, though, I know you and have marked you for revenge."

He finished the metamorphosis, returning to his true state, and the Jelk began to float away.

Ella rushed up, shoving the pronged weapon at him. Electrical currents passed between the prongs and the pulsating ball of energy. It stopped, appeared to try to move again, but failed.

"How's that feel?" Rollo shouted. "How do you like it, you little schemer?"

Screeching sounds came from the energy creature. The thing began to thin as its light lost luster. Then, as if sucked up by a vacuum cleaner, the energy creature flowed into the tube and filled the containment cube with roiling energy.

I plucked that out of the Jelk Catcher, staring at the trapped creature. I'm not sure what I hoped to see. Maybe two eyes peering at me, trying to ask for mercy. I had a machine. That's all. It wasn't living. It was fuel for an ancient gun. I kept staring, wanting to ask it questions, but now was not the time for that.

Finally, I slotted the cube onto my belt. I swear I felt warmth coming through my armored glove. I definitely felt movement on my belt.

"We have one," I said. "Now, let's get us a few more."

It took the others several seconds to recalibrate. They'd been watching me closely. Finally, each of them began scanning other, nearby battlejumpers.

"I found another," Dmitri said. "This Jelk is alone in his harem."

I linked to Dmitri's scanner. It wasn't a human harem, but a Saurian one.

"This is crazy," I said. "I always thought Claath had gathered a human harem because he looked like us. Now…I don't know what's going on. Are you sure that's a harem?"

"What else could it be?" Dmitri asked.

208

The Jelk on my belt continued to move as if still struggling against its new confinement. We were on a tight schedule, and we needed plenty of ammo for our Abaddon-killing weapon.

"Let's get another Jelk," I said. "Three, two, one…go!"

-32-

I should have remembered our ultimate objective. I should have thought about what we were doing more carefully. I hadn't paid enough attention to the differences. I was still thinking of this as a regular assault trooper attack, just with niftier weapons.

It wasn't anything like that…

We had T-suits that were thousands or possibly millions of years old constructed by the Ronin 9. The Ronin were extinct, and they had challenged the premier race in our galaxy. That race seemed to have the attributes of angels or possibly even gods. The Forerunners had built the artifacts, the jump gates and the Fortress of Light. This wasn't just soldiers shooting it out with guns. This was fantastic battle-wear for use against a possibly mythic adversary.

A trip to the center of the galaxy by jump routes would take years. I'd already been to Sagittarius A* and back, and that had taken less than a few days. Humans are incredibly adaptive. We could get used to just about anything. I'd already become familiar with the Fortresses of Light, teleporting suits and turning Jelk into balls of energy to power up a devil-slaying weapon.

So yeah, I should have thought things through a little more carefully before cavalierly, almost single-handedly attacking Abaddon's Super Fleet.

But the thing was we weren't attacking the fleet. We were ninjas, assassins, trying to slip in and out, taking out the head before the main fleet battle began.

My suit buzzed with power, and the gory battlejumper bridge disappeared. In a split second, I crossed space and appeared on another battlejumper.

Lounging Saurians were everywhere. A few splashed in a big pool. Others fanned themselves as they sprawled on cushions. A group surrounded a Jelk as he lay on a couch. He had his shirt open, showing a skinny, ridged chest. He even wore a gold chain with a glowing ball dangling on the end.

The area was as big as several basketball courts, with a high ceiling. It seemed strange now that a machine—a Jelk—worked furiously to collect money and indulge in such decadent living.

What motivated a Jelk to do that? Had the Curator told me the whole truth?

I lurched slightly, having appeared a little too high off the floor. One T-suited trooper fell from five meters up, splashing into the pool.

Rollo appeared perfectly in a crouch. His beam weapon glowed, and light speared out, striking a Saurian. The lizard exploded. I do not mean to say that it blew up. Instead, it exploded and grew with astonishing speed. Thick tentacles sprouted as a vast rubbery body took up ten times the space the "Saurian" had.

Instead of one of the Family facing us, it was an alien thing of incredible vitality. Then, I realized these transformations were taking place all around us. Each so-called Saurian exploded into the same sort of octopus monster-thing.

The ones in the pool moved faster than those on the dry areas.

The pool! I swiveled fast. Dmitri had landed in the pool. He hadn't come up yet. Instead, tentacles thrashed, slapping the water and disappearing from sight.

I roared an oath, charging the pool, beaming it. Steam hissed as the beam touched the liquid, filling the chamber at an excessive rate. Was that water? No! It was some other liquid that reacted furiously with my beam.

I skidded to the edge. I could see Dmitri down there. The tentacle monsters had him and were pulling hard, trying to rip off his suit. Why didn't Dmitri disappear? Maybe he couldn't think of it. The monsters had his arms and legs in vise-like rubbery grips.

I aimed my arm cannon and began firing careful shots. The liquid acted as a brake on the slugs, but not as much as one would expect—that must have been due to the density of each bullet.

I shot up one giant octopus-body and began on another. Black blood began spreading like a film from the shredded flesh. Soon, I wouldn't be able to see Dmitri down there.

I realized I was the fool. I concentrated, used my scanner, targeting the bottom of the pool, and teleported to Dmitri.

After wrapping an arm around Dmitri's torso—so I knew exactly where he was—I fired one dense shell after another into the nearby monsters.

Tentacles began sliding off Dmitri. Finally, the Cossack slapped my shoulder.

"Creed," he panted through the comm.

"Teleport out of the pool!" I shouted.

"Oh. Da. I do that now." Dmitri buzzed. I could feel it with my one arm. Then, he was gone.

The remaining tentacles lashed at me.

I also teleported, appearing beside the pool, staggering. The chamber had changed dramatically since I'd first viewed it. Steam roiled everywhere, as did a black mist. Oily blood slicked the floor as tentacles and rubbery pieces of octopus bodies writhed and humped. It was an ugly sight.

Rollo stalked the Jelk as Ella and N7 flanked him, beam-slicing the monsters and causing them to flop and tear apart with their bullets.

I cataloged two problems. The first was that we were using up Ronin 9 ammo at a prodigious rate. Could that be one of Abaddon's plans? The second thing was the Jelk. He was an elusive rascal, much more than I would have expected.

Rollo chased him, lunged, and the Jelk shimmered for a second. Rollo grabbed empty air as the Jelk moved from his spot a foot from where he'd seemed to be at the instant of Rollo's lunge.

I used a beam, but instead of striking the fleet-footed Jelk, he shimmered. The beam harmlessly passed him as he continued to scamper around the chamber.

That increased Rollo's fury, making him more determined.

It struck me suddenly. Abaddon had spoken to Ella in her sleep. The First One appeared to have read her mind. Abaddon knew our basic plan. Could he have set a trap for us?

My heart thudded with a grim certainty. We were using weapons we didn't truly understand. Yet that wasn't half as critical as facing an opponent we didn't truly understand. What did it mean to have lived for so long in another space-time continuum?

"Rollo!" I said, using the comm.

I heard Rollo's harsh breathing.

"Rollo," I said again. "The Jelk is screwing with you."

I heard a labored curse over the comm.

"You have to think or we're screwed, man. Stand down, Rollo. Stand down and *think*!"

Rollo hated aliens and Jelk more than most, yet he was a good soldier, the best assault trooper among us. He stopped and peered back at me.

I took a quick scan of the situation. Most of the giant octopus creatures were dead. The ones in the pool boiled out, but Dmitri retreated from them as he used the beam to good effect.

The Cossack was a master of the delaying tactic. Maybe it was in his genes.

The Jelk stopped as he studied us. Once more, I noticed the glowing ball dangling from the end of his gold chain. It was as if we faced a miniature playboy from the '60s.

What did the shimmering signify? He was always a little bit to the side of where we were shooting. Maybe the thing on his skinny chest was a distorter, a reflective device, showing him to be elsewhere than where he really was.

I laughed aloud. "Aim around him," I said. "He's not where he appears to be, but nearby. He's using our marksmanship against us."

So saying, I hosed on either side of the little red creep. Rollo did the same thing.

N7 and Ella continued to keep the last monsters off Rollo and me.

The Jelk got a scared look. He turned, tried to run and then screamed in agony. The beam didn't seem to touch him but his skin began to shrivel under the beam's intensity.

In another few seconds, his skin burst apart as a glowing ball of light rose from a location several meters from where I was watching him. At the same time, the glowing amulet fell to the floor, as there was no longer a flesh and blood creature to hold up the gold chain.

The energy creature seemed stunned, but I didn't think that would last long.

"Ella!" I said. "Use the Jelk Catcher before he gets away."

Ella started to run at him. The Jelk began to float away from her faster.

"Teleport in front of him," I said.

She did. The ball of light stopped in seeming shock. Before it could change direction, Ella slid the pronged device from her shoulders. She flicked it on and caught him—it. As before, the light dimmed. All at once, the Jelk energy ball was sucked up into another cube.

With a click, Ella turned off the Jelk Catcher.

I strode to her, extracted the cube and stared at the caught machine. This one shook harder than the first. Could it be angry?

As I hooked the ammo to my belt, the others circled me, killing the last of the octopus-like monsters.

"What happened here?" Ella panted. "We saw Saurians and—"

"What?" Dmitri asked her.

"Is this what Saurians really are?" Ella asked.

"I doubt that," I said. "The monsters were made to look like Saurians."

"Not look like," Ella said, "but were. It seemed as if they exploded out of their Saurian bodies."

"The Jelk had a device that distorted its actual position," Rollo said. "Luckily, Creed figured that out."

"That's not the problem," I said. "Why was this room set up like this?"

The others looked at me.

"It was a setup," Ella said, "a trap."

"Maybe," I said.

"It didn't matter in the end," Dmitri said. "We captured another Jelk. Let's get another."

"No," Ella said. "Let's get back to the *Santa Maria*. If they're setting traps for us…"

I looked at Ella, waiting for her to finish her thought. That's when I noticed the chamber's walls in the ultraviolet light range. They radiated with a strange pulsation.

"Ella, what were you going to say?" I grabbed her. "Ella!" I shouted.

"Creed," she slurred. "My mind…is slowing down."

I glanced at the walls again. They shined more dangerously than before in the ultraviolet range.

"Commander," Dmitri said, "I can't find the *Santa Maria*."

"Say again," I said.

"I can't see the *Santa Maria* with my T-scanner," Dmitri said.

"Is the wall blocking us?"

"No," Rollo said. "I can see elsewhere, but not our ship."

"Link to me," I said. I used my scanner, having found a battlejumper bridge. This one didn't have a Jelk unfortunately. "Is everyone ready?"

Something was very wrong, and I wanted to figure it out. But not here.

"Three...two...one...teleport," I said.

-33-

We appeared on the new bridge, dealing death to the Saurian officers and personnel. These stayed Saurians, at least.

There was nothing fair or nice about our attack. It reminded me of the time as a kid I'd cleaned our family barn of wasps with several cans of Raid. Locate nest, aim Raid, depress nozzle, watch the white stuff attach to the angry wasps and see them fall and curl and twist on the ground. If one was too lively, I raced away and waited for the Raid to do its magic.

On the battlejumper, we didn't race away and wait. We cleared the bridge of enemy and took up their abandoned stations.

Many years ago, we'd stormed and captured a Jelk battlejumper, so we were familiar with the controls for this one.

First, we sealed the doors so the rest of the battlejumper's Saurians couldn't storm us too soon. Then, we each went to our old stations, taking over the panels.

"The Super Fleet has moved," Ella said. "It is no longer in the one billion kilometer range of the *Santa Maria*."

I saw that too. The Super Fleet had moved away hard from the sixth planet and the hidden moon. It also seemed as if more time had elapsed than should have. Could that have been the reason for the glowing walls in the last battlejumper? Had it been some sort of time delay room, giving the Super Fleet enough time to pull off its maneuver?

"Abaddon knows that's our ship," Ella declared.

"I agree," I said.

"Let's use this battlejumper and start for the *Santa Maria*," Rollo suggested. "We'll maneuver back into the one billion kilometer range."

"That's not going to work," I said.

"Commander," Dmitri said. "Take a look at screen three."

I tapped my command chair, bringing up screen three. I saw it right away. The enemy was releasing T-missiles for a mass firing. If I were to guess, I'd say Abaddon was about to target the *Santa Maria*.

"That doesn't make sense," Ella said. "Why would he destroy such a priceless vessel? I'd think Abaddon would want to capture it."

I thought back to a fight in the Solar System many years ago. The Starkiens had come at us, launching T-missiles at our sole captured battlejumper. Those missiles hadn't used thermonuclear warheads, but had launched Lokhar space marines instead.

"Abaddon does plan to capture the *Santa Maria*," I said.

"With nukes?" Dmitri asked.

"No," I said, "with space-suited Kargs in the T-missiles' nosecones."

"Of course," Ella said. "That makes perfect sense. He will capture the moon-ship, us, our T-suits—"

"Listen to me," I said, sternly. "We have two Jelk. That's going to have to be it for now. We're getting out of here."

"How?" Ella asked. "The *Santa Maria* is too far away for us to teleport there."

"Okay," I said. "Listen up and listen good, 'cause I'm only going to say this once."

***

We teleported off the bridge onto a T-missile bay. The Saurian techs in there lasted less than a minute. Afterward, N7 opened his T-suit.

We each took up guard around him. This was a critical moment. If hordes attacked, if Abaddon should show up suddenly, we couldn't all pop out of danger.

N7 hurried to a T-missile. The android could do this faster than any of us could. Still, it was noble of him to have just done it. I had been about to ask when he'd started shedding his T-suit.

N7 detached the warhead from the missile. His fingers blurred over the manual controls as he reset it.

Ella clanked away from our protective circle to a panel. She brought up the *Santa Maria* on a screen, giving the exact coordinates to N7.

"I have it," he said.

"Then suit up," I said.

As N7 headed for the ancient suit standing empty on the deck, several side hatches opened. Saurian shock troopers in space marine armor charged in. They fired from the hip.

Instinctively, Dmitri and I maneuvered between N7 and the enemy. Each of us began using the Ronin 9 beam. It cut through Saurian armor, killing the lizards. Their slugs bounced off us.

Rollo roared a battle cry, disappearing. He reappeared among one group and used his hands and elbows, knocking and hurling Saurians everywhere.

"Get out of the way, Rollo," Dmitri said.

Rollo complied, appearing beside the Cossack.

Dmitri finished that group.

"I'm hit," N7 said.

My heart sank. I turned. A sluggish fluid dripped out of N7's shoulder.

"Can you still suit up?" I asked.

"I think so," N7 answered.

Those were a few tense seconds, but no more enemy lizards showed up.

"I'm in," N7 said.

"Let's the roll the missile," I said.

Ella had already opened an emergency hatch. The four of us carried the big missile down the corridor and into a hangar bay using the added strength of the exo-powered suits. Ella popped by the controls to open the main hatch to space.

The rush of escaping atmosphere lifted the missile and us, propelling everything outside. If this had been the first time we'd done something like this, we might have tumbled like debris. We were the veteran assault troopers now, however.

In short order, we found ourselves outside the battlejumper. There was plenty of space between each vessel. Still, I could see seven big enemy ships from here.

"I am activating the missile," N7 said.

"Grab hold, people," I said.

As we waited, battlejumper thrusters roared with energy. One by one, each big ship began to accelerate. I wondered where they were going in such a hurry.

The T-missile built up power, and we teleported away from the Super Fleet to near the *Santa Maria* in orbit around the blue gas giant.

Immediately, I opened channels with our ship. "This is Commander Creed. Can you hear me, Trask?"

"Loud and clear, Commander," said Trask, the acting captain.

"Lock onto our signal."

"There's a T-missile near you, sir. I'm locking on to destroy—"

"That's us, that's us," I said.

"Roger, sir, I'm leaving it alone. On no, sir, flocks of T-missiles are appearing."

"Get ready to transfer," I said.

"Transfer, sir?"

"Out of this star system," I said, linking my T-suit to Rollo's.

"Yes, sir," Trask said. "We're ready." They'd had standings orders to be ready to leave immediately.

"Rollo?" I asked.

"Now, Creed," he said.

Rollo vanished. I followed suit, sure that the others would follow me.

I appeared on the bridge to great excitement.

"There're thousands of them, Captain Trask!" a woman shouted. "They're heading for the ship surface."

"Transfer, transfer," I said. "We're all here."

The engines had already been building up. Two men pulled the main levers. The power spiked, and the old moon-ship transferred out of danger to a nearby star system.

My knees gave out as the ship reappeared in the empty star system. I sat down in the T-suit, smiling hugely. Yes, it seemed like Abaddon had known what we were going to do. What he'd failed to do was reckon with our deadliness and ingenuity. We had two dematerialized Jelk, two pieces of ammo for the Abaddon-killing weapon. That was less than I would have liked, but it was a great start.

"Let's put the suits away," I said.

"Commander," N7 said.

"Shoot," I said. "I forgot about your wound. How are you?"

"I am fine."

"I want you in the infirmary right away," I said.

"Commander," N7 said. "We have a problem. Ella is missing."

"What?" I said, spinning around. I was sure I'd seen four other T-suits on the bridge with me. "Where is she? Maybe she wasn't linked to Rollo's suit and appeared elsewhere on the ship."

An emergency process began as we started searching for Ella. It soon became clear that she wasn't on the moon-ship or anywhere within a billion kilometer range of our suits. Otherwise, we would have been able to talk to her.

Somehow, we'd left Ella behind when the moon-ship had transferred out of danger. We had to go back and get her before it was too late.

-34-

"If we go back," N7 said, "we risk having the Kargs and Saurians storm our ship. And do we know for a fact she didn't teleport with us? The *Santa Maria* is large. Ella could be hidden and hurt somewhere on the transfer vessel and we don't know it."

I hated N7's words as they caused hesitation in me. What if I was wrong about Ella being back by the sixth planet? Should I throw away our only real opportunity for saving humanity in order to possibly save Ella Timoshenko?

"We can look for her using the moon-ship's T-scanner," Rollo said.

I stared at my over-muscled friend. "Let's go," I said, teleporting to the room.

I shed my T-suit and began manipulating the viewing plate.

We'd transferred to a nearby star system *not* on the route to Earth. We learned right away that scanning from such a short distance used less energy than making a long-range scan. That could be important, but it didn't seem to matter right now. It also seemed to confirm the idea that Abaddon could use his mind powers more strongly the closer he was to the subject.

Soon, I saw the sixth planet of the star system. I zeroed in on the floating space marines, both Kargs and Saurians. It took twenty minutes before I found Ella. It wasn't her shape

223

or the suit that made her distinctive, but the red glow around her.

Several suited adversaries had situated heavy portables around her. Each of those bathed her in the red beam, perhaps to keep her from teleporting away.

N7 suggested the same thing.

I glanced at him. Dark fluid still dripped from the wound in the android's shoulder.

"Go to the infirmary," I said.

"Negative, Commander. One of us is in danger. I must stay on hand for when we attack."

I licked my lips, studying the scene. My heart sank then. I realized Ella had the Jelk Catcher. If we didn't get her back, we had no way of turning more Jelk into ammo for killing Abaddon.

"We have to go back," I said.

"There must be over twenty thousand enemy space marines out there," Rollo said. He stood by a panel. Thus, I assumed he'd used the computer to do the counting.

"We have to go back anyway," I said.

"Da," Dmitri said. "We must die for each other if we have to."

I smiled grimly.

Then I saw something frightening. As we watched, another creature popped into existence on the viewing plate. This one was big, maybe five times my size. It wore a black suit. Dread seemed to radiate from the being as I stared at him.

"Abaddon," Rollo whispered.

I glanced at the First Admiral. I didn't see rage on his face, but fear.

I looked at the viewing plate again. The big creature used a backpack thruster with consummate skill, maneuvering toward Ella.

In an instant, the portables stopped spewing their beams. The glow lessened around Ella, but didn't quit altogether.

The big creature—it had to be Abaddon right?—took Ella in a one-armed grip.

She squirmed, hitting his suited chest with her fists.

He put a big hand on her helmet. In a moment, her struggles ceased. What had he done to her?

Then, the big creature looked straight at me. That should have been impossible. We viewed this from a different star system many light years away. Still, he looked at me. I couldn't see his features. They were hidden behind a silvered visor, but I could feel his stare. It was eerie.

Commander Creed, a voice said inside my head.

I grunted painfully. The voice hurt as if listening to a thousand teachers scratching their fingernails along a thousand wet blackboards.

"What?" I said, hoarsely.

I have another one of your women, Commander.

"You're dead, Abaddon," I said.

You are a fool. You had a chance to serve me once. Now, I will collect your friends one by one and torture them for a thousand years.

I cried out in pain, grabbing my head, staggering backward.

"Get us out of here," Rollo shouted. "Abaddon is attacking Creed."

Know pain, vain creature.

I fell onto the deck, thrashing about, clutching a head that felt as if it was about to explode.

After that, I'm not sure what happened. The pain came in waves. As it did, I noticed something else, something more than just agony. I could read thoughts running through Abaddon's mind, faint and distant things that tried to duck out of sight as I observed them.

There is still danger. I must lure him near. Then I will—

Abruptly, the pain, the voices in my head and the hidden thoughts disappeared. I simply lay on the deck, panting, enjoying the respite.

Finally, I opened my eyes. Rollo stared at me. I turned my head, but couldn't see anyone else.

I tried to speak, but found that my mouth was bone dry. I licked the inside of my mouth, but that didn't seem to help.

Finally, I could feel my tongue again. There were splotches in my vision.

"Can you hear me yet?" Rollo asked.

I wanted to nod, but that would have hurt too much. I managed a, "Yeah."

"You look like shit, Creed. What happened? Did Abaddon mind-talk to you?"

"Yeah," I said again.

"N7 was right then."

"Yeah," I said for a third time.

"This is bad," Rollo said. "It's over."

"No," I whispered.

"I don't know how you can say that. We lost Ella. We lost the Jelk Catcher, and Abaddon knows everything we can do. I mean, that's a given, right?"

This time, I nodded. I had been right. The motion sent shooting pains through my skull.

"So what do we do?" Rollo asked.

I closed my eyes. I had to think, but we didn't have any time to think. Abaddon would tear down Ella's personality, ripping every thought from her. I realized I knew that because I'd seen the thought in Abaddon's mind.

Maybe that was one of the costs of using mind talk like that. The other being saw into your thoughts as well. I could see why someone like Abaddon would be reluctant to do that.

"Are you asleep?" Rollo asked quietly.

Without opening my eyes, I said, "I'm awake, and I'm thinking. You know, Abaddon may have given us our answer."

"What answer?"

226

"How to track him down," I said. "I think I'm linked to him. We have to go after him, Rollo. We have to do it right away or we'll miss our only chance."

"In case you haven't noticed, we didn't do too well today."

"He's afraid of me just a little," I said. "I have two disintegrator shots. Maybe that's all I'll need to blow Abaddon away."

"You want to just charge in and try to kill him?" Rollo asked, sounding dubious.

"Yes," I said. "That's exactly what we're going to do."

-35-

"Necessity is the mother of invention," as the old saying went. Here, necessity meant we had to roll the dice and hope everything went our way.

That's what I told the others. We met in N7's infirmary room. He lay on a cot with his arm in a sling. It wouldn't have to stay that way long, a few more hours at most.

Dmitri had turned his chair with his arms hanging over the backrest. Rollo leaned back so his was propped against a wall. I paced because of nervous energy.

It wasn't every day Abaddon invaded my mind. I was edgy and angry. I was also as close to depressed as I ever got. Abaddon had Jennifer, and now he had Ella. He knew our plan. He had our Jelk Catcher.

"He has deliberately goaded you," N7 declared. "It is Abaddon's plan that you act rashly."

"I don't know about that," I said. "He worked to defend himself from our super tech. I bet that's what he does best: taking care of his butt. We have two disintegrator shots at most. The—" I almost talked about the Curator. "The being who gave me the weapon suggested it might take several shots to kill Abaddon."

"Better make them pointblank shots to the head then," Rollo said with a scowl.

I nodded. "We're out of options. We have to move now while we know something about the enemy."

"Why move into a losing assault?" N7 said. "Why not go to Plan B."

"Which would be what exactly?" I asked.

"We must use the *Santa Maria* to slow down the Super Fleet," N7 said. "We must buy time for the Grand Armada to maneuver into a blocking position. In that way, we bring about a great fleet action. That will decide humanity's fate instead of these assassination attempts."

"Ella's as good as finished if we do it that way," I said.

"This is about humanity's fate," N7 said, "not just a woman we care for."

I wondered if that was true for N7. Did he love Ella the way the rest of us did? Maybe the android just knew how to choose the right words.

"You must take the long view on this," N7 added.

"I once did that on the portal planet when I left Jennifer behind. I've felt rotten about it ever since."

"Yes. But you saved your people and our galaxy. In the matter with Abaddon, you cannot allow yourself to indulge your emotions."

I glared at N7 but returned to my pacing. Each step hurt my head just a little. I wondered if Abaddon's mind talk had given me permanent brain damage.

What was the right answer? N7 suggested I rid myself of emotion in this. Rollo just sat there. Dmitri looked worried.

"Maybe emotion is what we have to use," I said.

"That is what an emotional man would say," N7 told me.

"I'm talking about trusting your gut," I said. "There are times you can make every calculation. Then, it comes down to running flat out for a Hail Mary pass."

"This is a football analogy?" N7 asked.

"I think this is overtime," I said. "We're losing, but we have a tiny window of opportunity. At such a point, you don't play it safe. You've already lost if you do that. Instead, you risk it all on a balls out attempt at victory. Nine times out of ten, you fail. It's that one time you succeed that is miraculous. We need a miracle, N7. Miracles don't come from careful calculations. They come from faith and going for it."

"Nice speech," Rollo said. "What does it mean in practical terms?"

I stared at my old friend. "We have to smash him down," I said. "We have to surprise him."

"I don't think Abaddon is ever surprised," Rollo said. "I think he's messing with you. Maybe he meant for us to capture the moon-ship from the beginning."

I didn't like that idea.

"Why would he have wanted us to capture the moon-ship?" I asked.

The First Admiral shrugged. "Beats the heck out of me, Creed. That's just what my gut is telling me."

I gave him a wintry grin.

"You said it right the first time," I told Rollo. "I have to get close and blow out his brains. While Abaddon is getting his people back to their respective ships, we need to go back to the star system, find Ella and the Jelk Catcher or find Abaddon, and teleport to either free her or to kill him with our two shots."

"There is problem we do that," Dmitri said.

"I'm listening."

"You mean to appear by the Super Fleet," Dmitri said.

I nodded.

"In that case, Abaddon's Kargs will storm the moon-ship as we did to the Saurians in the Solar System."

"I've already thought of that," I said.

"And?" Dmitri asked.

"We have to wreck the moon-ship's elevators and other interior maneuver systems, at least those connecting the lunar-like surface with the deep control chambers down here in the center. That way, the Kargs or whoever does the attacking will have to hoof it all the way to us. That's a long walk, which gives us time."

"Time to kill Abaddon?" Dmitri asked.

"That's first," I said. "Afterward, if we're still alive, we transfer to the Solar System. Earth Fleet and the Starkiens will storm the moon surface behind the Kargs. We'll hit the enemy front and back, eventually defeating all those foolish enough to have stormed the moon-ship."

Dmitri cocked his head as he studied me. "That is a good plan. I like it."

"It is risky," N7 said.

"I already said it was."

"What if Abaddon joins their assault?" N7 said. "What if he teleports directly to the moon-ship's bridge?"

"That's great," I said. "Then that's where I'll kill him as he's all alone."

"I do not necessarily mean that is what Abaddon will do," N7 said. "I am suggesting that he will do something we don't expect, as that is what he just did."

I snorted sourly. "That's the nature of war, my friend. We each try to pull a fast one. Someone wins and the other guy loses. That part isn't any different today. The only difference is what we're risking. But I still say this is the moment of decision. Our chances for success are worse than before, but I think they're better than anything else anyone else can think of."

"I cannot concur with your logic," N7 said.

"Rollo?" I asked.

"Did you say you read some of Abaddon's thoughts?"

"I did. I'm sure I sensed fear or unease concerning me."

"Could Abaddon have faked that?" Rollo asked.

I scowled, but finally said, "I suppose that's possible."

I didn't tell him that Abaddon wanted to lure me in. I would let myself be lured, but give him a bigger surprise than he expected. Knowing you're going to be ambushed is halfway to defeating the ambush.

"I'd say it's likely that Abaddon is faking you and us out," Rollo said. He tipped his chair forward and lurched to his feet. "But we gotta go for it anyway. I'm with you, Creed. I think this is our lone shot. That means we have to take it. We can't hang back like pussies because Abaddon makes us shiver."

"Yeah…" I said. "N7, you're staying this time. I want you suited up on the bridge, though. You're going to make sure the *Santa Maria* transfers home. If we die or Abaddon captures us, then you can implement your Plan B."

"I do this under protest," N7 said.

"But will you do it?" I asked.

The android looked at me squarely. "I will," he said.

"That's good enough for me. Now, let's get ready."

-36-

It took longer to get ready than I liked. I kept thinking about Ella, how scared she'd been before our commando assault. I'd told her not to worry, but she shouldn't have listened to me. What was Abaddon doing to her? What had the First One done to Jennifer?

My idea this time was predicated on the belief that Abaddon wouldn't risk destroying the *Santa Maria*. It was too valuable for him. Surely, Abaddon had many long-term goals. I had no doubt he hated the Curator. To reach the old man sooner rather than later, Abaddon would need the ancient Survey Vessel.

As we climbed into our T-suits, I thought about the Kargs. They were much different from Saurians or even Jelk.

I could almost hear an old voice in head. It wasn't Abaddon, but a Lokhar who had told me about the Kargs a long time ago. That had been the year we'd gone into hyperspace to search for the portal planet.

A Lokhar named Prince Venturi had told me, "*The Kargs are a devouring species, even more rapacious than the Jelk. They inhabit a much smaller universe than ours, with fewer planets per star. When that became too little space, they demolished the planets and used the matter to create Dyson spheres around the various suns. They annihilated all other life forms but their own. They are xenophobic to an intense degree, destroying everything they hate."*

Karg soldiers had barrel bodies with horny shells like beetles. They had triangular heads with the same tough substance and complex eyes like common Earth houseflies, with wet orifices for mouths with chitin teeth. They had two metallic tentacles with metal pincers on the end and three shorter tentacles on the bottom of the torso for mobility, allowing them to scuttle from place to place. Kargs spoke in clicks. They might have been designed as cannon-fodder creatures. They had served Abaddon faithfully enough. As to the Karg genesis, I had no idea. Maybe only the Curator or the Creator did.

It was likely that Kargs would be guarding Abaddon on the ship as we struck.

"I have the enemy fleet in visual," Rollo said hoarsely. He was using Holgotha's T-scanner.

Rollo tapped his controls as he zeroed in on the moth-ships. They rode the gargantuan mothership snowflakes. A moth-ship looked like a giant moth in many ways. The "wings" could move to a small degree. They were energy collectors. The "eyes" in the "head" glowed with an eerie red color. We'd seen destructive red beams pour from moth-ship eyes. We had yet to discover how they powered the red beams.

No one I knew had ever been aboard a Karg moth-ship before. We were going to be the first.

"How will we figure out which moth-ship holds Abaddon?" Rollo asked.

"I believe I'll sense him," I said. "I think the two of us are linked now. Maybe we have been ever since he talked to me in my sleep several years ago."

"I'm not sure I'm buying that," Rollo told me. "It sounds forced."

"Keep scanning," I said. "We'll find out soon enough whether I'm right or not."

I had the Ultrix Disintegrator hooked to my T-suit. Both Jelk-holding cubes were on my belt. The captured Jelk seemed more agitated than ever. I believe they had a good idea what this gun did and how they would each power a shot.

Rollo kept scanning one snowflake after—

"That one," I whispered, as a sharp pain spiked in my head. At the same time, I could see in my mind's eye Abaddon's head coming up sharply.

"Let's go," I said. "He can sense me."

Rollo stared at me hard. Finally, with his voice more hoarse than ever, he gave the command.

"We will transfer in four…three…two…one…now," N7 said through the comm. He was on the bridge. "We are transferring—"

The transferring sensations cut in. The moment the strange feelings quit, I tapped on my T-suit's scanner.

"Link to me," I whispered. I felt Abaddon a second before I saw him on the scanner.

He was huge, just like he'd been in his spacesuit. He was dark like clotted blood but had classically handsome features. The eyes swirled with power, with extreme menace and evil. I sucked in my breath upon seeing his eyes, working to tear my gaze free. He wore a metallic, iron-colored garment up to his neck. There were computer-like monitors on his chest and several big weapons on his belt. He was like some dark Greek god and seemed intelligent and forceful beyond anything I'd known. His appearance called to mind images of fictional vampire princes or the way humans imagine Satan might look.

Ella was chained by the neck and wore little in the way of clothes. The end of the leash was in Abaddon's left hand. She appeared downcast, defeated in spirit.

Several Kargs stood nearby with big rifles in their tentacles. I saw one other person, a tall woman with dark hair. She had elongated features and a sinister smile. Like Abaddon, she wore a metallic garment that did nothing to hide her womanly contours. It had to be Jennifer. She had a long knife in her hand, the blade gleaming with electric power.

"Are you seeing this?" Rollo asked over the suit comm.

"Ready?" I whispered.

"He's expecting us," Rollo told me.

"Do we have a choice?"

"No," the First Admiral said.

"Right," I said. "It's clobbering time."

-37-

Pressing the teleport switch was hard. My thumb seemed to travel for an eternity. I wondered if this was how it had felt in World War I. There, soldiers had heard a whistle blow. Then, they climbed up the trench ladder or scrambled up the trench on their hands and knees, and charged the enemy with a rifle and bayonet. They had walked or run across No Man's Land and crawled through reams of barbed wire. All the while, enemy machine gunners had mowed them down. How had the Tommie Boys found the courage to walk forward into the teeth of streams of lead?

Maybe a similar numbed courage moved my thumb. Maybe it wasn't courage, but soldierly stupidity. Maybe that's what valor was, part manliness and part craziness.

I moved my thumb against the switch, and found myself shouting as I appeared in Abaddon's chamber.

It was a big room with screens on the walls. I saw Abaddon peering at me on the screens. He'd known we were coming, all right, and he'd known the exact spot.

As I materialized, heavy slugs whined off my T-suit armor, staggering me. They knocked the Ultrix Disintegrator out of my hands.

"Surrender," Abaddon said in a dark voice full of authority.

Part of me wanted to grovel right there. How did one disobey the voice of a god?

I saw Dmitri throw himself onto his face before Abaddon.

"Put down your weapons," Abaddon ordered.

The Kargs kept firing, the heavy slugs hammering against me, making it hard to think.

I heard Rollo roar a battle cry. He fired back, and a Karg exploded into metallic and fleshy parts.

That helped me. I used my T-suit's beam and the gun, chugging shots, blowing apart the hated Kargs and firing at others. Then, I centered on Abaddon.

He jerked the leash so Ella cried out, pulled into my line of fire. The beam and slugs tore her into a rag of flesh. Afterward, the beam and slugs almost struck Abaddon. A force field kept them from reaching him, however.

"No!" I howled.

"You're a murderer," Abaddon said in a voice dripping with judgment.

If he thought that would break me, he was wrong. I went berserk instead. I'd killed Ella. I hadn't meant to, but she was dead anyway.

Jennifer—for who else could she be?—moved like greased death at that point. She reached Dmitri and yanked a power cord from his pack to the teleportation device. The Cossack tried to rise. Jennifer slapped sticky pods to him. They expanded with startling speed, wrapping him in a vile cocoon.

I was beyond speech or I would have warned Rollo to watch out. My best friend seemed to have lost it as well. He was down on one knee, blasting away, hammering Kargs into smithereens. Many of their slugs struck him, but it didn't matter. Rollo had braced himself against them, and the Ronin 9 body armor held.

I felt like the Angel of Death come to wreak retribution upon Abaddon the Lord of Evil.

I reached the Ultrix Disintegrator, picked it up, shoved a Jelk-filled cube into the chamber and targeted Abaddon.

"You're making a mistake," he said.

I felt him reaching out with his mind power. He struck, but I had steeled my will behind a curtain of rage. Despite the wateriness in my eyes, despite the throb of pain, I howled with battle-fury. I centered the Ronin 9 weapon and pressed the firing stud.

A silent screech cut off Abaddon's mind assault. I realized without knowing how that the Jelk in the cube was pleading for mercy.

It didn't matter. I kept my finger on the firing switch. In a swift act of justice, the disintegrator devoured the glowing machine ball. The Jelk fed the weapon power, and the thing discharged a short but savage beam of ultimate destruction.

Like a gush, it swept at Abaddon, striking him on the chest instead of his head as I'd aimed. The mighty Abaddon shouted with pain as he tumbled from his throne onto the floor. Smoke billowed from his form. The metal garment at that spot had curled away to expose the wound. Golden ichor flowed out of the rent, and I almost expected to see bone.

I raged joyously at his pain. I think I surprised him. I think Abaddon had forgotten about the Ultrix Disintegrator. Maybe he hadn't torn that from Ella's mind yet. Maybe he just thought his armor and force field proof against my weapon.

I'd just taught him otherwise.

I clicked the weapon. The spent and darkened cube tumbled onto the floor. I shoved my last captured Jelk into the chamber.

"Cretin!" Abaddon roared.

"Dead man," I said, targeting him.

Abaddon squeezed his eyes closed. I supposed he feared death. A halo appeared around him. What did I care about that?

I fired the Ronin 9 weapon. It discharged a ferocious gout of energy. Abaddon disappeared. The energy burned through the spot where he'd been, drilling through deck after deck until it must have reached the outer bulkhead.

At the same time, Abaddon appeared beside me on his feet. He had teleported. The halo must have had something to do with that. I thought it had been a last ditch protection against my gun.

Abaddon snatched the Ultrix Disintegrator from my hands. His shoulder muscles bulged, and more golden ichor flowed from the chest wound. With a grunt, he broke the ancient weapon. Then, he reached for me.

The result of my last shot saved me from those deadly hands. The gout of energy had burned through to the outer hull. Air whistled out into the vacuum of space, causing masses of debris to swirl into our chamber.

Abaddon swatted at things flying at his face.

I took that moment to backpedal, looking around. I'd failed. I'd had two shots, and I'd failed to kill Abaddon. I'd wounded him, though.

Jennifer raced to the hole, slapping something over it, sealing us from the vacuum. That caused the debris to fall to the deck.

Then, everything seemed to go crazy. Balls of energy oozed through the walls. Some of the pulsating energy balls halted. Others oozed back the way they had come as if running away. One materialized into a Jelk.

Right, I thought. The balls of energy had been Jelk in their real form. The one that cloaked flesh around it looked familiar.

I found myself staring at Shah Claath. He looked exactly as I'd remembered him. He wore a blue suit and fancy shoes. He had red skin and satanically intelligent eyes. He was the size of a tall child. I realized he was yelling at me, gesturing wildly.

Finally, his words penetrated my sound receptors.

"It's a trap, you stupid beast," Claath shouted. "Grab me and teleport back to your ship. Do it now before Abaddon regains his senses. Move, you brute. Do something intelligent for once."

The conniving creep infuriated me. I had no idea what the Jelk had in mind, but his words made sense after a fashion.

"Rollo, Dmitri," I said over the suit-comm. "Retreat to the *Santa Maria*. We have to regroup."

Rollo disappeared.

"Go," I told Dmitri. Then, I grabbed Claath, hugging his little body to my T-suit.

"You have lost," Abaddon told me.

I gave the Dark One the finger. Before Abaddon could respond, I teleported back to the *Santa Maria* with Claath as my prisoner.

-38-

I shoved the Jelk away from me as I materialized onto the bridge of the *Santa Maria*. Several officers gasped in surprise.

Trask turned to me. He was a small old man in a crisp uniform. "Commander, Karg squads have landed en masse on the moon surface. They have breach bombs and have entered the corridors. I estimate something in the nature of a million soldiers. We cannot possibly fight them off. Once they reach the engine rooms..."

A T-suit popped onto the bridge.

Claath whirled around. "Shoot him, Commander. It's one of Abaddon's creatures."

"No," Rollo said. "It's me, Creed."

I reached for the Jelk to shake him. Claath neatly dodged my suited hands and straightened his garment after stepping out of reach.

"What are your orders, sir?" Trask asked.

"Transfer," I said, dully.

"To what coordinates, sir?"

"The next star system," I said.

"You'd better go farther than that," Claath said. "Abaddon will reach you otherwise."

I stared at the Jelk, realizing he'd run to me for help. After all these years, wondering if I could ever hunt down Claath, the cunning schemer had run to me for succor.

242

"Transfer immediately, Trask. We'll pick different coordinates once there."

"Yes, sir," Trask said. The old man turned and began issuing orders.

In less than a minute, we left the Super Fleet, with at least one million Kargs working their way into the guts of the *Santa Maria*.

Claath was right about one thing. Abaddon tried another mind assault while we were here. It happened while Rollo and I shoved Claath ahead of us. We went to the viewing chamber.

I grunted and went to one knee. I resisted the mind assault by getting as angry as I could. Abaddon probed. I could almost hear him, but fought against it. Finally, the mind attack ended, and I climbed to my feet.

"You okay, Creed?" Rollo asked.

"No," I whispered. "But let's figure out where to transfer next. We have to move farther away from Abaddon."

"The First One must be hurt," Claath said. "You can thank whatever Deity you worship for that. Otherwise, Abaddon would have dominated your beastly mind like that." The Jelk snapped thin red fingers.

Rollo raised a gun at Claath. "Do you want me to waste him?"

"What good would that do you?" Claath asked Rollo. "You beasts have always baffled me. Why don't you start using your minds for once?"

I swatted Claath across the back of the head, making him stagger.

"We're not beasts," I told him. "I thought I taught you that a long time ago."

"You certainly act like beasts," he said, rubbing the back of his head.

Standing around and arguing wouldn't help anything, so we continued to the scanning room. In short order, Rollo and I chose another star system. We transferred again, around fifty light years away from the Super Fleet. I didn't want to take us to the Solar System, not with a million Kargs on board. I wasn't sure yet what kind of equipment they had brought with them. Could the Kargs launch off the moon-ship to attack elsewhere?

Claath cocked his head thoughtfully, finally nodding. "I think we're far enough from Abaddon." He grinned at me. It was a smile filled with toothy relief.

"Well done, Commander," Claath said. "That was astonishing. You have my full appreciation, believe me. I couldn't let you know that until out of range of the First One's filthy mind powers."

"What are you trying to pull, you weasel?" Rollo demanded.

The Jelk blinked at us in what appeared genuine surprise. "Surely you two cannot hold old times against me. Much has changed since then. We are allies of the gun, are we not?"

"What is that supposed to mean?" I asked.

Claath made a bland gesture. "It seems obvious enough. Abaddon has a larger gun than either of us. He has forced us to recalibrate our attitudes toward each other. Once, we considered each other as enemies. Now, we have become friends of the gun, friends of convenience, you might say."

"We're going to kill you," Rollo said.

Claath arched his eyebrows. "Whatever for? I have what you need. You have something I could use. We should work together in order to defeat Abaddon."

"Hold it," I told Rollo. "I want to get out of my suit before we start this. I need a drink, and I need to think. Guard him while I get out of this."

We traded guard duty as we each climbed out of our T-suit and bio-suits. Afterward, I wore my .44, and Rollo had a pulse gun.

We all went to a cafeteria, getting coffee and sandwiches. I'd like to say I was too sick at heart to eat after losing both Ella and Dmitri, but that would be a lie. I drank several cups of coffee and wolfed down three sandwiches.

Rollo did likewise, just more of both and as he glared at Claath with murderous intent.

Finally, I sat back. I couldn't believe I'd killed Ella. I couldn't believe I'd lost the Ultrix Disintegrator. At least I'd wounded Abaddon. The Lord of Evil had gotten a surprise there.

"I'm still trying to wrap my mind around what happened," Rollo said in a hoarse voice. "I can't believe we lost Dmitri."

"And Ella," I said.

"Ella was your assault trooper companion?" Claath asked.

I stared at him before nodding.

"She did not die," Claath said.

"Don't lie to me. I saw her die."

"You saw a robot likeness of her," Claath said. "She's too precious to Abaddon to allow you to simply slay."

"What?" I said, as hope raised its head in my heart.

"Commander, why do you think we Jelk rushed to Abaddon's quarters once we escaped our confinement?"

"What are you talking about?"

Claath put his fine-boned hands on the table. "Do you even know what happened on the ship?"

"Yes. I saw Jennifer."

"Who?"

"Surely you remember her," I said. "She was one of your nurses when you first came to Earth."

"Oh, the modified one," Claath said, nodding.

"We can't believe anything he says," Rollo said hotly. "He's a liar, at best telling half-truths to suit his agenda."

"Maybe his half-truths are all we have left," I said. "I mean, what else is there? We lost the disintegrator, the Jelk Catcher—"

"The what?" Claath asked.

"And we have a million Kargs on the *Santa Maria*," I said, ignoring our guest. "Maybe we'd better hear what Claath has to say. I know we both hate him, but maybe he has a point about being allies of the gun. We're losing our friends, and if we don't do something quick, we'll lose our great vessel, our last hope of saving Earth."

"No," Claath said. "You cannot save Earth. It is doomed. But you are correct about the ship. It is a lovely vessel. We can survive many long years by fleeing—"

I drew my .44, aiming it at Claath's head. "Listen to me carefully. I can still transfer back to Abaddon. I'll pop outside with my T-suit and leave you there. The First One can catch you and do whatever he was going to do to you Jelk."

Claath appeared thoughtful. "Yes. I take your point, Commander. I should be the one asking you what happened. This is the ancient Survey Vessel. You have Ronin 9 T-suits. The only place to have acquired those... Ah. This has become quite interesting. I had not realized you'd seen the Curator. Yes. This silly plan has his ineptness written all over it. I see he hasn't gotten any wiser over time."

"Who are you talking about?" Rollo demanded.

Claath raised an eyebrow and glanced at me.

"Start talking," I told him. "How come all you Jelk were prisoners? How come others weren't? Why did you run to me, Claath? What's going on here? Are you claiming to be Abaddon's enemy?"

"Of course," he said.

"Don't you remember the portal planet?" I asked. "You screwed us by helping Abaddon."

"That was then," Claath said with a shrug. "This is a new day. We are allies of the gun, as I said earlier. Don't worry about the past. Seek to survive the future."

"What's your story, Jelk? If you don't start talking—"

"Yes, yes," Claath said, interrupting, "enough of your beastly threats. Here in a nutshell is what has been happening with me..."

-39-

It was strange listening to Claath after all this time. Long ago, he'd turned us into assault troopers. He'd seemed so much larger than life then. He'd been the master of humanity's fate. Later, he'd become the man who controlled the system. We'd rebelled against Claath in order to win our freedom. Then, he became the renegade Jelk. He helped Abaddon reach our space-time continuum.

Claath was a survivor. That was the essence of his story. He'd learned to roll with the punches millennia ago. Abaddon had reached our space-time continuum with hopes of uniting his Kargs with the Jelk Corporation. Claath had slipped away from the First One, racing in a starship to warn his brethren. Thanks to Claath's timely advice, the Jelk Corporation had turned their power against this terrible enemy of everyone and everything.

Claath had risen high in the Jelk councils, showing the other Jelk how to defeat Abaddon and trick the raging Kargs.

"But…" Claath said. "We had forgotten the cunning of a First One. Among them, Abaddon was known for his cleverness. I think, too, the Dark One knew where ancient devices had been hidden. He couldn't trick the ancient artifacts. They were proof against him. That was critical. If the Forerunner objects had helped Abaddon, we would have had to serve him for eons. As it is…"

Claath cocked his head. "The ancient Survey Vessel was his latest find. I'm surprised—"

"Just a minute," I said, interrupting. "I've let you talk for a while. Now, I have some questions."

"By all means," Claath said, with his easy smile. "I am at your service."

I squinted at him. "Did Abaddon defeat the Jelk Corporation in the core worlds or did you decide to become allies of the gun?"

He winced slightly, looking away, and shrugged his narrow shoulders. "I would not say we allied with him."

"So…Abaddon defeated you?"

Claath glared at me. "Certainly not! We are the Jelk Corporation. Nobody *defeats* us."

"Sure they do," I said. "All those Jelk at the end had just escaped confinement—unless you lied to us about that."

"I have no reason to lie."

"I'm glad to hear it. So what happened? How did all you Jelk become prisoners?"

Claath pinched his lower lip. "We had a parley."

"What kind of parley?"

He frowned into the distance, speaking slowly. "We agreed to meet with Abaddon in the Onyx System. That's in the heart of the core worlds. The First One came with his masses, and we met him in our thousands. I'm referring to battlejumpers. For five weeks, he spoke with us, attempting to win us over to his plan. Oh, Abaddon was clever, but even more importantly, none of us recalled sufficiently his powers of mind.

"As he spoke to us in turn, using his charm, the First One secretly read our thoughts. Even more treacherously, he implanted ideas into our sub-consciousness. Slowly, we found ourselves agreeing with his ideas. They were so grand and glorious. After centuries of fruitless war against the religious-besotted Jade League, the corporation would rule the entire Orion Arm. Abaddon promised that us as our fief. He would conquer inward, using our mercenary armies.

"Yes," Claath said, "we planned to raise such a host as to startle the Curator and the inward races. They would know fear. They would rue the day they had turned on the Jelk, forcing us to flee to the savagery of the fringe zones. The corporation has worked tirelessly to raise the standard of culture and technology in the Orion Arm. Have any thanked us for our efforts? No. Always they resist, hating us, unwilling to give the corporation the due our hard work deserves."

"In other words," I said dryly, "the other races failed to treat the Jelk as gods."

"Yes!" Claath said, slapping the table. "Would that be too much to ask? We gave the other races so much. You cannot imagine how they groveled in ignorance before our coming."

"Creed," Rollo said, sullenly. "How does this kind of talk rid the *Santa Maria* of the Kargs? Maybe he's lulling us to buy them time."

"By no means," Claath said. "My intentions are honorable."

"What about the Jelk in Creed's disintegrator?" Rollo demanded. "Don't you care they died?"

"Ha!" Claath said. "Ahx Rax and Simi Baoji deserved annihilation, the traitors. They groveled to Abaddon, allowing the Dark One to place inhibitors in their being. They were no longer free agents, but slaves in the worst sense of the word. The rest of us went into confinement rather than to allow an inhibitor put into our essence. Yes, I am aware that they retained their Jelk-ness. Possibly, they could have multiplied later, thus eventually freeing themselves from Abaddon's control. I suspect that was their reasoning."

Claath shook his head at such stupidity. "The margin for error was too high. It was folly—"

"What are you talking about?" Rollo shouted.

Claath closed his mouth, sitting straighter. He glanced at me, and his smile returned.

"What?" Rollo asked, looking from me to Claath.

"The Commander understands me," Claath said, indicating me.

Rollo rose like a grizzly bear. I had the feeling he would attempt to rip Claath's arms from his torso. Instead, the big man turned, stomping out of the cafeteria.

"You do understand me, don't you?" Claath asked.

I figured I did. Abaddon had tricked the Jelk. They agreed to become his allies. In doing so, they fell under his power. Eventually, the Jelk realized their error. At that point, Abaddon gave them a choice. Take the inhibitor in their essence—becoming his slave until such time as they divided into renewed halves—or go into confinement.

"How did Abaddon confine you?" I asked.

"Partly though his amazing mind-powers and partly through ancient First One hardware," Claath said. "It is like a Forerunner object and like…" The little Jelk frowned.

"Like the original AI you escaped?" I asked.

Claath's head jerked as he stared at me. His eyes burned for an instant. His old villainy shone through, and he hunched his shoulders, hissing like a snake. Abruptly, he looked away, stood, shivered several seconds and slowly brought himself under control. He sat back down, facing me with a seemingly placid smile.

His eyes were hooded now.

"That," he said, "was long, long ago. I…do not like to remember that time."

"Okay," I said.

His eyebrows rose. "Okay?" he asked.

"You were slaves in the beginning, right?"

"No…"

"But you didn't like it in the original AI?"

He seemed to freeze, probably in an attempt to control his emotions.

"I did not like it there," Claath said softly.

"Why did the Jelk become the ultimate capitalists? Why do you seek riches and luxury?"

He blinked at me as if I were a cretin. "What else is there?" he asked.

I studied him.

"There is no such thing as a soul," Claath said. "That is an invention of you flesh creatures. It is a mind disease, in fact. The Jade League seethes with it."

"The other races are insane?"

"Yes! That is a good way to put it. They do not see reality as it is, as we do. Perhaps that comes from our original confinement. We see deeper than others."

"Or maybe you don't see as deeply," I said.

"That is preposterous," he said. "We are the Jelk, the ultimate realists. There is nothing but the here and now. The accumulation of capital, of things, is everything. There is nothing else but this delusion of souls. That is a false path for the weak-minded."

"Does Abaddon share your beliefs?"

Claath cocked his head. "That is a shrewd question," he said, with something like surprise. "I am unsure. He seeks power instead of riches. In the end, the two are different paths to the same end: comfort and enjoyment."

"Abaddon doesn't strike me as someone out to enjoy himself," I said.

"Perhaps you're right."

I raised my cup and found that my remaining coffee had gotten cold. I got up, tossed the coffee into the sink and brewed more. I returned to the table with the fresh cup, sipping the steaming liquid.

"So…" I said. "When I wounded Abaddon…"

"The locks on our cages came loose. We had been hoping for something like that. I suppose Abaddon is recapturing the others. I, with my greater knowledge and quicker ability to decide, realized I had to get far away from him. That left you as the only avenue for escape."

"You didn't fear my wrath?" I asked.

"To date, you haven't been able to kill a Jelk. Yes, with the Ronin 9 weapon, you did, but Abaddon destroyed the gun. Thus, it seemed that the most logical choice was to go with you and convince you to do the right thing."

"What would that be?" I asked.

As Claath started to answer, Rollo appeared in a T-suit. He aimed his beam at Claath.

"What are you doing?" the Jelk asked.

The beam poured from the orifice, striking Claath, burning into his flesh.

"Abaddon is controlling him," the Jelk shouted. "Stop him before it's too late."

Rollo kept beaming, and in a moment, Claath exploded into a ball of bright energy.

-40-

In my haste to get out of the way I spilled coffee on my shirt. At the same time, the ball of energy floated upward.

"Rollo!" I shouted.

Was he under Abaddon's control? Had the Dark One planted a post-hypnotic command deep in Rollo's subconscious?

The beam stopped and Rollo lowered his suited arm. He used a suit-speaker to talk to me.

"I'm sick of him, Creed. I'm sick of his haughty ways. I wanted to watch him die in the disintegrator's power chamber. That's all I could think about these past minutes—that we were cheated of our reward."

"Are you feeling…like yourself?" I asked.

"What's that supposed mean?"

"Claath suggested that you're under Abaddon's control," I said.

The beam-weapon arm lifted as Rollo re-aimed at the ball of energy.

"Don't do it," I said.

"Claath is slime," Rollo said in a tight voice. "He's trying to use us."

"I know that."

Rollo's silvered visor turned to me as if in surprise. "Why are you letting him then?"

"I'm not. I just understand that that's his goal. I have a different goal, though." I made a soft gesture. "Do you plan to keep on shooting him?"

"I've thought it over, Creed. It has to take energy to form flesh, to go from one state to another. If one made Claath change states over and over again, maybe that would eat up his energy reserves. Maybe that would be like starving Claath to death."

I tapped my chin, considering that. It was a novel idea, certainly.

"I hate him," Rollo said flatly, as he turned to watch the floating energy ball.

The energy changed color, becoming a deep red. Slowly, it took on a humanoid shape.

"I share your feelings," I quietly told Rollo. "But we need him, as I'm out of ideas. We have a million Kargs working down to us. Abaddon has Dmitri, Ella and Jennifer. Maybe the little…creep can come up with an idea. But he won't be able to tell us if you keep forcing him into his energy state."

"Yeah…" Rollo said. He finally nodded. "I'm done for now. You do what you gotta. Count me in for whatever it is."

With that, the T-suit vanished.

I touched the wet stain on my shirt. With a shrug, I returned to the pot, pouring myself another cup. I sipped and silently debated strategies as Claath pulled himself together.

After a time, I heard a chair leg scrape against the floor as Claath sat down.

I peered at him sideways. He looked different but it was barely noticeable. There was a slight discoloration on his right cheek and his nose seemed sharper than last time. Did Rollo have the right idea about "starving" Jelk to death by forcing them through repeated flesh to energy transformations? It seemed doubtful, but it was an interesting idea to have come from my meat-house friend.

"Was that a planned event?" Claath asked coldly.

"Ah, you're back," I said, facing him. "I hope that wasn't too painful."

"It was quite painful, and I resent it."

"Oh."

"Don't try to pretend. You already knew it hurt. Why else would any Jelk exhibit pain symptoms at his bodily demise?"

"That's a good point," I said, taking another sip of coffee. I was starting to feel shaky from the caffeine. Maybe I should stop for today.

Worry crossed his reshaped features. "Are we allies of the gun or not?" he asked.

I took my time answering. "That depends," I said.

"On?"

"On whether you can help me or not," I said.

"I assure you, I can."

"I'm not interested in assurances. I want proof. What should we do now?"

"What is the precise objective?" he asked.

"Freeing my friends and killing Abaddon."

Claath moved a saucer with his fingers as his features pinched up in thought. Looking up at me, he said, "We may not be able to free your friends."

"Why?"

"Because all this," he said with a wave of his hand, "is taking too long."

I raised my cup, made to sip and then hurled the cup and remaining coffee from me. The cup shattered against a far wall.

Claath jerked in surprise, staring at me. Then, he glanced about as if searching for Rollo.

"Listen," I said, putting my hands on the edge of the table, leaning toward him. "How do we kill Abaddon without a disintegrator?"

"I have no idea."

"You didn't have a plan for killing him?"

"We—meaning the Jelk Corporation—have had several plans. They all failed."

"If you don't know how to kill him, what good are you to me?" I asked.

"You don't understand. Killing a First One was always hard. They had powers no other race ever exhibited. But I think Abaddon has become greater than any other First One. He...*developed* in the other space-time continuum. He has become the greatest being alive. He's a danger to everyone. We thought—"

"Yes?" I said. "You thought what?"

Claath shook his head. "It doesn't matter. You had the greatest weapon ever made by another race: the Ultrix Disintegrator. It hurt Abaddon, which proves the Curator was right in giving it to you. Now, it's gone. Now, the Kargs are charging down here. Do you want my suggestion?"

"Let's hear it."

"We must rid the craft of Kargs and go to another galaxy. We can start over. Maybe in time Abaddon will come after us. Maybe ruling an entire galaxy will be enough for his vaulting ambition. In truth, though, I believe he is afflicted with the worst of the flesh diseases."

"What's that?"

"Abaddon seeks to kill the Creator."

I stared at Claath.

"Yet," the Jelk said, "how does one go about killing an imaginary being?"

That seemed to come out of left field. It surprised me. "How do you know the Creator is imaginary?" I asked.

"Commander, please," Claath said. "It is a vain and foolish concept. The Creator, as conceived, does not exist."

"How do you know that?" I asked. "Have you been to every point in the universe to check?"

"Clearly, I have not."

"Then how do you know He doesn't exist?"

"Bah!" Claath said. "I reject your argument. Here, I'll show you why it's futile. I believe there is a Cosmic Joker who causes each of us to trip and fall for his sick amusement. But you'll tell me that is a phantasm of my imagination. People trip and fall because they are clumsy. At that point, my eyes will gleam with righteous indignation. I will say, 'It is self-evident the Cosmic Joker exists. If you say he doesn't, I'll simply ask you if you've been to every point in the universe to check.' Obviously, none of us has been to every place in the universe. Does that mean whatever creature we concoct in our fantasies is true?"

"All right," I said, "you don't believe in the Creator. Frankly, I don't care if you do or not. I want to know how to kill Abaddon."

"I have already told you I don't know. Repeating the question won't magically force me to give you an answer I don't have."

I turned away. Was Abaddon unbeatable then? The Curator had given me the Ultrix Disintegrator—

I stood. I had my answer. If I didn't know, if Claath didn't know, there was still one person who might. I had to get back to that person and ask. I headed for the exit.

"Where are you going?" Claath asked.

"To the bridge," I said.

"A-ha!" he said, jumping up. "You have renewed your hope. I see it in your bearing. I am interested in this. I will join you."

I studied Claath. He seemed at ease.

"What just happened?" I asked. "Why are you so…boisterous all of a sudden?"

"It's not me. It's you. You've thought of something. I wish to observe how you operate. Time and again, you have done what I considered impossible. I would like to know your secrets in order to employ them myself someday."

As I listened to him, I realized something. It made me smile inwardly. I had an idea, but Claath wasn't going to like it. Neither was the other guy I planned to see. Everyone was going to be angry with me. But that was okay. I was pretty pissed off right now myself. When I got like this, I liked pissing off others.

Claath trailed me to the bridge. The crew stared at him for a time. Maybe they wondered why I was giving the Jelk so much freedom. Finally, the crew went back to work, plotting the coordinates to our next destination. I'd spoken quietly to Captain Trask, so Claath didn't know where we were headed.

I finally started for a chair.

"What is our destination?" Claath asked, following me.

I turned and told him. It left Claath stunned and then frightened looking.

-41-

The *Santa Maria* appeared at Sagittarius A*.

I came here feeling like we were a plague ship, as I carried a million Kargs. The last time we'd shown up, the Curator had threatened to use anti-force to rid the vessel of a few Skinnies in their electrical suits. I had a feeling anti-force wouldn't work against anti-life Kargs.

The problem was that it looked as if we'd transferred into the middle of a battle.

"We have to get out of here, Commander," Claath shouted. "The Ve-Ky are finally making good on their boast. They're storming the Museum."

From all around the accretion disk circling the supermassive black hole poured Vip 92 Attack Vessels. The lead energy ships already hammered the ancient structure with their energy-blob missiles. I did notice that none of those missiles teleported. They traveled the old-fashioned way, dissipating energy as they zipped toward the Fortress of Light. So far, a force field kept most of those missiles from the structure. In a small area, however, a few missiles flew through a visible force-field hole, slamming against the fortress directly. The armored spot had become red-hot and pulsated darker every time another missile struck.

"Commander," Captain Trask said, giving me a nervous glance. "The readings from those energy missiles are off the charts. If the Ve-Ky direct them at us, our vessel will explode in short order."

Claath shook his head. "It is a terrible pity. But I'm afraid the Curator is doomed." The Jelk made tsking sounds. "The Curator toyed with the Ve-Ky too long, it appears. He should have made peace with them or transferred his abode elsewhere when he had the chance. I deem it likely that he was too arrogant to contemplate such a rational course."

I felt like I had a crocodile beside me shedding false tears.

"Have you seen enough?" Claath asked me.

I ignored him, telling Trask, "We're going in."

"But sir—" Trask said.

"You spout madness," Claath told me. "The Curator is doomed. We cannot help him. We must save ourselves before the Ve-Ky turn on us. They might conclude you're considering helping the senile old fool."

"Shut up," I told Claath. "We don't have any choice in the matter," I said to Trask.

"Yes, sir," our acting captain said.

"You are a vain and foolish—"

"Don't say it," I warned Claath, certain he was about to call me a beast.

"You are vain, starship captain," the Jelk finished lamely. He seemed to reconsider his line of reasoning, nodding. "There are moments for brash actions. I concede the point. You have proven it on more than one occasion. This, however, is certainly *not* one of those times. Retreat certainly seems to be in order, don't you agree?"

I eyed Claath. He looked green around the gills, figuratively speaking, as he studied the vast fleet of Vip 92s. I wondered about that.

"How do you know about the Ve-Ky?" I asked.

Claath shrugged as if the matter was of no importance.

An "itch" in my brain blossomed into an insight. The Ve-Ky were material beings with energy ships and electrical combat suits. Jelk were energy beings who wore flesh and blood disguises.

"The Ve-Ky didn't have anything to do with your original escape, did they?"

Claath laughed nervously. "What a preposterous notion, Commander. This is the center of the galaxy. The laws here—"

"Tell me later," I said. "Captain, why haven't we transferred yet?" I'd seen two men yank the main levers to initiate the process.

"We should have," Trask said, frowning severely. "But something—"

The transfer took place then. It had been delayed for some reason, which seemed ominous. With a clang and a hard shake, the *Santa Maria* docked onto the Fortress of Light.

"Commander," Claath said in a rush. "This is a terrible, a grave and odious mistake. I realize now what you must have been thinking. The Curator seems like a kindly human, but I must warn you that he is a vicious meddler, a master deceiver and filled with the wickedest guile imaginable. We must run before he appears."

As if on cue, the main bridge doors swished open. Everyone looked up to see who was coming.

The big old man with the white beard and blue robe hurried onto the bridge. The Curator looked worried and angry, and he gripped a long metal staff in a gnarled old hand.

"Don't believe a word he says," Claath whispered to me. "He will try to dupe you, have no doubt about that. The vicious entity never should have interfered in matters that didn't concern him. He has a long and bitter memory. I suspect he has already threatened more than once to slay every one of you if you step out of line. That is his way, his evil, foul and despicable way."

261

"Commander Creed," the Curator said loudly. "What is the meaning of—?" The big old man stopped short, his blue eyes widening in surprise.

Claath slid behind me as if I could shield him.

"Commander," the old man said. "Is that a *Jelk* in your company?"

I grabbed Claath by the scuff of the neck, dragging him in front of me.

"It *is* a Jelk," the Curator said. "This is astonishing." He banged the end of the metal staff on the deck. It made a much louder boom that it should have. "Shah Claath, step forward."

To my surprise, Claath tore himself free of my grip as he woodenly began to walk toward the Curator. As he did, Claath turned his head as if his neck was rusted iron. He gave me an imploring look.

Claath's lips seemed sealed shut, but he struggled. Finally, he tore them open, shouting, "Please, Commander. Help me. Don't let him take me. This is wrong and vile."

I watched spellbound. What exactly was happening here?

"I'm sorry for everything I ever did wrong to you," Claath shouted. "I didn't mean any of it. Please, Commander, I once saved what was left of the human race. You owe me for that."

As much as I hated to admit it, he had a point. Certainly, Claath had never done anything that wasn't for his own good first. But he had chased off the Lokhar dreadnaught that would have finished off the last one-percenters.

"Curator," I said.

"This doesn't concern you," the old man said curtly.

I didn't like his prompt dismissal of me, but maybe the Curator had a point too.

"Creed!" the Jelk wailed. "I don't want to go back. Please, help me. I'll give you anything you want. I'll help you free Jennifer. I know Abaddon's secrets. I can help you destroy him."

"Then you should have spoken up sooner," I said. "I think it's too late for you now."

"No!" he wailed. Now, Claath tried to resist. His feet continued to move woodenly, though, as he twisted like a wet cat. Finally, almost against his will, the Jelk regarded the waiting Curator.

"I curse you!" Claath screeched.

"Don't you think I've felt your curses all around me for millennia?" the old man asked.

"You helped us once," Claath said.

"That was then."

"No!" Claath wailed. He threw his arms into the air. In a flash, his flesh and blood disguise vaporized, and he became his true self.

"It's about time," the Curator said. He aimed the top of the staff at the ball of energy.

Claath in his original machine self remorselessly floated toward the staff. The energy ball wriggled. It tossed. And then it zipped into the staff. For a moment, the staff quivered, turning red at the tip. The redness moved up the staff like a meal moving up a snake's belly. Finally, the redness faded until the staff was like before, a metal rod in the old man's left hand.

"Well, well, well," the Curator said. "That was unexpected. Shah Claath has come home. You must have surprised him by coming here."

I nodded.

The Curator smiled and then frowned, seeming to suddenly remember why he'd come down to us. "What happened, Commander?"

"Sir," I said. "I don't mean to be disrespectful, but haven't you been watching what happened with Abaddon and me?"

The Curator eyed my crew. He eyed me and then studied his staff before regarding me again. "Walk with me, Commander. You and I have a few serious matters to discuss."

263

-42-

The door swished shut behind us, leaving the Curator and me alone in the corridor.

"Sir," I said, "the Ve-Ky are attacking your Fortress en masse."

"How many times must I tell you? This is not my place. It is the Creator's Fortress. I am simply the caretaker."

"Yes," I said. "That's what I meant."

"Then please say what you mean. It will make things much easier between us."

"As you wish," I said.

He looked down at me. Then he looked up at the ceiling. "Perhaps I can use your appearance to my benefit. You have Kargs in the upper decks. That is disgusting, to say the least. They are vile creature with a killing lust you cannot conceive of. Oh. No. You *can* conceive of their lust to kill. It possesses you from time to time along with that apishly huge First Admiral of yours. In any regard, the Ve-Ky will soon beach my upper levels, as this is an unprecedented assault. Perhaps I can employ the Kargs for a time."

"Fight fire with fire?" I asked.

"That is an apt saying, perfectly apt," he said. "Now, wait a moment. I have to do this right." He swept his arms wide and stared at the staff in his grip as if it was a problem, then shoved the staff at me. "Hold this a moment, would you?"

I accepted the staff, and almost dropped it on the floor. It was incredibly heavy. I had to use both arms and still found it pressing down like the mythical hammer of Thor. What made this thing so heavy?

Freed of the staff, the Curator spread his arms and wriggled his fingers. As he'd done once before, he produced a ghostly control panel before himself. He began to sweep and tap gracefully. Images passed on ghostly screens. Flashes of light appeared and disappeared. I had no idea what was going on. He began to move his arms and fingers faster and faster. Finally, the process started freaking me out. I wanted to go home. I wanted regular assault trooper work. This stuff was too different.

"There!" the Curator said, clapping his hands. As he did that, the ghostly panel disappeared as if it had never existed.

He plucked the staff from me, tapping it on the deck several times.

"Thank you, my boy," he said. "Let us continue."

"Sir," I said, walking in step beside him, feeling absurdly like a boy walking beside his grandfather.

"Hmmm?" he said.

"If you don't mind me asking, what did you just do?"

"I don't mind. I don't mind at all. I had to reroute the Karg reality. It was much harder than you would expect. They are stubborn things, half alive and half machine. They're not cyborgs as you conceive of them, but a blasphemous mixture. It is quite revolting. In any case, the Kargs are no longer charging down here but flowing back up. They are seeing reality a bit differently from what it is. Soon, they will flow against invading Ve-Ky troopers. It will be a Karg bloodbath. Not that that will stop the Kargs from attacking. In that matter, they are well-suited for the present task. Their seemingly endless assault will give me time. I am sorely pressed, my boy, sorely pressed indeed. It was most fortuitous that you arrived when you did…"

The Curator stopped walking and talking to stare at me. He seemed a shade paler than before, and there was a hint of perspiration on his brow, which I found extremely odd. He used a sleeve to blot his forehead.

"What's wrong?" I asked.

"If you can't see it, I won't explain it."

I had a feeling I did see. "Are you saying my showing up when I did wasn't just by chance but by design?"

"That isn't important to you," he said.

"Maybe it is."

He nodded a moment later. "Yes, maybe it is, at that. I have underestimated you, Commander. Maybe it's time for me to stop doing that. How can I be of service?"

"Surely you witnessed everything," I said.

"Yes! You wounded the egotist. I find it very interesting that Abaddon turned on his Jelk allies. Ah, arrogance brings its own defeat, does it not? I don't mind telling you that that was our hope all along. The First One is the greatest of his kind. Now, he has more of your friends. And he destroyed the disintegrator."

The Curator tightened his grip on the staff. Finally, he lowered the metal rod, extending it to me once more.

"Grab hold, my boy. We're losing time standing here jabbering like monkeys. I'm beginning to understand the situation. The Ve-Ky are attacking in concert with Abaddon's assault on Earth. That's for a purpose. Likely, the Dark One wishes to keep me occupied just a little too long. Are you holding onto the staff?"

I held onto it with both hands.

"Don't let go," he warned.

I nodded.

The staff grew hot. We vanished, reappearing in the same wall-viewing chamber I'd been in before.

The Curator set the staff against a wall. He made several manipulations in the air. The wall-screen shimmered for a time...

"This is bad," the Curator muttered. He stepped away from the giant screen and plucked at his beard. Scowl lines appeared across his forehead.

266

"What's going on?" I asked.

"Shhh," he said. "Let me think." He plucked at his beard more.

His staff vibrated. He glanced at it. Then, he studied me out of the corner of his eye. He pursed his lips as if considering an idea. Finally, he strode to the staff, grasping it.

"Wait here," he said. A second later, he was gone.

What had that been about? I shrugged. It must have been a warning about the Ve-Ky that he'd gone to investigate personally.

I walked to the great wall-screen. It still shimmered. Suddenly, the shimmering lessened. Then, the shimmering lines faded away altogether.

I found myself staring at the Super Fleet. It had regrouped, moving as one toward the next jump gate. It would appear Abaddon was still headed for Earth.

As I watched, my attention kept going to a particular snowflake vessel, to one moth-ship on it. I stared at that ship, and faintly felt Abaddon.

The screen shimmered once more, and I saw into a vast room. Abaddon sat on a throne addressing several larger-than-normal Kargs. The First One grew still until he raised a hand. He looked up, gazing at me.

"Commander Creed," he said.

I noticed that Abaddon's lips moved. That was good to know, as I realized it wasn't mind-to-mind talking, which I would have avoided with extreme prejudice. We spoke person-to-person this time.

The First One had a rich, strong voice. The intelligence of his features added to the nobility of his appearance. He smiled sardonically at me, and his eyes shone.

"You took something of mine," he said.

I found it difficult to speak, impossible to tear my gaze from his.

"Ah..." he said. "You are in the Museum. Have you gone groveling to the old fool there, asking for a new weapon?"

Finally, I forced my lips apart. "What are you?" I said in a rusty voice.

"Your only hope," he said.

"I...almost...killed you."

He peered at me before spreading his arms and slapping his massive chest. "Do I look hurt to you?"

"No."

"No," he said. "I am Abaddon. I am the rightful ruler of this galaxy. Long ago, the others grew afraid of me. Surely, you realize that by now."

"Afraid?" I asked.

"I was too bold, too strong and willful. I dared to go where others feared. I learned more and grew stronger than they did. That is as it should be, as he who dares wins. I dared more than any other. Finally, I went to investigate the Karg Universe. The others were my anchor stone. Foolishly, I still trusted them. Do you know what happened, Commander? The old fool you call the Curator backstabbed me. He cut the connection between my anchor and me. He stranded me in the Karg Universe, hoping to be rid of his chief competitor.

"But I am Abaddon. I am the last of the true First Ones. I learned lessons that no creature should have to learn. The Kargs thought to tame me. The more fools them. I tamed them. First, I had to learn the hard lessons, become greater than I had ever believed possible.

"Oh, how I planned, Commander. How I readied the Kargs for the great and glorious conquest. I knew my day would come. I had merely to survive the eons. While doing so, I had to keep my fierce will alive. This, I have done. That old fool trying to use you has a reason to fear me. I will find him, and I will teach him lessons—"

Abaddon stopped in mid-speech. He stared at me as the hatred seemed to drain out of his eyes.

"You understand revenge, do you not?" Abaddon asked.

I nodded.

"Yes…" he said. "You have thwarted some of my ambitions, Commander. Very few in this life have done so. I suppose you believe that you are safe with that old schemer?"

I didn't know what to say.

Abaddon stroked his right cheek. He smiled, nodding as if with understanding benevolence.

"Commander," he said in a smooth voice. "What is it you seek?"

"The survival of my race," I said.

"I can give that to you."

"I want my people, too, Dmitri, Ella and Jennifer," I added.

I noticed movement to his left. A tall woman with dark hair raised her head. Her eyes burned with wrath.

"Jennifer?" Abaddon asked. "You want Jennifer, even after she has been my prize for so many years?"

"Yes," I said.

"She hates you."

"I don't blame her for that," I said. "She trusted me and I failed her."

"You failed her miserably," he said. "You left her behind. You said you loved her, yet you fled in safety without trying to rescue her."

"You know I couldn't. I was trying to save a galaxy from you."

"And look what happened," he said. "Here I am."

"Yes," I said. "You're here much weaker than otherwise. If it wasn't for me, you'd have trillions of Kargs and billions of starships. You returned with barely enough to hold off the Jelk until you tricked them."

His features become perfectly still. "That was then," he said.

"The past is the past?" I asked sarcastically.

It took him time, but he nodded.

"How come I don't believe you?" I asked.

He stared at me. Finally, he smiled. It was full of malice, full of hatred.

"You don't believe me because you know that for you, there is no forgiveness. Jennifer loathes you with a bitterness you cannot understand. She will cut open your belly and pull out your guts, laughing the entire time."

"That's nice," I said, feeling myself beginning to get angry.

"I have taught her things, Commander, wicked and evil things that have seared her innocent nature. She knows what it is to hate. You humans, you think you know how to hate, but you have little idea. It takes someone like me, a powerful, long-lived entity to truly grasp the concept. Too often, hate weakens a human. I have taught Jennifer the hatred that gives strength. It is like unto my strength."

"You hate me?" I asked.

"Yes," Abaddon hissed. "I hate you, Commander. I will wreak a fearsome vengeance upon you. You are already starting to realize this. I have taken your friends one by one. I will take more. They will all spit on your groveling form in time. Do you know, *Commander Creed*, that I shall kick your mewling form from one of my ships to another? There is nothing you can do to change this fate."

"I don't want to change it," I said. "I want you to hate me with everything you have. I thwarted you, Abaddon. I stopped your great plan of vengeance. I made sure you entered this space-time continuum as a weakling compared to how you could have entered as a conquering god. I did that to you, me, Commander Creed."

His eyes began to swirl with power.

I forced myself to laugh. "That's right, big shot. A mere human thwarted your will. You call yourself a First One. You're a fool. You're a dull-witted strategist. I didn't even do any deep thinking. I just showed up and, boom, everything you planned to do for countless centuries vanished."

"Bring them!" he shouted to his minions. "You!" he said, pointing at me.

I slapped my chest. "That's right, me, Commander Creed. I'm the guy who did you in, Abaddon. I'm the guy who shot you with the disintegrator, made you feel pain. And you know what? I'm going to make you feel pain again and again."

"I don't think so, mortal."

"I bet that's what you thought heading for the portal planet the first time. You told yourself how you could hardly wait to get back to my space-time continuum and kick some serious butt. How did it feel knowing the portal had closed on all your vast ambitions? Do you remember how you raged at me for that? Do you recall the sinking feeling in the pit of your pathetic gut?"

"Bring me his people!" Abaddon roared.

Abaddon had a volcanic temper. At this point, I didn't care. I hated him. I realized my helplessness to save my friends. I thought, I suppose, deep in my heart, that if I goaded him enough, he would kill them cleanly before they had to suffer a lifetime of torturous agony.

-43-

Suddenly, the wall screen shimmered again. It felt as if Abaddon's rage had grown so hot that he'd lost some of his mental control over the process.

The Curator instantly reappeared, almost as if he'd been waiting for this to happen. He dropped a bundle onto the floor, and he gave me such a look that I knew fear and trepidation.

I noticed something odd, too. He had a long handle stuck in his belt.

"We have little time," the Curator said. "I guessed right concerning you and him. Abaddon wants to torture you, Commander, almost as badly as he would like to do so to me. I am the one who cut his anchor, of course. I'm sure you've divined that by now."

I nodded.

"Do you willingly agree to become my effectuator?" he asked.

"I don't know what that means."

"Yes you do. Decide this instant, or it will be too late."

Strangely, I had a feeling I did know what he meant. He wanted me to become his errand boy, his troubleshooter. I'm not sure how long I was supposed to do that or in what capacity. I had a feeling it was going to take me away from the assault troopers and from Earth...possibly for the rest of my life.

By agreeing, I would buy an opportunity to kill Abaddon and free humanity from extinction. How could I say no? And yet, this would be a grave responsibility. I didn't seem like the right person for the job, not even the right kind of person.

"Yeah, I'm in," I said.

"You swear this?"

"I swear it."

"We must hurry, as we have seconds to do this. Put that on," he said, indicating the bundle on the floor.

I dashed to it, finding a jangling garment with metallic bands on the sleeves. I put it on, sealing the front against me, finding it much too big. Then the suit molded itself to my form almost like bio-skin until it fit from neck to toe like a leotard.

"What is this?" I asked.

"It is like your bio-skin in many ways, but it is more advanced and many times more powerful. You are going to need it in a moment."

Before I could ask more, the Curator took the handle out of his belt, handing it to me.

I accepted it. The handle had several buttons on it.

"That is possibly the last weapon I possess that might be able to slay Abaddon," he said. "Nothing else I have is as powerful. It is a Forerunner artifact, possibly more deadly than Holgotha. You depress the buttons in a selected sequence. A force blade of unbelievable magnitude will flow outward."

"This is a sword?"

"It is more than any sword, I assure you."

I stared at it as a feeling of awe made me shiver. "Is this like the flaming sword the angel waved while guarding Eden from Adam and Eve?"

"Your weapon has mythic properties," the Curator said. "Which is as it should be, as you will face a mythic foe. Do the two not suit each other?"

"I guess so."

The Curator breathed deeply. "Listen to me, my boy. The way is going to open soon."

"The wall screen is more than just a screen?" I asked.

"Yes."

"You're going to teleport me through to kill Abaddon?"

"Are you willing to do this?"

"Can I actually slay him?"

"You have the tools," the Curator said. "Whether or not you have the ability, even I do not know."

"Can you pull me back if I start to lose?"

"Not through the one-way teleporter," he said. "If I had more time—I am beset by the Ve-Ky. The Kargs haven't exited the Survey Vessel yet—"

He stopped talking, as the shimmering on the screen lessened.

"Good luck, Commander Creed. I bid you go in the Creator's name. Kill this upstart First One, and I can begin to repair the damage he wrought millennia ago."

"What if Abaddon kills me and grabs these Forerunner items?"

The Curator frowned as his shoulders slumped. "Then, I'm afraid, that I will never defeat him. In time, he will reach and kill me. This is it, Commander. This is the moment of decision. If you win, it is likely you can save your friends. Lose, and I'm afraid that Abaddon will take humanity and turn them into his chief servants."

"Do you have any last words of advice?" I asked.

"The combination to the force blade is two-two-three-one," he said.

"Got it," I said.

"Do not let him into your mind."

"How do I stop that?" I asked.

"By becoming so angry that your rage acts as a shield against his thoughts," he said.

Something must have caught his attention. The Curator glanced sharply at the wall screen. "No! The way is clearing too soon. I had hoped to surprise him. You have goaded him as only you can do, Commander. Ready yourself. Don't unleash the force blade until you're on his ship."

The Curator waved his arms, bringing a ghostly control before him. He tapped wildly as the wall screen became clear.

Abaddon was standing. Dmitri and Ella stood before him. Jennifer was to the side. Thirty big Kargs were in the chamber with them.

Abaddon peered at me, and shock filled him as he glanced at the Curator. "You!" he cried.

The Curator kept manipulating his ghostly screen.

"What are you doing, brother?" Abaddon shouted.

Brother? Were Abaddon and the Curator brothers? What was going on here?

"Go!" the Curator shouted at me. "It is time, and I can't keep the way open long."

"Open?" Abaddon asked.

I gripped the handle, gathered my resolve and shouted at the top of my lungs. Then, I raced toward my probable doom. This seemed like insanity. I dashed at the wall, jumping, and I felt myself flowing through. It felt as if I stretched longer and longer. I—

Stumbling into the great chamber on the moth-ship, I faced Abaddon. I could smell the Kargs as I began to press the buttons on my Forerunner artifact handle: two-two-three-one.

-44-

A pure force of energy grew from the Forerunner artifact handle. It radiated an intense bar of light about a meter in length while making a faint humming sound.

At the same time, my suit vibrated, filling me with strength and vitality. I felt light, as if I floated on the deck. I glanced down to see if that was the case. No. I stood just as I had been. Yet, my feet had a halo glowing around them. That must have been from the suit and obviously indicated something.

"Kill him," Abaddon said slowly, as if he had trouble mouthing the words.

I looked up as the big Karg leaders with their metallic tentacles leveled heavy slug-throwers at me. One after another, they fired, making garbled sounds. To my amazement, I could almost see the slugs flying through the air—they were streaks of motion. The astonishment almost froze me. I barely shook off the reverie in time, sidestepping the first bullet.

Was that right? Was that what I was doing? Everything seemed to slow down for me the longer I looked. Maybe it took a few seconds for the suit to fully power up. The Kargs moved sluggishly, Abaddon spoke in a garbled manner and my friends stood frozen in shock.

I sidestepped more slugs. It was becoming easier as they were no longer blurs in the air but actual moving bullets I could see.

I considered that as I slid to the left and right again and again. I didn't glance back to see where the bullets went. I was too focused on moving forward.

I'd speeded up. That was the only explanation that made sense. As I realized that, I wondered how long I could do something like this. I suspected this would tax my muscles and maybe my bodily systems. Once I took off the suit, would I ache for weeks, for months? Maybe I'd have a heart attack due to over-straining myself.

I gave a short bark of laughter. If this was it—a trade—my life for Abaddon's death and the life of my friends—I had no problem with that.

Let's get it straight. I didn't want to die. I yearned to live in those moments more than I ever had. I wanted to walk the Earth again. I wanted to free Jennifer from the horrors Abaddon had twisted in her mind. I wanted her to forgive me for leaving her behind those many years ago. At the very least, I wanted to tell her I was sorry for doing that.

I'm sure that might be hard for some of you to believe. I imagine that by the way I've told my life's story, more than a few of you think I was a self-indulgent jerk. Maybe that was true. Maybe I'd acted too harshly along the way, but that's what the situations had called for. Saving mankind hadn't been a task for a nice guy with nice manners.

My hand tightened around the Forerunner handle. I wanted to live. That's what you have to believe. But the old rage had ignited on the Fortress of Light. I burned with a desire to kill Abaddon. I'd goaded the big bastard. I wanted him to seethe with the desire to defeat me. That way, if I won, I could laugh in his face, and it would torment him immensely.

I was going to chop off his head if I could. I'd read the story of David and Goliath before. The shepherd boy David had used his sling to conk Goliath on the forehead. The big bad Philistine had crashed to the earth. That's when the shepherd boy scampered to the mighty champion and drew the giant's massive sword. With it, David had hacked off the head. According to the story in the Good Book, David had held Goliath's bloody head by the hair while he'd spoken to the Israelite King Saul.

That's what I wanted to do to Abaddon. I wanted to go back to the Fortress of Light and show the Curator—

A different thought struck. Abaddon was the Curator's brother. Maybe the old man in the center of the galaxy would take it ill if I showed him his brother's severed head.

I kept slip-sliding closer to the throne, closer to the Kargs, who ever so slowly shoved new magazines into their slug-throwers.

Dmitri had begun shouting my name. Ella's eyes were still wide at the sight of me.

I had become the avenger. I bore weapons of light against the monster of darkness.

Abaddon stood. He did it quicker than anyone else had moved in the chamber. The meaning of that hadn't dawned on me yet. I was too focused on my thoughts of holding his severed head.

The first faint flickering of his mind power touched my thoughts. It was an intrusion, like that noise in the night that made you wonder, made you frown and think about whipping off the covers so you could go check it out. The floorboard creak became like footsteps. Then it turned into a shout and an outline of a stalker in your bedroom, cradling a shotgun as he threatened to tie you up and rape your wife in front of your eyes.

I suppose any of a number of things could have happened at that moment. The suddenness of Abaddon's mind assault might have frozen me. That would allow the Kargs to riddle my body with slugs.

When I'd been in high school I'd had a bad dream. I'd felt as if I'd woken up and felt a grim presence of evil standing by the foot of my bed. It had watched me. I'd been frozen in fear at that, unable to move or speak. Then the curtains beside my bed fluttered. I'd known that someone was sneaking in through the window. With great terror, I'd shouted, lunging upward from my bed, trying to grab the intruder before he shot me.

Back then, I'd woken myself up from the nightmare. The curtains had been fluttering because I'd forgotten to shut my window. The presence of evil had also departed.

That same kind of evil feeling slammed against my mind now.

Creed!

Abaddon spoke in my mind.

I stared at the creature who was five times my size. His eyes burned with authority, with evil that threatened to steal my courage. I knew, though, that if I faltered, he would tie me up. He would do worse than rape my wife before my eyes.

Rage swept through my being. It was a righteous force that pulsated with desire. The demon from another space-time continuum had toyed with me for the last time. He had screwed with my friends for the last time.

My hatred blocked his mind talk. It sealed me in my own universe. I did not go berserk. Instead, a cold and ruthless fury motivated my actions.

Abaddon concentrated on me, as two left-hand fingertips touched his forehead.

I moved sharply to the right. I don't know what the Karg leaders saw. Maybe I moved in the flick of an eye to them. Reaching the first anti-life creature, I swung the meter-length force blade.

The Karg fell into two halves as gouts of machine oil spilled from his carcass.

The next few moments were a blur of action. I slaughtered Kargs. They were no match for the avenger from the Fortress of Light.

Jennifer leaped at me. She moved faster than the Kargs but slower than me. Her knife gleamed with electric power.

I swatted the knife with my force blade, destroying it. Then, I side-stepped her next leap. She fell toward the deck. In the slow-motion time it took her to reach the floor, I slaughtered another seven Kargs.

From the deck, she looked up at me.

I knelt beside her for just a moment. "I'm sorry," I said.

Her eyes burned hotter with anger.

"I should have gone back for you," I spoke, doing it as slowly as I could. "Now, I have come for you, Jennifer. After this is over, I'll take you away."

"Liar," she said slowly, as if she had to force out the words.

I didn't have any more time for her. Abaddon used another mind trick, this one a blast of knotted pain.

I shot to my feet and staggered backward.

You cannot win, Abaddon said in my head.

I slammed against a wall, lowered my head and let the coldness of my rage fill me once more. My tenderness toward Jennifer had given the First One an opening. With the rage, I shoved his thoughts out of my mind, sealing them behind a glacial wall.

My head rose and maybe my eyes blazed with cold fire. A new fervor had ignited in me.

"I see," Abaddon said, turning, heading for the back of his throne.

"Run, First One," I said.

"You are mistaken, puppet." He raised a long handle from behind the throne. His fingers pressed buttons. The long handle buzzed with noise. A flickering force axe appeared. His was not a pure energy like mine, but red and sizzling. His artifact felt older than mine, much older.

I strode at him, building up speed as I crossed the chamber.

"Look at him race to his death," Abaddon said. "He cannot wait to die."

I charged him, knowing that he was likely the greatest and most dangerous entity in existence. He had powers of which I couldn't conceive. A personal force shield protected him. He was huge. He could teleport, and I had no doubt he was many times stronger than me. What's more, his force axe could surely shred my amazing suit.

I would like to say that I didn't care, but that would be a lie. When fighting the prince of liars, it seemed like a poor policy to practice his strengths.

I was afraid, but that fear was in a citadel of determination surrounded by a vast moat of icy hatred. The fear watched from a distant vantage point inside of me.

He swung the axe. I dared to parry. The two energy forces crackled with power. His strength and speed caused me to fly backward and slam hard against a bulkhead.

Abaddon laughed with malice. "I had forgotten the joy of hand-to-hand combat. You are a gnat, Commander. You cannot defeat me."

I rose stiffly. I should have broken bones. Maybe the suit helped absorb some of the shock. The remaining Kargs seemed to move a little faster than before. Their bullets were streaks in the air again.

Was my suit losing power?

I couldn't worry about that. I was here to win or die, and I'd better win.

This time, I approached warily.

"Yes," Abaddon said, "you're learning."

At that point, two Kargs lying on the deck as if dead fired their slug-throwers. I heard the shots, turned and dodged the first bullet. The second ploughed into my suit's force field. That showed the bullet long enough for me shift aside. I also noticed an appreciable quickening in my opponents.

My suit couldn't do that too many more times, or I would be moving at normal speed again.

I would have raced to kill the Kargs, but Abaddon attacked, swinging the force axe.

I dodged. I parried indirectly, not taking the full brunt of the axe-blow, but using my force blade to redirect one of his swings.

More shots fired behind me. I couldn't turn, however. Abaddon pressed me too closely. At any moment, I expected to hear the sizzle of my suit's force shield and feel myself slow down.

That didn't happen.

Abaddon's force axe swished past me as I dodged and buried itself into the deck, crackling with power.

I used the opportunity, twisting around, wondering why the Kargs hadn't finished me. Both of them were slumped on the deck as if really dead this time, with bullet holes in them that leaked oil.

Dmitri raised a heavy slug-thrower. My friend had broken his restraints. Clearly, he had shot those two Kargs. Maybe he'd helped Ella, too. She picked up a slug-thrower from a dead Karg.

Abaddon tore the axe blade free. He bellowed and charged me.

The next few seconds were the most desperate of my life. I weaved and dodged, parried and kept death at bay by the barest of fractions each time. Twice, my force shield sizzled as his red energy blade sparked against it.

I staggered away as Dmitri and Ella fired slugs at Abaddon. The First One swatted a bullet away. Another made his force shield glow with power as it devoured the slug.

I think Abaddon realized it would hurt him having them firing at him while battling me. Thus, he halted, produced a halo around himself and disappeared.

"Look out!" I shouted.

The First One appeared by Dmitri, swinging. The Cossack tried to block with his slug-thrower. The force axe sheered through the weapon and sliced Dmitri in two, each half thudding bloodily onto the deck.

Ella scrambled madly out of the way.

"No!" I howled. "Dmitri!"

I charged Abaddon, and my rage was no longer cold, but hot. I attacked recklessly, my force blade a blur. Abaddon back-pedaled, blocked a swing, sidestepped and blocked another.

I felt myself tiring fast, but I wanted vengeance for Dmitri Rostov. The Cossack had just saved my life, and I'd let him die. I could no longer bear that.

"Fiend!" I shouted, lunging cobra-quick.

This time, Abaddon didn't parry or jump back fast enough. The tip of my force blade penetrated his personal shield. They both sizzled and sparked, and I felt stiffening resistance, but I was determined. With a grunt, I shoved my force-blade tip into his darkened flesh at the hip, burning into skin and muscle.

His force axe chopped down. Our two energy weapons roared with a flash. It hurled him backward and caused me to tumble head over heels.

I found myself panting on the deck. My Forerunner artifact lay several meters from me. The handle was molten and dripping, destroyed.

His longer handle still seemed whole, although the red-powered force axe was no longer in play.

With a groan, Abaddon sat up.

I tried to do likewise, but found that my muscles refused to obey my will. Was I already paying the price for over-exerting my body?

Abaddon worked up to his feet, panting, his face contorted with pain.

Ella aimed her Karg rifle at him.

"No," he told her. "Put it on the deck."

Ella moaned, trembling horribly, trying to fight the command. She could not, at last placing the rifle on the deck. She slumped after that, holding her face in her hands, weeping softly.

"You fought better than I expected," Abaddon told me. "But it wasn't good enough to defeat the greatest being in the universe."

He was right, but at least I'd hurt him. That was something, wasn't it?

As if to punctuate the thought, the huge First One put a hand on the hip wound, groaning as he did. He took his hand away. It was dark with blood.

"You will pay for this, mortal," Abaddon said. "You will—" He quit in mid-sentence, staring in shock at something behind me.

I twisted my head to see what the First One was staring at. My jaw dropped at the sight.

The Curator stood in the chamber. His blue robe glowed and his hair floated. He held his heavy metal rod with both hands.

"Brother," Abaddon said with scorn.

The Curator did not speak. His blue eyes blazed with wrath. He seemed the essence of grim justice. He aimed the staff as if it was a weapon.

I realized then that it had been buzzing. Now, a gout of power flowed from the end. The raw energy struck Abaddon in the chest. The First One howled in agony. I had the feeling his armor and personal shield had weakened, allowing this energy to strike his being directly. The giant First One howled and put his hands in front of the beam. He must have summoned something from inside of him, for he blocked the surge of power, shoving it back a meter from him. The power from the staff kept pouring out, however, beginning to incrementally push the block back at Abaddon. The First One's massive shoulders hunched and his head lowered. His blocking power bushed the gush of energy back a centimeter and then another. Could he shove the power all the way back to the staff? Would that destroy the weapon?

The Curator's fingers manipulated the metal staff. The buzzing sound quickened until the rod screeched with energy. It shook so violently it seemed the Curator had to fight to hold it, like a fireman wrestling a powerful hose. The gout of raw destroying force became a torrent. It shoved Abaddon's blockage back, back and back some more.

"No!" Abaddon howled. "None thwarts me! None!"

The facts proved otherwise. The raw power reached his hands, melting them. Yet still Abaddon resisted, using his mental strength. His face had screwed up into a mask of agony. Then, the staff's energy began to devour the First One's wrists, crawling up and destroying the forearms.

All at once, the blocking force collapsed. The torrent gushed upon Abaddon with full force. For a second, nothing happened. Then, a titanic explosion blew the First One apart. It was bloody and sickening and incredibly final.

Abaddon was dead and gone like that. It was amazing and unexpected. After all I'd been through, after witnessing Dmitri's horrible death, we'd done it, or the Curator had.

At that point, my forehead slumped against the deck as I fell unconscious.

-45-

I woke up in a bed. It was soft with smooth sheets and a smoother blanket. It felt good to be between them. Robins tweeted outside. They sang from the branches of an old oak tree.

I lay there absorbing the goodness, glad to be doing nothing at all. I'm not sure how long I lay like that. Finally, though, I shifted my position. I thought about Abaddon and the Curator's staff. What had powered the annihilating energy bolt?

Is that why the old man had sucked up Claath before? Had the staff used several Jelk to make that beam? Had Claath been the final ingredient, the final topping off of the gas tank, as it were?

I had a sneaking suspicion that was it.

As I lay there, I looked around the room. It reminded me of my bedroom as a teenager. There was the same dresser, the same tennis shoes on the floor. There was a poster of Josey Wales—Clint Eastwood—holding his six-shooters just as it had been in my old bedroom. There was another of my favorite Budweiser swimsuit model—

Wait a minute. This was *exactly* like my old bedroom.

I reached to whip back the covers. My arm, the muscles and tendons, were just a wee bit stiff. I wondered how long I'd been lying here. I moved my arm under the covers, flexing the muscles. It felt as if they had been sore, very sore, but had now almost recovered.

In any case, I pulled back the covers and checked out my bicep. It was huge, deformed long ago by steroid-68. That meant I wasn't in my old bedroom at home. It meant this all wasn't a strange bad dream I'd been having about aliens, bio-terminators and Forerunner artifacts. That meant—

The door swung open and the Curator stepped inside. I smiled until a terrible sinking feeling swept over me. I'd made an oath before leaving for Abaddon's moth-ship. I had agreed to become the Curator's effectuator, whatever that was supposed to mean. Did that mean I'd never see my friends or the sweet Earth again?

"How are you feeling?" the Curator asked.

"I'm alive," I said.

He pulled up a chair with an old leather jacket draped on the back. The Curator sat beside the bed as if he were my grandfather.

"You don't seem to be too happy about winning," he said.

"Is Abaddon truly dead?"

The old man's features clouded. At last, he nodded.

"Was Abaddon really your brother?"

"Come," the Curator said, "let us speak about other matters. That one is too sore for me."

I struggled to a sitting position. I was more tired than I realized.

"I fought for you," I said.

He took his time answering. "Yes and no," he finally said. "You primarily fought to save the human race." He grew thoughtful. "I might add that the Earth isn't out of danger yet."

"Why's that?" I asked. "We killed Abaddon."

"Yes. But the Super Fleet still exists. It is true there was a short, sharp struggle for power in the fleet, but a Karg Overlord has emerged. He is still taking the Super Fleet to

Earth. I would imagine so he can destroy the planet and humanity with it."

"The way you're saying this," I said, "it sounds as if you're willing to let me go back to help with the defense?"

"Why wouldn't I?"

I opened my mouth, reconsidered what I was about to say and closed it again. A feeling of shame bit, though. It was so foreign to me that I almost didn't know what it represented. The key word there was almost. I did know.

I sighed, wondering what was wrong with me. "Look," I said. "I made an oath. I'm your hitman or something, remember?"

"I recall the oath," he said. "But I believe I'm going to modify it."

"What does that mean? Wait. Before we get into that, I want to know more about Abaddon. I want to understand about the Jelk. Did Claath die in your staff so you could blast—?"

"Please," the Curator said, holding up his hands. "Let's deal with one question at a time. Yes, Shah Claath died. Yes, he and other Jelk powered the blast, as you put it. I had to wait to make my assault until you had drained Abaddon's power sufficiently. I also needed the Karg bodyguards out of the way. That was a courageous and cunning assault, by the way. I congratulate you, Commander. You are a dangerous opponent."

"I'm a *little killer*, remember? Now, I would dearly like to know what the little killers are?"

"Humans," he said.

"I understand that much. How did we become the little killers, though? What does that mean exactly?"

The Curator studied me, finally nodding. "You are little in comparison to bigger beings. In this case, that would be the First Ones."

"We're like you?"

He nodded.

"But...what are you?"

"The First Ones," he said. "I won't say more on the subject. We had our jobs. We did them, more or less, and some of us... Well, that doesn't matter today. You are like us in many ways, just smaller, weaker and not as intelligent."

"Thanks a lot," I said.

"Does the truth bother you?"

"Nice counter-punch," I said. "I suppose it does, but it shouldn't. The truth is the truth. But why were we called killers?"

"It's one of the things you seem to do better than any other race."

"Do you know why that is?" I asked.

The Curator shrugged.

"So...what happens next?" I asked.

"You will leave this place," he said. "I will also take back my Survey Vessel."

"Did you beat back the Ve-Ky assault?"

"It was difficult, but the million Kargs helped. Their vicious counterattacks gave me time to remember..." He smiled, shaking his head.

"You don't like to say more than you have to, do you?" I said.

"You're heading back to the fringe," he said. "Thus, too much knowledge can be a bad thing for everyone. By the way, I'll be taking the Forerunner artifacts like Holgotha back with me. I didn't have a way to enforce that before, but a few items from Abaddon's flagship will prove useful in that regard."

"Dmitri is dead," I said, feeling rotten all over again.

"That is true. However, if ever there was a noble death, it was his. He died helping to save the galaxy from an extended reign of evil. He died to give you a fighting chance to save the human race."

"Only a chance?" I asked.

"An extremely powerful fleet is headed to Earth. The Karg Overlord has decided he can't annihilate the Jade League without first eliminating the little killers."

I thought about that and about Holgotha's prediction concerning our odds if we could first eliminate Abaddon. Even given that condition, the Forerunner artifact had given us terrible odds for winning.

"Do we have more than a ghost of a chance of defeating the Super Fleet?"

The Curator plucked at his beard. "I dislike interfering in such matters, as I am the Watchman. I have studied the various elements, though. If the Grand Armada could reach Earth first, you would have a fighting chance. To bring that about, the Earthlings and Starkiens would have to slow down the enemy's advance to buy the Grand Armada the needed time."

"When do I leave?"

"In a few hours," he said. "I'll take you in the Survey Vessel, of course, leaving you on...Mars, I suppose."

I thought about that, about Dmitri and... "How's Jennifer?" I asked.

The Curator looked away.

"Is she dead?" I asked.

"That's an interesting question."

"Please," I said. "Let's stop with the veiled references."

"Fair enough," he said. "The Jennifer you know is long gone. The person in her body is quite different and will never... It's doubtful she will ever accept you no matter how well I can rehabilitate her. By that, I mean for her to see you will always mean her wanting to kill you."

"You can't ever change that?"

"Given a normal lifespan, I don't think so. In several hundred years possibly..." He shrugged.

"I'm going to live several hundred years?"

"No."

I frowned. "But Jennifer will live that long?"

"If she avoids any unforeseen accidents, yes," he said.

"But...how can she live that long? Did Abaddon modify her?"

"He did, but not in that way. She will live those extra years because I'm keeping her in the Fortress of Light."

"Hey," I said, sitting straighter.

"Calm yourself, Commander. It is for the best."

"But...I wanted to tell her..." I fell silent, brooding.

A person doesn't always get what they want. I'd wanted to defeat Abaddon with all my friends still alive. That hadn't happened. Good old Dmitri Rostov was dead. I would miss my old friend. I would miss his cheerfulness. It seemed so wrong that he was dead. He had been with me from the beginning of this grand adventure.

Now, Jennifer would be taken from me yet again. Yet...maybe only the Curator had the tools to restore her. Weren't my desires regarding her selfish. I wanted her to love me again. I wanted her to understand why I'd done what I had back at the portal planet. What did Jennifer want in this life other than slitting my belly? The Curator seemed like her best bet at becoming normal again. I should give her that.

I didn't have to feel bad about this then.

"Will I ever see her again?" I asked.

"Perhaps if I call you to my service," the Curator said.

I had so many questions I wanted to ask. The critical factor for me though was the Super Fleet. Despite Abaddon's death, it was still zeroed in on Earth like a guided missile. A feeling of deja vu struck. This seemed an awful lot like the Purple Emperor coming to destroy Earth three years ago. But this time I didn't have a way to end everything with a royal duel. This time, I'd have to defeat the enemy fleet with our supposedly inferior but more numerous starships.

I looked up at the Curator. "I have two requests before I go, and one before you take me back to Mars."

"What are they?" he asked.

I told him.

He looked away. "Your requests smack too closely of interference on my part."

"After what I've done for you, you can't do this for me?"

He glanced at me, frowning. Had I gone too far? "Very well," he said heavily. "But we will have to hurry."

-46-

Before I began my great task, I had an obligation to take care of. I'd been thinking about it as the Curator had spoken to me.

I would leave the Fortress of Light, but Jennifer would stay behind.

She hated me. I'd seen that with my own eyes. It had been difficult to take. Out of all of my actions during my life, leaving Jennifer behind on the portal planet had felt the worst. It rankled in my spirit.

I'd lived hard. I'd taken little to no crap from anyone. Yet, I had learned a lesson in life. When one was truly at fault, and when one accepted in his heart that he was a fault, it was good to admit it.

I opened a door in a special area of the Fortress. I walked softly, entering the dark chamber.

"Dim light," I said.

A dim light filled the room. I could see Jennifer asleep in a horizontal glass tube. Alongside her were banks of medical equipment and monitors. She had several medical tubes in her arms and a band over her forehead.

I approached the glass with a host of conflicting emotions roiling in my heart. For a brief time in my life, I'd had my true love. I looked through the glass at Jennifer. I hardly recognized her. Abaddon had done so much to modify her. Jennifer had never deserved this.

293

I swallowed hard.

I'd put her out of my mind many years ago because I couldn't stand the guilt otherwise. Now, gazing down at her—

I closed my eyes. For several breaths…what do you want to hear? I'd failed Jennifer. I'd left her behind in the hands of the devil. I hadn't had any choice in the matter. If I'd done otherwise—

I opened my eyes and I put both hand on the warm tube, looking down at her.

"I don't think you can hear me," I said. "But maybe in some manner you will know I came by. Jennifer, honey, I'm so sorry I left you behind. It was wrong. I had no choice. I wish you could forgive me. I realize you can't, and that's…that's what it is. I hope you find peace here at the Fortress of Light. I hope you find what Abaddon stole from you. I don't think you'd feel better after killing me, but heck, maybe you would. Maybe I should offer you my throat to show you how bad I feel."

I exhaled, turning away from her.

"I'm sorry," I said. "I love you, for whatever that's worth. Maybe someday we'll meet again after the Curator has healed your mind. Can someone untwist all the bad things Abaddon did to you? That seems like a monumental task. I'm glad the Curator is keeping you. I was going to have Ella put you under the Jelk mind machine. I think that would have been wrong, though."

I frowned. I was running out of time. What else could I tell her?

The door opened. The Curator looked in.

"Give me just a few more seconds, would you?" I said.

He nodded, closing the door behind him.

I turned and looked down at Jennifer for what could be the last time. My heart was heavy, but I was glad I could see her and tell her how sorry I was.

I wanted to open the tube. I wanted to kiss her, touch her and hold her tight. I wanted to stroke her cheek and tell her

294

that everything was going to be okay. Instead, as I'd done on the portal planet, I left her behind.

Does that make me sound bitter? I guess I was. I suppose it was impossible to fix every wrong. It left me determined to be grateful for what I had when I had it. I should have enjoyed Jennifer's company more in the little time we had together.

"Good-bye," I said.

Then, I hurried out of the chamber. I couldn't take any more of this.

***

The Curator stood beside me in the viewing chamber. He showed me the Super Fleet.

It was big, just as it always had been. Still, it was missing a few gigantic snowflake motherships and some battlejumpers. The old man had shown me the wreckages that had come from the brief power struggle.

Alexander the Great had been one of Earth's greatest conquerors. He had marched through the Persian Empire and later added parts of India to his vast realm. He'd had big plans for Carthage and the rest of the western Mediterranean but had died of a fever before he could implement them. Some figured he might have died by poisoning. Alexander had left some of the world's toughest generals behind, and they'd soon had a falling out with each other. The greatest of them had picked parts of the vast realm, setting up independent states. Those states had fought the Successor Wars.

My point is that Alexander's generals hadn't stayed together to increase the conqueror's realm.

Abaddon's Super Fleet was staying together. Clearly, there had been a short, sharp fight among some of the leaders. No doubt, the fight had determined who would rule, who would obey and who had to die. This Karg Overlord must be several times stronger, smarter, tougher or more ruthless than his competitors. He'd quashed them. That would seem to include whatever Jelk had remained with the fleet. Otherwise, those battlejumpers would have gone elsewhere with their Saurian crews.

I studied the enemy fleet. I made notes, recording them with my Lokhar-made tablet.

"Can you show me their likely route to Earth?" I asked.

The Curator looked down at me with an unblinking stare.

"Does that mean no?" I asked.

"You are stretching my limits," he said at last.

"I don't mean to."

"Nevertheless," he said.

I went back to studying the fleet, using what time I had left.

Then old man sighed, surprising me as he showed me the most likely route to the Solar System.

I made sure to keep the alien recorder going. I was going to use this data to try to figure out a way to beat them and save humanity once again.

-47-

So…Claath and Abaddon were dead. Jennifer was free from her enforced servitude and in the best place in the galaxy where she might rehabilitate her body, mind and spirit.

I'd achieved some of my greatest desires. The most important want, however, was yet to be fulfilled. The Earth, and humanity with it, was under a dire threat. As far as I could see, this was the big one that might solve a lot of our future problems. If the Jade League could annihilate the Karg-Jelk Super Fleet, we could finish off the Jelk Corporation for good. Humanity could then start thinking about colonizing the nearest Jelk frontier planets.

I had been to Sagittarius A* and back. I'd been in hyperspace before and another space-time continuum. I'd handled weapons and worn suits that belonged in a super-science museum. As Star Vikings, we'd teleported on a Forerunner artifact. Later, as Earth Force assault troopers, we'd teleported inside an ancient Survey Vessel and had used incredible T-suits.

In the end, though, I was back to bio-skin assault troopers, shuttles and starships, and I was back to the friends humanity had made these past years.

The Curator's Survey Vessel made a slight detour before taking us to Mars. It transferred to the Pollux System, the present location of the Grand Armada. It contained an even greater number of warships than the Super Fleet.

Our appearance caused a commotion in the vast armada until I spoke via screen to the commanding Baron Visconti of Orange Tamika. In the past, we'd worked together while facing Purple Tamika's monster fleet.

Visconti was a good tiger and one of the biggest I'd ever met. The Lokhar stood a good seven and a half feet tall, a towering individual. Even better, he had the widest and deepest chest I'd ever seen on a Lokhar.

Baron Visconti was the armada's Lord Admiral and wore a tight-fitting uniform with several medals for courage and cunning.

The Grand Armada had a multitude of vessels from the various races that made up the Jade League. It had masses of pursuit destroyers, hordes of strike and attack cruisers and an unbelievable number of mainline carriers. Yet for all that, its real power lay in the Orange and Purple Tamika specialty vessels. Orange Tamika fielded maulers. They were round vessels with five times the mass of a battlejumper.

All the Grand Armada's battlejumpers belonged to the Earth Force contingent, by the way.

In any case, maulers were heavy hitters, able to absorb an appalling amount of damage and still keep coming. Yet, they weren't the largest ships in the Grand Armada. That went to the Purple Tamika bombards. They had massively armored hulls and double-strength shields. Their weakness was a lack of speed. They were best used in massed battles.

In many ways, the Grand Armada was like an old-style Greek phalanx. It did best in head-to-head encounters. Many space battles, however, were more hit-and-run or hide-and-ambush affairs.

Could we get this mass in front of the Super Fleet and force the enemy to fight the way we wanted? Those were pretty big ifs.

"We have little time for such a delay," the Curator told me.

"Give me an hour with them, no more," I said.

"An hour," he said sourly.

I still spoke via screen to Baron Visconti and told him I'd like to meet on his flagship. He agreed.

Soon, N7 and I flew in a shuttle to Visconti's flagship mauler. It felt strange marching down a Lokhar battle-craft again. The old tiger smells, the fierce looks they gave me…it brought back memories, all right.

I wore my most stylish uniform with the .44 on my hip. The Lokhars viewed my Magnum with something approaching awe.

I entered a large conference chamber. I saw old Admiral Saris of Purple Tamika and others I recognized from years ago.

Baron Visconti approached. He'd put on weight since I'd last seen him, and there were streaks of white in his facial fur. He was still impressive, maybe more so.

We embraced and shook hands. Then, I scanned the throng. "I have little time," I told them. "And I'm not sure you'll believe all I've been through. Here's the key part. Abaddon is dead."

That created a stir and then bedlam.

After half a minute of excited chatter among those present, the baron rose. He'd sat down once I'd begun addressing the assembly. Visconti roared in a loud voice as only Lokhars can do, bringing silence to the great chamber. It was a good thing, too, as I'd been about to fire my .44 to get their attention.

"You said you are in a rush, Commander," Visconti said.

I nodded.

"And your moon-ship…appeared before the armada like a Forerunner artifact. It also fits the description of the attack vessel that raided many of our star systems."

I stared at the assembled tigers, Ilk and others. I'd been wondering for some time how to get them to listen and do what I told them without hours of convincing. Finally, I took out my recorder and showed them a holographic image of the enemy's Super Fleet.

That got their attention in a hurry.

"If you'll listen to me," I said, "I'll tell you how to defeat the Karg-Jelk Invasion Fleet."

"We are listening," Visconti told me.

I began to tell them how to do the improbable.

***

Afterward, I returned to the Survey Vessel. An hour later, the Curator brought us to Mars. He also returned the borrowed T-scanner to Holgotha. Then, the First One left, taking all the Forerunner artifacts with him. They had been staying near Ceres, protecting Holgotha.

The Curator had told the artifacts that they were in the wrong zone. From now on, each zone and cultural level would have to fight within the proper technological weapons it was allowed.

In case you're wondering, I'd asked him about the moth-ships and the remaining Jelk. They used highly advanced weapons and ship systems greater than this fringe zone should allow. The Curator had hemmed and hawed, finally saying that we had our advanced experiences to offset those powers.

That was just great. The Super Fleet was partly composed of ships from another space-time continuum. On various occasions, those moth-ships had done a number against Lokhar dreadnaughts and Jelk battlejumpers. They were the best fighting vessels for the coming encounter, better even than the Purple Tamika bombards. How could Earth Force and the Starkien Fleet slow them down long enough to bring the Grand Armada into play as I'd planned? Maybe as importantly, how could the Grand Armada defeat a Super Fleet only slightly less numerous than itself?

I had my answer, but I had to wait to let others in the Solar System in on it. First, I let them spout off in order to get it out of their systems. We met in a big auditorium on Mars, with a gigantic screen behind me. Earth's Prime

300

Minster was in attendance, the various flotilla chiefs, including First Admiral Rollo Anderson, and Baba Gobo and my old friend Kaka Ro, a Starkien war-leader.

Baba was the size of a baboon with similar fur. He had two yellowed canines at the end of a wrinkled muzzle and must have weighed ninety pounds. He had an old man's belly and a snow-white mane like a lion. Instead of sitting on a chair, Baba sat on a small raised dais where his chair would have been.

Beside him sat Kaka Ro, a younger, sleeker, darker-furred and very cunning Starkien commander.

We had Earth Force, the Starkien Fleet and several flotillas from nearby races. That was a pittance compared to the coming Super Fleet.

After hours of debate, I figured the time was right to start talking.

"We have one advantage," I told the assembled throng. "We know their destination—Earth. My suggestion is simple. We need to seed their path with massed drones and missiles, striking in such a way that they slow down to take care of each threat."

Using the screen and showing them the Super Fleet's likely path, I outlined the strategy.

There was silence afterward. The strategy called for a vast expenditure of missiles. That meant stripping them from every available source. I would take them from Earth's silos and from our battlejumpers and escort vessels. That would leave our ships and Earth's layered defense woefully short of missiles during the main battle.

"I do not like to disagree with you, Commander," Baba Gobo said. "But I believe that's too wasteful of our resources. It is also a grave risk, leaving us with too little on the day we will need everything."

"I agree with our good Starkien neighbor," Diana said promptly.

What was the old saying: a prophet was never honored in his hometown?

"On the day we will need everything," I repeated slowly. "That's exactly why we have to use our missiles wastefully and prodigiously beforehand. We're trying to slow down the Super Fleet so the Grand Armada will be here on the day of battle. Remember, wars aren't only about physical destruction. They're also about getting into the enemy commander's mind. We have to alter the Overlord's decisions. If we use our missiles as I suggest, the Overlord will start to get nervous. He might believe we have an unlimited supply. If he thinks every advance will be met with hordes of missiles, he'll go more slowly so he won't lose too many warships."

"Does a Karg think like this?" Baba Gobo asked.

He had a point. I wasn't sure. I hoped so.

"I don't know how a Karg thinks," I admitted. "But we're not only dealing with Kargs. Saurians make up a large part of the fleet. With massed missile attacks in every star system, we force the enemy to fight every step of the way. They'll be on constant red alert. They'll use up masses of PD shells and anti-missile missiles. Remember, they're a long way from home. They only have so much ordnance with them. We're near our supply bases. That made a huge difference when the English battled the Spanish Armada. Both sides ran short of gunpowder and shot back then. The English replenished their ships more easily because they were fighting off their own coast. The Spanish ran perilously low on both. Or take the Battle El Alamein in World War II. The Germans were trying to push through to Egypt, but they were at the long end of their supply route. Most of the badly needed fuel was burned up by the trunks bringing them their few supplies. The British massively—"

"Yes, yes," Diana said. "We understand the principle. It's the risk that is so daunting."

"This is a risk," I agreed. "The Kargs might push through, accepting horrible losses to get to Earth faster. I'm not sure the Saurians will feel that way. But why would the

Kargs accept such losses? They don't know how close our Grand Armada is?"

"Do you know that as fact?" Baba Gobo asked.

"No," I said.

"The Kargs might burn through your missile masses because they know exactly how close the Grand Armada is," Baba Gobo said.

"I'll grant you it's a possibility, although a small one."

"I suggest we gather all we have into one massive front," Baba Gobo said. "We will—"

"No!" I said. "The idea is to buy time. My idea most likely buys us time without burning up our ships and crews. Let the missiles do the heavy lifting."

"This is going to be bloody," Diana said.

"Let's not make it more bloody than it has to be," I told her.

There were further debates, more suggested strategies. Fortunately, Kaka Ro threw his considerable reputation behind me. That finally won over Baba Gobo. At last, grudgingly, Diana accepted the plan as well. We would do this my way.

Now would come the hard part, implementing the plan. A lot would depend on the reaction of this new Karg Overlord.

-48-

Our fastest advanced scouts found the Super Fleet in the Gamma AE System. That was a relief. It meant the Curator had been right concerning their path. That meant the Super Fleet would reach the Solar System through the farthest Outer Planets jump gate. My plan had been predicated on that being the case.

I planned to use the Earth as a lure during the tactical phase of the campaign, meaning in the middle of the massed fleet battle. Was that madness? Did I risk humanity for a possible small or even non-existent tactical advantage? Wasn't the better idea to destroy the Super Fleet as far away from the Solar System as possible?

Of course, that would be the better idea. I felt, though, that we needed every advantage to win decisively. We'd gotten rid of Abaddon. Now, could I get the Karg Overlord to act how I needed him to act?

In the Gamma AE System, the Super Fleet moved as before, like a giant school of sharks. They stayed together. I was betting the Karg Overlord was going to stick as close to Abaddon's plan as possible.

The Gamma AE System had ten planets, four terrestrial or Earthlike and the rest gas giants. It was a normal system in that the gas giants were far from the star. The terrestrial planets were in the inner system.

Five of our scouts far apart from each other rushed the massed enemy formation in the outer planets region. Their presence did nothing to halt the enemy's acceleration, which was too bad but not unexpected.

I remained far behind in our battlejumper, sending a scout ship back through the inner planets' gate to notify the rest of our advance flotilla what was happening. I kept the majority of the advanced flotilla in the next-door star system.

The five scouts heading toward the Super Fleet made a turning maneuver, using a gas giant to slingshot away from the enemy.

Over a billion kilometers away from the scouts, Jelk battlejumpers nosed forward, advancing ahead of the Super Fleet. They launched T-missiles. The scouts never had a chance. The T-missiles appeared among the five scouts, exploding with antimatter warheads. The blasts shredded the scouts as if they'd been built of tinfoil.

It was a good thing I'd used automated scout ships, as no humans had died. Still, sending the scouting force now seemed as if it had been a wasteful maneuver.

The rest of us immediately retreated through the jump gate out of Gamma AE. We moved through the gate to the Epsilon Indi System. Epsilon Indi was a mere ten light years from Earth in a straight line. Fortunately, the jump-gate route from Epsilon Indi led to the Innes' Star System.

I met an advanced flotilla of supply ships. As fast as possible, they unload their massed drones. As they did, the rest of us raced for the jump gate that would take us to the Innes' Star System.

It took a day and a half before the first enemy ships used the jump gate leading from Gamma AE into the Epsilon Indi System.

I smiled. It seemed the Karg Overlord had come down with a case of caution after all. That was heartening. We'd used five scouts. That many scouts might have indicated our main fleet was close by. It's what I'd wanted the Overlord to think.

To help solidify the idea, we had nearly five hundred thousand missiles and drones hidden in the Epsilon Indi System. We also had a hundred T-missiles ready and waiting.

After a two-hour scan of the system, an enemy battlejumper went back to Gamma AE. Soon, the Super Fleet began coming through the gate. Several hours later, it began accelerating for the jump gate on the other end of the system, the gate my battlejumper had parked beside.

Now began what was later called the Skirmish of Epsilon Indi. Our drones and missiles had the latest stealth technology. They remained hidden from the enemy as long as they stayed cold and still.

With a secret pulse from my battlejumper, the first thousand missiles near a gas giant accelerated into life. The enemy spotted them almost right away. A few enemy T-missiles popped off at strategic locations. Soon, our first thousand drones were slags of molten metal or useless hulks burned out by enemy EMP blasts.

I started another thousand at the enemy formation. The same thing happened.

For the next seven hours, I kept launching thousand-group missiles at the enemy fleet. At first, I wanted them overconfident. Then, I wanted them to wonder why we were so wasteful as to keep doing this hour after hour.

At the eighth hour, the enemy refrained from using up any more of their T-missiles. Maybe the Overlord figured that was our plan—to make him waste a precious resource. He was right. It was *one* of our ideas, but not the main one at the moment.

Our drones finally began closing in on the enemy formation, reaching the outer limit of their moth-ships' red beams. Those eerie beams drilled through space, destroying one of our drones after another.

It was at that point I launched the bulk of our antimatter-warhead T-missiles. We destroyed several battlejumpers and hammered a Karg moth-ship, blowing a vicious atmosphere into space out of a hull breach.

After that, the enemy became more deliberate, timing the rest of the T-missiles. This wasn't like Forerunner teleport tech. Our moon-ship and the Forerunner artifacts appeared whole in a second of time. Fringe-zone teleporting technology wasn't as good. It took several seconds for a T-missile to materialize into its new location.

That gave enemy gunners time to pour point-defense shells at the solidifying T-missiles. The missiles had to solidify before the warheads could ignite.

"Creed," Rollo said excitedly. "Do you see? Do you see?"

I saw, all right. I sat in my command chair, holding myself perfectly still. The enemy fleet was slowing down. The destroyed battlejumpers and the direct hit to the moth-ship seemed to have the needed effect.

We didn't have any more T-missiles in this system, but they didn't know that. We did have a lot more ordinary missiles. We would keep expending them. The key was the enemy reaction.

I could give a complete rendition of the entire skirmish. That might prove tedious, though. We had achieved our first and primary objective: the enemy fleet slowed to a crawl as our half a million drones continued to accelerate at them in one thousand and later ten thousand missile packs. We scratched another enemy battlejumper and managed to destroy a moth-ship, but that was it in terms of kills.

Yes, the expenditure was prodigious on our side. Maybe I'd used more missiles here than I should have. But nothing went perfectly in war. If nothing else, I forced them to expend masses of PD ammo and many of their T-missiles.

Now, I had to keep them at this crawl. If I could do that, my plan might actually work.

-49-

For eight more days, we expended missiles in one star system after another. It was clear we needed nine days, as the Grand Armada was not yet in position according to the original plan.

That meant I had to reach into my back pocket for Plan B.

"No one said we would live forever," I told my commanders in a packed conference chamber aboard Rollo's flagship.

"Are you talking about facing their entire fleet by ourselves?" an escort cruiser commander asked me.

"The Spartans faced the entire Persian Army at Thermopylae," I said. I was talking about the legendary 300.

"Those Spartans all died," the escort commander said.

"Yes," I said, staring at the man. "They died, but in doing so they helped Greece beat the invaders. Do we stand our ground to buy humanity life or do we run to save our sorry hides?"

The man licked his lips. I could see his inner turmoil. "We stand," he said softly.

"Yes," I said. "We stand."

The bulk of Earth Force and the Starkien Fleet waited in the Asteroid Belt near Ceres. Far beyond us, near Neptune, was a vast drone and missile belt a million strong. That had used up every remaining missile that humanity and the

Starkiens had left, including tens of thousands rushed from Earth's churning factories. The missiles in the silos on Earth and Luna were empty, as I'd said earlier. Earth and Luna Command only had beam weapons left to defend the homeworld. That was just like our starships. We had beams and PD guns, but had used up all our missiles trying to buy the Grand Armada the needed days and then hours to get here.

I no longer felt so sanguine about pulling this off. I kept reminding myself Claath and Abaddon were dead, and Jennifer was safe. Three out of four wasn't bad, was it?

"Look at that, Creed," Rollo said.

I studied the main screen. The Solar System's farthest jump gate glowed yellow. The first enemy ship was coming through. In reality, it had come through some time ago. We only saw this as fast as light could travel.

I closed my eyes. We needed just a little more time. I hated the thought of burning up our starships and seeing the entire Starkien Fleet destroyed. Even that might not be enough.

"We have to win this one for Dmitri," I said.

Rollo turned to me. Everyone on the bridge listened.

I opened my eyes and sat straighter. "We have to win this for Zoe Artemis and for all the people who died to give us this chance. Will they have died in vain?"

Rollo's thick features tightened.

"No," a weapons officer said hoarsely.

"Remember that when your guts turn to water," I said, loudly. "No matter what, we have to buy our people more time. The Grand Armada is close. If we can do this…"

I saw the determination in their eyes, but I also saw lingering fear. That would have to do.

The Battle for Earth began as the enemy fleet changed the basic set of its advance. Instead of the close-knit shark school, the Karg Overlord ordered his fleet to spread out. It came onward as a thin oval sheet, like a giant net heading toward the vast drone field.

The drones and missiles waited at a Neptune range. Those missiles were still billions of kilometers from the approaching enemy.

Hours passed, half a day and finally a day. The enemy fleet maintained its thin, widely spaced oval position. Each enemy ship was far enough from the other than a T-missile would have to pick and choose which one to attack. The moth-ships moved individually now, the bigger mothership snowflakes hanging back in a Uranus orbit.

Rollo and I had each slept since first sighting the enemy fleet. Now, we were back on the bridge. Ella was on Earth to coordinate any last ditch defenses. N7 was in a scout ship, hopefully by now with the Grand Armada.

The Grand Armada would enter the Solar System through a jump gate near Neptune. Would they do so before the Super Fleet reached Earth or after the third planet was a burning cinder?

"Give the order," I told Rollo.

Earth Force and Starkien Fleet drone operators began their business.

The last great drone and missile mass near Neptune began to accelerate toward the oncoming Super Fleet.

A million missiles all at once was an incredible number. Did the enemy realize it was our last missile barrage, or would they believe we had many more waves of missiles to send at them? For over a week now, they had faced these endless missile barrages. Could that be weighing on them? Or did they tell each other, "This is the last one"?

War was risk. War was playing your cards and hoping they were higher than the enemy's cards.

Red Karg beams burned thousands upon thousands of our missiles. Jelk battlejumper lasers and PD guns took down more. I found it interesting that the enemy didn't use any anti-missiles. Could they have run out of them?

On some moth-ships, the red eyes flickered and went out. I watched a missile slam into such a vessel, detonating. It made me grunt with appreciation.

The encounter seemed endless until the last missile blew apart from an enemy beam. There were almost a hundred enemy battlejumper wrecks drifting in space. Only a few moth-ships had been destroyed, though.

Remorselessly, the enemy formation continued to fly toward Earth.

"I thought the missiles would kill more," Rollo told me.

I was too tight-lipped to speak. I'd thought the same thing.

The Super Fleet kept coming. Finally, their most forward ships reached Jupiter.

"Now," I said, unable to hold it in. "Now, you have to start coming through now."

Nothing different happened, though. No Grand Armada starships came through the jump gate. I felt like a dismal failure.

The enemy's oval formation was halfway between Jupiter and the Asteroid Belt when Rollo shouted. Others took up his cry.

I'd grown sluggish, with my chin on my chest. I looked up, seeing the first Grand Armada ships finally coming through the Neptune jump gate.

I inhaled sharply, calculating distances and acceleration rates in my head. The conclusion was obvious. Likely, many on the bridge realized the same thing I did. The others began looking at me, waiting. If we could force the enemy to stop or slow down, it would give the Grand Armada ships time to catch up.

"Give the order to attack," I said.

The First Admiral went to his comm, giving the order. All over the Asteroid Belt, starships began powering up as we headed at the enemy. The final clinch was upon us. As our battlejumper began accelerating, I realized something else.

I grabbed an analyzer, punching in numbers. This was more than interesting. Renewed hope burned in my heart. We might have inadvertently stumbled upon a secret winning strategy. But to pull it off, we'd have to do the hardest fighting of our life.

***

One of the most perfect battles ever fought had been between Hannibal of Carthage and Rome. It had been the Battle of Cannae, and what made it perfect was that Hannibal's soldiers had surrounded the Romans on all sides. They'd squeezed the giant Roman host, turning it into a mob of men. The Carthaginian soldiers, with half the enemy's numbers, had butchered the legionaries in the tens of thousands that day.

We'd just surrounded the Super Fleet. Could we *squeeze* the enemy, though?

The day of battle was here. Earth Force and the Starkien Fleet had just become the screen trying to hold up the Super Fleet.

In the Battle of Cannae, Hannibal had used his Gallic allies to face the dreaded Roman Legions. Those wild Gauls had fought savagely. Even so, the grim legionaries had shoved them back, killing and advancing. The Gallic line had bent, came near to breaking, but had held just long enough for Hannibal's Libyan veterans to close the giant trap.

When the Grand Armada came into position, we would have to act the part of Gauls. That meant many of us would die today. The onrushing Super Fleet badly outnumbered Earth Force and the Starkien Fleet. Could we force the Kargs and Jelk to slow down?

***

I'd planned to use the asteroids in the belt like trees in a forest. We would have used the rocks to shield us, leaning out like snipers to hit individual enemy vessels.

Now, Earth Force and the Starkien Fleet took up a giant cone formation. The largest Starkien shark-shaped vessels formed the outer rim of the cone. Those ships had the strongest shields and hull armor. They would take a pounding, no doubt there. Their job would be to protect the

312

rest of us. Then, the cone would pour massed fire upon individual Super Fleet vessels, destroying them one by one as fast as possible.

It was a ragged cone. Rollo and other flotilla commanders gave constant orders. Starkien leaders did likewise. Our cone had accidents. Several ships had to fall out. Still, we advanced toward the vast mass of dots ahead of us.

"This is insane," Rollo confided to me in a whisper. "We're all going to die."

"Everyone dies," I said.

Rollo stood beside me as we watched the enemy formation. Minutes passed and became a half hour. Space battles always took a long time to unfold.

"Sir," a sensor officer said.

"I see it," Rollo said. He turned to me.

I watched stoically. Inside, though, I was grinning.

Originally, Holgotha had given us a five percent chance of victory, provided the enemy did something stupid. For stupidity to help us, however, first the great Abaddon had to die.

Abaddon was dead, along with some of the most important Karg leaders. I'd slain some of those Karg leaders myself with the Curator's force blade. Many of the most cunning Jelk were dead, gone or imprisoned by the Overlord. The cleverest Jelk of all was gone, Shah Claath.

How cunning was the Overlord? Maybe as important, did he have anyone on his side to bounce ideas off of? Maybe his best warlords had perished by my hand.

That was a nice thought. Seeing this was even better.

The Overlord made a move we desperately needed. He'd faced endless drone and missile assaults now for days upon days in every star system. How was he supposed to know we'd run out of missiles? For all he knew, he had to battle hordes more before he could reach Earth. Now, though, the Grand Armada was behind him and coming on fast. He was encircled after a fashion, something no space commander wanted.

Still, the Overlord clearly wanted to destroy Earth, but it now appeared he did not want to sacrifice the bulk of his moth-ships to do it. Thus, he made one of the worst blunders on the battlefield.

He began to split his forces.

While some of the greatest captains in history had done that and gotten away with it, the Overlord wasn't one of those geniuses of battle.

He let the Jelk battlejumpers continue to advance upon the cone. Meanwhile, the moth-ships made a turning maneuver. It appeared as if the moth-ships were trying to do an exit stage left, maybe to swing wide and avoid the Grand Armada behind them.

I had an idea of what the battlejumpers were supposed to do: get close enough to Earth to launch whatever T-missiles they had left. Maybe some of those warheads would contain bio-terminators.

Before the enemy battlejumpers reached the range of our cone and its beams, they launched T-missiles. Those vanished, reappearing far away from us but near Earth and Luna. I hoped Ella could take care of them.

Now, the Jelk battlejumpers began a hard turning maneuver, following the Kargs well ahead of them.

As I sat watching, I nodded in appreciation.

The T-missile attack on Earth reminded me of the Japanese at the Battle of Midway. They'd tried to take out Midway airfield and the American carriers at the same time. That had been a terrible mistake. Concentration of effort was one of the key rules of war.

That was the lure of Earth I'd talked about before. The Karg Overlord had just tried to destroy Earth on the cheap at the worst possible moment.

An hour later, as our cone formation gained on them and as the Grand Armada accelerated, the Karg Overlord appeared to change his mind once again. Maybe his monitors showed him the T-missiles had failed to take out Earth. Ella had done her job with beams and fighters, having lost a quarter of her pilots in the process. The Overlord now re-maneuvered to try to bring his split fleet together again. I imagine he planned to blast through us and destroy the Earth before facing the Grand Armada.

It wasn't the worst plan.

It gave us time to close the trap and possibly die.

The Super Fleet had become two smaller ovals. The battlejumpers slowed down and changed heading. That allowed the Kargs to catch up with the Jelk-commanded Saurians.

During that time, we changed the heading of the cone, coming at the reunited oval. The Karg-Jelk maneuvering had cost them precious time.

The Karg red beams struck farthest. It was like a thousand angry moths. They smashed against the front rim Starkien shark-ships. Shields glowed, stood fast for a time, buckled and finally collapsed one by one. The beams tore into those heavy hulls. The Starkiens didn't have super-hulls, but these had thick ones. The red beams burned deeper, making molten work of them.

The first giant shark-ships went critical, exploding, taking three others down with it. Fortunately, the force shields behind them held fast.

Now, the moth-ships began to destroy the outer rim Starkiens with fierce regularity. No enemy T-missiles appeared. No regular ones slid to the attack.

What did happen was that the ragged cone reached its beam range.

On our flagship, Rollo gave curt commands. The engines purred. Our heavy beams joined hundreds of others to make one giant fist. Like an annihilating light, it smashed against an enemy battlejumper. The force shield and hull went down fast, causing an explosion.

There was little for me to do but observe. It was hard because I watched the enemy destroy the cone ship by ship.

We hammered them, though. We devoured what seemed like an endless supply of Jelk battlejumpers.

Hull debris, water vapor, bodies—far too many of those—coils, spent casings, shredded bulkheads and other junk drifted by. The cone was gone. The oval net was coming around us. We had become bait, and the enemy ate our vessels.

"Creed," Rollo said, staggering to me as a shuddering explosion rocked our battlejumper.

"Keep fighting," I said.

Rollo nodded. He issued the same order to his ships.

The cone died. Our Earth Force ships were shattered. The Starkien Fleet had all but vanished from existence. There were a few of us left. We beamed, killing another enemy vessel, and we watched, drained of emotion, as the vast net sucking the last life from us quit firing in our direction.

We'd bought our side time. It had cost us dearly, but we had stood our ground like the ancient 300 at Thermopylae. It was a terrible and glorious thing.

The Grand Armada had finally come within firing range of the rearward Kargs.

I'll give the Overlord this. He didn't bother anymore with our handful of surviving vessels. He threw everything at the Grand Armada. I think he believed he could beat them, and maybe with the moth-ships he could have.

The two sides fought it out with brutal savagery, showing a blizzard of beams on our main screen. I began to wonder if the Overlord was smarter than I'd given him credit for. Those horrible red beams devoured the forward bombards and maulers. I couldn't believe it. Once they died, nothing could stand against the moth-ships for more than few seconds. After all my work—

"Creed," Rollo said in a harsh voice. "Do you see that?"

I rubbed my eyes. It was a grim decision, but I think I understood.

Baron Visconti must have ordered his fast strike cruisers and pursuit destroyers into the van of battle. Standard battle procedure called for them to stay on the sides and nip at the enemy. Instead, these cruisers and destroyers with their light hulls rushed to the forefront. They had the speed to do it, but no shields or armor to speak of, not compared to maulers and bombards. Those light starships died in droves, but by doing so they absorbed the fury of the red Karg beams.

The butchery made me sick.

What it did, though, was give the bombards and maulers time to close. Once near enough to the enemy, their heavy beams finally began to puncture Karg hulls.

That's when it became the Grand Armada's turn to butcher the enemy.

The next hour and half became legendary. At far-range, the moth-ships outmatched the maulers and bombards. At close range, they become equals. Our greater numbers and freshness told then.

It was brutal. It was a slugfest, and in this kind of encounter numbers counted as much as high technology. For once, we held the advantage, and Visconti never let it go.

What seemed like a lifetime later, the terrible battle entered the mop-up phase. We had taken terrible losses, almost three-fifths of our starting numbers if one included both fleets. But we annihilated the enemy. The Karg-Jelk Super Fleet was no more than a handful of vessels racing for a jump gate.

That day, we won the greatest battle in the Orion Arm in a thousand years. In fact, the Jade League-Jelk Corporation War was over. The victory was decided in the Solar System in what became known as *Fortress Earth*.

Rollo clapped me on the shoulder. I punched him in the chest. Then we began the sober task of searching for survivors.

After years of intense suffering, it looked as if humanity might finally breathe a great sigh of relief.

-Epilogue-

A year and several months later, I sat on a bench in New Saint Petersburg, overlooking the Baltic Sea. The city was twenty kilometers from the blasted site of Old Saint Petersburg.

Russian birds sang in nearby fir trees. They had yellow breasts and tweeted louder than I could believe. Maybe they were happy to be alive. I knew I was.

A grand year and a half had passed since we'd destroyed the Super Fleet. Our scientists had scoured the wreckages for months, prying loose the advanced Karg systems. We had finally begun to implement some of the more interesting Karg technologies and were working on the rest.

I'm sad to report that there had been rumblings in the former Jade League. Instead of everyone rejoicing for the next century with glad tidings all around, former friends had begun to get angry with each other. It was simple, really. Now that the Jelk and Kargs were gone for good, former allies finally began to realize what bastards their neighbors really were.

History has taught us that that was the nature of wartime alliances. Once the enemy pressure left, people remembered past injustices. People—all aliens, I suppose—followed the path of their own self-interest.

It was the way of the universe, so why fight it? Still, it left me feeling sad. We'd all gone through so much together.

We'd all sacrificed for the greater good. Now, lesser people squabbled and restarted old feuds.

On the home front, Diana was still our Prime Minister. So, we were doing pretty well in the scheme of stellar things. We'd already claimed several choice old Jelk frontier planets as ours. Nobody in our neck of the Orion Arm cared to mess with the little killers. I guess we had a pretty scary rep, especially now. Diana knew how to use that.

Me? I'd written a big fat book about my adventures. Most aliens believed me as well as Marco Polo's contemporaries had believed him, which was to say not at all. Still, the aliens and humans had bought lots of copies of my adventures. That meant my bank account was doing fine.

For the first time in years, I felt as if I could unwind. I'd left the assault troopers several months ago, becoming a private citizen. For two months, I'd hiked in the wilds, tramped through our new cities and went to a few book signings, drinking too much coffee and eating endless donuts.

I didn't know what I wanted anymore. No more aliens were breathing down our collective necks. And...

Okay. I'll level with you. I kept thinking about Jennifer. I wondered about the Curator, the real scoop concerning Abaddon, the Ve-Ky and the Creator. What was it all about anyway? What did the Forerunner artifacts do in the center of the galaxy? How come our galaxy was split into zones?

I sighed, stretching my legs, watching sea gulls wheel overhead. I guess I'd never know those things. That had started to bother me.

Maybe twenty minutes later, I saw a babe walking down the path from the nearby university. She knew how to use what she had, all right, and those breasts straining against her blouse...

"Hello, Creed!" Ella shouted, as she waved to me.

I stood up, waving back.

Ella ran, slowing as she neared me. Finally, she held out her hands. I took hers. I wanted to hug her, but I didn't know if I should.

"What's the matter, Commander?"

I shook my head. "It's just Creed these days."

She looked into my eyes. "Do you want to sit down?"

"Sure."

Ella sat beside me on the bench. After a time, she threaded an arm through mine, snuggling up next to me. We watched the sea gulls.

"You keep thinking about her, don't you?" she said.

I didn't answer.

"Creed, you need to find something to do."

"Like what?" I asked.

"I think Earth has become too small for you."

"Come on," I said. "That's bogus."

"No. I think that's the curse Abaddon gave you. You killed him—"

"The Curator did that."

"Only after you softened up the most dangerous being in the galaxy," Ella said. "Anyway, as I was saying. Abaddon cursed you. Remember in your book how you said the Curator said Abaddon corrupted everything he touched?"

"I remember."

"He's corrupted you."

I didn't want to believe that. "No," I said. "I already was corrupt."

"Not like that," she said. "I mean being able to enjoy yourself. I don't know if you can anymore. You need adventure, the spice of terrible adventure."

I wondered if that was true.

She squeezed my arm. "I have to go. I have an appointment. Will come to my place later?"

I shook my head.

Ella let go of me, standing. She glanced into the distance and then studied me closely. "Why do I have the feeling I'm never going to see you again?"

"What? That's ridiculous."

"Good-bye, Commander Creed," Ella said. "It has been an honor knowing you." She bent low and kissed me on the cheek. When she straightened, there were tears in her eyes.

"Ella, what's gotten into you?"

She swallowed. Then, she glanced behind me in the distance, turned back to the university path and hurried away.

I thrust my hands into my pockets. That had been weird.

Five minutes later, I heard the scrape of shoes behind me. I didn't turn. I didn't want to see who was there.

A massive old man with a huge white beard and dressed in a great coat came around to sit with me on the bench. For a time, the Curator and I simply watched the waves.

"I spoke too prematurely some time ago," he told me.

"Yeah?" I asked.

"I am going to need your services after all."

"As your effectuator?" I asked.

He nodded.

"What about Jennifer?"

"We will deal with that if and when it comes up," he said. "For now, you will be far from the Fortress of Light."

I turned to fully face the old man. "What does an effectuator do anyway?"

The Curator considered that, finally saying, "He helps me take care of delicate problems."

"How?"

"With his mind, with his cunning and sometimes with barbaric weapons," the Curator said.

It was crazy, but I felt a new excitement well up in me. I hadn't felt this way since...since we'd beaten the Super Fleet. Maybe Ella had it right. I needed to do something, something important to feel right.

I stood up. So did the Curator.

"Are you willing to come with me?" he asked.

"Sure, why not?" I said.

"Then, let's go. I don't like leaving my ship on automatic any longer than I have to."

I walked with the Curator, wondering if I'd ever see the green hills of Earth again. The feeling didn't last long, though. My curiosity about what lay ahead took hold. I could hardly wait to get started as the Curator's newest galactic effectuator.

The End